Dear Pat,

How to Marry a Rogue

by

Anna Small

This book won 6th out of the top 100 historical romances for 2015! Please enjoy!

Love, Anna xoxoxo

How to Marry a Rogue

Cover Art by *Rae Monet, Inc. Design*

The Wild Rose Press, Inc.
PO Box 708
Adams Basin, NY 14410-0708
Visit us at www.thewildrosepress.com

Publishing History
First English Tea Rose Edition, 2014
Print ISBN 978-1-62830-356-8
Digital ISBN 978-1-62830-357-5

Published in the United States of America

Dedication

Dedicated to Walter, for his loving support and never shirking from Mr. Mom duties while I'm lost in a book.

For Megan, who is my greatest inspiration and comic muse.

For Connor, who makes me laugh and brings me joy.

And to Don, Lisa, James, Chelsea, and Devon, with love.

My thanks also to my best friend, Carolyn Sarah Leister, who graciously allowed me to use her name in the creation of Mrs. Leister, even though Mrs. Leister is a notorious tart of the British stage!

Chapter One

"Your husband is the most insufferable brute who ever walked the earth! He simply must allow me to go abroad with Aunt Adele."

Georgiana Lockewood emphasized her frustration with a sharp stomp of her foot on the thick Aubusson carpet.

Her sister-in-law, who nearly always gave in to whatever Georgiana asked, sank lower in her chair, her attention focused squarely on her knitting needles.

"Jonathan has your best interests at heart, Georgiana," Sophie said. "He doesn't want you to be so far away when…" A blush stained her cheeks as she laid a light hand upon her belly.

Georgiana swept an irritating lock of hair from her shoulder with so much force a breeze stirred her skin. "I want to be here when the baby arrives, but Aunt Adele said this would be her final trip to France. It may be my last hope for any sort of fun before my dearest brother chains me to some…" She waved her hand as if she could pluck the proper word from the ceiling. None presented itself. With an elaborate sigh, she sank beside Sophie's chair, her silk skirt tangling around her legs. She slapped a fold out of the way. "Please, Sophie. You must talk to Jonathan. He always does whatever you say."

Sophie's eyebrows rose so high Georgiana

wondered if they'd touch the soft brown curls skimming her brow.

"My relationship with your brother is not suitable for discussion, my dear. Besides, you are wrong. Jonathan has his own mind, and if he thinks you should stay here in town, you should obey him."

It was the *obey* Georgiana could not bear. She was getting nowhere, and quickly. Sophie was her last hope against the brother who had been more of a father to her since their parents died years before.

Father? She grimaced. More like commander. Sometimes she wished Jonathan had allowed her to live with their late uncle's wife, their scatterbrained, though well-meaning, Aunt Adele. The sweet old dear would have permitted all sorts of adventures, not locked her away like a criminal. True, her cage was filled with elegant furnishings and outings to town, but it was not enough.

When her brother married, Georgiana had hoped for an easily swayed ally in his new bride, but the demure, soft-spoken Sophie had proven to be as dominating as he was. While she was grateful for the security they provided, Georgiana had experienced the drawbacks of living under their roof more than once.

She watched Sophie for any miniscule sign of wavering, but her lips remained firmly pressed together.

"I had hoped I could be gone for the season," Georgiana announced, adding an elongated sigh for good measure. "There are certain people whom I'd rather not meet at Vauxhall or a ball." She swiped her cheek in a pretense of tears, hoping her reference to a most indelicate situation two years before would cause some reaction in Sophie. An indelicate situation she herself had instigated, but she couldn't dwell on it now.

Just as she'd hoped, Sophie's lips trembled. She knitted with such a sudden ferocity Georgiana feared the baby cap would turn out lopsided. "Please, do not think upon that...that terrible person. Besides, you probably wouldn't see him in any case. Jonathan said he is not in town." Her needles stopped clicking, and she met Georgiana's stare. "Jonathan made some inquiries before we left Fairwood Hall. He didn't want things to be difficult for you, either."

"How thoughtful of him," Georgiana muttered. *Fiddlesticks.* It was her last card in this tricky game she was trying to play. She plopped down into a chair opposite Sophie and picked at a loose thread on the watered silk covering. Her brother's home in Grosvenor Square had always been a veritable playground of delights, situated in the middle of everything exciting and bright in London.

But she couldn't enjoy herself this year, try as she might. Vauxhall Gardens held no enchantment, and she'd tired of strolling through St. James's Park, no matter how many treats Jonathan bestowed upon her. Even the promise of attending Almack's proved uninspiring, despite Jonathan's gift of several new gowns and baubles. This was her first grown-up season, but she had spent it aimlessly roaming the corridors and criticizing everything from the cakes at tea to the way the chambermaid kept her room.

She leaned her head on her hand in an exaggerated display of despair and peeked at Sophie from under her lashes. "I shall wither away and die here in London, and neither you nor my brother will shed a tear if I do."

"You look healthy enough." Jonathan entered the

room and kissed Georgiana's forehead before sitting on the arm of his wife's chair.

She thumped a pillow so hard a tiny feather poked out of the stuffing and floated in the air. "You will have your laugh at my expense."

"I am not laughing, Georgiana." He crossed his arms and regarded her with the stern look she'd always thought resembled a grumpy old owl interrupted from its dinner of plump mice. "Two helpless females crossing the Channel and trekking across a foreign country is nonsense."

"Aunt Adele is strong for her years, and I am no trembling ninny, afraid of her own shadow." She gave him a defiant look before he could make fun of her. "You make it sound as if we will paddle across the sea in a rowboat and tramp across fields and brambles in our stockinged feet. The packet ships to France are safe, and Aunt Adele's sister's home is less than a day's journey from Le Havre. We won't require lodgings and can go straight on once we land."

He shook his head, but his frown indicated a possible change of mind. A splinter of hope penetrated her anxiety, though only by a slight margin, as Jonathan's reasoning was long-winded enough to make even Job clap his hands over his ears.

"It's not safe."

"The war is long over. Did you not mention at breakfast you hoped to take Sophie to Paris next year? And you've always told me to broaden my horizons."

"With books and study. With music and art." He stood and crossed the room, pacing like a caged monkey she'd owned as a child. His forehead beaded with sweat, a good sign he was losing his footing.

"Besides, you're too young to go abroad."

Clenching her fists, Georgiana pushed up from her chair to face him. "I will be twenty in a month! Nanny Halifax left us years ago, in case you haven't noticed. All I want is to…to see some of the world before you'd have me locked away for the rest of my life."

A scowl crossed Jonathan's usually amiable face. "You would compare marriage to prison?" He glanced at Sophie. "If the gaoler were as beautiful as my own bride, I should welcome Newgate."

She gave him her best withering stare, but his expression remained immobile. She tried to catch Sophie's eye, but her sister-in-law remained unnervingly focused on her knitting. "Yours is a happy marriage, but that is not the case for everyone. Please, brother, I wish to go to France. If you allow it, I promise…." She crossed her fingers behind her back. "I promise to address the loathsome subject of which you have been trying to force upon me lately."

"The loathsome subject?" He gave a short laugh. "With an attitude like that, you will hardly be a bride worth winning." He hooked his fingers into his waistcoat, a sign implicating he was about to make a decision. "I merely want you to become acquainted with my plans for your future, Georgiana. You will not have to marry…oh, for at least another year."

A year was eons away. Aunt Adele sailed within the month. Who knew how Jonathan might change his mind until then? And there was always Sophie, dear Sophie, who could twist him around to her way of thinking if she really wanted to help her poor sister-in-law. "Whatever you wish, my dear, wise brother."

He lifted his hand. "I have one caveat, before I give

my consent. Aunt Adele is hardly a suitable companion to escort you. Two helpless females..." He turned to Sophie with a look that hinted he wished her support. "Do not you agree with me, Sophie?"

She shrugged just enough to placate them both.

Jonathan sighed. "I cannot consider all the logistics right now, Georgiana. Ask me in a few weeks."

"We don't have a few weeks! I've already made inquiries for our passage, and I have more than enough financial security. Aunt Adele's sister lives in a chateau, Jonathan—not in a dilapidated cottage in the woods. Please." She considered dropping to one knee, but he would not take lightly to dramatics.

"My dear, make her see reason." Jonathan gave his wife an encouraging little nod, but she only lifted her knitting higher as if she had trouble seeing the small stitches.

Georgiana stared at her so hard she knew her sister-in-law could feel her gaze.

Sophie's cheeks blushed a rosy hue. She looked up at her husband. "Had I owned the support of my family to venture abroad at nineteen in the company of a beloved aunt, nothing would have stopped me." She winked at Georgiana. "Especially a stodgy older brother."

He snorted.

Georgiana hopped from one foot to the other.

"Is that a yes?" she cried. "It is a yes! Sophie agrees with me, and you've always said how clever she is, Jonathan."

Jonathan looked from his wife to his sister, as if searching for a weak spot. "Very well. But..." He silenced another exuberant outburst. "Aunt Adele and you will not travel alone. I will find a suitable escort. The last time that poor woman ventured to Bath, she'd gotten the date of the rooms all wrong. I won't have you stopping at various inns because of her lapse of judgment."

"Thank you, my dear, dear brother." Georgiana skimmed the carpet as she crossed the room to embrace him.

He held her at arm's length, his dark brows furrowed. "Do not thank me, yet. You may only go if I find someone trustworthy." Deep in thought, he faced the hearth, picking up various statuettes as if the answer to his problem lay hidden in miniscule marble carvings. "He must be a gentleman who is capable and courageous. Someone who will lay down his life to protect you. A man above all manner of reproach with a sound moral compass." He replaced a figurine of a boy playing a flute and hefted a statue of Hercules.

Sophie and Georgiana exchanged amused grins behind his back.

"Why, my dearest, you've just described yourself," Sophie said. "Does such a man exist in the entire kingdom besides you?"

He gave a rueful laugh as he faced them. "Unfortunately, no. But there's one who might do the job." A tremor rippled through him, causing the silver threads in his brocade waistcoat to shimmer in the lamplight. "If I can persuade him to leave his"—he cleared his throat—"pursuits."

Chapter Two

Jack Waverley licked the corner of his mouth and tasted blood. No whiskey for him later, as it would mean a hell of a burn in his torn mouth. He shook his sopping hair from his eyes, spraying the rowdy men with sweat and droplets of blood. Taking a deep breath until his ribs creaked, he rubbed his battered left fist with his right.

His opponent glared at him, and the two circled each other to the shouts and taunts of the inebriated crowd.

"Had enough, yer lordship?" his opponent jeered.

Jack grinned, his pulse pounding with a new burst of energy. "Not quite yet. After I lay you out, I intend to take on your brother." He shook a strand of hair from his eyes. "And then I'll take your sister."

With a roar, the fighter lunged at him, but Jack stopped him with a clean uppercut to his jaw.

The man's eyes rolled comically back into his head and he keeled over like a fallen tree.

Jack dusted off his hands and searched among the sea of faces for his second.

Talbot Reynolds handed him a clean towel, his face beaded with sweat from the pressing heat. "Good show, there, Jack. He didn't see it coming."

Before Jack could reply, a woman in a low cut dress and no corset gripped his ears and pulled his face down for a smacking kiss tasting of cheap wine and an unspoken promise only a man could detect. Had he not been exhausted to the point of falling down, he might have invited her into a side room somewhere. As it was, he merely offered a courtly bow.

"Yer a right strong brute!" She squeezed his biceps with forceful fingers.

Talbot pried her off him and sent her on her way with a smack on the bottom for good measure.

"Thank you, madam." Jack's gaze wandered after her retreating figure.

Talbot nudged his arm. "That's another five hundred you've won tonight."

Jack sponged off his sweaty face, scowling at the traces of blood smeared on the towel. "Five hundred to the good, but it nearly cost me a tooth." He gave a tentative wiggle with the tip of his tongue. "I'm through with this lot for the night. How about a drink?"

"Or a long soak in a tub. You stink, Waverley."

Jack spun around at the familiar voice. "Lockewood!" He gripped his friend's hand, pumping it vigorously. "What the hell are you doing here? Did you see that last match?"

"Match, you call it?" Jonathan brushed at his sleeve where an overeager patron had clutched him in a fit of excitement, leaving a greasy smear on his spotless coat. His upper lip curled in disdain. "Looked more like a brawl."

"Yes—but a brawl has no money to be won."

"True; but the end result is the same." Lockewood's stare took in all of Jack's bruises and bumps. Jack grinned.

"I never expected to see you in one of these places,

Lockewood. Do not tell me you've reconsidered the charms of boxing? You're strong enough, you know." He gave his head a slight shake. Poor Lockewood looked as if he'd rather be anywhere else than in the roiling boxing dens.

"Thank you for your assessment, but I am here on another matter. I do hope you will assist me."

"Anything, my friend. But let's speak outside where the smell is decidedly less pungent."

They walked outside, and Jack sucked in a lungful of cool air, wincing with every movement of his ribs. Talbot helped him with his shirt, and he gingerly stuck his arms in the sleeves. Jonathan handed him his topcoat.

"Do you still visit your grandfather's winery across the Channel? Or has he bestowed that duty upon another?"

Jack's mouth twisted. "My grandfather will only trust me to see to his business, no matter how much I loathe leaving my fascinating life here. Unfortunately, I will be off to Bordeaux at the end of the month, there to suffer under the spells of guileless young women and flowing juices of the vine." He fastened the last button on his shirt. "Are you interested in a few cases?"

"No, although I wish it were as simple as that. Georgiana desires to go abroad with our aunt Adele in a month. I am seeking a strong male escort." Jonathan flushed. "I hate to ask you, Jack, but if you were already going…"

"I would be delighted, Lockewood. Grandfather wants me there within three weeks or so. I can easily alter my plans to fit yours."

Jonathan's shoulders straightened as if Jack had

removed a great burden. "Thank you, Jack. You don't know how much this means to me. If anything were to happen to her..." He shook Jack's hand. "Come by my house in Grosvenor Square later, if you are able. Perhaps we can share a drink and talk of old times."

Jack grinned wryly. He had a full evening already planned involving the company of his latest mistress—an Italian Cyprian named Donatella. Or was Gabriella on the menu tonight?

"I fear I would not be suitable company for your sweet bride, banged up as I am. Come to my set at the Albany later. It's probably a lot quieter than Grosvenor Square, with all your women clacking about. As I recall, Georgie could talk the ears off an elephant."

Jonathan laughed. "She has not changed in that regard. But we do not call her Georgie anymore. She's all grown up now, as she never fails to remind me. Shall we say ten this evening?"

Jonathan walked to his waiting carriage. Jack stared after him.

"What have you agreed to, Jack? Is not his sister a child?" Talbot asked.

"She should be—oh, I don't know—about sixteen or so. No, eighteen." He chewed his lip. Had it been two years or more since he'd last visited Fairwood Hall? He saw Lockewood on occasion but had missed the wedding due to pressing business. Maybe he'd been too wrapped up in a winning streak at a gambling hell to notice. He really should pay more attention to his friends. He had few left in the world as it was.

"Hard luck, Jack. I wouldn't want to escort a chattering chit and troublesome old matron across the Channel."

"I don't mind. Georgiana was always an amusing girl." He caught a glimpse of himself in a storefront window and frowned. "I hope my nose looks more like its old self before the journey. I would hate to scare the ladies."

****

"Is domesticated bliss boring you to tears already?" Jack regarded his friend as they sat before the fireplace in Jack's bachelor quarters. The room was tidier than usual, as Jack had spent the past few nights tied down at a gaming table or pursuing the delectable Mrs. Leister, an actress at the Haymarket with whom he'd once shared a dalliance in his youth.

"On the contrary, my dear fellow," Jonathan replied archly. "Marriage was the best thing that ever happened to me. You should be so lucky."

As much as he enjoyed teasing his old friend, Jack had to agree. "You and Sophie are very fortunate. I've never seen you happier."

"You should set your mind to a similar place, Jack. One cannot find happiness in those gaming hells and dens of sin you frequent."

"Marriage has spoiled you for these low establishments, Lockewood." He waved his hand, lazy from the cozy fire and a rich supper. "I have not your penchant for domestication. I shall not stick my neck willingly into the parson's noose."

"Do you not ever think of settling down, Jack? Putting all of this"—Jonathan motioned toward Jack's crooked nose—"behind you?"

"The noose will be around my neck soon enough." Jack tried not to dwell on the last conversation he'd had with his grandfather. "Alas, I cannot find anyone suitable."

"You have, no doubt, been looking in the wrong places."

Jack smirked. "Perhaps I should visit your bride's family. Does she not have a few pink-cheeked sisters still at home?" Jonathan shuddered, and Jack choked on a laugh. "Do not worry, Lockewood. You and I would make disparate brothers-in-law."

"I agree with you there. You would be better off allowing someone else to find a respectable bride for you, Jack. Sophie can always inquire amongst her friends. Nice girls, the lot of them."

Jack twisted the glass between his fingers, sloshing the dark amber liquid around the edges. "That would be delightful if we were talking about a cottage by the sea or a piece of horseflesh. Thank you for the thought, but I prefer to find my own bride."

"Has your grandfather been threatening you again?"

Although he grinned, Jack detected an air of sympathy in his friend's voice.

"He is of the opinion a wife will end my wicked ways. To that effect, he has threatened to halt my allowance by my thirtieth birthday if I do not produce a marriage license." He stared into the bottom of his glass. "And a wife to go with it."

"The dreaded thirtieth birthday ultimatum." Jonathan sighed. "I don't envy you. To be forced into marriage, well..." He finished his brandy. "I know we both experienced many diversions in our youth, but I am glad to have settled down. I never thought I'd say it, but I am truly happy. I wish you would find that kind of happiness, Jack."

He couldn't resist snorting. "What? Attach myself to a rich little heiress who will try to bend me into her mother's ideal of a perfect husband? Staying home every night at the beck and call of a shrill-voiced viper while delightful temptations wait around every corner?" He tapped the rim of his glass. "You don't remember what it's like to have a different woman in your bed night after night. As lovely as Mrs. Lockewood is, I would not want to come home every night to the same woman."

Jonathan shook his head sternly, but a corner of his mouth twitched. "One day, you will eat those words, Jack. I will wait for the day when you spout poetically of the haunting creature who has beguiled you down the aisle."

"When that day comes, I give you permission to hang me from the nearest tree."

"Why so down on love, Jack? Now that I think of it, I've never known you to lose your heart. Even to the actress we all knew, years ago. Sarah, was it? I thought she was the one for you, despite the fact your grandfather would have disowned you on the spot for sullying the Waverley name."

Jack fidgeted with his cuff buttons. "It's complicated."

Jonathan sniffed. "There is no complication. You refuse to open your heart to anyone, as friendly and caring as you are. What do you fear? That someone will actually love you?"

"I haven't seen you in nearly three years, and all you can do is preach steadfast monogamy? Come, man! I remember when your heart was torn between the delightful Lady Selfridge and her sister. Neither of them knew you were courting the other. Do not speak to me about true love. Besides, it does not exist."

"It does not?"

"No. It's a fabrication intended to ruin the lives of otherwise contented bachelors." Jack rose to stretch his legs and peered out the window at the rain pouring off the roof across the street. The green hills of Bordeaux would be a respite after the sodden London spring.

"I will not attempt to change your mind, Jack. And, for God's sake, I do not mean to preach. I would have you happy."

"I am happy." Jack turned away from the window and forced his frown to vanish. "As happy as I can expect to be. Enough about me. Tell me more of your sister's upcoming adventure away from the safety and security of your hearth. I'm surprised you are allowing her out of your sight."

"Georgiana wishes for a change of scene. I admit an ulterior motive in asking you to escort her, Jack. I hope you can talk some sense into her while you're traveling together. She has always looked up to you, and I think hearing advice from someone she admires will help my purpose."

"Oh? What has she done now?" Jack recalled Georgiana's mischievous antics as a child, often driving her patient brother to distraction.

"She refuses to discuss any possibility of marriage. I have found several likely suitors for her, but she will have nothing to do with them. I'm at my wit's end, and Sophie will not take my side."

Jack hid a smile. "She's still very young. Can she not wait a few years?"

"She'll be twenty in a month. She has not

entertained any suitors this season. If she continues like this, no one will want her."

Jack laughed. "She's beautiful, intelligent, and enormously wealthy. Anyone would have her, should he meet your impossibly high standards. Tell me the list of candidates for your future brother-in-law, and I will foster my own opinion as to speaking to her."

Lockewood numbered them on his fingers. "There is Winston, the son of Lord Jarvis."

"Not very bright, but he has around six thousand a year and will not interfere with your controlling his wife's every move. Next?"

"The Earl of Rochester's boy."

"The one who was caught in a compromising position with his sister's governess?"

"No, the other one." Jonathan's face flushed.

"Ah. Roderick. Big ears to match his equally big inheritance. Decent dancer, but I've encountered him at enough gaming hells to know you do not want him visiting Fairwood Hall at Christmastide unless you lock up your scullery maids. Who else have you selected, or are they all as promising as this lot?"

Jonathan's left eyelid twitched. "Viscount Richmond's eldest. Herbert. He's rather big-boned, but he's a steady fellow. Likes horses."

"Only because he shares their appetite." Jack steepled his fingers. "Georgiana will not tolerate a gambler, nor will she accept that oaf, Richmond, regardless of the fortune. Why are you going to so much trouble in procuring a husband for her? Surely, with her own fortune, she may remain on the shelf for a good many years before taking that fateful plunge into the abyss. She has you and your wife, and her other

Lockewood cousins." He peered intently at his friend. "It must be for another reason."

Jonathan fidgeted with his watch fob. "Do you recall that repugnant incident about two years ago?"

"Involving a man whom you considered a brother?" Jack tensed, every muscle contracting as if he were in the boxing ring and not in his drawing room. "I do wish you had brought me along to Gretna Green, Lockewood. I'd have seen to it that Mitford took his food in liquid form the rest of his life."

"That is precisely why I did not bring you." Jonathan's frown deepened. "Georgiana was overwrought. She begged me to spare his life." He snorted. "As if I would sully my soul with that man's blood on my conscience. Were it not for our lengthy friendship, I would not have been as merciful as I was."

"He took advantage of your friendship, Lockewood, and of Georgiana's innocence. Why, he was at Fairwood Hall almost as much as I was in our school days."

"Yes, but you did not try to seduce her."

"Only because your father had a knack for hiring fetching dairy maids." Jack winked, which eased a smile onto his friend's face.

"I still find it hard to believe I was blind to his designs on her. He had us all fooled."

"Don't blame yourself. *Mouldy Mitford* turned into the biggest scoundrel of us all. And he had quite the competition." He tugged at his cravat.

"Speak for yourself."

"Fear not, Lockewood. I will beat him for you, next time I see him. I have not heard of his being in town. Perhaps he's done us all a favor and dropped off the earth, or is currently living amongst cannibals on some island."

"We should be so lucky." Jonathan's face clouded. "Georgiana is lonely, Jack. She denies it, of course, but I can see it. Yes, she is happy—Georgiana would find happiness in any kind of decent company. She has Sophie and me, as you said, and cousins and friends. Aunt Adele is a faithful companion. But it is not enough. A young woman, with such a big heart—" He hastily rose from his chair and poured another finger of brandy. "Mitford, that scum, preyed on her trusting nature. Thankfully, I found them before…" He drained the contents of his glass in a single gulp.

Jack ran his hand through his hair. It had been difficult—damnably difficult at the time—to forgive Lockewood for not allowing him to beat Edward Mitford into a bloody pulp for his devious ways.

When he'd next seen the scoundrel in a gaming room at White's, he'd called him out, but Mitford made such a scene of Jack's being inebriated nothing came of it. Still fuming, he resolved to answer Mitford's unpardonable behavior toward the Lockewoods one day.

"That is why I wish her to marry," Jonathan said at length. "Before she is, as you called it, *on the shelf* for too long, and no one will want her. She deserves to be happy with the right man. To be a wife." He cleared his throat. "To be a mother."

Jack chuckled at the idea, and Jonathan's frown eased. "Can you imagine Georgie a mother? She would be just like her children—running around the garden and dragging them into her mischief. They would beg you to tell Mamma to come down from the branches of the highest tree."

Jonathan returned to his seat. "I always hated heights. I was so glad you volunteered to climb that great oak after her. What was she—about six or so?"

"More like five. Her dress was tangled in the branches, and she'd lost her slippers. She saw me and pretended she hadn't been crying." Jack grinned at the memory. "I was a skinny lad and don't know how I managed to bring her down. Her little arms were tight around my neck. I said to her, 'Pudding Face! Let me breathe a moment, or else we'll both fall!'"

Jonathan laughed with him. "She was always getting into trouble, but I think it was so she would be rescued by one of us." His smile faded. "She wasn't even surprised to see me, when I came upon her and…and that blackguard. She never said a word on the ride home but held my hand the entire time. It was as if she'd known I would come."

"You've been brother and father to her for a long time, my friend. I don't know how you do it."

Jonathan shrugged, and a trace of the carefree boy he once was appeared on his face.

Not for the first time did Jack inwardly scold himself for not visiting more often, taking some of the responsibility from Jonathan's shoulders. The Lockewoods had provided a loving home for him in those first, terrible years after his parents died and his grandfather had sent him away to school.

"I had no choice. But I would not have it any other way. God knows what ruin she'd have come to if Aunt Adele had taken her under her wing. I'd have spent the rest of my days dueling one scoundrel after another. Aunt Adele caused my parents no end of headaches after my uncle died, for all that she's so kindhearted. That's another reason I want you to escort them. One impetuous woman in the family is one too many."

Jack raised his empty glass. "To heroes and rescuers of little girls, whether they be prizefighting rogues or landed gentlemen. Or both."

Jonathan imitated the gesture. "To you, Jack. And for what it's worth, you like to play the rogue, but I know you. I wouldn't trust anyone else with Georgiana's safety, you know."

"Strange, I do not remember saying I would go."

"Strange, indeed. I thought you had."

Jack rose from his chair, and Jonathan did the same. "So I did." They clasped hands firmly. Jack held his friend's gaze. "I will guard her with my life." He laughed shortly. "After all, what kind of mischief can she find in the quiet countryside?"

Chapter Three

"I hope you do not sleep the entire way to Portsmouth." Georgiana prodded Jack's boot with the toe of her shoe. Her eyes narrowed as she watched him feign sleep.

He'd been that way for the last half hour, and the monotony of Aunt Adele's snores and the jostling of the coach had distracted her to irritability.

He cracked open an eyelid. "As if anyone could sleep with your relentless chattering, Georgie." He muffled a yawn with the back of his hand and stretched against the padded seat.

"How many times must I remind you to refrain from using that dreadful nickname?"

"You are still the pestering little girl I remember so well. It's hard to remember you're all grown up." He arched his eyebrows. "*Georgiana.*"

"You're grumbling because you're tired. You should not have been carousing all night, but resting in anticipation of our journey."

"I'll have you know, I was counting sheep well before midnight." He regarded her suspiciously. "Since when did you become so bossy, miss? I recall a more respectful girl. You used to sit at my knee and beg me to tell you of my wild escapades."

"Perhaps when I was ten I admired you," she said crisply. She purposely scanned his slouching figure, noting his rumpled linen and drooping neckcloth. "I hardly recognized you this morning. Do you not have a proper valet? I notice you do not travel with one."

"I can dress myself, thanks." The corner of his mouth twitched. "I have a suitable houseman in Bordeaux who doubles as valet when the occasion calls for it. What about you? A grown up woman should have someone to attend her. Or do you still have a nursemaid?"

She gave him her best disdainful glare. "I will have someone at Lady Priscilla's home attend me. A respectable man should live as one. You have sunk low in this world, Jack Waverley."

His lips twitched as he fought back a smile. She tingled inside. She'd always enjoyed their repartee. It was why she'd always looked forward to his visits at Fairwood Hall. That and his ability to make her laugh even at her darkest moments. He'd been a great comfort when her mother had died. She'd crawled into his lap and slept for hours when he found her, alone in her father's big chair. Nobody else had the time to come looking for her, but Jack stayed at her side, ready with a tug on her curls or a sweet hidden in his pocket, distracting her from her sadness.

"Not so low I cannot escort an innocent maiden and her chaperone across the Channel." He adjusted his collar and cuffs with the assumed air of a judge. "I warn you, I may rescind my offer to your brother and send you packing. None of this gallivanting about the Parisian streets for you, Georgie. Think of all the parties and balls you will miss!" He clucked his tongue against his teeth. "And all because of your low opinion of me."

She laughed, genuinely happy for the first time in weeks. When Jonathan and Sophie moved to London for the season, they'd hoped the excitement would drag her out of her doldrums. Instead, she'd hardly left the house except to accompany Sophie on a few obligatory visits to those ladies of the *ton* they could not ignore. The daytime visits were not too bad; she had no chance of meeting Edward in the places where matrons and children dwelled. An outing to the theatre or a ball might put her in the same company of the one person she could not bear to see.

She'd nearly ruined herself over an infatuation with Edward Mitford. With his flirtatious grin and wicked charm, he resembled her idea of all that was romantic and exciting. When he'd asked her to elope after stealing a kiss, she'd hesitated for only a moment.

It didn't take long for Jonathan to forgive her, and she had sincerely tried to please him in the last two years since her escapade. She was the model sister-in-law and confidante to Sophie, and truly looked forward to becoming an aunt. Although nobody outside her immediate family knew of *the incident*, as she and Jonathan referred to her near-elopement, she was aware of how close to ruin it had brought her. Never would she put herself in such a position again. She imagined meeting Edward in public and snubbing him, while he stared after her in hurt surprise.

"There's that smile I've missed. How have you been?" He regarded her with a brother's concern.

"I have been very well, thank you, Jack. I will admit I was determined to get away. This trip could not have come at a more opportune time."

"Ah." He nodded understandingly. "Your brother

mentioned your reluctance for of stepping out." He cracked his knuckles. "Do not fear, Georgie. When we return to London, you can lure Mitford into a wood, where I'll lie in wait. And then I will pummel him within an inch of his life until you tell me to stop." The wicked spark she remembered from childhood glinted in his eyes. "However, I would applaud you if you strode right up to the bastard and belted him in the eye. I'll hold him down for you."

Georgiana gaped at him in horror, then doubled over with laughter. "You are impossible." She wiped the corners of her eyes. "Oh, but if I could." She laughed again. "But that would mean I still cared about…" Like her brother, she could barely speak the dreadful name. She shook her head slightly. "Indifference is the opposite of caring. That is what Jonathan told me. So, I am indifferent to him."

"Bravo."

"It is very kind of you to accompany us, Jack," she said when it seemed he might take another nap.

"I am pleased to renew our acquaintance again. When did you grow up?"

The faintest breath of heat rose up her throat to fill her cheeks. A mild stirring of something curious and alarming formed in her chest. She'd always seen Jack as her brother's friend, if not a brother of sorts himself. But the distance of a few years had changed things. He was no longer the teasing boy, the rescuer. He was a man, with a life separate from what she'd known of the rambunctious lad who'd spent his holidays at Fairwood Hall.

"Naturally, I am grown up. Did you expect me to stay a child forever?"

"No, but I am certain your brother wishes it." He cleared his throat. "Have you given marriage a thought, Georgiana? Your brother hopes…"

She crinkled her nose. "Did Jonathan ask you to speak to me about marriage? Please, Jack, do not begin preaching the merits of marriage to me. You should have been married long ago, yet you scorn the very thought. I have never heard you discuss marriage without a sneer or joke."

He opened his mouth to protest, but she noted his guilty look. "It's not that I scorn it, Georgiana. Marriage is perfectly suitable for some people. I just do not understand the draw. Really—one mate for the rest of your life?" He shook his head, his eyebrows raised in mock astonishment. "Ridiculous."

"The Reverend Franklin would shake his fist if he heard you," she admonished, but was disturbed she almost agreed with him.

"Is the Reverend Franklin a happily married man?"

She chewed her lip. "He is a bachelor, I believe."

"There you have it. Who is he to command others to marry?"

"I see your point, skewed though it may be." She played with the beaded fringe on her reticule. "I hope you will not be too busy in Bordeaux. I will have no other company but Aunt Adele and her sister, Lady Priscilla."

"Rest assured I will have plenty of leisure time on my hands." He studied her for a moment. "Perhaps I will fetch you occasionally and show you the countryside. There are some picturesque villages and towns you might like to see."

She pursed her lips. "I do not think I should

accompany you without a chaperone."

"Put your worries aside. I trust you will not compromise me."

She laughed. "You are terribly wicked, Jack. You know what I mean."

"Yes, I do know. But why should it matter if you are *sans* chaperone with me? I'm as close a brother to you as Lockewood."

Her smile remained, but she wanted to protest his statement. Since seeing him that morning when he'd come to her brother's house to join her and Aunt Adele, she'd had to reconcile her memories of the playful older friend with the image of the grown man he'd become. Who'd have thought skinny Jack would broaden in the chest and shoulders the way he had? That the round face would melt into curving cheekbones merging into a chiseled jaw?

In seconds, the image of the boy she remembered was replaced with a man who was almost a stranger. She didn't feel quite herself, and was conscious of what she said or if she laughed too loudly or too often, as if she must impress him. She had to keep reminding herself not to arrange her pelisse over her knees or glance down to see if the ruffled trim on her bodice was drooping. Annoyed suddenly, she leaned against the side of the carriage.

"I suppose it will be all right for you to chaperone me." She was still a little girl in his eyes. How much had Jonathan told him about *the incident*? Worse, why was he taking on Jonathan's cause and pushing her toward marriage? "Besides, we shall probably not meet any of our acquaintance in Bordeaux. Aunt Adele said it is rather unfashionable at the moment."

"I promise not to shame you should we meet anyone."

She scowled. "I know you would not shame me, Jack, even if your nose looks a bit smashed. And what is that bruise beneath your brow? Did you walk into a door?"

His eyes narrowed. "You have a sharp tongue, Georgiana. I'm not certain if I like this grown up version of the little doll I once knew."

"That doll is gone, Jack. I am quite the adult now. I even walk downstairs by myself."

"Well, that is a relief." He grinned slowly. "I can see we are to have ourselves an enjoyable time. I'm tired of women who cannot keep a conversation going, unless it is to try and convince me to give up my scandalous ways."

"Are you saying you enjoy being insulted every five seconds?"

"Coming from you," he said, sighing, "I take it as a compliment."

Silence overcame them, and she wondered if it would be proper to close her eyes and sleep, as Aunt Adele had done. She met Jack's gaze, her stomach twitching when she realized he was still looking at her. "How much further, do you think? It seems like we've been cooped up in this coach for ages."

"Goodness, Georgie. Are you going to complain the entire crossing?"

She blushed at his familiar teasing. "I merely inquired. If you do not have the answer, you may say so."

"About three more hours. The sea crossing will be tons more enjoyable. You'll be able to walk around the deck and take the air. With a proper escort, of course."

She rolled her eyes, making him smile. "I've never been on a ship before." She sat up straighter. "Will it be a rough crossing, do you think?"

"Not too bad, I suppose. But you will have to contend with the sea monsters. If you're very good, I'll toss you overboard so you can swim with the mermaids."

"Are you going to insist on treating me as if I were six years old?"

"Come now, Georgiana! Who else entertains you as well as I?" He reached across the coach and patted her hand. "We will have an enjoyable crossing and an equally marvelous journey to Bordeaux. And I will be there to protect you, should you require it."

"You are every inch a gentleman, Jack Waverley."

He pulled the brim of his hat down over his eyes, and she knew she would not be able to disturb him this time.

"Why do you and your brother always say that with a hint of mockery and not a little surprise?"

****

The deck heaved and rolled beneath her feet. Georgiana lost her footing and hurtled against the railing where she banged her hip. Her gloves and most of her pelisse were soaked with the sea spray springing up from the waves every few seconds, but she held on grimly. Standing on the deck of the packet ship *Essex* was the only thing that kept her from joining the other passengers, below in the cabins, seasick and miserable.

She'd left Aunt Adele doubled over a bucket but realized the open deck wasn't a better choice. Glancing around the crowded deck teeming with sailors and a few other like-minded souls, she searched for Jack but didn't see his telltale figure anywhere.

The ship slammed into a higher wave, and she sank to her knees, her cheek pressed to the rough wood that smelled of fish and saltwater.

Strong arms lifted her, and she turned to protest but sagged against Jack as he lifted her to her feet. "I thought you said the crossing would be smooth."

His laughter vibrated from his chest. The roar of the sea and the noise of the crew had drowned out any sound. He bent his head, and a breath of warm air skimmed her forehead.

"Alas, I have no skills in predicting bad weather or seas. It is a smooth crossing, relatively speaking. A sea captain once told me about rounding the Horn. Now, that is a voyage you would never wish to take."

She gripped his coat while he led her to a bench between some sturdy looking barrels, where they sat. She fell forward when the ship rocked again, and he reached his arm around her waist to steady her.

"I must say, Pudding Face, you are rather green around the gills."

"How is it you are not ill?" She released his coat to hold her middle and prayed she wouldn't humiliate herself by being sick all over her shoes.

"I have made this trip many times in the past few years. My grandfather's heart is too weak for him to make the voyage. So, it has fallen to me."

"You're very good to do it." She was grateful for the conversation, as it kept her attention off the horizon dipping over the bow.

"He pays me well." He gave a wry smile. "I do not mind the journey. There is usually a little business to see to, and then I have an extraordinary amount of spare time to waste in the gambling halls and salons of Paris. If only you weren't so young, I would take you."

She choked. "My brother would have you strung up by your bootstraps!" But her heart panged for a moment. How exciting it would be to attend a ball with someone as exuberant as Jack.

She remembered Jonathan's halting words to Sophie about Jack's—what had Jonathan called them? "Truly, Jack; you must find some more wholesome pursuits."

"Look at the little girl, lecturing me! Yes, I should. I will stop in for tea with you and Aunt Adele twice a week, and you can teach me knitting."

"I do not knit." She would have said more, but another wave almost sent her hurtling to the deck. Instantly, he pulled her close to his side, and she gritted her teeth, hiding her face in his coat. "Oh, God, make it stop."

He brushed his hand over her cheek, just under her bonnet. "Close your eyes, Georgiana. It will make it a little better. I'll hold onto you so you do not fall. This weather cannot last."

His right hand rested on his knee. She gripped three of his fingers as hard as she could. "Keep talking to me, Jack. It's not so bad when you're talking too me."

"What shall I talk about?"

Already, she felt a little better, with the familiar scent of his hair pomade and cologne in her nose, and his arm, heavy and safe, about her. He'd comforted her so often in the past it was perfectly natural to lay her cheek on his shoulder. For a moment, the hard muscles in his arm disappeared, and she felt the reassuring familiarity of his body. Grown or not, he was still the dear friend who'd always protected her.

"Tell me about the naughty things Jonathan and you did at Cambridge." She fought a rise of bile as the ship bucked and danced over another crashing wave.

"There are so many. I hardly know where to begin."

His broad, thick fingers clamped around her palm. She focused on the scars—some old, some more recent. Jack's hands could tell stories her brother's never could.

"Just...just think of something. Did you not wake up drunk on the steps of a chapel once?"

"That is hardly a suitable bedtime story for such a proper young lady. Your brother will not like it."

She pinched his hand. "My brother is not here. Besides, I've already heard it. I especially like the part when you dropped unconscious at the Latin master's feet after insisting you were dry as a monk. Tell it to me again."

Sighing elaborately, Jack made a show of settling her against his side in preparation of telling a great tale. He brushed a drop of sea spray from her cheek. "Lockewood should not have told you these unsavory things about me. I wouldn't want you to lose respect for me."

"I lost respect for you long ago, so you are safe."

He pinched the spot on her cheek he had just dried. "This is going to be a long voyage if you maintain your attitude, miss."

"I promise I'll be good," she said demurely, patting his hand where it rested on his knee.

He turned his hand over and clasped her fingers. "How many times have you broken that promise?" he chided.

Chapter Four

"Terra firma at last!" Jack called out, helping Georgiana assist Aunt Adele, whose legs shook from her exhausting seasickness. They emerged from the cabins below, blinking in the bright morning sunlight.

"My poor nerves," Aunt Adele murmured, clutching Jack's arm with one hand and leaning on Georgiana with the other. "I dread our return, my dears, if the crossing is anything like what we've just endured. I know not how all these poor boys make the trip." She nodded at the sailors, who scurried about the deck and gangplank with aplomb.

"The journey should be better at the end of summer," Jack assured them. He winked at Georgiana. "You bore up quite well, miss. You should have seen her, Aunt Adele. She was a pillar of stoic fortitude. At one point, I rather feared our little girl was going to shove the pilot aside and take the wheel into her own hands."

"I was not," she corrected, but gave him a grateful look when Aunt Adele cracked the merest of smiles.

"My grandfather's carriage should be waiting for us," Jack said. "We'll ride in comfort to Bolbec. You'll have your land legs back in no time."

Georgiana gazed up at him from beneath her lashes. His chest tightened, but he shook off the feeling. She was a good girl, and it was kind of her to be at her aunt's disposal. He forced himself to picture her in a starched pinafore, her long curls bouncing down her back. She'd been beguiling back then, too, able to convince him and Jonathan—though less Jonathan and more so Jack—to play one more game. One more push on the swing beneath the giant oak standing guard in the park. Jonathan would allow a few more minutes, but Jack had been the victim of her charms too often. He'd once spent several hours patiently braiding daisies into crowns for her dolls, and another time had crawled around on all fours while she pretended he was her pet dragon.

Aunt Adele's discreet cough brought him back to the present. He assisted Georgiana in situating the older woman on a bench outside a lading house.

"I'll help you organize our things. We have so many trunks and boxes I fear you might leave one behind in your haste to be rid of us." Georgiana took his arm before he'd offered it.

"I would never be so hasty as to leave the company of two pleasant ladies." He swept a bow to Aunt Adele, who waved weakly.

"Off you go, my dears. As soon as I'm sitting by the hearth and drinking a cup of hot tea, I shall be as good as new."

Jack led Georgiana through the throng of sailors and passengers swarming the crowded docks. He was mildly amazed at her ease in moving through all classes of workman and passenger, but it was the Lockewood goodwill in her. She looked around, her eyes shining with excitement. A twinge of sympathy filled him. She had suffered much because of Edward Mitford. One day, Mitford would receive his just reward. Jack fervently hoped he would be there to see it.

"What a lovely day," Georgiana commented, after they'd given instructions of where to send the luggage. "I feel as if I am truly on holiday."

Her earlier paleness had vanished. The salty, fresh air brought out a rosy hue in her cheeks reminding Jack of her younger self. Little else reminded him of how she used to look. She was taller than he'd expected but possessed natural curves no amount of tight corsetry could hide. Her blue eyes flashed before she turned away to look around at the bustling crowds.

He cleared his throat roughly, as if the gesture would also clear his mind.

Months ago, he'd been eager to start this journey, aware of the delights awaiting him. He'd made the acquaintance of a bored, married countess on his last visit. She'd written him several times, promising his latest trip would be one he'd remember. Before Lockewood had secured him to escort the ladies, the countess had filled his every waking thought. He glanced down at the gloved hand gripping his arm and couldn't remember what the countess looked like.

Georgiana met his gaze. "I'm so glad you're with me, Jack." She tucked her other hand over his arm in a sort of embrace. A blush swept across her cheeks as she caught her breath. "I mean with us. With Aunt Adele and me."

"As am I," he said, before he could utter a teasing response instead.

****

Aunt Adele's sister, a widow who had spent the last several years abroad, lived in an old chateau hardly deserving of the name. Mossy and overgrown, the gardens had seen better days, and Georgiana hid her disappointment as she stepped from the carriage. This was not the picturesque haven she'd envisioned. Her trepidation eased as Jack fussed over Aunt Adele, helping her from the carriage with the concern of a son.

Their journey from the harbor to Bolbec seemed too short. Every passing mile brought the moment of Jack's departure closer. As relieved as she was to reach their destination, she was reluctant to say goodbye. He, on the other hand, seemed eager to be off, to an estate a few miles away his grandfather kept for such visits.

"We cannot thank you enough." Aunt Adele took his hand and pulled him toward the house as her sister emerged. "I do not know what we would have done without you." She turned to Lady Priscilla, who resembled her down to the wobbling chin and graying curls beneath her cap. "Sister, Mr. Waverley was a godsend. I don't know how we would have borne the journey without him."

The two women fussed over him for a few moments, and Georgiana hid a smile at his discomfited expression. But he wiggled his eyebrows at her when the others weren't looking.

"It was my pleasure to have been of service to you and Miss Lockewood. I will call on you as soon as my work permits. If not, I will see you in three months, when we return to merry old England."

"You must have some tea and rest after your journey." Lady Priscilla took his other arm.

Georgiana stifled a laugh as they tugged his arms at the same time while he remained in place.

"Alas, I have business that cannot wait." He pulled free and swept into a courtly bow.

Georgiana blocked his path to the carriage. "You are going to take me around, are you not? I do so wish to see some of the countryside. And Paris, too, of course."

She bit the inside of her cheek at the petulant whine in her voice but couldn't help her peevishness. He was almost desperate in his attempt to be rid of them. She recalled Jonathan's warning that Jack was a man with many diverse appetites, and would probably not wish to associate with her once they were in France. At the time, she hadn't cared either way, until she realized the voyage and the carriage ride were all the time they'd have together. Three months without his wit and conversation would be an eternity.

A blush seared her cheeks. Wit and conversation? Was that all she was going to miss?

His steel gray eyes fastened on her, and she glanced away, embarrassed as if he'd caught her doing something naughty. He gave her a replica of his earlier bow. "I will call on you, Miss Lockewood, by this time next week. I thought two days in my company was enough to last you a lifetime."

"Oh, my goodness, no, Mr. Waverley!" Aunt Adele shook her head. "It is rare to find such a likeable young man. You must come again."

"I accept the invitation, dear ladies. I must be on my way now."

"Then we will say goodbye, sir. Please come and see us soon." Aunt Adele kissed him on the cheek and walked inside with her sister.

Georgiana met Jack's expectant gaze. She'd never been at a loss for words in his presence, but her voice seemed frozen. Bidding him goodbye with a joke would sound immature. A formal adieu, too matronly. She stooped to pick a wilted rose from the tangled bushes lining the path.

"You're not going to behead all these roses, are you?"

She straightened. "My brother and you have remarkable memories, sir, in that you recall my childhood exploits at every opportune moment."

"I remember your howls when your nurse scolded you after you destroyed your mother's garden."

She tucked the rose into his buttonhole. She didn't remember her sobs so much as she remembered who had comforted her. Not Jonathan, who'd agreed with the nurse in her punishment. Jack had tossed her onto his shoulders and galloped around the corridors until her sobs turned to laughter. She stood back to admire her handiwork and plucked a drooping petal.

"I hope you'll come and visit us." She tried to keep a jolly air, but her voice caught. The excitement she'd felt at the outset of the journey paled at the reality of their separation.

"I will, but only if you assure me you will not be too busy with all the excitement around here." A sweep of his arm took in the empty road and the quiet countryside. A bird chirped in the branches overhead.

"I promise to tear myself away from it somehow." She held out her hand uncertainly. How did one take leave of a gentleman who was neither relative nor admirer?

Jack solved her dilemma. "Are you not going to kiss me goodbye? I understand it is the custom in France."

"So is eating frogs and snails. If you like, I'll go

into the garden and hunt them for your tea." As if the slimy creatures dwelled within her middle, her stomach quivered and jumped. Her chest rose and fell too rapidly as he closed the last bit of space separating them.

"Save them for me. I must dash."

Before she could speak or think, he placed his hands on her shoulders and dipped his head. He brushed a light kiss across each of her cheeks, and she wondered if he'd felt the heat of her blush on his lips.

"Goodbye, Georgie. Look for me at week's end, and we shall have a grand time." He bowed quickly and climbed into the carriage. The driver urged the horses forward. She returned Jack's wave until the carriage vanished behind the hedgerows.

She must have walked inside to where Aunt Adele and Lady Priscilla were, and she must have drunk a little tea and eaten a bite or two of an apricot tart, but she could not remember a thing except Jack Waverley had kissed her.

Chapter Five

Nothing at the *vignoble* had changed since Jack's visit a year ago. He strode through the rows and rows of fragrant barrels while his grandfather's foreman, Gaston Gironde, droned in heavily accented English about the shipping schedules and a particularly bad harvest the year before.

Jack walked beside him, hands clasped behind his back, nodding now and then as he listened with half an ear. Georgiana's softly floral scent still clung to his collar when he'd leaned in close for a mocking kiss goodbye. The remembered pressure of her downy cheek against his lips distracted him to the point where he nodded affirmatively to a question Gaston asked. Apparently, he gave the wrong response.

Gaston's thick eyebrows rose on his forehead. "But surely, Monsieur Waverley, you cannot mean to throw eighty barrels away! We usually turn it into a cheaper wine we sell locally. That is how we have always done things here."

Shaking his head to dispel the image of Georgiana's wide blue eyes staring up into his, Jack observed the motion did little to force her out of his thoughts. "Do as you wish, man. I do not intend to make any changes. We both know my presence is so my grandfather can pay me in the guise of noble employment."

Gaston nodded briskly. "Wine it shall be." He motioned toward the offices in the back of the building. "I will show you the books, Monsieur Waverley, and have your signature."

"Lead on," Jack murmured, stifling a yawn. He'd always wondered how his grandfather could be involved in the mundane business world but now realized it was easy when he could send his grandson in his stead.

At the office, Jack sat in the heavy carved chair at his grandfather's desk. Long ago, his grandfather had taken frequent jaunts to oversee the *vignoble*, run in partnership with his friend, Gaston. When an old war wound prohibited him from taking the trip, Jack's father had stepped in. After he died, Gaston managed the daily operations. Now, the job had fallen to Jack.

He glanced around the office as Gaston mentioned the latest problems with transportation and increasing port charges. His gaze drew upward to the portrait taking prominence on the wall. His mother's painted blue eyes gazed down at him.

She was posed in a rose garden fabricated by the artist, since roses had never grown so lushly at Stoughton Park. Her slender white arms and neck, as well as her sweeping chestnut curls, had not emerged from the artist's imagination. If he stared at the painting, he could almost hear her voice or see the sparkle in her eyes.

When he was high enough to reach his father's knee, she'd abandoned them. The lingering memories were vague blurs. Were it not for the sole remaining portrait, he didn't know if he would have forgotten how she looked. Grandfather had all the other portraits and her possessions burned the terrible morning they discovered her betrayal. This painting had escaped his tirade, having been transported across the Channel a few years before. It was one of the reasons Jack didn't mind coming to the *vignoble*.

"You've kept it after all these years." Jack motioned toward the portrait.

Gaston shrugged. "I see no reason to take it down. Your father told me this was the only place he could visit her."

He averted his eyes, and Jack realized it was because his own face must have displayed all the stifled agony her disappearance had caused. Grandfather had forbidden mourning his daughter-in-law, and once when Jack had asked where Mamma had gone, he'd received a sound slap.

He'd managed, as children can, to fill his life with games and friends, but his father had taken her absence hard. He'd turned to drinking at all hours of the day and was found in a field a few months later. The official word was that his horse had thrown him, but Jack knew his mother's abandonment had caused it. A sudden pain gripped his chest, and he ground his teeth, waiting for it to dissipate.

"Monsieur?"

Jack gave his shoulders a little shake. "Yes, yes. What do I need to sign?"

Gaston set a leather-bound book before him, and Jack dipped his pen in the inkwell, signing where Gaston pointed. He could have been signing away state secrets to some French upstart for all he knew. When he was done, Gaston handed him a stack of letters. One particular letter on buff-colored thick paper caught his eye.

"What's all this?"

He recognized the owner of the handwriting the moment he took the packet. The Comtesse de Mirville was expecting him. Staring at the letters brought back a flood of memories, which consisted of too much wine and not enough clothes for either of them. An odd sense of regret overtook him. He stuffed the letter inside his coat.

"Your grandfather's letter is here, monsieur." Gaston pulled a missive from the pile and placed it meaningfully before Jack.

"You can forego all the *monsieuring*, Gaston. You've known me since I was wet behind the ears. These formalities give one a headache."

The older man's lips twitched, and he bowed smartly. "As you wish, Ambrose."

"I'd prefer *monsieur*, after all." He pushed away from the desk. "We both know you are running this place handsomely by yourself, and my presence is only a formality. Shall we call an end to this dreary meeting? I have other things to do." Being in the room with the reminder of his beloved father's death staring down at him was suddenly too much.

Gaston arranged the papers on the desk into neat stacks. "Fortunately, the *vignoble* manages well on its own."

"If that is the truth, I wonder why my grandfather sends me here at all."

The Frenchman's thick black eyebrows drew together in a line. "Perhaps it is so *monsieur* will have meaningful employment and not waste his time on frivolous living."

"Amazing, Gaston. You didn't even mutter that under your breath but boldly stated my grandfather's opinion verbatim."

Gaston bowed smartly. "We share the same opinion." His wizened features lost some of their tightness. "I have known your family since before you were born. I do not ask your pardon for speaking plainly."

Restraining a laugh at Gaston's seriousness, Jack rose from the chair. "I would not expect any less from you or my grandfather." He clapped his grandfather's old friend on the shoulder and gave his mother's portrait a fleeting look. "Show me from this place, Gaston. It's time I returned to my wicked life so you may carry on your more important work."

Outside, Jack ordered his driver to take him to his grandfather's chateau. He leaned back against the velvet padding and removed Danielle's letter.

She'd spared no amount of graphic English and French words to describe exactly what she proposed for their reunion. Le comte was conveniently abroad, and she was alone in her sprawling chateau on the outskirts of Bordeaux. Jack tried to remember small details of her face and figure, but could not. Fleeting, scented memories of Georgiana flooded his mind instead.

How she'd clutched his coat on the ship, her lithe body pressed against him when a most opportune wave sent her flying into him. The way her full, rosebud lips moved when she spoke or laughed. The mischievous glint in her eyes as she'd teased him on the way to Portsmouth, obviously relieved to leave England behind.

He should send word to Georgiana that,

unfortunately, his business in Bordeaux would keep him too occupied to pay a visit. She was a reasonable girl, and doubtless Lady Priscilla had many outings and enjoyable times planned to keep her busy enough she would not give him a second thought. Perhaps she might even attend a ball and have an innocent love affair. Something to take her mind off that dog, Mitford, and throw her back into the world again.

He almost sighed with relief as his plan unfolded. He'd send word to Danielle and tell her to expect him before nightfall. He could sup with her, though he did not remember eating or drinking much when they were together. He waited for his ardor to stir; for the expectant ache in his loins to grow as he anticipated a night in her arms.

Nothing.

"Perhaps Lockewood is right," he muttered. "I've taken too many blows to the head to think straight." When the time came to go abroad this year, he'd paced the floor in his impatience for the journey to commence. Now, so close to sating his desire, he was almost disturbed the burning passion he'd felt for the saucy brunette had vanished.

Better to avoid both women and any complications they might cause. He intended to enjoy himself on his grandfather's gold the short while he was in France. An anonymous love affair was what he needed. Perhaps he'd go to Paris and find someone for a few nights' passion and then return to Bordeaux and the tedious business of the *vignoble*.

He crumpled the letter into a ball and tossed it out the window, where it caught on a gust of wind and rolled into a ditch.

Chapter Six

"One does become used to the simple country ways after a time," Lady Priscilla said, fanning herself lazily while Georgiana and Aunt Adele took tea with her in the garden.

Georgiana sipped her lukewarm tea and tried to look more interested in the conversation, which had alternated between how to keep lace from drooping in the humid weather and the trouble with garden moles, who were very much the same, it turned out, as English ones.

"I can see why you prefer living abroad," Aunt Adele said with a sigh, closing her eyes and leaning back against the plump chair cushions. "I thought you would come home to England when your Jean-Luc died."

"Oh, la," Lady Priscilla replied. "I have everything I want right here. There is no end to amusements of all sorts."

Georgiana glanced around the garden. Except for the chattering of a few birds and the occasional hum of a bee, all was quiet.

"What amusements?" she asked politely.

Lady Priscilla blinked, as if surprised to see Georgiana was still there. "We have many balls—rather like our assembly balls back home, though much more enjoyable. And the food is far better, though they have never heard of white soup. It's not the same, really, when there's no white soup at a ball." She went into a discourse on a menu she'd sampled once, and Georgiana waited impatiently for her to continue about the ball. She seemed to notice Georgiana again and smiled suddenly.

"My husband's nephew, Alphonse, is attending one tonight. I will ask him to take you along, if you like."

Before Georgiana could accept, Aunt Adele spoke up. "She cannot go out unchaperoned, dear sister." She fanned herself hastily, glancing at Georgiana as if to say, *I saved you from unspeakable danger*. "We should send for that wonderful Mr. Waverley. He is the dear friend of my nephew, Mr. Lockewood."

Heart quickening at the mention of Jack's name, Georgiana picked at an orange, peeling it with her nails. "Jack doesn't have any time for us, Aunt Adele. He sent word he was too busy to entertain us."

She tried to sound as light and nonsensical as the two ladies but swallowed a bitter taste in her throat. More than two weeks had passed since he'd left them in Bolbec. When Jack didn't come for her at the end of their first week, she'd put it down to his being occupied with the winery. The following Friday arrived, and instead of Jack's broad shoulders gracing the chateau doorway, he'd sent a messenger.

Aunt Adele nodded. "Oh, yes. I'd forgotten. Fine gentlemen are always so occupied with more important things." She turned to her sister. "Perhaps your husband's nephew can take her, if Georgiana wishes to go. Is Alphonse an amiable sort of man?"

"Oh, yes. In fact, he is going to join us for an early supper before the ball. Georgiana, dear, you may use

Marceline to help you dress and do your hair. We are a bit more fashionable here in France." She patted the sides of her gray ringlets dangling from beneath a soft linen cap the same as her sister's.

Georgiana ate a segment of the sweet orange. Her disappointment at Jack's absence faded as the realization she would go to the ball unchaperoned began to form in her mind. She could spend the entire night dancing with whomever she pleased, as often as she wished, without a guardian's stern eyes upon her. Her French was very good, and she was eager to try her conversational skills upon people younger than seventy.

"Thank you, Lady Priscilla. I'm looking forward to it."

She finished her orange as the women forgot her again. When it was clear she would not be missed, she excused herself and went upstairs to her chamber. Sweeping open the lacy woven curtains, she breathed in the warm, fresh air of the gardens below. Softly rolling hills stretched beyond the horizon, dotted with other estates and wooded areas as far as the eye could see. The countryside was peaceful, and the local village filled with friendly people, who'd bobbed a curtsy or tipped their hats to her and Aunt Adele when they'd taken a drive at the beginning of their trip.

Other than that, they had not left the chateau, which seemed to suit Aunt Adele just fine. Her cold had returned, and she'd wrapped an old piece of flannel around her throat, even though the day was warm. Lady Priscilla, plump and pretty, did not care for exercise, and the two sisters spent their days in the sunny garden, drinking tea like two British matrons rather than the worldly travelers they liked to pretend they were.

Georgiana sighed, her breath disturbing the curtain, which was so sheer it resembled a spider's web. The buzzing bees in the roses and hyacinths below the window hovered lazily at their task. Her eyelids fluttered, and she had to rouse herself. If she didn't do something soon, she would become as lazy as the white cat in the garden. Fat on mice and garden moles, it had flicked its whiskers at her once before closing its yellow eyes and going back to sleep.

She turned from the window and hastened to her dressing room, where she quickly chose a ball dress for the evening. The silvery blue color complemented her eyes and skin, and she preened before the mirror. She imagined she was dancing with a handsome Parisian around a ballroom ablaze with a thousand candles. She closed her eyes in a peaceful daze, and almost heard the strains of violins. Her body swayed to the music in her head, and she struggled to put a face to her partner.

One of the gardeners in Lady Priscilla's employ had dark, gypsy-like eyes and long black hair. He'd winked at her a few days ago when Aunt Adele wasn't looking.

Humming a tune, she twirled in a small circle, enjoying a slight breeze on her legs as her skirts floated around her. The gardener was spinning her about a grand ballroom, his full red lips turned upward in a smile. She lost herself in her reverie and gave a spontaneous giggle at an imagined compliment. Before she could stop herself, her phantom dancer's dark eyes lightened to the color of the sea on a stormy day. Jack's rakish grin transformed her fantasy Frenchman. The dark hair vanished, changing to burnt gold. Her eyes flew open, and she threw the dress down with a murmured oath.

"Oh, get out of my head, will you?" she snapped. She began rifling through her jewelry and hairpins, as if it were the most important thing in the world to be perfectly accessorized.

Chapter Seven

Alphonse was a droopy-eyed, sad-looking fellow with lank black hair and a perpetual frown. Georgiana wondered if she should bring some smelling salts in case her escort collapsed during the evening. Lady Priscilla and Aunt Adele cast each other significant glances, and Georgiana stifled a laugh at the idea of being courted by someone as dull as Alphonse. No matter he was the first Frenchman she'd met and her salvation from her mundane life so far. He was not the least bit interesting, and she earnestly prayed her aunt was not thinking of matchmaking the pair of them.

He sat opposite her in the carriage and stared out the window, refusing conversation. She'd tried her French on him but gave up when all she received was a noncommittal grunt. Not bothering to stifle a sigh, Georgiana smoothed the wrinkles from her gown, which shimmered in the waning sunlight. As dreadful as her companion was, she anticipated her first night out. What a treat not to worry about Aunt Adele watching her like a hawk, or Jonathan hovering over her shoulder every time a potential dancing partner emerged from the crowd.

She'd been sheltered most of her life, but that was not uncommon with young ladies of her class. Her mother had been a successful debutante, catching the eye and hand of her father at her very first ball.

Georgiana had no such conquests. After *the incident,* she had refused to make her debut, much to her brother's grievous concern. She didn't see the point, really, which was for a debutante to meet her future husband while in the guise of attending as many balls and events as possible. Marriage was the furthest thing from her mind. Tonight, she was going to have fun.

She turned away from the window and started a little when she met Alphonse's penetrating gaze.

"You are a long way from home," he commented in near perfect English.

"Yes, I am. Have you ever been to England?"

He shrugged, and she thought she'd imagined he'd ever spoken at all.

A few more moments of silence followed, and she cleared her throat. "Will you meet some friends at the ball?"

"No."

Her heart sank. Lord above, would she have to remain at his side the entire night? She nearly wrinkled her nose at the odious idea. She was looking forward to dancing with as many partners as she chose.

"Perhaps…one friend," he said at length, watching her carefully. She nodded encouragingly, as it seemed he wished to convey a confidence. Even coming from Alphonse, it was the most exciting thing she had heard in a fortnight.

"A young lady?"

"She is the daughter of a miller. My aunt and my parents frown upon the match."

"I see." Georgiana didn't know why she should be shocked the same prejudices existed in France as they did back home. "Well, I believe you must follow your heart in these matters, Monsieur Alphonse." She smiled, but he only seemed dourer, if that were possible.

"I have not the freedom to make my own choice, Mademoiselle Lockewood." He gave her just the slightest smile in return and looked out the window again.

She could think of nothing else to say and was almost relieved his melancholia had been based on yearning for love rather than a dull personality. "My brother wishes for me to marry," she said, then cringed at her lack of propriety.

His thick black eyebrows flicked upward with interest. "Are you in love with your fiancé?"

"I have no fiancé just yet."

Her palms sweated inside the sheathlike gloves. How much time remained before Jonathan insisted she marry one of the suitors he'd chosen? He hadn't mentioned any by name, but she'd seen important looking cards coming to the house with various crests and arms embossed upon them. Once, she'd caught him and Sophie whispering in the breakfast room, and when she'd entered, Sophie had beamed at her, nodding once at Jonathan and exclaiming, "He would be perfect!"

Thinking they were talking about a new stallion Jonathan coveted, she'd dismissed the conversation. Now, she wondered if she'd missed something much more important. She'd promised Jonathan she'd consider marriage if he allowed her to go abroad, and he'd kept his word. She must keep hers, regardless of the outcome.

"I shall not marry for love." Whenever she tried to imagine the nameless suitors Jonathan had brokered, she could only see bland, nondescript features. No romantic notion filled her heart. Her back stiffened against the padded carriage wall.

"Why not?" He leaned forward, as if she were a fascinating specimen on a table, and he was about to dissect her.

"Because it is not real. Because it does not last."

He turned away with a smirk. "English girls are very strange."

"It has nothing to do with being English." She bit her tongue to keep from saying more. The last thing she needed was for Alphonse to go back to Aunt Adele and report her scandalous words. She cleared her throat delicately. "Perhaps it is an English thing."

"You have not been in love before, mademoiselle. If you had, you would not say that." He looked a little too smug for her liking. A sharp image of Edward flashed through her mind, searing his dark eyes into her brain before she could prevent it. She gulped almost painfully.

"Perhaps you are right. I have never been in love before." How easy to lie to a stranger. Her stays crushed her ribs with her rising anxiety. She glanced out the window but couldn't concentrate on the pastoral countryside. Several coaches were parked along a stone wall, and their driver slowed the horses.

"That is unfortunate." He ran his hands through his hair, but the gesture only flattened it. "We are here," he announced, rather unnecessarily, as the coach came to an abrupt stop outside a gaily-lit building overcrowded with couples and groups of people dressed for a ball. Georgiana took the footman's hand as he helped her out, and she waited for Alphonse to offer his arm and escort her inside, but he was indifferent. He seemed to be looking for someone, and she guessed it was the miller's daughter.

His sour expression suddenly brightened, and he called out something in rapid French that she barely caught. A pretty girl in a pink dress and white roses in her hair skipped across the lawn to him and threw her arms around his neck.

Georgiana gaped in surprise, then allowed the couple their privacy and walked into the building along with the others. Not one word of English did she hear, and she realized quickly that for all her proper conversational French, she did not understand the idioms and local dialect very well. Groups of young girls fluttered about in pairs or trios, flirting blatantly with handsome young men, who pinched their cheeks and stole kisses left and right.

Excited but wary, Georgiana got caught up in a group who herded her into a refreshment room. She'd already had her supper and usually had a light appetite, but the intriguing smells and sights of so many delicacies forced her to sample a slice of cake and some bonbons. Someone jostled her elbow, and she nearly dropped her plate. She turned as a tall, dark-haired man struck the head of the man who'd bumped her.

Her gallant knight grinned down at her. He swept into a low bow, and when he straightened, she met his mesmerizing black eyes. She curtsied, lowering her head so he wouldn't see her blush. He was the living vision of her phantom dancer.

"Forgive me, mademoiselle," he said in a rich, low voice. "I hope that fiend did not distress you."

"He did not."

"Do you dance this evening? A lady as *tres charmant* as yourself should be dancing." His eyes twinkled in the light of the candelabra on the tables and overhead. A tiny voice in the back of her mind told her to refuse. Surely, a man with such wickedly handsome good looks and bewitching eyes could mean nothing but trouble. She should find Alphonse and request a dance with him, even though he was probably deeply involved with his illicit romance.

The stranger held out his gloved hand expectantly. Before she knew what she was doing, Georgiana set down her plate and allowed him to lead her to the main room where a quadrille was already forming.

How delightful to have such an attentive partner, and no suspicious chaperone clucking in disapproval. For the first in a long time, Georgiana felt a rush of freedom. *This is what it must be like for Jack.* Her head spun as she whirled around the room.

The dance was over before she knew it, and her partner took her hand and held it almost possessively. Excited by the vibrant music and the general gaiety of the other dancers, Georgiana didn't mind when they were at a table spread with more sweets and bowls of punch. He offered to get her a glass, and she nodded happily, looking forward to the rest of the evening. More than a few young ladies had glanced at him, and she was proud he'd chosen her.

She toyed with the idea of inviting him for tea the next day and giggled when she realized she didn't know his name. How positively liberating to be so carefree and improper! He returned with the punch, and she held the cup to her lips, eager to continue dancing.

The glass slid from her gloved fingers and crashed

to the floor, sending crystal shards and rose-colored liquid to spatter the hem of her gown. She ought to have minded the murmured words of concern from her partner, who knelt to pick up the worst of the pieces, but she was unaware of his or anyone else's presence.

Save one.

Across the room, a man returned her stare, the corners of his mouth twitching as if he were about to speak. The thick black brows flickered up in surprise, then lowered as a smirk spread across his face. After an interminable time, he turned his back in a pointed manner and continued his conversation with his companions.

Impossible.

Her frozen heart melted at the sight of his broad back. Had he always been so tall, so broad-shouldered? Had his hair always curled just a little bit, onto his collar? Had the sharp cheekbones always looked as if carved from marble?

She didn't realize the dull ache in her chest was a sob rising to her lips. Stifling a gasp, she pushed past her concerned partner and stumbled out onto an empty veranda. Before she could give in to tears, rough fingers grabbed her arm while another hand groped at her breast. She jerked away, only to collide into another man. The stale stench of his breath nauseated her.

"Mademoiselle, where are you going?" He pulled her hard against him.

She raised her hand to strike his face, rage burning through her, but he caught it as easily as if it were a mouse in a cat's paw. The other man was behind her, pressing against her.

Panicking, she threw back her head to scream, but

a grubby hand closed over her mouth. Swiftly, they moved toward the corner, taking her with them in some unspoken understanding. She lifted her knee and narrowly missed her attacker's groin, but he only laughed. His fingers fumbled with her bodice while his companion worked on raising her gown.

Her attacker's expression turned from intent leer to one of absolute terror. A silver blade glittered against his throat. At first, she thought he had a red ribbon tied around his neck until a thin, bright stream of blood dripped from where the blade pressed his throat.

"Release her, and I might let you live." A very annoyed, heavily accented English voice speaking French reached her through the blood pounding in her ears.

The man let her go and backed away, his swarthy face even darker from his suppressed anger. His partner joined him, and they stumbled backward, making their way off the veranda and disappearing into the night.

"Jack!" she stared at her rescuer with a mixture of shock and relief. Her legs gave out, and she would have fallen had he not caught her.

"Are you hurt? Did those bastards touch you?" His big hands patted her roughly, as if he could assess any damage with his bare fingers. She shook her head, a hysterical laugh rising to her lips.

"No, I am unhurt. Your arrival was very timely. How long have you been here?" She suddenly found it difficult to stand on her own. He gripped her elbows and gave her a little shake, his head suddenly close to hers.

"Long enough. What are you doing here alone? Where is Aunt Adele?"

She looked around, feeling as helpless as if she were a child lost in the woods. The shock of her near attack must have been telling on her, and she merely stared beyond the veranda into the dark landscape.

"She is at home. She wanted me to go out for the evening and enjoy myself, but I'm afraid I lost my escort."

"Who is your escort?"

"Lady Priscilla's nephew, Alphonse." She hiccupped, and a nervous, frightened giggle burst from her. "I do not know where he is. I was dancing with another gentleman. I do not know his name."

"Dancing with a stranger, Georgiana? And no escort, save a lovesick boy?"

"How do you know he is lovesick?"

"Because all Frenchmen are." He shook his head. "Never mind. I'll take you home, and we'll sort this out in the morning. Lady Priscilla's nephew deserves a good thrashing for abandoning you, and I'm just in the mood to give it."

He led her through one crowded salon to another, until they reached the main hall. He collected his hat and ordered his carriage. She turned back toward the ballroom to see if Edward had remained where she'd seen him, but he was gone. She longed to give in to a good cry, but Jack was already ushering her into the carriage in a brisk manner, not unlike a mother hen she'd once seen at Fairwood Hall, when her chicks had gone astray.

****

Jack smothered the curses lurking in the recesses of his throat. He resolved to see her safely home and then planned to return to the ball and find the two ruffians.

And when he did—

"I cannot go back to the chateau. Aunt Adele will have a fit if she hears about this. She will insist we return to England immediately, or write Jonathan about it. Either way, I will have to go home, and I'd rather not. It is not Alphonse's fault he abandoned me. He was making a tryst with a young lady to whom his parents object. She's a miller's daughter."

"Hush, Georgie." His voice was gruff with agitation. He tugged at his neckcloth. The pressing air inside the stuffy coach made his coat seem as if it was made of leather. "We shall have to inform your brother, regardless."

"He will demand my return. No, Jack." She shook her head stubbornly. "You can chastise me about making bad choices in the morning if you like. But I will not go home. Not yet." Her lip trembled. "I'd rather not entertain the thought of suitors at the moment."

"Perhaps you would be better off with a husband's protection," he reasoned, but she only pressed closer to the wall of the coach. "Your brother cannot always be there to protect you, nor can I." He thumped his fist on the side of the door. "What would have happened had I not been there to stop those brutes? And what of dancing with a man whose name you did not know? He could have set them up to..." He swore below his breath. "You are not in England anymore. You are too trusting for your own good."

"Then why not spend the rest of my life locked in a tower? You and Jonathan will never have to worry about poor, helpless Georgiana dragging you away from your gaming tables and boxing matches." She sniffed deliberately. "Or women."

"So elegantly put, Georgiana." He forced back his temper. She was upset, and understandably so. "But you must see reason. Sooner or later, you *will* have to marry."

"And why should I? What does it matter if I marry or not? Perhaps I should go into a…a convent. There's a lovely one down the road from the chateau. Perhaps I should knock on their door tomorrow and demand sanctuary from you and my brother. I speak French quite well and will fit in nicely with all the other lost girls."

Before she could burst into tears, he tucked the rug around her knees, but she pushed it away. A light beading of perspiration dotted her forehead, and he opened the window to allow a cool breeze to filter inside the coach. He patted her shoulder.

"Do not worry about a thing, Georgie. Perhaps we do not have to inform your brother. You aren't hurt, after all."

He tugged her earlobe, a gesture he'd done repeatedly in the last several years since she was a girl of five. Normally, she would rejoinder with an irritable slap on the hand, but she only stared at the landscape as the black shapes of buildings gradually faded and the dark patches of fields and cypresses surrounded them. She rubbed her hand across her eyes and met his concerned gaze.

"I'll be perfectly fine."

"Of course you will." He forced himself to remain calm, when all he wanted was to seek revenge on the blackguards who'd attempted…

She sniffled and he forgot his anger. "Try and rest.

We'll be at my chateau soon, where we will discuss all sorts of devious plots for vengeance on those louts."

A bare smile touched her lips. "Thank you, Jack." The shock slowly dissipated, and she shivered. When he tucked the rug around her again, she did not shrug it off.

Chapter Eight

"I'll send a man to Aunt Adele and inform her you're with me." Jack walked ahead of her and lighted the lamps throughout the house as they passed. "I think you should stay here until I am assured of your safety. Your brother would never forgive me should you go astray while I am supposed to be protecting you." He kicked a wine bottle on the floor, and it rolled beneath a settee. "Pardon the mess. This place is only opened when I make my annual sojourn. I'm not used to visitors."

The house was eerily silent, and Jack explained most of the servants lived nearby, with only a cook and a few scullery maids in the back rooms. "It's very quiet here. Peaceful. Nothing like the hustle and bustle of town."

He was making awkward small talk, and she realized it was because she'd been so silent. She tried to think of something to say, but nothing entered her mind. All she could think of were Edward's black eyes as he'd stared right through her. As if she did not exist.

She skimmed her hand along the cool marble balustrade as they walked upstairs. The chateau, like Lady Priscilla's, was a little shabby, but she didn't mind. France had suffered since the end of the Revolution, even though many years had already passed. Jack's chateau had the air of a bachelor's home, with its sparse décor and dirty glasses on the sideboard.

He pushed open a door in the middle of a long gallery and indicated she should enter first. He placed the lamp on a table, and she glanced around a large bedchamber. He strode to the window, pulling open the curtains so moonlight filled the room.

"You can sleep in here. The linens are fresh. There's water in the ewer, I think. You'll find a nightrail in the wardrobe, just there." He motioned to an armoire against the wall. Her tongue felt glued to the roof of her mouth. His efficient look faded.

"Georgie, I say—are you quite well? Shall I fetch a doctor?" His face blanched. "Are you certain those men did not hurt you?"

She blinked, nodding slowly.

He snapped his fingers. "Wine," he said with a tone of relief. He dashed to a sideboard, scrambled about the cluttered sideboard for a clean glass, until he simply brought her the bottle. He held it to her lips. "Have a long drink of this, sweetheart."

His voice was low and encouraging. He'd never called her anything, ever, besides Georgie, Pudding-Face, or her least favorite, Miss Chatterbox. She choked and sputtered as he tipped the stem, forcing her to take a healthy swig.

"Better?"

Her knees wobbled, and he gathered her in his arms, swinging her up as easily as if she weighed no more than a child. He deposited her on the bed, and for a frightful moment, she couldn't bear the thought of being alone.

"Please, Jack." She clutched his coat with her stiff fingers. "Do not leave me." A shiver ran through her.

Despite the stifling, warm air filtering in through the opened windows, her body ached as if she stood in a tub of icy water.

"Georgie, you're safe here. No one can come in. Besides—" He gently pried her fingers loose from his lapels. "I will kill anyone who ever tries to hurt you." A shadow crossed his face as he spoke, and she believed him. "Now"—and he was all business again—"kick off your slippers and go to sleep. My chamber is the first door we passed, should you need anything. We'll have a good, long talk in the morning, where we will discuss appropriate punishment for the nephew, if Lady Priscilla doesn't do something to him first. We must also decide how to keep this a secret from your brother. Cracking the nephew's head will be a sight easier than facing Lockewood."

With a parting wink, he left the room before she could speak again.

****

She eased the door open. Jack's heavy, comforting snore echoed through his chamber, bouncing off the tapestried walls. A candle on a side table cast a feeble light in the room. He lay sprawled on the bed, his coat and waistcoat carelessly tossed over a brocade settee. His boots were on the floor, and a stocking remained on one foot. His white shirt, creased and marked with sweat, was unbuttoned, revealing an expanse of tawny, muscular chest.

If he were any other man, she would not be standing in the doorway of his bedchamber as she had done so often as a child. Had it been Jonathan lying asleep, she would not have dared cross the threshold, as her brother was always quick to send her back to her room to battle nightmares alone. But Jack usually slept so heavily he never noticed her presence at the foot of his bed. Even after Jonathan scolded her for disturbing their guest, and Jack urged her to let him sleep in peace, she persisted in sneaking into his room whenever a nightmare or sad feeling took effect. She'd take care to be gone before he awakened, and Jonathan and he were none the wiser.

Such behavior was permitted of a motherless child, but somehow, she didn't consider herself too grown up to run to Jack for comfort. Nor did she care about a possible scandal should a servant spy her actions and report to Aunt Adele. She glanced down the corridor again. The house was silent save for his heavy snores.

Without hesitation, she padded across the carpet and crawled onto the bed, curling up at the foot as she used to do. An act she had done a hundred times in the past still felt right so many years later.

Time had changed a few things. He was taller now, and she barely had enough room without the footboard pressing against her nose. She scooted across the bed to lie beside him, straightening his arm to curl around her shoulder as she snuggled close. She rested her head onto his chest and listened to his heart reverberate in her ear. When she was younger, his chest was a massive thing she could barely reach across. Now her arm reached around him quite easily. Her head was no longer at the level of his collarbone, either, but touched his jaw. Although he had grown and changed, his natural scent was the same. The tears she'd stifled while he was awake fell freely, sliding down her cheek and across her nose, until they dropped onto his shirt.

Never had she thought to see Edward again. Had

she not avoided the places in London he was likely to visit? Foregone the usual stream of parties and balls so as not to risk the sight of him? She could have laughed at the irony of coming all the way to France only to see him at a ball, but every trace of humor had abandoned her.

Not much of his appearance had changed since she'd last seen him. The black curls, tumbled over his forehead, the sharp outline of his cheekbones against his pale skin. He looked a little fleshy, as if he'd over imbibed in food and drink, as Jonathan had once prophesied he would. The present image of him only forced her to remember in sharp detail the man she'd given her heart to, what seemed years ago, but had only been two summers past.

Jonathan wanted her to marry so she could forget Edward altogether. When she'd asked him if any of the suitors were handsome, he'd merely replied, "What is handsome compared to financial security?"

She sniffled and wiped her damp face lightly into Jack's motionless side. Why was Edward in Bordeaux? It was fortunate for him Jack had not spotted him first. How terribly Jack might have beat him, and in front of all those people. Spitefully, she almost wished he had.

Her head ached from the evening's events. How relieved she'd been to see Jack peering over her attacker's shoulder. She could still see the scarlet line he'd drawn across the man's throat. If he'd applied any more pressure, she was sure he would have killed him.

Shivering, she fumbled for the quilt. She wished she could awaken Jack to talk about what happened, but he would likely scold her for being upset over seeing Edward. To stifle her sobs, she pressed her face into his side. She must have pressed too hard, because he flinched and sprang upright a moment later with a noise that was a cross between a snore and a yelp.

"Good lord, Georgie! What are you doing in here?"

Her tears came freely now. She sat up when he did, catching hold of his arm before he could pull away.

"I saw him." She hiccupped, trying to hold back a fresh sob.

His anxious frown indicated he wasn't partial to tears. He fumbled with the small buttons on his shirt. His bare chest gleamed in the solitary candlelight and she turned away a second longer than she should have.

"Who did you see? The men who attacked you, do you mean?"

"No, no." She shook her head. "Before the men." She took a few gasping breaths. "Him…" She nearly choked on the name and pressed her hand to her mouth. After a moment, she breathed, "Edward."

"Mitford?" Jack's voice was hard. In a moment, his arm wrenched from hers as he sprang from the bed. "What the devil is the bastard doing here? How could he…?" The words tore from him in sputtering bursts. "I blame Lockewood for not slitting his throat when he had the chance. The bloody bastard!" He picked up his boot and flung it across the room, where it collided with a marble bust, sending it clattering to the floor.

Georgiana blinked. Jack had always possessed a marvelously volatile temper, but she was unused to coarse language. Fascinated, she listened to him rant for a few more moments, during which time he tossed his other boot, sending the bust's twin crashing to the hearth. The nose broke off and skittered across the marble until coming to a stop at the edge of the carpet.

Chest heaving, Jack faced her. "You are mistaken. How the devil would he have the means for such a journey? He spends his money faster than I do, which is saying quite a lot."

"I don't know." She bit her lip. "Perhaps he saved some money for his passage."

Jack snorted a most inelegant snort. "He couldn't save a wooden farthing if his life depended on it." He uttered another curse, looking decidedly fierce. She shrank against the headboard and clasped a pillow to her chest, though she was not afraid.

"It was not him. Your eyes were playing tricks. I'll bet my life on it." His face softened. "And you know how much I love to gamble."

He brought the wine and sat on the edge of the bed. "Have a drink, Pudding Face." His voice was softer, more natural than the raving madman of a few moments before.

She took the bottle and swallowed a mouthful of wine. She handed it back, and he took a long drink, then regarded her with sleepy eyes.

"To what do I owe the pleasure of your company this evening?" He patted his shirt. "And why is my shirt wet?"

"I couldn't sleep. This house is so big and empty." She never realized before what true quiet was, having lived at Fairwood Hall with more than fifty servants always present.

"It does feel like one rattles around the walls a bit." He rose from the bed and replaced the bottle on the table. "But you cannot sleep in here, much as I don't mind the company." He winked. "It will be just my luck you'll tell your brother I compromised you, and he'll lure me into the marriage trap. Perhaps that was his idea all along, and you're part of his conniving, scheming mind."

His teasing tone stirred something in her. She drew the quilt up to her neck. "Oh, please, let me stay. I'll sleep on the settee, or the floor. I don't want to be alone." She purposely swiped a stray tear from her cheek and sniffled loudly.

He heaved a sigh. "If you were not so tall, I would throw you over my shoulder and carry you back to your own chamber." He indicated the settee. "Throw me a pillow, will you? I suppose I've had worse beds than this."

"It's only for one night." She tossed him a pillow. He blew out the candle.

"It had better be. I did not sign up for this journey as a nursemaid, much as I would love taking you across my knee and giving you a well-deserved spanking for all the trouble you cost me this evening."

"Nursemaid Jack," she sang softly. He snorted, and she laughed quietly. "Was she very beautiful?" She'd spoken before she'd given it a thought. His personal life was none of her business.

"Who?"

"The paramour you had to leave tonight on my account."

He snorted. "There is no paramour." He punched his pillow in the darkness.

"You came to the ball alone?"

"Yes. I often attend balls unaccompanied. One has a damnably difficult time meeting new paramours if one is attached to another. Why the interest in my activities, she who ventures to balls in a foreign country with no chaperone?"

"I assumed there must be some reason to have kept you from visiting Aunt Adele and me." She bit her lip, scolding herself for sounding petulant.

"I apologize for not coming to see you. My grandfather will accept nothing but absolute perfection. And if there was a paramour, Miss Lockewood, this is less than suitable talk from one as young and innocent as you."

"When I am one and eighty, will you still consider me a little girl, I wonder?"

"You will always be my friend's little sister, dear Pudding Face."

His voice held a barely perceptible warning. She lay back on the pillows and snuggled beneath the quilt. "I should tell Jonathan you compromised me. That will be fine revenge for all the times you called me Pudding Face. He would be forced to call you out, and you will feel so guilty you'll allow him to kill you."

He harrumphed loudly. "I can imagine that duel. He would talk me to death before I could get in the first blow."

"If you promise to take me somewhere tomorrow, I promise not to mention what happened tonight to my brother."

"That's called blackmail."

She echoed his snort. "Call it what you will. I want to enjoy myself while I'm away from home. It's my last chance."

"You've seen what trouble you've found in having so much fun, haven't you?"

"I will not be in trouble as long as you're with me."

His laughter rang around the darkened chamber. "I

will think of somewhere harmless to take you in the morning. There's a bee farm nearby. Or perhaps we can stroll through a garden, if you promise not to disturb the butterflies, although I do fear for the safety of the roses. You might prick yourself on a thorn and bleed all over the place."

"I have never had a bad experience with a flower."

"Then I will ensure you have them in abundant supply while you're here. Good night, Georgie. Pleasant dreams."

"I shall dream of you, Jack. My rescuer." She'd spoken the words before she'd thought of them. He was quiet for a few seconds.

"Throw in a few bottles of wine, and I'll allow it."

"I shall also throw in a freshly starched cravat. Your linen is not very tidy."

He laughed again. "Perhaps I will dream about you, Georgiana."

She gasped with shocked amusement. "You are no gentleman, Jack Waverley."

"On the ship, you told me I was every inch the gentleman. How fickle is the mind of woman."

"So now you are admitting I'm not a child anymore."

"I admit no such thing."

The mattress sagged as she moved toward the edge. His outlined form on the settee was comforting in the darkness.

"I'm glad you were there tonight."

The settee creaked beneath his weight as he made himself more comfortable. "You may thank me properly in the morning. I have no cook on Sundays, and prefer eggs and sausage. Toasted bread, as well."

She drew the quilt up to her neck. Already, the night's frightening events had faded somewhat. She was safe now. Jack's scent wafted from the sheets and pillow, enfolding her in a sea of musk and spice. His presence was like an invisible shield, protecting her.

"Perhaps you are partly a gentleman."

He grunted. "I shall endeavor to become a full gentleman, if it pleases you."

She stroked the wrinkled linen pillowcase, imagining Jack's golden hair fanned across it. Shaking her head at the alarming thought, she merely sighed.

"Not a complete gentleman, please, Jack. I could not abide you too stuffy, like Jonathan."

"I am terribly unique, I admit."

He was trying to take her mind off her ordeal, and she smiled despite her troubled heart. "You are in a class all by yourself."

"As are you, Pudding Face. As are you."

Chapter Nine

Jack rubbed his neck as he dragged himself to a sitting position. How the devil had he not made it into his own bed the night before? He'd hardly touched a drop, yet here he was, clad in breeches, shirt, and stockings, with a perfectly good bed a few feet away.

A perfectly good bed with a sleeping woman nestled among the covers.

There could be only one reason a woman lay sleeping in his bed while he was on the settee.

"Georgie! You lazy chit! Time to wake up." He strode to the bed and yanked the quilt off her.

With a muffled yelp, she sat up, looking around the room as if she were lost. "Jack?"

"Good morning to you, too. If you don't mind, I'd like to bathe and dress, and your presence makes both tasks interesting though terribly inconvenient."

She pulled the neck of her nightrail closed and threw back the coverlet. He caught a glimpse of her slender leg until her gown covered her to the floor when she stood.

"I'd rather not return to Aunt Adele just yet, if you don't mind."

"By all means, stay as long as you like. I'll be gone until supper."

He moved around his room, checking his watch fob and ringing the bell to summon Philippe, his one servant who acted as valet whenever he was in France.

"Where are you going?"

"To my grandfather's winery."

"Whatever for?"

He exhaled loudly. "I do take my responsibilities seriously, contrary to what you may believe." She continued to stare at him, and he scowled. "You needn't look so surprised, Georgiana. You have that look of shock I saw so often on your brother's face whenever I did anything that smacked of respectability."

She held out her hand. "Forgive me, Jack. I didn't know you had serious pursuits."

"You mean besides boxing and throwing away money on paramours?"

"Yes. I mean, no, of course I don't think those are your only occupations. But if you have such good employment here, why would you waste your time with the other things?"

"Because listening to my grandfather's foreman lecture me all day and tasting numerous glasses of wine is not the romantic life it sounds."

"May I go with you?"

He blinked. "Why on earth would you want to go to the *vignoble*? There's nothing to see. Besides, it's harvest time, so it will be very busy. No one will have time to entertain you or suffer your presence underfoot."

"Oh, please, Jack! I promise not to disturb anyone. Least of all, you."

"I don't know..." There were a hundred good reasons why he should return her promptly to Aunt Adele's safekeeping, but he could not think of one. Perhaps it was a good idea to show her the *vignoble*.

She could return to her brother with a glowing description of the flourishing vineyards he oversaw. "Although I'm certain I'll regret this, you may accompany me. You must hurry and dress. I was supposed to be there before noon, but your snores kept me awake half the night."

His words did not have the desired effect, and she rewarded him with her trilling laughter at his stern voice. Taking her by the shoulders, he steered her from his chamber and pointed to her chamber door.

"You'll find some clothing that may suit you in the wardrobe inside. I'll send Marie to attend you, but mind you don't keep me waiting. This is a work day, not an afternoon visit."

She rose on tiptoe and kissed him quickly on the cheek before he could react. "Thank you, Jack."

He didn't answer, and only realized he hadn't once she'd closed the chamber door behind her.

****

Softly rolling hills covered in trailing vineyards filled the view outside the carriage window. Georgiana pushed at the brim of her hat so she could see it better. The hat was among a suspiciously large collection of garments she'd found in the wardrobe. She glanced at Jack, who seemed to be studying her. She raised her eyebrow to give him her best haughty look.

"Am I entertaining you, sir?"

"Yes, since you asked. Your head is bobbing back and forth like a cockerel in the yard, looking for a lost seed."

She tossed her reticule at him and regretted her actions when he tucked it inside his waistcoat with a comical grimace.

"That is all the money I have in the world, Jack. Give it back." She couldn't help but lose her stern demeanor.

"I will not. You threw it at me, which is, in effect, the same as giving it to me. If you end up having to sing in the streets for your passage back to England, you have only yourself to blame."

She settled back against the padded seat and folded her hands in her lap. "Very well. I shall sing outside your window every night, and you may throw a few guineas down at me until I have enough for my passage."

"I will compose a list of my favorite tunes. If you learn them well, perhaps you will earn your money back. If not, you will make a very good scullery maid at Lady Priscilla's chateau." He patted his chest where her reticule lay.

"To thank you for your cockerel remark, I'll have you know I was enjoying the countryside. A certain gentleman promised he would take me out, but I was left to languish these past weeks at Lady Priscilla's house. The only excitement I've had was last night at the ball."

"Yes, and such appalling excitement, Georgiana. What were you doing with that tall Frenchman before you saw the abomination himself?"

She fanned herself with her gloved hand, basking in the memory of the stranger's smile while ignoring the troubling fact of Edward's presence. "He asked me to dance, so I danced. Had you been true to your word and taken me out yourself, I would have been dancing with you all night and not strange men."

"Do not place the mantle of sainthood upon these

shoulders, Miss Lockewood."

"But they're such broad, capable shoulders, Mr. Waverley. My brother will be pleased to hear how you saved me."

He shook his head. "God, woman! Do not ever tell Lockewood about last night. He'll have my head and Aunt Adele's for our negligence in allowing you to run around the ball unescorted."

"Then you had better be nice to me, or I will write him immediately and report how you abandoned me at the mercy of two elderly ladies and their inept views on chaperoning."

"And one of the elderly ladies' inept nephews."

"Oh, yes, let's not forget about Alphonse."

"*Alphonse*." Jack repeated the name under his breath. A flush spread across his jaw, and his hands tightened into fists. Good heavens, poor Alphonse was doomed if she did not defend him quickly!

"He is not to blame for what happened to me last night, Jack. Those ruffians could have struck at any time. You do not have to worry about chasing him down and breaking his nose."

"I should do a lot more should I ever meet the nincompoop." His gray eyes glittered as shards of steel were imbedded in them.

Her heartbeat quickened, and she gulped back a breath of excitement. What would have happened last night had Jack not found her in time? She fought the urge to throw her arms around his neck and squeeze him as tightly as she could. The thought she might actually enjoy embracing him struck her. She changed the subject.

"I am fortunate to have such a friend as you."

He pulled the brim of his hat below his forehead and leaned against the wall of the coach in preparation for a nap. "You'll forget I exist the moment you return to England and all the leering fops who pass for eligible bachelors are vying for your attention."

She shuddered elaborately. "Ugh! You make courtship sound so inviting, Jack. You must promise to accompany me to Almack's and fight off anyone I do not fancy."

He snorted. "Your brother will be pulling them forward with one hand whilst I fight them with another. If I were in your place, Georgie, I'd find the richest of the lot and marry at once. Tear yourself away from the good intentions of your noble brother."

"Jonathan has my best intentions at heart."

"I'm sure he does." He looked as if he would say more but chewed his lip without uttering another word.

"You don't agree?"

He straightened, as if resigned to the notion she would not let him nap. "I will speak frankly, if I may. He doesn't want you to throw yourself after another fool like…like the previous one. He's worried if you do not marry soon, you will give your heart to the wrong man."

"How is a man the wrong man if I'm in love? Did he say this to you?"

He shook his head. "He didn't have to. It is twenty years of friendship speaking now. And I must say, Georgiana, you were quite the impetuous child, running away with Mouldy Mitford the way you did. You have too much to offer a husband that you'd waste it on him."

She leaned forward, fascinated in his knowledge of

the world. How fortunate her brother had chosen Jack to escort her to France. She would learn all manner of things from him if she chose her words correctly.

"What do I have to offer? You mean my inheritance?"

His mouth twisted. "Lord, no, you goose! Any man would be happy to have a woman like you as his wife. Not for your fortune, but for your..." His words broke off as he made a vague motion at her face and somewhere in the vicinity of her chest. "This is not suitable conversation. If you want compliments and flattery, we should find the stranger who monopolized you at the ball. I'm sure he'd have plenty of pretty things to say to you."

"Were you spying on me? Was that another of my brother's requests?"

"I was not spying. I happened there on my own accord from circumstances that had nothing to do with you. One could hardly miss you, Georgiana. You do have a way of standing out, with your loud laugh and twirling about so every male in the place couldn't keep his eyes off you."

"I was enjoying myself in a way I never can in London. You should have escorted me if you didn't want everyone staring at me, as you claim. Why did you not greet me, instead of leaving me in the hands of handsome strangers?"

"Handsome?" He rolled his eyes. "That man was slippery as an eel. I was keeping an eye on him as well as you."

"You still have not answered my question."

He shifted in his seat, a dark flush spreading across his jaw.

She giggled with triumph. "I understand now. You were going to have a tryst of your own!"

Tugging his hat brim low, he crossed his arms over his chest and closed his eyes with an attitude of finality. "Do not speak of grown up things, Georgie. I'll strap you good and proper and send you to bed tonight without your supper."

She bit back a retort because his words hinted he almost expected her to stay with him. She leaned her head against the window and sighed. The day was turning out to be rather beautiful.

Chapter Ten

Georgiana was duly impressed with the sprawling *vignoble* and showed enough enthusiastic interest in whatever Gaston told her about the latest vintage that Jack's barely visible scowl seemed to lighten. Without his offering it, she took his arm, folding both her hands around it as they followed Gaston through the warehouses. He laughed as she followed Gaston's instructions on how to properly taste the samples he'd laid out for them.

"You may impress your brother with your newfound knowledge when we return home. Perhaps he will allow you to stock his wine cellar."

She savored a mouthful of wine before expertly spitting it into a bowl set aside for the purpose. "I may have found my new calling, Jack. Perhaps your grandfather will allow me to take over your duties here, and you may stay in London sorting through all those dreadful suitors."

"No, thank you. I prefer my French jaunts. One feels a sense of freedom here."

Strange, that a man as worldly as Jack should not feel free to do as he liked. She'd always assumed wealthy bachelors were in the best position than anyone else. He didn't have to worry about an arranged marriage, or if his hem was cut the right length, or if he'd danced too often with the same partner at

Almack's.

"Well, I for one do not miss England at all. I would stay here at least a year if I could." She forgot to spit out her next taste, regretting her actions when a wave of dizziness rolled through her. She'd forgotten to spit more than once, and had swallowed at least two glasses worth. A giggle escaped her, and she clapped her hand over her mouth when one of Gaston's inky black eyebrows arched slightly. "Thank you for the tour, monsieur," she said, walking with Jack again as they strolled out toward the fields.

Vines as far as the eye could see filled the landscape. Puffy white clouds rolled lazily across the bright blue sky, so dazzling she had to shield her eyes with her hand. She gave a start at a group of women standing in open tubs, their feet pounding rhythmically while they held their skirts up to their knees.

Jack noticed her stunned silence. "They are stomping the grapes into juice."

"It looks like enormous fun! Have you ever trampled grapes before, Jack?"

She released his arm to tug on his hand, which clasped hers as naturally as if they'd been fitted for each other, like a pair of gloves.

He'd held her hand a thousand times before, as she'd always claimed him the moment he'd crossed the threshold of Fairwood Hall on those precious holiday visits. But this time was different. He was not helping her down from a tree or escorting her into dinner. The hand holding hers did not retain any of its youthful plumpness nor was it covered in scratches. His grown up hand was broad and secure, reassuring as it always had been.

A pulse of energy seemed to have shot through her palm and gone straight to her center when she took his hand. She marveled at how every curve and bumpy bone in her hand found some willing spot in his palm and fingers. Distracted, she had to glance up at him to register his words.

"It's stomping grapes," he was saying, "and no, I have not. My grandfather did not consider it dignified enough for his grandson, regardless of how much I begged for a turn."

"That is a shame, for it looks like great fun." She sighed and fiddled with the ribbon ties on her bonnet. "May I try it, Jack?"

He blinked. "What, stomp grapes? Are you mad? That's all I need, is your brother to hear…"

"He need never hear of it, Jack! My goodness, you do carry on as if I'm running to him every five minutes to hide behind his coattails."

She batted her eyelashes for good measure.

His fingers tightened around hers, and she squeezed back.

Finally, he shrugged. "Do as you will. As if I or anyone can stop you from doing precisely as you wish."

He left her with some of the workers, who took her into a building to change her gown. When she emerged some minutes later, he had to look twice to realize sedate Georgiana Lockewood had transformed into an attractive peasant girl. The result was quite distracting, and he pretended his attention was needed elsewhere.

He bowed to her quickly before chasing down Gaston, where he took the startled man by the shoulder and led him back inside the office. After Gaston answered the few simplistic questions he'd asked, Jack went out to the yard again, where Georgiana had clearly stolen every male heart present, from the youngest boy to old Marc, ninety next winter.

Her skirt flew above her bare knees, displaying her slim calves. Juice stained her legs and skirt, and sweat darkened her bodice, outlining a bosom that did not require assistance to stand out. Her hair hung in a thick, heavy mass over her shoulders, the bottom tendrils forming curls from a mixture of juice and sweat.

He remained in the shadowed doorway, where he could watch her without danger of anyone seeing his face.

He did not see the little girl who'd wrapped his heart around her finger. The child was gone. He didn't know whom he saw now.

Whoever she was, he was staring at her in a way her brother would never allow.

Or forgive.

Chapter Eleven

"Please, Jack, permit me to stay a few more days. I shall go mad if I'm stuck in that ridiculous old chateau much longer. I should rather have stayed at Fairwood Hall than come to France, if you're going to force me to suffer out the rest of my visit there."

Despite the workers' best attempts to keep her exercise mild, Georgiana bore traces of her rambunctious exercise among the grapes. Rosy-cheeked and bright-eyed, she was the very picture of the delectable country maid he normally came to France to pursue. Crossing his legs to disguise his body's inopportune reaction to this fact, he shook his head as firmly as he could, steeling his will as he stared directly into her eyes so she could not dissuade him.

"Absolutely not. You have interfered with my salacious endeavors of seducing pretty French girls long enough. Besides, do you know what kind of a scandal you may be brewing? People will say you've sequestered yourself with a notorious rogue, and you'll have ruined yourself forever. None of those jackanapes your brother has lined up will want you if word gets out."

She crossed her arms as she had done as a child when she didn't get her way. The gesture did nothing to tame the persistent fire growing in his belly. Her crossed arms forced up her uncorseted breasts. He purposely turned his head away to clear his thoughts, but the passing scenic countryside did nothing for his state. He re-crossed his legs, but the image persisted. He rubbed his hand over his face, but she mistook the gesture as his being exhausted by her.

"Good! I wouldn't have to marry any of them."

"Lockewood will kill me, Georgie. It's not worth the headaches, the…"

"Am I such a headache for you, Jack? I thought we were having loads of fun. It's like being children again, but with none of the adults pestering us to wash our hands or go to bed early."

"It is all fun until someone finds you out." He shook his head. "As close to your family as I have always been, I am not a relation. You are Aunt Adele's charge. I am only your escort. Besides, I sent word to Aunt Adele to expect you today."

"If you do not want me, just say so." Her eyes took on a sheen he realized was tears.

"It's not that." He chewed his lip. "I have enjoyed this time with you, my dear, truly. Too much time has passed since I saw you last, and I am thankful Lockewood asked me to escort you here."

"But," she said with a scowl.

He fought the urge to reach across the carriage and pat her leg.

"Yes. But." Sighing, he turned his attention to the window again. They would be in Mirville soon. One of his servants mentioned a fête there lasting all week. They could stop on the way to Lady Priscilla's. It would lift her mood, making her less contrary to his wishes. "When we return to London, I will be the first in line to dance with you at all the balls and parties you're missing. And if none of Lockewood's choices come to fruition, I will escort you to as many amusements as you like."

His voice had taken on a cajoling tone, and he nearly winced at how obvious he sounded. Lording it over her, as if her very presence was suffocating his—he almost laughed at her brother's phrase—pursuits. Yet, better she think him bored than discover the real reason why he hadn't visited Fairwood Hall since she'd started growing at an alarming rate. Or why he couldn't wait to see her safely off to the boring but secluded chateau of Lady Priscilla. Let her spend her remaining days in France drinking tea with old ladies and arranging flowers. So long as she stayed safely away from other men. And him.

"I can see you no longer desire my company." Her lower lip trembled, but her eyes glinted icy blue. "By all means, deposit me at Lady Priscilla's immediately. I have no wish to forestall any of your wild adventures, Jack."

"Adventures?" He laughed. He should placate her, or, at least, reassure her of his brotherly responsibility to both her and Lockewood. Instead, he was almost relieved she'd read him wrong.

Even though she would never know how far from the truth she really was.

****

It was late afternoon when she emerged from the guest chamber, telltale smudges beneath her eyes. He pretended not to notice and bowed when she descended the staircase to the foyer below, where he waited.

"Do not worry, Jack," she said sweetly, breezing past him toward the open door where his carriage stood at the ready. "I left my chamber exactly as I found it. None of your…" She paused delicately, in an exact imitation of her brother. "…*guests* will ever deduce another female spent the night. Your reputation is securely intact in that regard."

"How very thoughtful of you, Miss Lockewood."

He took his hat from a servant and clapped it on his head before following her into the carriage. She ignored any help and clambered inside, her gaze focused on the view from the window so she wouldn't have to see him. He allowed her to stew for a few minutes.

"I will speak to Aunt Adele and inform her of your desire not to remain cooped up in the chateau during the remainder of your trip. You just name the days, and I will come and rescue you from the fortress of *ennui*."

The pinched lips loosened, and she turned to face him so quickly a long curl draped over her shoulder bounced.

"Do you promise?"

"Yes." His heart began pounding, and he cleared his throat. Uncanny how just a look from her rounded eyes had an unsettling effect on him. "In truth, I have an entertaining day planned for you this very afternoon, at the end of which I will deposit you at the door of said fortress."

She clapped her hands. "How exciting! What are we going to do? Where are we going? Paris?"

He snorted. "Not Paris. As if I would take an innocent child like you to Paris! There is a fête at a village just outside Bolbec. I thought you might like to dance with some more handsome Frenchmen and see the town. There will be fire-eaters and perhaps a gypsy to tell your fortune. Best of all, it is unlikely we shall meet anyone we know, so people will not question your being out alone with me."

"I detest the lowly way people think. You are as good as family."

"I agree, Georgie. However, I would like to keep your reputation secured, regardless of your opinion to the contrary."

"I do not mean to imply I enjoy flouting the rules of society." Her brow furrowed. "No matter how ridiculous people can be."

"Ridiculous or not—" he began, but she cut him off with a wave of her hand.

"Please refrain from lecturing me again, Jack. You're as bad as Jonathan with your endless lectures."

"Then change the subject, by all means."

Her smile returned. She indicated her gown, one of Danielle's favorites. She'd spent a few days with him the last time he visited, and this dress had been lost behind the bed after a rousing evening. "Am I overdressed, do you think?"

He took in the tight burgundy silk bodice, the loose skirt of dove gray edged with black velvet. It was the most respectable of the lot, but she'd been pleased to have something new.

"You will be fine." He hated to tell her that every male eye above the age of fourteen and under the age of…well, no limit, he supposed…would be on her no matter what she wore.

"And you look the very image of a successful winery owner, Jack." Her gaze swept approvingly over his buckskin breeches and polished black top boots. He'd ignored his usual convention and chosen a starched white shirt and neck cloth and hadn't realized until now that his waistcoat was also burgundy silk, matching her.

"Successful winery owner's grandson."

"But it will all be yours in your inheritance, will it not?"

He nearly guffawed at her mistake. "Should my grandfather ever remember he has a grandson who is supposed to inherit, then, yes, it will be mine."

Those penetrating Lockewood eyes were fastened upon him, and he could not escape her gaze. "Are you not close?"

He eased his fists open and clutched his knees. "No."

"Just, no?" She imitated him, but he could not return her mirth. Her smile quickly faded. "I'm sorry, Jack. I assumed…."

"Assumed the old curmudgeon who sired my father should dote on me as much as he did his son? Why do you think I was always at Fairwood Hall on school holidays and not at Stoughton Park?"

"I am sorry." The color deepened in her cheeks. "Have you no other family? I always assumed you must have somebody."

"There's no one." He sighed. "Please, change the subject back to my dreadful lectures. I've no wish to open a door to my darkened and mostly uneventful past."

"You're all alone," she murmured.

He did not respond and glanced out the window. His fist clenched on his knee quite by accident, and he did not look up when she reached across and covered his hand briefly with hers.

The rub of her glove on top of his made a chafing

sound, but he fancied he could feel her warm skin through the layers of kid.

Chapter Twelve

"Do not leave this spot. I will inquire as to where the gypsy carts might be." Jack walked away, whistling beneath his breath.

Georgiana was unable to help her broad smile as she looked around the decorated village square. Vines and wildflowers entwined in a hodgepodge of color adorned shop doors and windows, and even the cobblestone streets looked polished. A maypole stood in the village square, and she hid a smile at the confused children, who scampered in the wrong direction and got tangled in the long ribbons that shimmered in the sunlight.

A barefooted girl ran up to her and thrust a yellow rose into her hands. Georgiana curtsied, laughing as the girl's knobby knees dipped in perfect imitation.

"You are so pretty, mademoiselle," the girl said in French and skipped away before Georgiana could answer.

She held the rose to her nose and inhaled deeply. The scent flooded her mind with thoughts of home, of Fairwood Hall's lush gardens, and of her mother. What would Mamma have thought of Jonathan's pestering her to marry? Doubtless, she'd have allowed her to stay at home another year, ensconced in her music room with her pianoforte to keep her company. Why have a husband come along to spoil it all?

She should not frown upon marriage. She forced the guilty thought from her mind. Were not Jonathan and Sophie blissfully wed, and with a baby on the way? Her parents had also been a love match, and she'd always fantasized of meeting a wonderful man like her father or brother or…

Jack.

The rose trembled in her hand. Why would Jonathan not consider Jack as a potential suitor for her? He had wealth and station, and had not caused too many scandals. At least, none that lingered past the time he'd kissed Clementine Forbes during a Christmas party at Fairwood Hall. Luckily, he was underage, so nothing more than a box on the ear by Clemmie's older brother had sufficed, rather than a forced engagement.

So why not Jack? She stiffened. What if Jonathan had asked him, and he'd refused? Perhaps he did see her only as a young girl who'd always fallen into one scrape or another. He was tired of helping her out of sticky situations, or always taking care of her when there was nobody about. Had he not looked eager to depart the last time they'd met, when she was fifteen? She'd practiced his favorite piece for hours on her pianoforte, but he'd hardly stayed still long enough to listen. The childhood friend had become a stranger.

"Georgiana Lockewood! What a surprise to find you in Bordeaux! I should think you'd be enjoying yourself in town."

Georgiana spun around as Lady Richmond, one of Aunt Adele's acquaintances, approached and kissed her on the cheek, followed by a fond embrace before Georgiana could react.

"My son, Herbert, and I are joining the rest of the

family in Paris, but we'll be in London by month's end. Are you here with your brother and his wife?" The woman scanned the crowd with an interested air.

Georgiana glanced around for a glimpse of Jack. Why had he chosen now of all moments to abandon her? Lady Richmond might take the wrong idea and spread some malicious gossip about her being without a chaperone. She regained her composure. "Jonathan and Sophie are back in England. I came to France with Aunt Adele."

"How is that dear creature? I have not seen my old friend in months. Is she having a rest inside one of the shops? It is very warm today."

Before Georgiana could answer, a well-dressed, big-boned young man sauntered over to them, a pastry clutched in his hand. He stared unabashedly down the front of her bodice before meeting her startled gaze.

"This is my eldest, Herbert. We've been speaking with your brother about your future, my dear." She prodded Herbert forward, and Georgiana had to control the revulsion clamoring inside her at the crumbs and bits of food on the side of his cheek. His bleary eyes never left hers, and she wondered if she should risk insulting the Richmonds by running away as fast as her flimsy little slippers would carry her.

"My future…?"

What possible reason could Jonathan have with the Richmonds?

Oh.

"Georgie, I've found the gypsy tent." Jack was beside her before she'd noticed. His hair was blown about his face, and he'd loosened his neckcloth according to his habit. He stared at Lady Richmond and

Herbert, seeing them for the first time. "I beg your pardon, ma'am." He bowed, and she dipped into a slight curtsy, her brows knit together.

Her silence spoke volumes. Glancing from one to the other, the woman finally settled upon Jack, her upper lip twitching into a sneer she didn't bother to hide. "I am Lady Richmond, an old friend of Georgiana's family. This is my son, Herbert. And you are…?"

Frozen into silence, Georgiana watched Jack's jaw clench a few times.

His lips parted to speak, and he glanced down at her as if she held the answer.

Frantic, she clutched his sleeve, picking at the fabric in a desperate attempt to provoke some sort of reasonable response from her brain, but she was helpless. How could she explain her presence at the fair without the accompaniment of Aunt Adele? How to explain being in the sole company of a man like Jack Waverley, with his openly teasing air and his unfastened neckcloth? A man who'd been born into an honorable family of means, yet who gambled and boxed whenever he chose?

"Jack Waverley, your ladyship," he said at last. "I am also an old friend of Miss Lockewood's family." His hand fidgeted toward his loosened neckcloth, but fortunately, he dropped it at his side when she gave him the slightest nudge in the kidney.

Georgiana held her breath. It was too much to hope the simple response was all Lady Richmond required. They should say goodbye then leave before the woman could tell if they were figments of her imagination or flesh and blood.

"An *old friend*?" Lady Richmond's eyes seemed to penetrate through Georgiana's forehead as if she could see into her thoughts.

Lady Richmond was powerfully connected to the patronesses of Almack's. One wrong word, one innocent slip, and Jonathan and Sophie would be ruined. It wouldn't do her any good, either.

"He's…we're…Jack is…." Her stuttering did more harm.

Lady Richmond's breath caught, and Georgiana wondered if her lips could pinch together any tighter.

Jack pressed his hand over hers, but panic rose inside her until she thought she would burst.

Herbert forgot his pastry for the moment and appeared somewhat interested in the conversation. He leered at Georgiana and she shrank into Jack's side. He clasped her hand tightly.

"Forgive my silence," he said abruptly. "Miss Lockewood and I are recently married. We are on our honeymoon."

Too terrified to look at Jack lest her amazement betray his lie, Georgiana's breath left her in such a rush the lace trim on her bodice fluttered against her skin.

Lady Richmond's eyes widened until Georgiana wondered if they would pop out of her head.

"You…are…married?" A tremor vibrated through her, visibly shaking the ends of her spencer. She swallowed a few times, her throat working against the hat ribbons tied beneath her chin. "Well, I must congratulate you both." She nudged her son in the ribs, and he bowed, showing none of his mother's anxiety. "I had no idea there were…other arrangements. Your brother made no mention of this in his last letter."

"My…my brother?" Again, she was unable to complete a full sentence. Jack's outrageous statement was shock enough for one day.

"Your brother and I have been discussing your future, Miss Lockewood." Her graying brows drew together. "Of course, nothing was set in stone, as it were." She threw back her shoulders, then, with a short curtsy, took Herbert's arm. "Good day to you both."

Georgiana bounced on the balls of her feet, her earlier impulse to run far away coming back. "Good day, your ladyship."

She could not look at Jack. What unspeakable horror would she see on his face? What wild lunacy had possessed him? Just as she'd been about to introduce him as her cousin, the shocking words had issued from his lips like rain from thunderclouds.

They were alone. Georgiana counted to five before risking a glance at his face. Besides one eyebrow arched to the point where he resembled a lopsided owl, he looked very much the same as before.

"We should go now. Yes, that's the best thing. We will go to Aunt Adele." The exposed inch of skin above his collar was as crimson as his waistcoat.

"Whatever you say." She almost stammered her reply.

Her hand remained on his sleeve as they walked away from the center of town.

The gypsies had settled on the outskirts. Their ponies grazed nearby, shaggy and soft looking, their hair thicker than English horses. Were this any other occasion, she'd have gladly gone to them, to explore the enticing area that was the gypsy camp. But she dared not leave Jack's side.

His face resembled an aubergine. In another moment, she feared his eyes would burst from his sockets.

He appeared to be struggling to say something, but no sound escaped him. With a sudden, muttered oath, he seized her hand and pulled her behind a sheltering wall. He placed both hands on her shoulders and peered into her face.

"What in all that is sacred possessed me? I expected you to have said something ridiculous, but for me to have..." He pushed away from her, pacing in a quick circle before clasping her shoulders again and shaking her once.

Georgiana pulled from his grasp and tried to regain some of her dignity. "I was going to say you were my cousin, if you don't mind."

"Why did I not think of that?" He grabbed a handful of his hair and tugged it to stand on end. "God, Georgie! I do not know how I lost my sensibilities. This will not bode well, mark my words."

He closed his eyes and lowered his head, pressing his forehead against hers so firmly she had to break away before she fell backward. She clutched his waistcoat for balance, his heartbeat thudding against the backs of her hands.

"It matters not," she began, but he pressed his finger to her lips.

"It does matter, Georgiana. I should have said I was your...your uncle, for God's sake, but the thought left my head when I saw her son." His eyes were wild. His cheek muscle twitched, and a large vein throbbed upon his brow. "I can stand many things, but at that moment, I could not stand the thought..." He ground his teeth and pulled sharply away to strike the wall behind her. "Lockewood was wrong, wrong! I should have put an end to his plans to throw you away to a tosspot like Richmond!"

Wincing in pain for him, Georgiana seized his hand and pressed her lips to his knuckles while he groaned.

"Oh, Jack…"

Shaking his head, he groaned again. "Tosspot or no, I've ruined your chances! Your brother…Oh, God, your brother! Lockewood will kill me, and deservedly so."

"What are you talking about?"

"Part of the reason your brother desired me to escort you to France was to convince you of your duty." He grimaced, but the scorn soon vanished from his face.

Why did he and Jonathan always speak in riddles? "What duty, Jack?"

He gently pulled his hand from her grip. "You were meant for…for that loathsome oaf, Richmond. And now, because of me, you will have no one, once he and his mother return to England and tell your brother what has happened." He stared at her in silence.

She gave him a reassuring pat on the chest. "Do not worry so. I'm certain Jonathan will understand." She didn't want to admit she was partly to blame. If she'd only listened to him and gone back to Bolbec without a fuss, they wouldn't have bumped into the Richmonds.

Sighing, he took her hand and threaded it through his arm. "Let us go. I'll try to solve this dilemma whilst we ride."

She forced a downcast look on her face, although she sensed her horizons had just widened considerably.

She would not have to marry a pig like Herbert Richmond. Had they not been in public she would have kissed him for thanks. How utterly brilliant Jack was! He'd saved her from a fate worse than death, twice in as many days.

"I'm sure you will think of something," she said. It probably would not be too maidenly for her to rejoice in the fact Jack had singlehandedly destroyed all her brother's future prospects for her. With any luck, Lady Richmond would inform Almack's patronesses that Georgiana Lockewood was not suitable for marriage. She could live her days the way she wanted: in perfect freedom without any limitations imposed by a dreadful husband.

The throbbing vein diminished on his forehead, but his color was still high. "The best solution would be to drink my hemlock now, before Lockewood hears of it." He contemplated her for a few seconds before shrugging. "Either way, we should not go to Aunt Adele. I fear the poor lady will have an attack should we tell her what happened. I'll send word you're ill and will be staying with me until you've recovered. In a few days, I'm sure I can think of some way to salvage your reputation."

She hid her pleasure at avoiding another dull week with Aunt Adele and Lady Priscilla bemoaning the state of the cakes. Still, she possessed a slight fear of what the sweet old dear would say to her if word reached her. Despite protesting against the *ton's* ridiculous rules, she knew she should not have ignored them. Jack was perfectly suitable company in private, but not in public.

Jack stared out the window as they rode back to the chateau. Georgiana couldn't help but pity him, for he looked so distracted.

He seemed to sense her gaze upon him and spoke without looking at her. "You may stay with me under one condition. No, two. Firstly, you will not question my habits or try to rearrange things. I am used to being alone, and prefer it that way. Secondly, you will keep to the house and gardens. I cannot risk anything else happening to you whilst you're under my protection." He grunted. "For all the good it has done you thus far."

"Goodness, Jack! How you and Jonathan flutter about, like two squawking hens. I am perfectly able to take care of myself."

"Harrumph!"

"Oh, yes, forgive me, Jack. It was I who invented that preposterous lie to Lady Richmond."

He poked the air. "Do not look so pleased with yourself, Georgiana. At least, you may be reassured you're better off without Herbert Richmond. That aside, you can be certain your brother will have it in for us both."

"You are probably correct."

"More than probably, I fear. I have few friends in this world, your brother being the oldest and best of the lot." He sighed heavily. "Why did I not say I was your cousin?" He pounded the side of the carriage, causing her to jump at the noise.

"I know why."

He scrubbed his face with his hands. "Pray, tell me, since you know so much."

"You do not want me to marry anyone."

He stammered and sputtered a reply but could only make a feeble noise.

She wanted to laugh at his reaction. "You still

insist on seeing me as a child, Jack! That's why you didn't want Herbert Richmond to marry me."

He pulled at his collar. The knot in his neckcloth was a loosened circle of fabric about to come apart completely. He tugged at the window and stuck out his face. The scent of lavender from nearby fields wafted into the carriage. When she objected, he shut the window with more force than was warranted.

"That is precisely the reason."

She merrily picked through a packet of sweets he'd bought her earlier in the day, popping them into her mouth one after the other.

****

Despite the potential scandal about to effectively destroy her chances of ever finding a husband, Georgiana almost danced across the threshold of Jack's chateau. Jack apprised his servants, Philippe and Marie, that she would be a guest for the long term due to illness in Bolbec, and Marie set about preparing a chamber. It was not her previous room, but further down the corridor and away from Jack's suite.

She had little to unpack and joined him for supper in the dining room. Although the meal was superb, she picked at her food, finally giving up on the lamb and selecting a crusty roll. Her stomach writhed as if something was knotted and twisted inside. When he still had not started a conversation, she took the lead.

"For all we know," she said, tearing the roll into little pieces, "Lady Richmond will not say a single word. She might be so insulted Jonathan didn't tell her about us she will remain silent."

"There is no *us*," he growled, draining his second glance of wine.

Picking at the bread helped her avoid looking at him. He hadn't touched his dinner except to stab a boiled potato a few times.

"Well," she said at length, glancing at him before lowering her eyes again, "it's possible nothing will come of it. We can go back to England and act as if nothing happened."

He carefully set down his fork, leaned back into his chair, and regarded her as if she had just announced she was going to sprout wings and fly.

"And what will you do, should she accuse your brother of going back on his word? A broken engagement is nearly as bad as your going about with no chaperone but me."

She groped for her glass and took a sip of wine. "I don't know." She tried to smile and gave a little hopeful shrug. "Whatever happens, I shall always be grateful for what you did. At least I won't have to marry her grotesque son."

He raised his glass to her. Only a smear of wine remained on the bottom. "Huzzah for that." He set his glass down and folded his hands on his chest. "I'll write Lockewood myself in the morning. With any luck, he won't have enough time to plot my death before we go home."

She giggled, but her laughter died at his continued serious expression. "Just tell him I made the blunder. He can be angry with me all he likes, and you will be innocent."

"A fine thing to do—blame my terrible lack of judgment on a child." He pushed away from the table and stepped around to the back of her chair to pull it out while she stood. "To bed, Georgiana. This time, I pray you—do not venture down the corridor and sneak into my bed. I can only tolerate one scandal at a time."

A rapid blush seared her face and tingled through the rest of her at the vision his words inspired. "I…I won't go to your chamber," she stammered.

He offered his arm while they walked upstairs. "We'll have a fresh start in the morning. Perhaps we'll go for a drive. I always think better when I'm moving."

He opened her chamber door and remained outside while she stepped in. She turned to face him and pressed her hand to his chest before she could stop herself. He glanced down at her hand but didn't move it away.

"Do not trouble yourself, Jack. I know it will be all right."

A shadow of a smile touched his lips for a moment, though the crease in his forehead remained. He lifted her hand and kissed it, then gave it a little shake.

"I'm sure it will. Sleep well," he said, his eyes twinkling. He added unexpectedly, "Mrs. Waverley."

It took her a second to catch what he'd said, but he'd already turned away, heading to his own chamber. He closed the door behind him, and she followed suit, although she didn't go to bed for a long time afterwards. Instead, she sat by the window and stared at the full, bright moon.

Crickets and frogs chirped in the garden below until the night echoed with their cacophony. An owl hooted by the stables. A low yowling of the resident tomcat indicated he'd found a mouse. But all she heard was Jack's voice, repeating over and over—

Mrs. Waverley.

Chapter Thirteen

Georgiana greeted Jack at breakfast. By his red-rimmed eyes and unkempt hair, it was obvious he'd had just as sleepless a night.

Although she was grateful for the end to Jonathan's matchmaking, she dreaded facing her brother. As if Jack read her thoughts, he patted her hand from across the table.

"I'll send word to Lockewood about meeting the Richmonds. I'll say it was a terrible misunderstanding on Lady Richmond's part. Perhaps she will remain quiet about seeing us together, and you'll be back in the marriage game with none the wiser."

"I am grateful to you, Jack, regardless of how cross Jonathan becomes with me." She smeared a dollop of jam on her croissant. She'd had a restless night, alternately dreaming of Jack as a gypsy, riding a shaggy horse and fighting off wild beasts for her sake, and of Herbert Richmond, who had metamorphosed into a giant cake monster with two raisins for eyes. "I will say it until I die, Jack, but I am eternally grateful you spared me Mr. Richmond. I should have made him as miserable as he would make me."

"I heartily agree with you, for once." Jack made a sandwich of his eggs on a piece of toast and then stuffed it into his mouth so she would laugh at his crude manners.

"Love is nothing but pain and misery. Poor Alphonse! He is forbidden to marry the woman he loves, and all because her father is a miller. For all we know, he is the best miller in France, but it matters not. He and the girl shall be miserable for the rest of their lives."

He dabbed at his lips with his napkin. "They will not be miserable. She will be married off to another miller's dullard son, and your poor Alphonse will find happiness with a snobby heiress." He waved his napkin at her. "Perhaps Lady Priscilla and Aunt Adele have plotted for you to be his bride. That would be a good excuse for your breaking it off with Richmond. Imagine, Georgiana; you may be the next Madame Alphonse Whomever-the-devil-he-is and will have to look over your shoulder for a spurned miller's daughter come to do you harm."

She scowled. "I am not part of any wedding plot. A plot of Lady Priscilla's, anyway. As if I would marry someone like Alphonse. Besides, he is in love with the miller's daughter." She shook her head. "It is tragic two people in love must be apart, when those who do not love each other would be forced to marry."

Jack dropped his napkin on the table. "All this talk of millers' daughters! Love is not the problem, Georgiana. It's the timing. I, for example, have never experienced the wretched invention. I see a woman I want; I court her. If she will not have me or when I grow tired of her, it is over. Finished. No broken hearts, no weeping eyes. No tear-soaked pillows." He gave her a meaningful look, and she bristled.

"I did not cry into your pillow the other night."

"I heard the odd sniffle now and then."

"Perhaps it is this drafty old place. You need to have your windows seen to."

"Bother the windows, Georgiana. You are still in love with that miserable sod, Mitford, and you will not admit it."

"I am not in love with him anymore." She lifted her chin defiantly. "I do not believe I ever loved him."

"You gave a very good impression of being in love with him."

She glowered at him. "I grew up with him the same as I grew up with you. I am not in love with you, Jack Waverley. I merely sought an escape, and Edward happened to be there."

He shook his head slightly, his lips pursed in amused irony. "Say what you will, Pudding Face. If he had married you before the mighty Jonathan discovered you, you would be lamenting the state of your marriage, chained to that worthless wretch."

Despite the excitement of first love spurring her to a horrendous lack of propriety or common sense, she was relieved nothing more had come of her botched elopement than a disgraceful journey back home with her brother. To his credit and her infinite relief, he'd been gentle, sympathetic even, and had not mentioned the matter to her again after his initial lecture urging her not to waste her love on a man like Edward Mitford.

A shiver ran through her. Imagine if she had married him. She'd be cursing her state from the first day, as he'd already caused a few scandals involving young heiresses who'd been as taken with him as she had been. Only they didn't have as good a brother as Jonathan, and one girl had gone north to distant relatives, never to be heard from again.

She resumed her preparation of her croissant. "If ever I do marry, it will not be to anyone I am in danger of loving. I will find an old fat man with gouty legs and a sour disposition. He will leave me alone, and I shall not bother him. Then, I shall be as happy as I can be."

"That will never do, silly girl. Even an old man with gouty legs will wish some attention from you."

His knowing look caused her to blush. She gave up on her ruined croissant and dropped it on her plate. He shrugged.

"You need to marry someone quiet and kind. Not a Richmond or a Mitford, God forbid. Someone with as much money as you, so you may be assured he isn't using you. You need a man who's steady, and patient." He sipped his tea and added another spoonful of sugar to his cup. "A blithering fool, in other words."

She stirred her teacup. "Someone who is your complete opposite, you mean."

"Precisely." He made a face at her.

She giggled. "I should marry you, Jack. Then I won't have to be afraid of anything ever again, because you will always be there with your sharp knife."

"Don't forget the swords. I'm awfully good with a sabre."

"And your fists. Jonathan told me about your boxing matches."

"He talks too much." But he smirked with pride.

She stifled another laugh. "Why have you never married?"

He sighed and concentrated his attention on his cup. "I may very well have to, and sooner, rather than later. My grandfather recently informed me I must marry before the tender age of thirty, or he will cut off my allowance. I'm a good fighter, but not that good." His eyebrow arched in self-deprecation. "I rely on his money, and he knows it, damn him. Of course, I can always tell him to take his money and go straight to the devil. Then, you will have to visit me in my little den beneath a bridge. Perhaps you can bring me a hot supper once a week so I do not starve to death."

"Oh, dear." She couldn't imagine Jack living in poverty any more than she saw herself married to Herbert Richmond. "How terrible, Jack! And what are you going to do?"

He drank the last of his tea and set the cup on the table with a clatter of china. "I'm going to enjoy myself as much as I can in the little time I have left. I think in about—oh, three years, I should be ready to settle down. Perhaps I'll marry a little goose like you. Have you any rich friends interested in a man who only wants them for their dowry?"

"No friend quite so desperate as to settle on you. I know Jonathan wishes for me to marry soon, but I am not about to give up my own freedoms, just as you don't want to give up yours."

"I did not know you were a pugilist."

"I am referring to being able to play my music whenever I like and not be at the beck and call of some bothersome man who can't decide how to tie his neckcloth."

Jack indicated his bare throat with a flourish. "Which is why I scorn the blasted things."

"Here in the country, you may scorn them all you like. When you return to England, you'll be buttoned up and tied around the neck just the same as the rest of us."

"Then I shall never go home." He reclined in his

chair and closed his eyes with such a comical expression on his face she laughed. "I have an idea, Georgie. I will find a boringly suitable husband for you, and you may find an equally loathsome bride for me. That way, Jonathan and my grandfather will leave us alone. We can meet once a year for luncheon and chortle over a pot of tea at how we tricked them both, while our long-suffering spouses remain at home."

She exhaled slowly, studying him. "As much as I would enjoy seeing you trapped forever in matrimony to a shrew, I know just the proper girl for you, Jack. Do you know Veronica Fielding? She has a tidy inheritance as well as her father's charming house in town."

"Hmm…can't say that I've heard of her." He leaned forward, interested. "What does she look like?"

Veronica's sweet smile and well-endowed charms came to her mind. The image of Jack's muscular arms sweeping Veronica into a darkened bedchamber unsettled her. She quickly shook her head. "Never mind her. I forgot she is missing her front teeth and has an appalling laugh."

"Really? What does her laugh sound like, then?"

"Have you ever heard a pig in a sty when its brethren have pushed him aside?"

Jack shook his head, his lips tight.

"Well," she said leisurely, cutting a piece of sausage into slices, "that is what she sounds like."

"There must be other girls you know who won't mind being chained to me for the rest of their mortal lives. Can you think of any others whose laughter does not imitate barnyard animals?"

"Only women who would disappoint you and test your limits of reason, I'm sad to say. I would suggest

Leticia Haversham, but she has sworn to join a convent if she can't marry her father's footman."

"He must be the perfect specimen of footman if she would refuse a man like me. Perhaps I should eschew boxing and learn a lowly trade in taking care of carriages and horses." He cocked his head to the side. "You know of nobody else?" She shook her head, and he sighed. "It is hard to believe you know so few eligible ladies, Georgiana. Where did Lockewood send you to school? A dark castle in the middle of the Bavarian forest?"

She divided her sausage slices into little rows. "It doesn't really matter, does it, Jack? Any woman you marry would be unsuitable."

"How do you mean, pray?"

She echoed his sigh. "You enjoy drinking, gambling, and fighting. Not many wives would put up with such behavior."

"Oh, you'd be surprised with what a woman puts up with if there's a promise of five thousand a year."

"Not if she fell in love with you. A woman who loved you would make your life miserable."

He leaned his elbows on the table and stared at her. "Yes, I see your point. Better I choose someone who has no interest in love, but a cold-hearted, soulless fiend who will let me do as I please, regardless how lowly and sordid. Is that what you suggest?"

She nodded once. "Exactly. Someone who feels the same way about love and marriage as you do."

"You should do the same. Find a scholarly man more interested in what lies between the pages of a book than in making you happy."

"I shall stay here with you, then. Nobody bothers

one here in Bordeaux. Even the servants stay out of sight. It's as if we are the only two people in the world."

"Your brother will want you soon, Georgie. Baby Lockewood is on his or her way any day now. You shall have to go home. I'd love to hear you explain to your brother how you managed to spend the remainder of your holiday abroad sequestered in my palace of sin. Lady Richmond has probably composed a half dozen letters to him as we speak, informing him of our recent marriage."

She ignored the last part of his sentence and sipped her tea instead. "You are correct. The baby will arrive, and I'll have to go home." Her heart sank, which confused her. She didn't particularly care for France one way or the other. The food was wonderful, of course, and the countryside picturesque. But she would miss Jack's humorous comments and the way he made her laugh.

She would miss him.

The thought shocked her enough that she upset her saucer when she placed her teacup on the table. Eventually, she would be someone's wife. No self-respecting heiress would stay single when there was a family name to uphold. What if her brother's other choices were worse than Herbert? She lowered her head for a moment to fight a wave of panic. There was only one possible solution to her quandary. It stood before her in all its simplistic, obvious glory.

"Will you marry me, Jack?"

He stared at her as if she'd just announced she was a mermaid. "I've always admired your mischievous nature but never believed you to have such an absurd sense of humor as that, Georgiana."

The thought grew in her mind the more she studied him. She almost smacked her forehead at the brilliance of her idea and only wondered why she hadn't thought of it sooner. "It's the perfect solution, for both of us. Do you not see?" Her voice rose in excitement. "You will be able to present a bride to your grandfather and keep your allowance, and Jonathan will abandon his list of suitable suitors, who are completely unsuitable. Lady Richmond can write a dozen letters, and they will not mean a thing."

"I thought I told you earlier I would never marry. We were just discussing…"

"But it would be different with me." She rose from her chair and hurried over to him, dropping to her knees and upsetting his cup when she gripped the tablecloth to steady herself. She took his hand and held it fiercely, as if she would press the idea into his skin. "I will not be the kind of wife you detest. You may box all you like, and drink, and make merry. I will never ask you where you've been, or with whom. We can even have separate homes." Her voice rose in her excitement, while her plan formed before her in all its glorious simplicity. "You will have my dowry when I marry. All I ask is a lovely little house in town, or else in the country. It matters not. What does matter is I shall be left to myself, with my music and my own mind to command. You may live wherever you wish. Do as you wish. We are the best of friends and know each other well enough to leave each other alone. It's the perfect arrangement, and you must say yes."

She finished on a breathless plea. He glanced down at their entwined fingers. His jaw moved once or twice as if he were about to speak, but her heart sank when he shook his head.

"It will never work."

"But why, Jack? You are so stubborn." She pushed his hand away, not trying to hide her disappointment. "Give me one good reason."

He dropped another spoonful of sugar into his tea and stirred it four times. He then added a slice of lemon into his cup, carefully removing a seed that floated on the top. She almost held her breath awaiting his response.

"Because you will fall in love with me, and there goes my freedom. It will be over between us before it starts."

Her lips parted with a rush of air. "You are so conceited, Jack! I will never…"

He caught her hand as she struggled to her feet, her legs tangling in the twisted folds of her gown. "Listen to me, Georgiana." He seldom used her full name and she reluctantly met his gaze, although she ensured her lower lip trembled.

He sighed. "I know you, my dear. You will say now it is for convenience, or we are great friends, or what have you. But eventually, you will be like every other woman who fancies herself married. You will begin questioning my whereabouts, and search my linen for any telltale scents of foreign perfume. You'll beg to accompany me regardless of where I'm going, and you will put an end to my boxing." As he spoke, she interjected with a few shakes of her head and verbal denials, but he only silenced her. "It will never work. You will be unhappy, and I shall be unhappy because I've made you so." He brushed a wayward strand of hair from her hot cheek. "The last thing I ever want in this world is to hurt you."

"You would prefer I marry a blithering fool, as you called it?"

His gray eyes darkened with a sudden shadow. "I would see you happily married to a loving man who deserves you." He lifted his cup but did not drink. "I regret I am not that man, as would you, if you were so foolish as to see this idea of yours to the finish."

She chewed her lip, her thoughts racing as she tried to change his mind. "What if I do not fall in love with you and our marriage is exactly as I promised? What if it really is possible for us to marry, and you may continue with your bachelorhood existence? Prizefighting and paramours from morning 'til night? And you may have all my money. I just want…" This time, her voice trembled of its own accord.

His eyes narrowed, and he finally drank his tea, draining it while he studied her, his face inscrutable. "I'd be wealthy beyond words with all your thousands. I'd be the happiest bachelor husband in all of England, with a beautiful wife who allows me to spend my days in idle pleasure, while she lolls around her pianoforte all day."

Her breath hitched. "Does this mean you have changed your mind?"

He groaned, but she heard his stifled laughter. He scrubbed his face with his hands, then blinked at her as if he'd just awoken from a dream. "How do you do it?"

"Do what?"

"Use those big blue eyes of yours to get whatever you want? God help us should you ever use your powers of persuasion for evil deeds. It would be the end of the world."

Her breath trapped in her throat. "So—it's a yes?"

"Against my better judgment and my conscience screaming vividly into both my ears…" He paused for effect. "Yes."

Laughing with delirious joy, she threw her arms around his neck. "Thank you, thank you! You have saved me yet again. Oh, Jack, you will not regret it!"

He patted her back then held her at arm's length. "It is not so easy to marry here in France. Better we wait until our return to England."

"We cannot wait, Jack! Jonathan will forbid it."

"The laws of France require a bride be over the age of one and twenty. You are underage."

"I shall lie."

"To a priest?" His eyes were comically serious. "While I would love to help you, it just will not do. You need a guardian's permission, and your brother, thankfully, is absent."

Was he trying to change her mind? Frantic, she blurted out a name. "Aunt Adele is my legal guardian while abroad. She can give her permission."

"That dear woman will not risk your brother's wrath."

Her one chance of escaping the future her brother planned was almost gone. "She will if you threaten her." His eyebrows arched, and she hastened to explain. "I mean only if you tell her Jonathan must know about Alphonse abandoning me at the ball. She will do as you demand."

"Machiavelli." He shook his head, but the ghost of a smile lingered on his lips.

She held her breath and counted the ticking of the

clock on the mantelpiece.

Eight seconds passed before he finally sighed. "Very well. But…" and he held up his finger when she reached for him, ready to embrace him. "There can be none of that, Georgie. If I'm to remain your husband-of-convenience, we shall keep our friendship intact. Any…intimacy will only confuse the matter."

She gulped back her laughter and took her chair. "I hadn't thought of that."

"It will just make it easier for us if we remain friends." He paused. "And by us, I mean you."

"Why just me? Is your heart made of stone, Jack Waverley?" She giggled but stifled it at the flash of pain that flickered across his face. Like a shadow fading in the dusk, she wasn't sure she had seen it.

"Not stone. You would not be happy loving a man like me."

She nearly sighed with relief. "Then you have nothing to worry about. I am not in love with you, and I promise not to fall in love with you, ever."

"Good." He cracked a wry grin. "And I swear never to fall in love with you."

She'd hoped the very thing. Love and its wicked twin, jealousy, carried too much sorrow and despair. Besides, who needed love when one could live as free as one chose, able to come and go as she pleased? She wanted to leap for joy she would be spared any further heartache.

She would never have to endure the pain a man like Edward Mitford had caused. She would not have to sacrifice her soul by marrying someone like Herbert Richmond, either.

Jack was fun and full of life, and understood her

heart and mind. What better husband could there be? Meeting Lady Richmond was the best possible answer to their mutual problems.

"So, Jack," she said at length, relief pouring over her as fresh and bountiful as the tea in the pot, "are there any more gowns upstairs that would pass for a wedding dress?"

Chapter Fourteen

Georgiana waited for the elderly woman to regain her composure before releasing her hand. She'd only told Aunt Adele moments before about their sudden betrothal, and the poor dear looked as if she were about to faint. Not that she blamed her. Just hearing herself say the words aloud was madness.

After what seemed an interminable amount of time, Aunt Adele nodded slightly. "Forgive me, my dears. My head is spinning. I thought you were ill, and staying at Mr. Waverley's because you were not strong enough to travel. I was in quite a dither when Alphonse returned home without you." She fanned herself with a handkerchief. "Dear me, I hope I did not do wrong when I did not send for you directly."

Her worried look turned into suspicion. Georgiana shook her head. "Jack was a complete gentleman, if you are concerned I was compromised. Indeed, my visit at the chateau only prompted feelings that have lain dormant for ever so long." She gave Jack a meaningful look and he hastily agreed with her, although she wished he could refrain from giving such a sardonic smile.

Aunt Adele patted her chest as if she had to catch her breath. "You wish to marry Mr. Waverley, Georgiana?"

"Yes. Shall I send for some tea?"

"Thank you. I do feel a little out of sorts."

"I'm not surprised," Jack said wryly. "I confess I nearly fainted myself." Georgiana gave him a warning look, but he only grinned.

"But why now, why here? Can you not wait until we return to England? Your brother will be most…" Aunt Adele hesitated, and Georgiana imagined all sorts of descriptive phrases regarding her brother's reaction when he heard. "Disappointed."

"Do not worry, Aunt Adele," Georgiana said with more bravado than she felt. "Jonathan will not mind. After all, he wishes me to marry soon, and Jack is an old friend."

"Which is why my death will be nice and slow, rather than swift and to the point," Jack muttered.

"In any case," Georgiana said, shooting him a warning look, "I must have your permission, since I am underage to marry in France. Will you help me?"

The older woman twisted her hands together and glanced around the parlor, as if help were on its way. "I…I do not know if I should."

"I do not know which will alarm Jonathan more," Jack said, smiling pleasantly as he sat beside Aunt Adele, "how you permitted Georgiana to go without a proper chaperone to a fiasco of a ball where she was nearly ravished, or that she has married a respectable gentleman." He hesitated for only a moment. "Meaning myself, of course."

"Oh, dear," Aunt Adele murmured.

Georgiana pressed her from the other side. "Jonathan need never be told what happened at the ball. Will you grant your permission, Aunt Adele? It will mean the world to me." If she had become too theatrical, she tried not to notice.

Aunt Adele glanced from one to the other and finally placed her hands over each of theirs. "Are you so in love you cannot wait? I know your mother would have wanted a fine wedding for you, Georgiana. Here, you have no friends, no relations, except for my sister and me."

"It will be splendid," she said quickly. "I have a lovely gown and bridal clothes. Besides, with my brother's child on the way, I wouldn't have time to plan something extravagant. All the attention is on the baby." She hoped this final plea would work. Aunt Adele gave a drawn out sigh, and Georgiana couldn't help but feel a little guilty about her part in duping the poor woman.

"What about love?" Aunt Adele glanced at Jack and appraised him with a sharp eye. "Do you protest your love for my niece? As much as I do like you, Mr. Waverley, you must admit this is highly irregular." She chewed her lower lip, and the hand covering Georgiana's trembled slightly. "Highly irregular."

"I have always loved her," he said firmly.

Georgiana gave a little start. She glanced at him, shyness striking her as if she were a wallflower at a ball.

His jaw seemed to tense for a second. He winked. "And she loves me. You may have no doubt of that, dear, dear Aunt Adele." He lifted the woman's hand and kissed it loudly.

At last, she nodded. "I suppose I cannot dissuade either of you. Georgiana will not bend once her mind is set." Georgiana held her breath until she nodded again. "I grant my permission."

"Thank you." Georgiana flung her arms around her.

Aunt Adele returned her embrace, while Jack rose to order tea. "I only hope you do not have any regrets."

"I won't." Georgiana looked quickly at Jack. "And neither will Jack."

"Tomorrow at noon, then," Jack said, and Georgiana beamed at him.

"Tomorrow."

They sat with Aunt Adele for the remainder of the afternoon, discussing her plans to remain in France with her sister.

"You will have no further need of me once you have Mr. Waverley to protect you." She dabbed her eyes with a lace handkerchief.

"But who will protect me from the charming Miss Lockewood?" Jack murmured, low enough so only Georgiana could hear.

She wanted to return his teasing, but his eyes glittered back at her like diamonds in a crystal bowl. The full realization she was about to tie herself to him for the rest of her life silenced her.

The remainder of the hour passed with Aunt Adele's pleasant chatter about her future life in France, but Georgiana heard little. She couldn't help but study Jack, noticing every tiny detail about him that had evaded her before. The curve of his ear was barely visible beneath his shaggy curls. His scarred hands were more noticeable when poking out from his white cuffs. She'd always thought him well built but had never noticed the muscular line of his legs, taut in his buckskin breeches.

A wedding day would mean a wedding night. Even

if they were to maintain a companionable relationship rather than one based on love, they would not be truly married unless…

Something in her middle quivered, and she nearly faltered when Aunt Adele asked her a question.

"Yes," she murmured in reply, staring at Jack's bicep flexing beneath the taut wool sleeve of his coat when he reached for the teapot.

"Really?" Aunt Adele replied, sipping from her cup. "I thought you'd rather wait a year before starting a family."

Chapter Fifteen

"Are you ready, Georgie? The priest won't wait forever, you know."

Jack paced the wide corridor, while tapping his fingers on his thigh and glancing at her door every few seconds. What could be keeping the girl? It wasn't as if this were a state affair, or hundreds of guests were awaiting their arrival. She didn't even have a proper wedding gown, just something one of his paramours had left behind.

She'd found the peach-colored silk gown hanging in the back of the wardrobe and had fallen in love with the plunging neckline and yards of Belgian lace around the hem. Had it belonged to Danielle or Francine, another lady whose company he'd briefly enjoyed? He shook his head, slightly ashamed he could not remember the delicious creature with whom he'd spent a memorable fortnight.

He glanced at his reflection in a large mirror hanging in the corridor. Deep lines marked his forehead, which was a burnished golden color from careless years of outdoor sport. His coat was a little tight around the shoulders, and he knew it was from lack of exercise since being away from his boxing club. He slapped his hand on his abdomen and sucked in his stomach. *Too much rich food.* He spun around as a familiar giggle broke the silence.

"I never fancied you for a dandy." Georgiana emerged from her chamber in a rustle of silk. Her ivory skin, flawless as an alabaster statue, glowed as if lit from within. The lowcut gown revealed more than a hint of cleavage, but she had tucked a lace-trimmed handkerchief in the front.

Marie apparently possessed the skills needed to arrange a lady's hair, and she'd done a marvelous job on Georgiana, twisting her long, golden curls into a mass of spirals. Some were piled high on her head, fastened with his own jewelled stick pins, as she hadn't travelled with any of the Lockewood jewels. He couldn't help but stare at her; the full red lips, smiling at him with confidence and her eyes holding the slight look of adoration he'd noticed when he'd met her for the first time. She hadn't given him a moment's peace since.

"Have you lost your ability for speech?"

He marvelled at how much she had changed in the few years since they'd last met. She'd been all sugar and sweetness then, ready to bring him his favorite pudding when he and Jonathan returned from riding or some other sport. Once, she'd swiped a taste of the almond-flavored cream on a cake, leaving a smear on her face. He'd called her Pudding Face ever since. Where had the girl gone? In her place was a goddess, for all that she was unaware of the spell she cast on those around her.

He straightened his collar in the mirror. "I hardly notice my appearance, unlike some. I seem to have sprouted more silver at my temples, and the creases around my eyes multiply daily. You, however, probably enjoy the dazzling sight of your own visage every time you pass a mirror. I've noticed you never fail to glance at your reflection."

She reached up before he could stop her. She brushed his unruly hair from his eyes, and he jumped as if her nearness had sparked something in him. A blush spread rapidly across her face, but she laughed.

"You are a schoolboy no longer, Jack. I rather like the look of you now—all respectability and properly tied neckcloths. You could be a responsible landowner and not a celebrated fighter."

He snorted. "Believe me, it is only for the next hour. The moment the priest leaves, I'll be back to shirtsleeves and boots."

"What a shame." She clucked her tongue. "You look very dashing all cleaned up. I'm surprised women aren't crawling all over you."

"They were, before you insinuated yourself into my chateau."

She laughed, and it was the loud, hearty laugh of the Lockewoods, though rare in her brother.

At the thought of Lockewood's reaction when he found out what they had done, Jack was tempted to utter a prayer. He offered his arm in a grand gesture. "My lady, our very drunk and overpaid priest awaits in the rose garden. But you'll have to walk through an overgrown patch of weeds to get there, and I'm afraid there's a rather large puddle we have to cross."

She took his arm, linking both hands around it as she used to when she was a little girl. It was her way of making him stay for just one more game, one more story, when cards and brandy beckoned with Lockewood and his friends. One more ride on his shoulders, because Lockewood never would. And Jack always did.

"Is Aunt Adele downstairs?" she asked.

"Yes, along with Lady Priscilla and a rather sallow-looking fellow I can only assume is the ignoble Alphonse. She spoke to me privately."

Georgiana fidgeted with a button his cuff. "What did she say?"

"She is having second doubts, Georgie. Despite our protestations, she is not convinced of our sincerity. She intends to write your brother, and I fully expect an inquisition upon our return that will make the Spanish one look like a garden party." He scowled. "Presuming, of course, Lockewood is not already on his way here to slit my throat. A letter from Lady Richmond might have reached him by now."

Her brow furrowed. "Why should Aunt Adele object? She likes you well enough."

"She thinks I've seduced you." He could not recall blushing since he was in school but felt uncomfortably warm. He'd blame it on the sun, dazzlingly hot this fine summer day, but they were still indoors. "As if I came all the way to France to take the innocence of my friend's sister."

"I shall write Jonathan today and inform him otherwise."

"You shall do no such thing. Better to return to England in a few weeks, rather than the months we've planned. Of course, Aunt Adele may not write to him after all. I was rather—vocal—about her trusting that fool, Alphonse, to escort you to a ball, wherein he abandoned you the moment you arrived. I told her I rescued you from an unsavory situation, which might have resulted in your death, or ruined reputation, which is quite the same thing to her."

"Oh, Jack!" She clapped her hand over her mouth, but he heard her escaped laughter. "You didn't frighten the poor thing, did you?"

"I simply told her the prospect of your being ravished by two scoundrels was infinitely worse than attaching yourself to me for the rest of your life."

"But not much worse."

He glanced sideways at her. "No, not too much worse than that."

They walked outdoors, blinking at the invasion of bright sunshine hitting their eyes. She lifted her skirts to avoid a muddy patch, and he had to force himself to turn away from the enticing sight of her trim ankle as she leapt across.

"Your grandfather's chateau is rather a mystery. One finds the most curious things. To whom did these clothes belong?"

He didn't want to tell her about the gown's owner, although earlier he'd thought to tease her for wearing a courtesan's gown. For some reason, the idea of teasing her no longer appealed. Especially when those great blue eyes were turned up at him.

"I'm not certain. My grandfather used to allow guests to stay here if they were passing through." A little lie would never hurt. He couldn't recall the last time his grandfather set foot in Bordeaux, and the old man was not known for his hospitality.

"It's pretty, but it smells a bit. Like garlic and perfume."

The end of her button nose crinkled, and he had to restrain himself from pinching her cheek. He also had to restrain himself from doing more. She was awfully tempting in the flimsy gown.

"The entire house smelled like that when I got here. You get used to it after a while," he lied. *Francine*. Now, he remembered. They'd fed each other garlic and wine-soaked mushrooms. His groin ached at the memory. Had it only been a few weeks since his last tryst with a courtesan whose name had left his memory?

"That must be the puddle you mentioned. Looks more like a lake."

They stopped at the edge of the flooded garden. Before he could think about the damage he would inflict on his boots, he turned abruptly and lifted her.

She squealed in surprise and wrapped her arms around his neck. "This is like in a storybook, Jack!"

"Well, you're no little girl lost in the woods." He hefted her with an exaggerated grunt. "You need to avoid so much pudding with your supper."

As she pressed against him, he caught the scent of the fragrant soap she'd used in her bath, as well as the faint garlic odor clinging to the fabric. She was featherlight in his arms, just as she'd been years before when he'd carried her across a field to her home when she'd sprained her ankle. Lockewood and he had taken turns carrying her, but she had fallen while chasing him, so Lockewood insisted Jack do the honors. Her skinny arms had clung to his neck, and she'd chattered into his ear the entire time, making up a song at one point and singing it for him and her brother.

Her arms held firm about his neck, one hand combing through the back of his hair. The tickling sensation it produced was distracting, and he jiggled her a bit to make her stop. He glanced down once and got an eyeful of her full bosom, pushed up by the tight bodice. Gritting his teeth, he sloshed through the water while she continued touching his hair.

"I forgot one slight matter." He tried to distract his attention away from her bosom and focused on her face, so close to his.

"What is that?"

"I haven't got a ring. Had I expected to find a bride on this trip, I would have been better prepared."

Her skin flushed all the way to her lace-trimmed bodice. "I don't mind. I wasn't expecting to find a husband abroad, either."

He set her down on the dry grass. Aunt Adele and Lady Priscilla sat on chairs the servants had dragged out for the occasion. A makeshift altar stood before the hollyhocks. Alphonse stood with his hands behind his back, an almost bemused expression on his angular face. Jack longed to say something to him but didn't want to spoil the moment. Besides, the trouble he had brought Georgiana was nothing compared to what Alphonse had done.

The priest was a relative of Philippe's and had been persuaded not to ask too many questions. If persuasion was a close cousin to bribery. He nodded, a broad grin on his face. "*Bonjour,* monsieur! And this must be *la mademoiselle!*"

Georgiana curtsied and Jack bowed, although he felt a bit ridiculous. He wore his best suit with a more or less clean shirt, and her gown was that of a successful courtesan. Marie and Philippe and a few other of his servants were also present, and he noted one's bare, dirty feet.

"Could you not find an English minister?"

Georgiana whispered.

He fidgeted with his neckcloth. Perspiration beaded on his forehead and dripped over his eyebrow to sting his eye. "I was hard pressed to find this one. Fortunately, he didn't mind being paid in my grandfather's wine."

The priest opened his prayer book and began a shortened, simplified version of the wedding service. Jack's French wasn't too bad, and Georgiana spoke it better than he. So he was surprised when the man pronounced them man and wife, and Georgiana remained frozen beside him.

"That's it, then," he muttered, shaking her hand which had been clasped in his for the duration. "We did it, Pudding Face! Well, aren't you going to start ordering me around as your new husband, or has the cat got your tongue?"

She raised misty eyes to him, and promptly brushed at her face as if she had a dustmote in her eye.

The hair lifted on the back of his neck as if he were caught in a trap. He gulped hard. Georgiana Lockewood was no trap. She was the sweetest girl he knew, and he would die to protect her. Any lingering doubts for what they'd done faded when he stared at the pale rose blush of her cheek and her eyes, round and wide and blue as the grapes in the *vignoble*. He was so glad that, if anything else, he had saved her from the likes of Richmond.

"*L'embrasser*!" Marie cried, clapping her hands. "Kiss him, madame!"

He grinned down at her. "Yes, *embrasse-moi*, Georgie. The priest will question our motives if you do not." He'd meant to tease her, but his heart pounded erratically as he waited along with the others for her to do something.

She drew a shaky breath, her slim shoulders vibrating with the action. She placed one hand lightly on his chest while the other remained clasped around his. She rose on tiptoe and he had to stoop to meet her halfway. He turned his cheek slightly toward her, as she'd always kissed him there, but she turned at the last second and met his lips. He jumped back as if stung.

"*Felicitations*!" the priest sang, nodding at them both. The servants led him away. Jack looked down at his new bride. Ought he to embrace her? To kiss her again, but this time, the way she ought to be kissed, and not an innocent peck on the lips?

The warmth of her hand penetrated through his shirt when she'd given him a little caress. He glanced down, half in wonder, half bemused, to stare at her oval fingertips. Mistaking his look, she pulled away and was silent.

He'd made many mistakes in his life. Some of them, fully knowing the risks, as when he'd seduced the Marquise de Burgoyne at a party in Paris years ago while her husband gambled in the next room. Or when he'd lost one thousand pounds on a bet, won it back, then promptly lost it the following night. Other mistakes were not as clear to him at the time he'd made them. He hoped this was not one of those times.

"Congratulations, my dears, and blessings, too." Aunt Adele kissed them both. She fanned herself with a feeble hand. "I apologize for not staying longer, but this warm air does make one tired. If you will forgive me, Georgiana, I will return with my sister to the chateau."

"Do you need any assistance?" Jack offered his

arm, but Alphonse had already stepped forward.

"I will see the ladies home, monsieur." He bowed smartly to Jack and turned to Georgiana. "Congratulations, madame. I am happy you changed your mind." He bent and kissed both her cheeks in the airy custom Jack found so annoying.

"Changed your mind about what?" Jack asked, but she must not have heard, because she didn't reply. They walked back to the house where Aunt Adele declined any refreshment, citing the coolness of Priscilla's chateau as her most dire need.

As they saw the ladies and Alphonse into their coach, Aunt Adele pressed Jack's hand. "I will not write to Jonathan yet, as you requested, Mr. Waverley. He will take the news better coming from his sister's husband."

He forced a cheerfulness he didn't quite feel. He could just imagine Lockewood's eruption if he ever received *that* letter. "I quite agree with you, *Aunt Adele*." He punctuated this last, and the old dear gave a gratified smile.

Georgiana was silent the entire way back to the house, and he would normally have pointed that out but did not have the heart. The strong bonds of friendship had evaporated into the tenuous strings of marriage.

He didn't feel like a bridegroom. He had not courted nor seduced her. There had been no endless meetings with her brother and aunt to compose his suit for her hand, and he had not received a dowry in exchange for turning a Lockewood into a Waverley. He was almost too nervous to glance down at the quiet girl at his side, but when he did her deepening blush and the tiny smile on her lips brought him no end of relief.

Perhaps he was not the best choice of husband for her, but he would never hurt her, like Mitford had, nor would he ever treat her coolly, as Herbert Richmond might have, with his overbearing mother.

He wanted to ask her thoughts, but the answer might not be to his liking. Strange how just a simple ceremony of words and gestures could transfigure one so.

The cook had prepared an outlandish wedding feast for just the two of them, and Jack inhaled the aromas of a fine meal, relieved that eating would be a suitable distraction.

Georgiana followed him toward the dining room, and paused.

"Are you hungry?" he asked.

She shrugged, then quickly nodded, her eyes wider than usual. "Aunt Adele brought my trunks with her, so I'll just change out of this dress. The smell does irritate one so."

"Good idea. I did promise to remove my neckcloth the moment the ceremony, such as it was, ended. If it does not offend you." He'd almost added, *madame*, at the end of his sentence, but bit off the word at the last breath. New bride or no, Georgiana Lockewood was very much a mademoiselle.

They walked silently upstairs, and he gave her a little, almost foolish bow when they reached her chamber. She hastily closed the door, and he went to his own room, whistling soundlessly between his teeth and drumming his fingers onto his thigh while he walked. He was a stranger in his home, and this bewitching girl was now the mistress of all he surveyed.

Once inside, he glanced around his bachelor

quarters. Dirty linen lay strewn about, as he eschewed the services of a proper valet except when in London, as the Parisian gamblers and roustabouts he associated with were more concerned with the contents of one's purse rather than the cut of one's coat. He glanced at the messy bed and winced. It was hardly a bridal chamber, if he could dare assume she should be compelled to go along with the other trappings of marriage.

Stopping short in his tracks, he stared at the bed, trying to imagine sleeping entwined in Georgiana's arms during the hot, sultry night. Just as his body reacted in its typical manner, he laughed. Georgiana was too proper a lady, too innocent to consider such a thing. Especially when he had been so close to her in the past. Why, they were almost family.

Except that they were not.

He ran his hands through his hair, tugging it violently. He'd hoped before their meeting at Fairwood Hall last month that she would not look as he remembered her. He'd prayed for her slim curves to have made way for gluttony. For her clear blue eyes to squint. Although why her eyes would not remain their remarkable shape, nor her figure to bud into a woman's soft curves, mystified him.

A loud groan escaped him, and he paced the room, unsure of what to do next. Did he dress for dinner or remain casual as he had all week since she'd been at the chateau? Did his newly married status require he brush his hair or polish his boots?

He opened the wardrobe and surveyed his clothes with a frown. Nothing would do. They were all evening or riding clothes. Evening for when he sought female companionship and riding for the odd occasion when the gardener brought round the finest horse in town so he could attempt some sort of exercise. He was seldom active during the daylight hours and hardly knew how to act or dress in sunlight.

Either way, he could not go down to dinner in his shirtsleeves. He slipped off his shirt and pulled on a clean one, then selected a waistcoat and frock coat. If only for tonight, and because he respected her family, he would wear a neckcloth. Suffer through with the wretched thing, but wear it nonetheless.

If his hands shook slightly when he tied the material into a semblance of respectability, he ignored it. If he cursed more than usual while searching for a clean pair of boots, he put it down to frustration with the neglectful housekeeper.

As he had done earlier that day, he regarded his reflection in the mirror. His hair had thinned a little at the temple, and despite what Georgiana had said, the few silver hairs mocked him that his days of boxing and sitting at a gaming table all night were ending. Perhaps marriage was the right thing for him. With luck, he could persuade Georgiana to bear a few offspring and they'd buy a suitable home in the country, near Fairwood Hall.

His hands froze on his neckcloth. He hadn't considered where they'd live. He still had his set of chambers at the Albany, but ladies were not allowed. Besides, more than a few questionable females possessed keys to the back door.

"What the hell were you thinking?" He yanked off his neckcloth to retie it. He'd forgotten he'd made certain arrangements with more than a few of his usual lovers for when he returned. How to cancel them now? Before he could dwell on it further, there was a knock on the door. He should have expected her.

Georgiana stood in the doorway, her own gown adorning her curvaceous figure in a shimmering column of ocean blue that exactly matched the color of her eyes. Her elaborate hairstyle was still in place, and her bare throat and décolleté glowed pale pink from the heat of the day.

He caught his breath while trying to maintain an air of bored civility. The little vixen had to know the effect she had on him.

"I didn't know if you were coming down yet. Perhaps we may walk together." Her voice was a breathy whisper, as if she were trying not to wake a sleeping person.

"I'm almost finished here."

Suddenly, they were two strangers who'd been thrown into a desperate situation. Stranded at sea, or lost in a forest with no help in sight. She took a step forward, stopped, then proceeded to walk to him. Before he realized what she was doing, she took the ends of his neckcloth and tied it for him.

"You look…different." He'd almost said beautiful, but stopped himself in time. Georgiana Lockewood…correction, *Waverley*, always looked beautiful.

A blush stained her cheeks, and she smiled, her full lips trembling like a rose petal caught on a breeze.

"All the other gowns in the wardrobe are just as odorous. Their owner must have soaked them in perfume."

He fought the rising embarrassment at her words

but managed to look her in the eye. "Perhaps it was Marie's way of keeping the room smelling fresh. The chateau does have a closed up smell about it when there's no one here." He tapped his finger at the air near her shoulder. "You look nicer in your own clothes. As your new husband, I will see to it you have plenty of new gowns, bonnets, and slippers. Your brother has kept you attired like a child. It's time you dressed like a woman."

Her eyes sparkled. "I would love some new clothes. But, Jack, I do have my inheritance. Now that I'm married..." She blushed, gulped, and continued, "we will have control of my money." She patted his lapels. "There. You could pass for Beau Brummel's own brother now."

He was about to jest in kind, but his tongue felt plastered to the roof of his mouth. Although he tried to avoid it, he couldn't help but notice how her neck sloped down to an obscenely perfect bosom, or that her lower lip puffed out just enough to spur him to thoughts he'd rather not have now.

She continued fiddling with his buttons and adjusting his waistcoat until he realized it was because she was suddenly too shy to look at him. He wanted to take back the entire morning; indeed, their whole conversation that had brought them to this. What in God's name was he doing with a bride? Only days ago, he'd been anticipating a sojourn into Paris to enjoy a week of debauchery and all manner of scandal-worthy behavior.

He could not go back on his word. He'd saved her so many times in the past that rescuing her was second nature. This was the last in a long string of rescues, and one he could not avoid. She lifted her head and gazed up at him. Trusting, secure. He could give her that, if nothing else.

He offered his arm. "Does Beau Brummel have a brother who fights?" He led her out of his chamber and toward the staircase.

"If he does, I'd wager you could beat him." She linked both hands around his arm and walked with him downstairs to their awaiting feast.

Chapter Sixteen

"I've arranged for our passage home at the end of the month." Jack picked at his wedding luncheon much in the same way Georgiana was. Beyond a few requests to pass the saltcellar or to inquire if she wanted more wine, he had not said much.

"To avoid any issues with Lady Richmond?"

He nodded. "Better we leave from Calais and have a civil marriage at the British embassy. I do not know the legitimacy of a ceremony performed by a drunken priest on French soil."

"Whatever you wish." She dabbed her lips with her napkin and looked expectantly at him.

He tugged at his neckcloth and loosened his collar. Why did the room seem so much warmer whenever those deep blue eyes were fastened on him?

She took a sip of wine, deeper than her previous tastes. "We should also consummate our marriage, so should Jonathan demand our separation, my loss of virginity will make me a less viable candidate for those wretched suitors he's chosen."

Jack sputtered a mouthful of wine across the table. Random purple dots absorbed instantly into the white cloth. He choked on his breath and pounded his chest until he'd regained speech.

"I sincerely and utterly beg your pardon?" he asked as calmly as he could.

Georgiana regarded him with a serene, almost angelic innocence, as if she had just asked if he'd like another helping of potatoes. Her lips trembled slightly, but her gaze never wavered.

"I think you heard me, Jack. And given your infamous reputation, which, as you boast, is deservedly earned, the idea should not come as a total shock to you." A faint blush rose from the crest of her bosom to her throat, finally reaching her cheek.

He watched it in fascination before blinking rapidly to clear his vision. "You are probably correct in your opinion of your brother's reaction. Even if we did consummate it—" He nearly choked again. "How are we to prove it? He will only have our word. Ought we to save the sheets?" She blanched, and he instantly regretted his crudeness. "Forgive me," he muttered. "That was indelicate."

She airily waved his words away. "Not at all. I'm actually considering the prudence of that very thing. I can bundle them up and pack them in my trunk." She rose from the table, her fingertips pressed to the edge, as if for support. "So…" She swallowed audibly. "Do you have any disagreement?"

He bit back a laugh. She was trying so hard to be mature, and all he could think of was when he'd climbed up a tree and rescued her. He'd been sixteen then, and she eight. Her skinny arms had clung so tightly around his neck, he almost choked. When he set her on the ground, she laughed in his face. "Do it again!" she cried, holding up her arms to make him lift her because Lockewood refused. Come to think of it, there was not much Jack had ever refused his best friend's little sister. This day was living proof.

"None at all. In fact, your suggestion has another benefit." He stared directly into her eyes, forcing her gaze to hold. This would be her way out, he decided. Shock her, and she would flee the room—the chateau, if he were fortunate enough, and forget she'd ever brought up the insane notion in the first place.

"What benefit is that?" she asked, as cool as if she propositioned men every night.

"As you said, I am a man of fearsome appetites. Since your arrival has caused me to forego my normal pursuits, I have been—shall we say, lonely. Your arrangement would take care of both our problems. Lockewood will never force you to leave our marriage if he knew you'd been tainted by me, whereas I will not have to look for a French doxy with one hand in my purse and the other on my…."

"I see your point," she said quickly, loudly.

"Then we have only to decide on the time."

"The…the time?"

"Why, yes. Do we retire upstairs now? Or would you prefer to wait a few days to better prepare yourself and stir my ardor into a raging fire?"

Her face burned as red as the tomatoes on her plate. "Prepare myself?" She huffed. "It is not an expedition I'm suggesting, but the normal routine between a husband and wife." She frowned. "Why, is there something I need to prepare for?"

"That depends on your definition of routine."

"I don't want to wait. Tonight, after supper." She chewed her lip, and some of her blush faded. "After the pudding. I smelled chocolate when I passed the kitchens earlier."

"Excellent suggestion. One tantalization before the

other." He leaned back in his chair, his gaze still burning into hers. "Your chamber or mine?"

"Yours. No, mine. Yours is not very tidy."

"Dressing gowns or *au naturel*?"

She rose halfway from her chair, ablaze with his indignant attitude. He mentally congratulated himself.

"If you are trying to mock me…."

"Never." He rose from the table and brought a bottle of wine from a sideboard. It wasn't quite noon, but somehow, the conversation seemed to call for one or both to be out of their heads. He poured two glasses. After a moment's pause, he gave hers another healthy glug. "I am at your disposal, mademoiselle. Forgive me—*madame*."

She raised her glass, and the wine sloshed a little. "Should we not have a toast?"

"By all means." He lowered his glass, as he was about to have a drink, and lifted it in her direction. "To a satisfactory union."

"*Satisfactory*?"

Had her lips always been the color of ripe cherries? And why was she arching her brow in such a coquettish way, as if to hint that it would be more than satisfactory? His coat suddenly seemed too tight, and his breeches…He'd have to pay a visit to his tailor when he returned to London, to add another inch or two in his waistband. He hadn't noticed how little room he had in the crotch.

"I shall endeavor not to disappoint you."

"Disappoint me?" The flirtatious look slid off her face as quickly as it had appeared. "I hardly think…"

"That you will know the difference?" He grinned broadly. "Miss Worldly, sitting so calm and collected as if she propositions unassuming gentlemen of low means every night."

Her glass hit the table with an audible clink. "I apologize for not being the sort of woman you're used to. I asked Marie about the gowns in the wardrobe today, and she assured me they were not here before your arrival. I suppose that is why you were too busy to visit me at Lady Priscilla's."

Her flushed face unsettled him. Shifting in his chair, he motioned at her with his glass. "You are already meddling into my affairs as I predicted; all your protestations to the contrary. I have not led a saintly existence since arriving in Bordeaux. Would you rather I regale you with the sordid details, or leave the past to itself?"

"Leave the past," she muttered.

"I hate to remind you, but did you not promise that one of the stipulations of our so-called marriage was my continued freedom in the life I am accustomed to living, as are you free to do as you please without interference from a bothersome husband?"

"Yes, yes." She appeared quite exasperated, but he could not resist.

"I will remove all those troublesome garments from your chamber on the morrow, Georgiana." He reminded himself of her precarious position. First, under the thumb of her older brother, and now tied to him for the rest of her life. The thought was positively ghastly. "I would not have you any way but what you are, Miss Lockewood. Forgive me—Mrs. Waverley."

"And what way is that?" At any moment, he feared she would flee the room. She blinked a few times and he wondered if her eyes glistened from tears or just a trick of the light.

"Sweet and innocent, and utterly charmed by me."

The joke worked. A wavering smile touched her lips, and she drank her wine when he did.

They ate the rest of their meal in silence. Jack tried to make small talk but quickly gave it up when he realized evening was only a few hours away.

And how long, really, did it take to eat one's pudding?

Chapter Seventeen

She did not recall leaving the dining room or walking beside him up the staircase. She couldn't tell if he was walking faster than usual, but they reached the top landing in no time. She'd tugged his sleeve to hold him back in a moment of panic. He placed his hand at the small of her back to guide her toward her chamber. She walked woodenly into her room, which seemed unfamiliar and threatening now his broad shoulders filled the doorway.

His presence dominated the room. He was a head taller and had always seemed so big in comparison to her, but then, she'd been a child when he used to visit. The muscular arms that had swung her around the park or tossed her over his shoulder were now the arms that would carry her to bed. At least, she assumed he would carry her. Wasn't that how a marauder about to ravish a maiden behaved?

If he suffered any of her reticence, it didn't show. He sat on the settee, leisurely pulling off his boots. She stood in mute fascination watching him undress as if he were perfectly at home. Although she'd seen him countless times without his boots and certainly without his coat or waistcoat, it was an entirely different thing altogether that he should remove these items in front of her. He glanced up at her and gave her an easy grin, as if he'd been caught doing something naughty. In the flickering lamplight, his skin had taken on a golden hue, and his hair blazed with glinting highlights. She wondered if he were fully aware of his effect on women. His easy grin, sparkling eyes, and the boyish cleft in his chin were irresistible.

Well, irresistible to some, but not her. She unclasped her single bracelet and placed it on the table, unable to follow him in removing more of her garments. She chewed her lip, unsure of what to say. How did one start a conversation with one's new husband, whose reputation for fast living and ravishment of all kinds far preceded him? She'd feared this moment, just a bit, but annoyance replaced her worry now that he was actually going through with her hastily thought up suggestion. If he were any sort of loyal friend or noble protector, he'd have talked her out of it. Not strode inside her chamber as if he couldn't wait to take her up on her outrageous, ridiculous…

"Shall we get this over with in the traditional, yet effective way, or would you rather enjoy yourself?"

A rapid blush heated her face. He did have a way with words. He pushed up from the settee, setting his boots aside, an expectant look on his face as he waited for her reply.

"Whatever you're used to."

His eyebrows rose in a bemused fashion. "That would entail you with your skirts up over your head, bent over the nearest convenient table."

Was he trying to shock her? Her belly quivered. "That doesn't sound very…pleasant." So why did her mind whisk up a vision of Jack, behind her in some questionable position, as she gripped the old Etruscan desk in the drawing room?

"Then it is to be passion, romance, and kisses?"

She nodded uncertainly. "All of that, but no kissing."

"Why ever not? I neglected to eat the onion soufflé for your benefit. Besides, I have heard on many occasions my kisses are exemplary."

"That is precisely why I do not wish to kiss you. Kisses bring feelings, and feelings bring love—a thing which neither of us desires."

"Good point. You have a very practical mind, Georgie."

Her arms had begun trembling, and she chafed her skin. "You must not call me Georgie anymore. I am a married woman."

"What shall it be then? My darling? My sweetheart?" He tugged at his neckcloth. Of course, he would begin removing his clothes. She fought the urge to turn away and gave in to her curiosity. The more of his clothes he removed, the more naked she felt.

"Don't be ridiculous."

He draped his coat over a chair and removed his neckcloth a second later. "Tell me what I may call you. Frankly, this is more conversation in a bedchamber than I'm used to having."

"Anything but Georgie. It sounds like a little boy's name."

"Mrs. Waverley? Will that be allowed?" He unbuttoned his waistcoat, and she realized his shirt did not require elaborate tucks and pleats, but his own physique filled it out.

"Only in public. Mrs. Waverley would sound odd at the breakfast table. What do you usually call a woman you're about to bed?"

"Expensive."

Swallowing back a sudden lump that had appeared in her throat for no reason at all, she gave him her best arch look.

"I meant women you did not have to pay, but otherwise seduced."

"My powers of seduction, while ample, I assure you, are not as flagrant as your brother and you believe." His waistcoat joined his other garments. He wiggled his finger.

"Yes?" She thought her heart would pound its way out of her chest.

"Are you going to remove your gown yourself? Damned tricky things, those tangled laces."

"I suppose I am fortunate you have had so much practice in removing a lady's garments." She turned her back. Breathless, she waited for a touch, a caress...anything. How would it feel to be touched for a purpose other than dancing or being handed from a carriage? How would it feel for Jack to touch her, in a way not meant to play or tease but something else? She wasn't sure he had touched her until the tiny hairs on the back of her neck prickled at the whisper of his breath on her neck.

The laces and buttons were no match for his swift fingers. The gown slid down her shoulders and body in a rush of silk and pooled about her feet in a shimmering puddle. She crossed her arms over her chest, too nervous to face him. Would he continue to tease her? Comment on the size of her breasts? She suddenly couldn't remember if she were well endowed or flat chested. Would he care either way? After so many women in his bed, would he even notice?

She should have asked Marie for advice. Though the girl was about her age, she'd seen her emerge from the shadows in the gallery more than once with Philippe, who always seemed contented.

"Turn, please." It was a soft command, but one nonetheless. She gulped audibly and turned.

"I…I need a nightrail."

"For what purpose?"

She shrugged, biting her lip because she could think of no words. How had she ever thought this would be a good idea? Discussing lovemaking downstairs over supper was one thing. On the verge of being soundly ravished by Jack Waverley was another.

"All right—you may keep your chemise. For now." He cleared his throat, obviously relishing the moment. "Lights lit, or doused?"

"Doused." She shook her head. "No, lit." She could find an escape route if necessary in the lamplight.

He cocked an eyebrow. "It is more interesting when one can see what the other is doing. Good choice."

"I want to see what you're doing."

"You won't see much. Your eyes will be squeezed shut in ecstasy through most of it."

She fought back a new blush but didn't think her efforts worked. "I am a little curious, if you must know. This is one more…experience I shall have." Her face felt as hot as if she stood inches from a flame. "Besides—I want to…to admire your physique. If that would not embarrass you." Perhaps he would reconsider at the thought of his own vulnerability.

"No, no. I am rarely embarrassed." He pulled his shirt over his head. "And the last thing that would embarrass me would be a little thing like you, ravishing me with her innocent eyes."

She held her breath as she scanned the broad expanse of his chest. Muscles she never knew existed formed ripples and planes across his abdomen. A myriad of scars and old bruises covered his ribs, and when he turned to fling the shirt over a chair, she noticed long lines on his back.

"What happened to you? Were you once mauled by tigers?"

"Close. A very enthusiastic countess once clawed my shoulders at a most inopportune time. Her husband got me with a rapier point when he decided to defend her honor." He paused for a moment, as if reliving the memory. "Come to think of it, he was rather a little late for defending her honor."

"Did my…" She gulped, not knowing if she really wanted to know the answer. "Did Jonathan ever participate in these antics?"

He laid his right hand across his heart, but there was a sly gleam in his eye. "Your brother is a most exemplary man who kept his nose buried in his schoolbooks, while yours truly was out carousing like a tom cat."

"*Really.*"

"Must we discuss Lockewood anymore? It rather stifles a man's ardor if he's forced to consider his brother-in-law." He removed his watch fob and began unbuttoning the fall on his breeches.

Georgiana had the sudden urge to flee from the room, but something building inside her kept her firmly where she was. She was as intrigued as she was anxious, excited as she was alarmed. When she looked at him, she could still see the boy, forever a smile on his lips, always a prank or joke for her. How she'd looked forward to her brother's homecoming from school at Christmas, for he always brought Jack Waverley with him. She would tag along when they were shooting or riding, and once even heard a whispered tale of something about one of the scullery maids she couldn't wait to tell Mamma. Jack had bribed her with sweets not to tell that she became ill for two days.

And now he was her husband.

He was no longer the big-eared, skinny youth who pulled her hair and made little boats for her dolls to sail around the pond. The humorous look still occupied his eyes, and she suspected it would never vanish, but there was something else there now, too. It was as if he'd grown up and was both amused and horrified at the prospect. He had shaved that morning, but dark whiskers now shadowed his face, making him look even more roguish than ever before. She wondered how his rough jaw would feel against her skin, and trembled. She couldn't stop trembling.

She turned away before he unfastened his breeches. Her fingers were stiff and useless as she fumbled with her stays. Her inept fingers tangled the laces into a knot.

His hands were on her shoulders, heavy and warm. She'd always admired his hands. They seemed so capable and strong. He'd held her hand a hundred times, but this was different. He was not touching her now in the way a youth protected a little girl. There was a possessiveness to his grip that had never been there before.

"I hope you are not embarrassed, my dear Georgie—I mean, my dear Mrs. Waverley."

"I'm not to be Mrs. Waverley in the bedchamber, either." She tried to make her voice sound crisp, but the words rushed from her in a single breath.

"I will call you my lovely one, then. Because that's what you are. My God," he breathed. "You're so beautiful, Georgiana."

A gasp strangled in her throat when his lips, unmistakably his lips, brushed against her ear, sending a thousand sparks flying throughout her body. She'd forgotten how to breathe or stand or think… She sank back into his arms just as his hands left her shoulders and wrapped around her waist.

"What…what are you doing?"

"You wanted love-making, did you not?"

His lips trailed deliciously hot kisses down the side of her throat. A shiver coursed through her and this time, she did wobble as she stood.

"I don't know." She'd forgotten everything they'd discussed. At supper, it had seemed so practical and simple. *Consummate the marriage.* It was an arrangement between old friends, for heaven's sake. A physical act as old as time, predictable and mundane.

If it were so mundane, why did her body feel as if a thousand tiny explosions were searing her from the inside out? Why had she lost the sensation of firm ground beneath her feet?

"Well," he began, turning her to face him and holding her against his bare, hard chest, "if you like, I can make this very quick and less satisfying for you, though infinitely easier on me."

She wasn't sure what he was talking about but sensed he was teasing her. Her chin lifted as some of her confidence returned.

"I do not want it to be easy for you."

"Then you must not object to my…appreciation for your many charming attributes."

Before she could ask what he meant, he undid her laces so quickly the stays dropped from her body and landed between them.

"It would be much nicer if you'd let me kiss you." His voice was soft and low, lulling her into a dreamlike trance. One of his arms remained around her waist, and she was grateful for the support. His other hand trailed up her arm and skimmed her breast, causing her knees to bend as she nearly fell backward at the shock of his touch.

She didn't want the night to end. Didn't want any of it to be quick and, heaven forbid, easy on him. His lips were inches away, and she stared at them, mesmerized. "We should not kiss. I don't want to fall in love. Remember what we said?"

The moment she said the word *kiss*, it was the only thing she could think about. Had it only been a few weeks since she'd greeted Jack at her brother's home, eager to start their journey and resume their friendship? They'd gone from old acquaintances to husband and wife in the space of a heartbeat. A wave of gratitude swept over her. Were it not for his sacrifice of his bachelorhood, she might be having this same evening a year hence, but with Herbert Richmond or someone equally as loathsome fumbling at her instead of Jack with his sure, knowing hands.

"I remember. But do you think people fall in love over a mere kiss? I have it on good authority your sister-in-law did not kiss Lockewood once until they were betrothed. Do you think they didn't love each other until the very second they kissed?"

She swallowed to moisten her dry throat, but it didn't help. "So…if we kiss, we will not fall in love?"

"Not in the least. It is another part of lovemaking. I've kissed hundreds of women and not fallen in love with even one of them. And you wanted the full experience, did you not? I mean, if this is going to be our one night together, you might as well make the most of it. Do you not agree?" He tilted up her chin with the tip of his finger.

She hadn't meant to look from his mouth to his eyes and then back to his mouth again. In truth, she couldn't help but stare at it. His lips were full and soft, as much as she'd seen them drawn back in a sneer or in anger. The scent of wine lingered on his breath, and the chocolate they'd eaten. She'd barely touched hers, but he had eaten as heartily as if he had not a care in the world.

"Then…" She inhaled slowly, her breath catching in her throat. "Kiss me, Jack."

A grin touched his lips, then vanished just as quickly. The last thing she saw before her eyes closed was the sight of his heavy lashes lowering over his gray eyes. His warm breath breezed across her lips before his mouth joined hers, and she froze in her shock and delight.

She'd thought his lips would remain pressed to hers and unmoving, but they were caressing, drawing her lower lip between them. She gasped for a breath, not realizing she was holding it, and his tongue entered her mouth. A quivering rush of warmth flooded her limbs, leaving her legs weak and trembling. Dazed, she collapsed against him, and he slid his hands beneath her arms and raised them around his neck.

She'd been kissed before. Edward had attempted it once or twice, on the desperate ride to Gretna Green what seemed like an eternity ago. But his breath had reeked of stale wine and tobacco, and she'd turned from him. Edward had been almost wild, groping at her, but Jack's hands on her back were steady.

His tongue stroked alongside hers, and when she responded, he groaned low in his chest, like a bear she'd once seen at a fair. The rumble seemed to come from deep inside him and echoed in her head. She lost track of time and would not have been able to say if they had been kissing for a minute or if an hour had passed. Each caress of his hand on her face, his lips brushing across hers, awakened new sensations she had never before imagined were possible.

He broke away abruptly and before she could wonder why, he removed his breeches and stood naked before her.

"Oh…my."

She wobbled but regained her footing. The only naked men she'd ever seen were the marble statues in the British Museum. But ancient models of Greek and Roman gods were nothing compared with a breathing, flesh and blood man. Who would have thought such a broad chest could sit atop a slim waist and muscular thighs? Or a chest could be as smooth as oiled marble, but with a mass of dark hair trailing down a navel to the object she could neither look at nor tear her gaze from?

"Have I appeased your curiosity?"

She nodded mutely.

As if he waited for her signal, he swept her up into his arms so quickly she forgot to compare him to a marauder or anything else. All she could do was hold onto him as he carried her toward the bed.

Chapter Eighteen

One sweet caress blended into another, each more daring than the one before. Georgiana alternated between clutching him and pushing him away, excited and terrified and then thrilled again as his lips traveled over her throat and between her breasts. When had he removed her chemise? But no, it still clung to her damp skin. He'd tugged on her ribbon ties and slid the garment to her waist. She crossed one arm over her chest but he pushed it aside so quickly she wasn't even aware she'd done so.

"Hold onto me." His breath seared her throat.

She lifted trembling arms and pinned them around his neck. His mouth sought hers and she was powerless against his invading tongue and urgent lips. He'd wedged himself between her thighs, until her hips felt as if they'd snap their joints. The demanding hardness of his arousal mixed with the gentle caress of his hands until she was lost in a swirling waterfall of emotion. She was gripping him too hard; he broke the kiss, his mouth an inch above hers.

"I won't bite," he whispered, and she laughed, mildly hysterical, but also ready to explode with the rush of desire his touch inspired. "Don't fight me, my dearest."

"I'm not…"

"You are. You're struggling against me. Just…just

breathe."

"Give me a moment." She struggled to match the rhythm of her breathing to his. Every inch of his body was covering hers. How could Jack be so heavy yet so light at the same time? Her fingers tangled in his hair, luxuriating in the soft waves from his heated scalp. His whiskers rasped lightly against her forehead.

"How are you now?" Each strained word puffed from his lips.

She nodded. "I'm fine."

"Good. Your moment is up."

She cried out with the shock of it, and he lay on top of her, heavy and still, propped on his elbows. She was vaguely aware of his sweaty palm on her cheek, her hair, smoothing her forehead and skimming her eyes and the bridge of her nose. He was whispering something soft, almost melodic. She detected the soothing words she'd heard him murmur to her cat once, when it gave birth to a litter of four kittens on top of a favorite gown she'd left on the floor.

She blinked, and the sharpness vanished. It wasn't a pain, exactly, but she was aware of the strange sensation of being connected to him. Surely that single thrust couldn't be all there was. Restless, she shifted beneath him, and he grimaced.

"Are you hurt?" The idea she could hurt powerful Jack Waverley was laughable.

"No." A drop of sweat rolled down his nose and onto her cheek. "I was waiting for you to get used to it."

She sucked in a shaky breath. Moved a slight inch or two. "I think I'm used to it now."

"Thank God," he murmured, and kissed her.

A steady, low throbbing ache had begun exactly

where his body pinned hers. The slightest movement even from his breathing stirred an ember of passion that expanded into full-blown fire. Her breathing quickened, and she released his neck. She'd always enjoyed watching his hair sweep around his face, and now twined it through her fingers, holding the silken strands like tiny ropes. He continued to gaze down into her eyes, although his eyelids flickered as if they would close a few times.

"Shall I move at all?" Her voice caught in her throat.

"By all means, love. Move as much as you like."

He moved the slightest bit, and she arched against him spasmodically. He gave a grunt of satisfaction and covered her mouth with his, sucking lightly on her tongue while his body stroked smoothly into hers.

She forgot about the exuberant French woman who'd scarred his back with her fingernails in a moment of passion and did the same, digging into his velvet soft skin and kneading the granite muscles that quivered beneath her questing fingertips.

He was gasping her name now, but it wasn't *Georgie* or any childhood nickname. It was her full name, spoken by a man to a woman. He was no longer her brother's teasing friend but her husband, her lover. She nearly cried with the realization of it and knew that somehow, inexplicably, she had been waiting for this moment all her life.

"Something has happened." Her voice broke in a joyous cry of release. His arms eased about her, and his kiss softened to a mere caress. She trembled violently, rocking against him as the force of her climax astounded her. He laughed softly and kissed her forehead.

"Not a bad first time, eh?"

His voice broke through the stillness. They'd kicked off the coverlet and sheet, and his skin glowed in the lamplight. She dragged her foot lightly over the back of his calf, and he trembled.

"Not bad at all. I expect you'll congratulate yourself later."

She caught a glimpse of his grin before his face disappeared to nestle between her cleavage and throat.

"I'll let you thank me later." His strokes resumed, bolder now, and she lifted his head and framed his face with her hands, to better watch his reaction.

His brow furrowed and his mouth gaped open, and then his eyes closed tightly and he groaned.

A rush of heat flowed deep inside her, and it occurred to her that, while they married for the convenience of doing as they pleased the rest of their lives, there was the chance they could conceive a child.

He rolled onto his side, his chest heaving against hers. His lips were warm and languorous on her mouth. She hadn't stopped marveling at the infinite variety of kisses. He was absolutely right. His kisses were a thing of wonder. Soft as a feather one moment then firm and demanding another.

She sighed as he lazily stroked her breast, kneading it with his fingers as if it were a plaything.

"Is it always like this for you?" She instantly regretted her words. Did she really want to imagine him bedding anyone else? The shock of that truth struck her to the core.

"You mean as noisy?"

A dusky glow of moonlight filled the room,

blurring the edges of furniture and walls. In the semi-darkness, she had the luxury of studying his face. The hard curve of his jaw softened and his mouth wore a bruised look about it, as if he'd been boxing. The sudden need to kiss him fought against her sensibilities, but she held back, not wanting him to tease her.

"No, not noisy." She lowered her eyelids, suddenly too shy to look at him, even though their bodies were still pressed together. "I meant…" *As earth-shattering, heart-rending*—"thrilling, I suppose."

"Thrilling?" He slid his hand down her waist to her hip. "I must say, Georgie…*Georgiana*, this was the most thrilling moment of my life."

"Truly?" She picked up his hand from her hip and held it between them. Her fingers were lost inside his large, wide palm.

"Shall I say you're the only woman in the world for me?"

She swallowed nervously. How had she turned a perfectly normal friendship into something teetering on the edge of disaster?

"I wouldn't want you to make up pretty things to flatter me." She turned abruptly on her side, scrabbling for the sheet to cover herself. She heard him sigh, but he could have laughed.

"You've gone and done it, Pudding Face." He scooted close and drew her to him again.

"Done what?" She scowled, but it was lost on him, because he couldn't see her.

His arousal pressed into her bottom, and she writhed away from him, but he clasped her in his arms, his laughter now audible.

"Your platonic experiment is a disaster. You may

as well admit it. I will not hold it against you."

Her heart pounded against her ribs, and she knew he felt it because his hand had captured her breast. He turned her over to face him and lifted her thigh around his hip. As their bodies touched, she clutched his shoulders before she could stop herself.

"Admit what?" But it was a breath whispered against his lips. His tongue slid against hers and she arched toward him. His strokes were slow and gentle, and she stifled the moan rising to her throat, lest he think she was being wanton.

"We two are not meant for mere friendship." His lips vibrated against hers. "You are in love with me now."

Tears filled her eyes. He was mocking her. He was the same, teasing Lothario she'd always known he was. He was probably enjoying the satisfaction of thinking he'd triumphed. That what he'd said all along would happen had, indeed, happened.

"You are mistaken, Jack. We are only friends. I'm just…just a little overwhelmed. It's France…and the wine. That is all."

"Of course, it is. Blame everything on the wine. I always do."

She found his lips again, kissing him feverishly as the force of her desire tumbled her headlong into a black, empty chasm.

****

His breathing slowed in heavy sleep. His arm lay heavily across her, and she lifted his hand to her lips. She almost kissed him but decided against it in case he awoke.

The first streaks of purple light signaling dawn

peeked through the gently blowing curtains. They'd rise soon, ready to begin their new lives as a married couple. Only, they wouldn't have a life like Jonathan and Sophie's, where words of love were freely spoken and the anticipated birth of a child brought them closer. What kind of life would they have together?

She snuggled into his side as he turned in his sleep. His body curved around hers as if they'd been made for each other. It was nice to share a bed with Jack. More than nice, if she admitted the truth. She could hardly get over her surprise at how events had transpired. When had friendship—childish adoration, even—blossomed into love?

And what in heaven's name was she going to do about it?

It couldn't be love. Impossible. Had she not sworn never to love again? It was her very reason to have wanted to marry him in the first place. His conquests and reckless living were the deciding factors in making him the ideal husband. With so many women in his life, he would never become attached to her, and she would never again have her heart controlled by foolish lovesickness.

So why did she anticipate the next time they made love? Why did she want to shower his grizzled cheek with kisses and press her ear to his chest to listen to his heart? Was this platonic love for a man who'd been like a brother for years?

She closed her eyes so she couldn't stare at him anymore. It wasn't love at all, just the novelty of sharing a bed with a skilled, enthusiastic lover. What else could it be? Perhaps her first time with Edward might have been the same. She shuddered. Somehow, she couldn't imagine holding onto Edward and returning passionate kiss for kiss as she had with Jack.

"You talk in your sleep."

She twitched with surprise, relieved she had not kissed his hand. He most surely would have teased.

"I do not."

"You wouldn't know, would you?"

"What did I say?"

"Mostly my name. Just as I expected."

He yelped when she pinched his thigh. "You are conceited, Jack Waverley."

"And you love me anyway, Mrs. Waverley." He sat up to straighten the sheet over them. "We should have ample evidence to show anyone who questions the legitimacy of our union."

She glanced at the spotted sheet and blushed furiously. He only laughed and pulled her back onto the bed when she tried to rise.

"I should have known you would be..." She choked despite her resolve to be aloof and worldly.

"That I would be what?"

He stretched over her with obvious delight. She pushed against his chest, but he captured her hands, drawing her arms over her head and pinning them to the pillow.

"You have not a bit of compassion in you, whatsoever. You are only interested in teasing me, when last night was so...so..." She bit her lip, and he quickly kissed her, framing her face in his hands.

"So what?" he murmured, his lips trailing across her mouth and to her throat.

"You know what I'm trying to say."

"Of course it was wonderful. I told you it would

be, didn't I? Have I ever lied to you?"

She struggled against his hold, but he was so warm, and his musky scent invaded her senses that she didn't want him to stop. He released her hands and she wrapped her arms around him.

"One of my governesses told me a woman had to endure her husband's…you know." She chewed her lip. "I'd always thought sharing a man's bed would be a trial."

"Well, we can always do it again, and I can try to be inconsiderate and loathsome."

A single curl had drifted over his ear. She twined it around her finger. "I'm trying to say that you were…that it was…just perfect."

His jaw worked for a moment, and she half-expected a teasing reply. The corners of his eyes crinkled. "I just wanted you to have the full experience. That way, when you run back to Fairwood Hall, you can have something to write about in your diary."

Again, the devilish grin. Her heart pounded almost painfully. "Are you not coming home with me?"

"What?" His eyebrows darted up in feigned shock. "And face your brother? Are you mad, woman?"

She slipped her legs around him and watched the grin fade into the same look of devout seriousness she recognized from the night before. "We can always send him a letter."

He chuckled, but she sensed his interest lay in other matters for the moment. "I will go with you, then. After all, I can hardly trust you on the road home by yourself. Who knows what sort of mischief you'll find? Besides, I did make that promise to your brother." He sighed elaborately, as if it were only the fact he'd promised Jonathan and nothing else that changed his mind.

Relieved, she almost kissed him but smiled instead. He'd already slipped inside her, like slick satin wrapped in a sheath of velvet. Her mind fogged.

"Thank you, Jack."

"For this?" He nuzzled her breast, dragging his scratchy whiskers across her throat until she had to stifle a giggle.

"For...for sacrificing your bachelorhood."

"I'm sure I will be forgiven by all the other bachelors who will curse me for breaking the code."

"There's a code?"

If there was, she did not care to hear it. From his heavy breathing and muttered expressions of delight, he did not care to explain.

Chapter Nineteen

"Where are you going?"

She lifted her head from the pillows, her body heavy. They'd spent the entire day in bed, and she didn't know if it was morning or night. What's more, she didn't care. The curtains were open, and a faint, hazy light entered the room.

He paused in buttoning his shirt. "Contrary to popular belief amongst the Fairwood Hall set, I did not venture to France merely for base pleasure-seeking. I do have actual business to attend."

"Of course, you do." She wanted to ask if he were going to the *vignoble* but did not want to pry. Even though she'd spent several waking hours under his loving attention and several asleep on his chest, their agreement did not give her the right to ask.

"I will be home in time for supper. You may spend the day guessing my favorite dishes and concocting an excellent menu with my capable cook."

He pulled on his waistcoat. She caught her breath. He cut such a striking figure. His muscular arms were hidden beneath the flowing sleeves but his heavy, lean thighs strained against the seams of his breeches. He winked at her.

"What is that frown? Missing me already, Georgie?"

She thumped her pillow and pretended she was

more interested in comfort than staring at him. "I shall miss your incessant teasing and bad manners. As for your supper, we shall have my own favorites. I hope you like pickled pig's feet."

"How did you guess my favorite?"

She groaned. "What time is it?"

He padded across the carpet and sat on the edge of the bed. "It's just past six. In the morning." He cocked an eyebrow. "I'm not surprised you're awake. You snored all night to awaken the dead. I don't think I slept more than two hours. Every time I tried to push you away, you'd scurry back across the sheets into my arms. Just think—you no longer need steal into my bed, but may become a welcome visitor."

She bit back a retort, only because he was stroking the side of her face, and his touch soothed and aroused at the same time. His hand skimmed her throat and slid under the sheet. She tried not to gasp when his palm covered her breast, but did so anyway, reaching for his hand and holding it in place. He leaned forward and kissed her gently, almost sweetly, on the lips.

"God, it pains me to leave you. Truly pains me." His gray eyes sparkled with their familiar mischievous gleam. "But I look forward to spending another glorious night in your arms." He frowned suddenly. "That is, if you'd still like the full experience of the oft-touted honeymoon, Mrs. Waverley."

Forgetting her resolve to remain aloof, she sat up, allowing the sheet to drop to her waist. She pressed into his chest as his arms reached around her.

"That is not an unpleasant idea."

He combed through her tangled hair with his broad fingers, caressing her scalp as he did. Her eyelids fluttered closed, and she sighed. She felt his soft laughter like a gentle breeze on her mouth when he kissed her.

"Good. I'm glad last night was as non-unpleasant for you as it was for me."

A rush of heat surged over her limbs until the blush reached her forehead. "You must stop teasing me so, Jack. If anyone heard us, they would think I'm a little ninny, following you around like a puppy, while you laugh and smile at me."

"I shall frown at you then and quite often. You grew up in too good a household, I think. Not enough shouting and spirit-breaking, in my opinion."

She finished buttoning his shirt, her fingertips lingering on a patch of bare, warm skin. "You would do better to spoil and pet me." She straightened his collar with a firm hand, hoping her voice sounded authoritative. "I can be very easily persuaded into generosity."

"I do not want your thousands, Georgie. I married you to save your reputation and keep you from the loutish Mr. Richmond."

His tone was light, but his eyes hardened suddenly. He pulled away, but she grasped his shirt.

"I meant with my affections." She'd tried to be flirtatious, but her attempt was regrettably pitiful. She swallowed, suddenly nervous, as he continued to look at her. "Which are, of course, yours to command."

He laughed loudly and pulled her to him a little roughly, but she clung to him anyway. She felt him inhale the scent of her hair, and then he lifted his head and kissed her soundly. "I shall command them, then. But, tonight, when I return. I have no time now, as tempting as you are." He continued to dress. "In your absence, and between excruciatingly boring lectures from Gaston, I will endeavor to think of more endearments for you. I can't go on calling you Mrs. Waverley."

She didn't want to express too much pleasure at the thought, but nodded in agreement. "And I will think of something for you besides Casanova or Don Juan."

"You compare me to such as them? I do not know whether to be insulted or flattered." He scowled comically, then sat on the settee and drew on his boots. "They have nothing on me, my darling." He winked at her. Within minutes, he'd tied his neckcloth and finished dressing. He held his arms open. "How am I? Suitable for French wine merchants?"

She giggled. "You're a proper dandy. Jonathan will tease you to no end when he hears about it."

He gave her what she thought was a mildly reproachful look, and she laughed again. "And how will you spend your day, Georgie? Besides pining for me."

"I will not pine for you, though you may think so if it appeases your vanity. I intend to play that marvelous pianoforte you've neglected all these years. I may also take a stroll around the gardens, and perhaps even go into town." She did not intend to do any of it but didn't want to admit how much she was going to miss him. The realization troubled her. Restlessness overcame her, and she got out of bed, hastily drawing on the shirt he'd discarded the night before.

He whistled through his teeth. "That looks much better on you than it does me." He paused at the door before leaving. "As a special request, Georgiana— please do not leave the premises alone. I will be on the other side of town and not able to rescue you. You seem to attract all manner of trouble wherever you go." He lingered at the door. "Including your recent attachment to me." Another wink and he was gone.

She stood silently in the middle of the room, hugging her arms around her. When she bowed her head to her chest, she could smell his scent—a mixture of woodsy spice and sweat—clinging to her skin. She summoned Marie to help her bathe and dress, suddenly unwilling to be alone. As she soaked in a fragrant tub, she realized he had not kissed her goodbye.

And was mildly disturbed he had not.

****

Twice he mistakenly categorized a shipment of barrels. Next, he spilled a glass of wine across a stack of freshly written invoices. As Jack patted the mess with a towel, Gaston snapped his fingers for assistance from an underling and took Jack's elbow.

"Perhaps a walk outdoors, Jack. The rest is just bothersome paperwork I can do later."

"I know, but my grandfather expects me to do some work around here besides walking around the vineyards and drinking his wine."

"We shall not tell him, then," Gaston said, winking.

Jack grabbed his hat as they walked through the door. He inhaled the clean-smelling, fragrant air of the *vignoble* and stood with his hands on his hips as he looked across the gently rolling hills of grape. A year ago, this was all he'd wanted. The thought someday he would be the master of his grandfather's enterprise appealed like nothing else. All his boxing and gambling was to secure him financially until that moment. He would make his own way in the world, and nothing would interfere with his plans.

Nothing had until he'd agreed to escort a certain golden-haired chatterbox of a girl across the sea. And there was the slight matter of his having married said girl without her brother's consent, approval, or blessing. He doubted he would receive any of them. Especially after last night.

He could still feel the light weight of her body against his, each dew-slicked breast beneath his hands. Her moans and sighs fluttering in his ear as they joined, again and again. Her slender fingers, shy and hesitant for only a moment before she touched him as boldly as he touched her…

Gaston's laughter broke into his thoughts. "She must be quite a goddess, for your mind to be elsewhere."

"Hmm? Oh, no." Jack waved off his comment with a breezy hand, nearly choking with embarrassment at what Georgiana's image aroused in him. "I was merely thinking about the new shipment."

"Of course, of course." Gaston shrugged. "You may go back to your chateau, Jack. I will handle all the details here. You may return at the end of the week when the shipment is ready. You can put your seal on it."

"Thank you." He shook Gaston's hand. "Perhaps I shall bring her by."

"Ah! La comtesse will enjoy the new vintage."

The rush of heat burned Jack's face before he could compose himself. "Not la comtesse, Gaston, but my new bride. Miss…" Again, he fumbled over his words. "Miss Georgiana Lockewood." He couldn't resist adding, "The enthusiastic grape stomper from the other day."

Gaston's eyebrows flickered upward for only a moment, but he gave a little bow. "Forgive me. I had not heard. My congratulations. Your grandfather will be very proud."

"I'm certain of it," he said drily. He could almost see the wheels turning in the Frenchman's head and wondered what Gaston would write in his report to his grandfather. He planned to write his own letter but did not want to seem as if he had only married to appease the old man. In truth, it was his original intent, but the friendly companionship she'd promised had gone by the wayside in the newly discovered fact they were so compatible in the bedchamber. He clicked his heels together in a mock salute and walked toward the gates where his carriage waited. He had to stop himself from mentally calculating how long it would take to reach the chateau.

He slowed his pace, sweat breaking out against his collar. What if Georgiana wasn't waiting for him in a state of heart-pounding desire, but dreading his return? She might be having doubts, especially after last night. She hadn't been ready, now he thought of it. He'd frightened her, and she'd kept silent to spare his feelings. What he'd assumed were gasps of delight had really been groans of horror and pain. The clawing fingernails hadn't rent his skin in passion, but as a defensive move. Her kisses had been panicked responses to his assaulting mouth, not desire.

Perhaps he wasn't returning to a love nest, but a bleak house where a regretful girl was going to tell him she'd made a terrible mistake and they must return to

England immediately. Perhaps there'd be time to spare her reputation, if he could invoke Aunt Adele's silence. No one need ever find out about their hastily arranged marriage, and Lady Richmond might be convinced it had all been some fantastical joke. Besides, until it was sanctioned by English law, it wasn't really a marriage, anyway. They needn't go through the embarrassment of annulment, but could simply pretend it had never happened.

He climbed into the carriage and fell back against the cushioned wall. Right now, Georgiana was tossing her belongings into her trunks, frantic and distraught. Perhaps she'd already contacted the shipyard and arranged passage home. Or worse, she'd summoned her brother, and Jonathan was on a fast sloop intent on rescuing his sister from yet another who'd betrayed his trust.

By the time the carriage stopped at the chateau, Jack was dry-mouthed and out of breath, as if he'd run the length of the *vignoble*. Quelling his urge to tear through the house to ensure she was still there, or worse, observe her despair, he walked briskly but calmly through the courtyard to the front door.

As Philippe greeted him, a strain of music from his father's old pianoforte reached him through one of the open windows. Without saying a word to Philippe, he abruptly turned to crunch and squash his way through the flowerbeds and hedgerows to the side of the house.

Pushing aside a clinging ivy stalk, he peered into the drawing room. Serene and lovely, Georgiana sat at the pianoforte with her profile to the window, her golden hair pinned up with one long, loose curl hanging over one shoulder. Her gossamer silk gown skimmed her body in a dusty shade of periwinkle, and the white lace at her collarbone and shoulders only emphasized the delicious creaminess of her skin. He watched in mesmerized fascination as her slender fingers danced across the keys. Now and then, she paused, seemingly staring into space, before jotting down a notation or two on the music sheet in front of her.

She was not packing her belongings and flying about the house in a mad frenzy in her haste to escape. Her eyes were not swollen and puffy from rivers of tears at the loss of her innocence at the hands of a rogue. On the contrary, a faint blush stained her cheek, and she seemed relaxed.

She resumed playing a light, dainty piece he'd often scorned as too romantic and soft, but now he wanted to sway in time to it, his chest expanding with a feeling he hadn't experienced but once in his life.

The last time he'd seen her play was at Christmastide, when she was a gawky girl of fifteen. The Lockewood charm lurked behind her eyes, but she was unaware of her potential emergence as a butterfly trapped in the cocoon of long, coltish legs and a flat chest. He'd sensed her hidden power from the moment he walked through the front door of Fairwood Hall. Normally, she would run to him when he arrived, and this day was no different. But she'd stammered and blushed as she greeted him, and he'd restrained from kissing her, sensing she had changed, or was changing.

She was no longer the child who hung from his arms while he swung her wildly into the air. A young woman had taken her place. He'd sensed her gaze upon him whenever they were in the same room together, and he'd avoided her, explaining away his guilty feelings with the thought he had no time to spend on an impressionable girl. Mitford had been present and lavished much attention on her, flattering her and dancing with her every night, while Jack made an excuse he'd hurt his ankle riding. He hadn't wanted to risk anyone sensing the real reason he could not bear to be in her company. Why he didn't want to feel her lithe body in his arms as they danced. Why he didn't want to smile down at her impossibly beautiful face, all semblance of fraternal feelings gone as if they'd never existed.

She'd asked him the next morning why he hadn't danced with her, as his limp had mysteriously vanished. He didn't have an answer then, but he knew it as clearly as if it were written in the white puffy clouds overhead.

And damned if he knew what he'd do about it.

He crept from the bushes and back onto the path, straightening his neckcloth when he reached the front door. Sliding his hand through his mussed hair, he walked into his house with the casual air of a lord, although he was certain Philippe hid a smile as soon as his back was turned. He did not care for his supper. Not just yet. Suddenly, he had an intensely fierce desire to listen to his wife play the pianoforte.

Chapter Twenty

"Have you been shut up in here all day with the ghosts of old composers?" Jack announced from the drawing room door. He crossed the room to where she sat and leafed through the music on top of the case.

"Some of us are not carousing all day and night." She played blindly, not caring what tune emerged from her fingers.

"Some of us are not doing that, either." He picked up a stray sheet and held it to her. "What is this? I didn't know Mozart illustrated his work."

She glanced carelessly at the paper and gasped in dismay. At the bottom of the sheet she'd drawn their entwined initials, complete with tiny hearts and an attempt at a rosebud. She snatched the paper from him and crumpled it up.

"I was bored."

"Hmm." He went to the cabinet against the wall and removed a violin case. "I'll wager you don't know this about me."

"Which of the myriad fascinating things about you do I not know?"

She bit her lip in feigned concentration, picking out the tune almost effortlessly. Normally, her excellent playing was a source of pride, but since coming France, she took no pleasure in it. All she'd done since his absence was daydream and draw silly pictures. She was grateful she'd burned the last one before he came home—a little sketch of his lips she'd spent an hour drawing.

He unlatched the case and removed a violin and bow. He held it up to her, almost reverently. "This."

"Was it left behind by one of your grandfather's guests? The one with the smelly gowns, perhaps?"

He frowned comically, but she sensed a touch of bashfulness. "It was my father's, if you must know. I did learn other accomplishments besides drinking and seducing daughters of groundskeepers while at university."

As she watched in semi-stunned, amused silence, he placed the violin under his chin, took a breath, and closed his eyes as he drew the bow across the strings. The familiar strains of Boccherini poured from the instrument, as effortless as her own playing had been.

She snapped out of her dazed confusion and accompanied him on the pianoforte. As he played, he walked slowly toward her, his gaze locked with hers. Their playing was harmonious. Neither of them missed a note, and he even nodded briefly before playing a little faster, but she kept up.

With a flicker of his gaze, he indicated she should move over on the bench, and she did, without losing her place on the keyboard. He sat on the edge, his back against her shoulder as they continued to play. His hair brushed her face a few times, and she inhaled deeply, her breath catching as her pulse sped up. Sensual memories of the night before threatened to disrupt her concentration, and she had to consciously will her hands to hit the right keys. When the piece ended, he rested the violin and bow on top of the pianoforte and faced her.

"I had no idea you could play! Why did you not say something before? We could have played duets when you and Jonathan were home at Christmas."

He grinned. "That is precisely why I did not say anything. Besides—I would much rather listen to you. You always played for me, Georgie."

She turned toward the keyboard again, fiddling with a loose D-sharp key. "How you will flatter yourself." Her heart pounded so hard she feared he could hear it. Perspiration broke out under her arms, and she shifted on the bench, wishing he would get up and move away from her so he wouldn't detect the effect he had on her.

He chuckled. "I am speaking the truth. The last time I was home with Lockewood, you were—what, fifteen? You found out my favorite piece and learned it for a week. At the Christmas party later, you played it and stared at me with those big blue eyes the entire time. I still remember you wore a white dress with a pink bow tied in the back."

She sniffed. "I was probably watching you drink all the wine punch and fawning over Lady Ellenton's daughter."

"Ah, yes. I'd forgotten about Clementine Ellenton. I wonder whatever happened to her?"

His hand rested on the keys. She dropped the lid, banging his fingers. He drew them back with a sharp yelp, and then looked into her eyes. She tried to return his grin but failed. Surely, he could see the helpless jealousy and naked emotion on her face. It was useless to pretend anymore. The feelings she'd had as a lovesick girl—unsated by even Edward's flattering attention—were unabated where Jack was concerned.

She started to rise from the bench, but he caught her wrist, turning her body as he placed her hand around his neck. Her fingers curled into his hair of their own accord. The desire she'd experienced the night before—the yearning ache as she'd clasped him in her arms—rushed back in a torrent. She pushed at his shoulders, but it was more for show.

"If you want to find out about Miss Ellenton, perhaps you should write her. I'm sure she would love to hear from you. Perhaps you could visit her and let her nibble on your neck with her rabbit teeth."

He shook his head, his face displaying his amusement. "I have no wish to see her. It's your teeth I want nibbling on me." He pulled her into his arms.

"You ignored me the last time you saw me. You refused to dance with me, leaving me to…to Edward's devious plans." The accusations tumbled from her and she thumped his chest, but he caught her hand in a strong grip. "You used to spend time with me, but that Christmas you avoided me as if I were leprous."

The teasing grin faded rapidly from his lips. His gaze burned into hers, and she forgot to struggle. After an interminable moment when she'd nearly given up on him saying anything, he spoke.

"I didn't want to see you all grown up. You were so…uncomplicated then."

Her throat dried up. "Am I so complicated now?"

"I don't know what you are." He shook his head, his eyes glowing with wonder. "I hardly know you like this, Georgiana." He drew a breath, his chest shuddering. "But I know I want you."

"You want me?" She wasn't sure she'd heard him

correctly. Her hands slid behind his neck, her fingers locking together before she could stop herself. Without replying, his mouth captured hers, pressing and urgent. His hands slid from her waist to her hair, pulling it free from her modest chignon and then streaming it through his fingers.

"Yes, I want you, you tempting little creature. All day, I've thought of you and nothing else. You've distracted me to the breaking point." His lips brushed across her cheek and toward her ear.

She arched against him with an overwhelming wave of desire that rose from his slightest touch. "I thought about you, Jack." She would never tell him how much, or that she'd spent half the morning in his chamber, sorting his neckcloths and tending to the slightest mending of his shirts and linen, even though she had never sewn a stitch in her life. He had an appalling number of shirts missing buttons and stained with what resembled rouge, and she'd thrown those away, her stomach roiling until she'd had to lie down.

He lifted his head to gaze into her eyes. His breathing had thickened, and his eyes had a smoky gleam to them.

"Did you?"

She nodded, her eyes drawn to his mouth again. How was it possible that unsophisticated, ill-mannered Jack Waverley should have the most kissable lips in all of England? And probably in France, for all his boasting. She drew in a shaky breath. Her arms trembled as he pulled her onto his lap.

"I know we had to share a bed last night to ensure our protection from your potentially overwrought brother, but I cannot help wondering if…"

He played with a long curl that hung over her shoulder. A delicious shiver ran through her.

"If what?" She could barely breathe. Didn't want to breathe, or move, or do anything if it meant leaving his arms.

"Well, I was thinking perhaps you might rather enjoy a second time." His gray eyes twinkled with their familiar wickedness. "You know—without all the anxiety and nerves of last night."

She held back her laughter and began unbuttoning his shirt. "I was not anxious or nervous at all. That was your conceit playing upon your mind. Again."

"Indeed." His mouth twisted as he held back his own smile. "In that case, perhaps we should have another go because I was so anxious and nervous last night."

"You…you were nervous?" She tried to laugh in a worldly way, but her voice only cracked.

"Of course. It's not every night a man is a bridegroom with such an irresistible bride in his bed, demanding all sorts of wanton experiences. I'm surprised I could even walk this morning."

The laughter died in her throat. There was nothing the slightest bit humorous in what he was doing to her now. He traced an invisible line down her throat, ending at the top of her cleavage. Her breathing grew unsteady, and she leaned toward him dizzily, searching for his mouth even while he looked like he would speak again. He clasped her to him, one hand seeking her breast, which she felt through the layers of her clothes.

"Shall we…shall we go upstairs?" she whispered, her lips fluttering against his.

He shook his head and lifted one of her legs over

his until they faced each other on the narrow bench. Her elbow banged the keyboard, and a dissonant chord broke the silence.

"Later. Right now, I just want to…feel…you…"

His words cut off by more kisses, until he stopped speaking altogether. Her lips parted to his tongue, and she tasted his mouth. His hand fumbled between them, and she realized he'd unfastened his breeches. A gasp of admonition rose to her lips, but she pushed the thought away, and released his neck to help him. He laughed into her mouth but continued kissing her deeply. The seconds flew by, and then he had taken her hand and gripped it around him.

A strange quivering rattled her bones, and the same helpless kind of yearning deep in her soul echoed through her again. She heard a faint sound of whimpering and realized it was coming from her. She hadn't known he'd raised her skirts until his broad, warm hand was beneath her thigh, caressing her and lifting her onto him at the same time.

"Ah, Georgie," he groaned, and she gave three short gasps the moment they joined.

"You—must—not—call—me—Georgie."

"I thought—" He gulped audibly. "—that rule pertained only in bed. And we are not in bed at the moment."

It was his turn to hit the keyboard, and soon, in their frantic struggle to remain on the bench, a discordant cacophony rattled her eardrums. Her feet were on the floor, so she was able to keep her balance while he held her hips, guiding and steadying her.

Any trace of modesty that might have lingered, unvanquished from last night, deserted her. She nearly rose to a standing position with the crushing force of her climax, his head between her breasts while she clasped him there, unable to move or speak. She froze in the timeless moment, and felt his release a second later.

Sinking down again, she remained in his arms, shaking with emotion and physical exhaustion. He ran his hands down her back and up again, finally framing her face and pulling away slightly so he could look at her.

"Georgie and Jack," he murmured, a tender smile on his lips. His flushed face glistened with perspiration. "Who would have thought it, eh?"

He was still hard and inside her. She tried to talk, but nothing would come out. Her body spasmed around him one last time, and her head fell back as she let out a soft cry of completion. He held her close, rocking her slowly back and forth on his lap until her quivering dissipated and her breathing calmed.

"Never...never, in a million years," she finally replied, closing her eyes and laying her head on his shoulder.

Chapter Twenty-One

A week of sharing sensuous nights with her new husband had come and gone. They could barely face each other across the dining table without his sweeping her from her chair the moment the servants left the first course. She'd stopped wearing a corset because it was easier to breathe without it, especially when she was so breathless whenever he was around.

Georgiana lay in bed, blinking in the morning sunlight streaming through the opened windows. The night had passed in a blur of almost surreal passion, shared and spent. They'd hardly spoken a word to each other after supper the night before and had stumbled upstairs and into her chamber, falling onto the bed and dissolving into oblivion. He'd long stopped asking if he could share her bed and just assumed he could.

Not that she had any objection to this new arrangement.

Swiping her tangled hair from her face, she surveyed the ruined remnants of their bed. Half the quilt had spilled onto the floor, and she vaguely remembered him tearing one of her silk stockings in his haste to disrobe her.

Sighing and stretching, she hugged his pillow, drawing his scent deep into her lungs as if she could store it there for future reference.

"Where are you?" she murmured into the pillow.

Her thighs twitched at the remembered pressure of his weight, and she groaned aloud, then laughed. Kicking off the sheets, she sprang from the bed and rang for Marie to help her dress. Perhaps Jack was in the garden or had gone for a quick drive and was on his way back home. He couldn't have gone too far. He hadn't even said goodbye, which was unlike him.

After selecting a mint green morning gown, she stood like a statue while Marie dressed her. He should be home by now. How long did it take to check the grounds or instruct a servant? Her ears strained for a sound, but no echo of banging doors downstairs or Jack's jovial voice ringing through the house ordering all sorts of delicacies for supper reached her.

Marie asked how she wanted her hair arranged, and she shrugged, a sudden wave of unease tickling her stomach and making her hands shake. What if something had happened to him? Or worse, he'd had second thoughts? Even now, he could be on his way to the harbor, intent on abandoning her. She'd be stranded in France with only herself to blame. Had she not learned from *the incident* never to trust her heart?

She shook her head, and Marie questioned the movement. Georgiana motioned at her hair. "It's fine. Whatever you think."

Marie continued dressing her hair while humming softly beneath her breath. "You look beautiful, madame," she said, settling a glossy curl to hang over Georgiana's shoulder. "Monsieur will not be able to take his eyes off you." She glanced archly at the disheveled bed. "Or his hands."

"Cheeky," Georgiana began, laughing despite the worried ache in her chest. Before she could say more,

Philippe rapped on the door and entered the room. A folded piece of paper lay on a tarnished silver tray. It was probably from Aunt Adele, asking when they were going to visit. She took the note and scanned the hastily scrawled words. She read it twice before realizing it was from Jack. She'd never seen his writing before.

The message was brief and impersonal. He could have been writing to a casual acquaintance. Crumpling the note in her hand, she forced a smile that belied her feelings. "Please inform *le chef* not to order anything special for supper. Monsieur will be dining out tonight."

Philippe bowed and exited with Marie, but not before Georgiana noticed their exchanged looks. She tossed his note into the fireplace. She should be relieved her amorous husband was absent for the night, attending a ball he'd claimed was a business meeting. She pressed her hand into her lower back and stretched, a slight groan emitting from her lips. Too much rolling around the bed with his heavy body pinning hers had left her weak. She really could not complain, as he was only doing what she had encouraged. He could remain a bachelor, though legally her husband. She'd given him free rein to bestow his favors on anyone he chose.

She frowned, her heartbeat quickening. She'd never thought he'd actually take her up on it.

Before this week, her experience was limited to the few, fumbling kisses with Edward, which she'd bestowed mostly due to her excitement at the dramatic enchantment of the whole elopement, and not for any real desire to kiss him. She'd actually found kissing repellant, with the rasp of a rough chin on her cheek, the reek of another person's breath in one's nose, and the foreign invasion of a probing tongue.

But that was with Edward. She'd almost dreaded kissing Jack on their wedding night, much as his breath was quite pleasing and the shape of his mouth intriguing enough she'd wondered what it would feel like pressed against hers. She'd worried kissing one man was the same as kissing another. What a relief to discover kissing Jack and kissing Edward were two entirely different things.

She leaned her face against her palms as she stared almost blindly into the mirror. What did Jack see when he looked at her? He was used to more experienced women. The sort who wouldn't blush when he came to them and who probably didn't lie motionless beneath him, afraid to make a sound in case she sounded wanton.

The hairstyle Marie had arranged suddenly appeared too girlish, innocent. Frowning, she tugged at a few hairpins and allowed a long curl to drape over her shoulder. Jack seemed to like twining his fingers in her hair, and she enjoyed being petted by him, almost as if she were a lazy cat sitting on his lap. She met her gaze in the mirror. Did she look more worldly now she'd shared his bed for a week? Did her newfound experience show in her face, in her eyes? If another man beheld her, would he know she was no longer a virgin, but a girl who'd crossed the invisible line into the world of men and women?

She pinched her cheeks to redden them but need not have bothered, since her thoughts alone were enough to make her blush. Was she enough for Jack, or had he quickly tired of her? He might be out now, seeking the company of women he was used to, before she'd practically coerced him into marriage. A worldly man like him would not be content to remain at home with a novice like her. He was probably relieved to be away on some semblance of business, no matter how contrived it sounded.

A ball, indeed.

Her cheeks reddened again. She frowned at herself in the mirror as if she could tell the girl looking back at her not to worry. The girl apparently didn't understand. The blush spread from her collarbone to her hairline. There was no other choice. She would have to enhance his pleasure while at home, so he wouldn't seek it elsewhere.

Marie's laughter reached her through the open window. Rising from her chair, Georgiana leaned on the casement to look for her. Standing over a flowerbed, Marie leaned close as Philippe stooped to kiss her.

Georgiana ducked back inside her chamber before they noticed her. She left her chamber to seek Marie, who, being French, was surely an expert on love and all things related to it.

Not that she intended to fall in love with Jack, but learning a few things to amuse him in bed would be good for a laugh.

So why did she feel not the least bit amused?

Philippe bowed quickly when she came upon them in the garden, but Georgiana hoped her smile was reassuring. He left on some pretext or other to do with locks and latches, and Marie regarded her suspiciously.

"Does madame require anything else?" Her gaze took in the mussed hairstyle over which she'd taken such pains.

"Oh, no. I mean, I came to ask you something." Her throat suddenly dried up. Perhaps she was overstepping. Marie was not much older and possibly lacked the same knowledge as she did. She might be offended Georgiana had assumed…

"Yes?" Suspicion changed to curiosity.

"I was wondering…" She chewed her lip, trying not to stammer. "I mean, if you happened to know…"

Marie took Georgiana's hand and led her to a marble bench surrounded by a rose bower. Swatting at a bee, Georgiana sat beside her.

"What is it, madame?" Something in her round brown eyes told Georgiana she already suspected what she was going to ask.

"A…a friend of mine, back in England, was recently wed. She asked me some questions before I left, but I did not know how to respond." Gulping, she pressed on. "Questions of an intimate nature."

"I see." Marie arranged the folds of her linen work dress around her. "She wanted to know how to please her husband."

Georgiana bit her lip to fight back a blush. "Yes. But I thought…" She indicated Marie with a weak hand. The rosy cheeks flushed, but the older girl merely nodded.

"I have been in love with Philippe Bertrand for two years. He refuses to marry me until he has enough money to buy a house. My father is crippled and depends upon me." Her slim shoulders rose in a shrug. "That does not mean I keep Philippe at a distance. We will be married someday."

As if she expected censure from Georgiana, she crossed her arms over her chest. Georgiana patted her hand.

"I hope you will be able to marry soon, Marie. I will speak to my…to Jack about it. Perhaps he may do something. There must be a little house around here you could have."

Marie's eyes lowered. "*Merci*, my dear madame. I would not ask for myself, but…."

"Say no more about it," Georgiana said, her heart swelling with generosity. She could afford to be generous when she was so happy. Correction, she thought, the nagging hint of fear and uncertainty creeping back into her mind. *Could* be so happy.

"About your friend's situation," Marie said, after clearing her throat and blinking back what Georgiana realized were tears, "she should be as open and loving to her husband as he is to her."

Georgiana leaned forward, as if being closer would make the words stick in her mind. "What do you mean?"

"She should not wait for him to come to her. She can be…" She hesitated, as if her next words were too daring to speak. "Seductive."

"Seductive?" The word slipped from her mouth, foreign and strange. "How so?"

Marie arranged the long curl over Georgiana's shoulder, flipping up the end. "She should greet him like Delilah, adorned in flowers." She plucked a rose from the bush beside her and tucked it into Georgiana's hair. "Your friend should abandon her nightrail…and wear something…" Her eyes skimmed Georgiana's body, as if determining what sort of clothing would best fit the situation. "Something alluring. Such as his shirt."

"I see." Hadn't Jack mentioned his shirt looked

better on her than it did on him? Her pulse raced with excitement. "What else?"

"Philippe likes the windows open, and candlelight. Not the darkness." Her blush returned, but she laughed when Georgiana smiled. "I think it is the same for most men. The fresh breeze on the skin and being able to see what lies waiting for them."

Georgiana wished she had something on which to write Marie's advice. Hopefully, she would retain most of it. "Seduction, then, is the key." It seemed almost too simple. Of course! Had not Jack seduced her right from the beginning? Starting out slow and then dragging her along with him into a pleasurable world she had never known?

"Yes." She brushed her fingertips across Georgiana's cheek. "But you have nothing to worry about, madame. Monsieur is madly in love with you."

"I…what? Who? I was speaking about my friend." She shook her head. "And you are mistaken, Marie. Jack is not in love with me. Nor I with him." The shock of what she'd just said tasted bitter. She'd made her marriage sound like a joke, a sacrilege. "I merely sought your advice, because…"

Marie stood, pulling Georgiana's hand as she went. "Come, madame."

"Where are we going?"

"To your chamber, to find a dress for the ball tonight. Philippe will escort you and help you find monsieur."

Her steps faltered. "He is at a business meeting. I should not disturb him."

"Yes, you should."

Georgiana regarded her with new admiration.

"What will I do when I find him?"

Marie squeezed her hand. "You'll know."

****

A few minutes later, Georgiana was knee deep in gowns and petticoats, tearing through her selection of evening gowns for the perfect dress. She held up a silk gown the color of fresh cream and tossed it back into her growing pile with a muttered oath. Virginal white was not what she wanted tonight. She would confront him at the ball and then…

And then she knew not what.

She sagged among the sea of silks and lace, drawing her knees up and pressing her head to them. How could he have predicted this exact thing would happen? What piece of her heart had betrayed her into falling in love? She neither wanted nor expected it to happen and had given her assurances—nay, protestations—to the contrary. She'd assured him he was free to seek out the company of whomever he wished. Now that he had, she wanted to take back everything she'd said.

Their arrangement was perfect for Jack. She'd said so herself. What man wouldn't take her up on her offer? In a five-minute ceremony, he'd gained freedom from his grandfather, the freedom to do as he pleased, and all while receiving the full blessing of a wife with a dowry of thirty thousand.

The clock chimed the hour. Nearly five, but she was not the least bit hungry. She wondered if she could ever eat again. Jack would not be home until very late, if not until breakfast. Perhaps he was postponing his return because he couldn't bear her company. Worse, he was too busy enjoying the company of someone else.

Gulping back her misery, she decided to forget Marie's plan and simply have a light supper and go to bed. As she pulled free of the pile around her, a dark blue gown caught her eye. She shuffled through the garments until she grasped it.

The bodice was far too low to be respectable.

The fabric so sheer one would appear exposed.

Anyone foolish enough to wear it in public risked censure.

It was the perfect choice.

She struggled to her feet and shook out the dress. A faint whiff of garlic and heady perfume clung to the fabric. It was one of the many gowns left to molder away in the wardrobe by its mystery owner.

"And he has absolutely no idea to whom this belonged," she muttered. She stood before the mirror and held the dress up to her bosom, turning from side to side to appreciate all angles of what she might look like wearing it. The sharp blue brought out the color of her eyes. The silk would float like gossamer against her skin.

Although not conceited, she was very aware of her effect on men. Of her effect on Jack. He could tease with silly nicknames and tug her hair all he wanted. She knew the look in his eyes was not that of a boy teasing a girl. Marie's words filled her with renewed hope. She would surprise him for a change, until he was begging for release. He would never desire to go back to any of his paramours.

She would make herself as irresistible to him as he was to her.

Damn him.

Chapter Twenty-Two

"Your luck is appalling, my dear fellow. If it does not spend itself quickly, I fear you will have to accept my wife as payment for my debts." Le Comte d'Oursy tugged at his lace cuffs before taking a pinch of snuff.

Jack leaned back into the stiff brocade chair and cracked his knuckles. "Your wife is too thin. I would prefer your eldest daughter, monsieur. Clarice, is it?"

"Careful, monsieur. My sense of humor is as fickle as your mistress's affections."

He snorted. "Which one?"

"I know you have many." A nod of his head indicated the door. "Here comes one now. I have not seen this one before, but she must be new, as she appears to be spitting daggers at you." He smirked. "She's quite fresh and lovely, Jack. I applaud your exquisite taste. When you tire of her, please send her my way." He gave an extravagant bow and tossed a roll of banknotes at Jack. "I bid you adieu, until the next time we meet." The comte pushed away from the table and straightened his coat.

"Perhaps you will win it all back from me, though I doubt it." Jack tucked his winnings inside his coat before he prepared to face Danielle. He ran his hands through his hair and half rose from his chair, a silent curse on his lips. He'd meant to write her, informing her of his newly wed status, but had been distracted of late to do so.

Calling Georgiana distracting was like calling the sea enormous.

Which was why he'd invented the excuse of dining out to spare her another night of passion. He'd sensed their growing closeness, despite both of their protestations they were merely friends. But it was hard to be friends with a woman who clung to his neck while she squirmed deliciously beneath him half the night. Impossible to remember they were friends, not lovers when her lips parted for him the moment they kissed. He was alarmed at how often he came up with a new excuse every night to escort her to her chamber. He'd checked the lamps, the chimney flue, and even a suspicious damp spot on the ceiling so many times she surely saw right through him.

"I would have called on you sooner, my dear…" His words broke in mid-sentence as he turned to face his scorned lover.

"Indeed? Then I have come at a most opportune time." Georgiana's clipped tone was contrary to her garish costume.

He almost laughed at his audible gulp, hiding his gleeful surprise she'd found him. God, he'd missed her, even if it had only been half a day since he'd seen her last. He'd wanted to put some distance between them but had spent most of the day lamenting her absence and counting the seconds until he was in his carriage heading home. He straightened to his full height, and she had to tip her head back to glare at him.

"What the devil are you doing here, Georgie? Has the house burnt to the ground, and you've come to fetch me?" He scanned her figure and did his best to look nonplussed. "Apparently, all your clothes are lost, and this is the best you can do."

"The house is fine." She spoke evenly, but it was through quivering lips. "You can come and go as you please, and I should have the same allowance."

"I never said you were chained to the hearth, Mrs. Waverley." He chewed his lip to restrain himself from laughing. The only thing worrying him more than Lockewood's sister at a soiree of the most questionable kind was meeting Danielle at the same locale. She knew d'Oursy well and was a familiar guest. A quick scan of the ballroom assured him of her absence. The strange feeling he was walking blindly into a trap pervaded the air around him, even though the woman doing the trapping was an innocent little thing he could master at his will.

At least, he used to.

"If you desire a night of excitement, I would prefer you take it elsewhere. The opera, perhaps. We'll leave for Paris on the morrow, and you may have your fill of adventure. But this is not the place." He took her elbow and led her from the salon, where she was already causing many a raised eyebrow.

She tugged her arm free. "I like it here, Jack. And if you recall our *agreement*"—she said the word as if it were a mockery—"we are both free to do as we please."

"That is so, my dear"—he regained control of her hand—"but you may do as you please elsewhere. Your brother would have my head on a platter were he to learn you came here. D'Oursy's parties are notorious."

"I thought you were here on business. Besides, I am a married woman now and need not answer to my brother. Either way, you can protect me."

"I was meeting an especially wealthy client here, and besides, the gambling is marvelous. I do not have the luxury of keeping an eye on you." He took her arm deliberately, ignoring her movements to free it. "Come, let me take you home. I've had enough of gambling and free-flowing spirits for one night. You should be tucked into bed with your nightcap tied securely beneath your chin, not gallivanting about with this dreadful society." He gave a short, mocking bow. "Present society excepted, of course."

"Are you going to tell me a story, or sing me a lullaby, dear Papa?" She batted her eyelashes at him followed by a snort of disgust. "I am my own woman, Jack. You did promise to show me around and have neglected your promise. I've been a prisoner in your house for days and days and am dying to have some fun."

"From all the howling emerging from our bed the past week, it seems to me you've had more than enough fun, miss."

"It's *madame* now, Jack. Do not confuse me with one of your mistresses."

The plump lower lip quivered. He muffled a curse. She had heard the big-mouthed comte. He'd wring the man's neck the next time they met.

If Georgiana didn't kill him first.

"Impossible I should confuse you with anyone, dearest. We can stay another hour and dance, if you like. But that will be the last I'll hear of it."

He was certain her arched eyebrows were equal in height to his. Was the girl actually mocking him?

"I thought you were above giving me orders, *Mr.*

Waverley."

"Only when it concerns your safety and welfare, *Mrs. Waverley*."

She planted her hands on her hips. A fire burned in her eyes, and her lips parted in a sneer. The gaudy lace on her bodice fluttered with each intake of breath, skimming across the top of her ivory bosom. He suddenly had the urge to scoop her over his shoulder and carry her to the nearest darkened corner where he could have his very satisfactory way with her. He shifted his stance, uncomfortably aware of his growing need. Damn, but the girl possessed some kind of wicked charm controlling his every breath. Perhaps he could cool both their tempers in the carriage ride home. The image of Georgiana perched upon his lap the duration of the ride back to the chateau was almost excruciating in its vividness.

"You didn't object to the original intent of our agreement, Jack, which was for us both to remain independent."

He wanted to protest, to say his feelings on the subject had inexplicably changed, but caught himself in time. A certain hesitancy in her look convinced him she did not believe a single word she'd spoken.

And that was good enough for him.

He closed the space between them. "Please, Georgiana, come home with me without a fuss. I can take you to finer places than this. You shall have your parties and dancing, and all you desire. I'll even allow you to dance with black-eyed Frenchmen some of the time."

He couldn't help glancing around the salon again for a sign of Danielle. A new crowd of guests had entered, and a woman's laugh was familiar. Danielle's usual tactic was to arrive very late just when he'd given up hope of seeing her. By then, his ardor was stirred to distraction. He scowled involuntarily. Danielle had a practiced, sure knowledge of seduction. How did this little chit know what strings to pull?

A stranger caught Jack's eye and smirked, making an obscene motion with his hand. Flushing, Jack steered her toward the door.

"I'm afraid I will stand on convention and the laws of this land as your husband and command you to accompany me the hell out of here."

"The commands of a husband do not pertain to me, Jack."

"Did you not vow to obey me? I recall hearing those words spout from your lips in a garden last week."

"I'd have said anything to get out of marrying Herbert Richmond, but now I think I may have made a mistake."

Before he could respond, a woman swept into view, her green eyes spitting fire, her red lips already muttering foul curses his way. He closed his eyes for a second, but the apparition was still very much in focus when he opened them again.

"Who is this woman, and why is she wearing my gown?" She poked her finger at Georgiana, who was mute with, Jack supposed, horrified surprise. He resigned himself to what would surely be an unpleasant end to his otherwise droll night.

"Calm down, Danielle," he soothed, but she turned on him.

"You do not come to me. You do not send word to

me. I left a letter for you with your man at the *vignoble*." Her skin stretched taut over her sharp cheekbones. "Why is this so, Jack?"

"Who are *you*?" Georgiana asked pointedly, her face flushed and her lips red as burgundy wine. Jack quickly stood between them when Danielle's gloved hand flew up to strike.

"I should ask the same of you, *mademoiselle*," she spat. "Why are you wearing my gown?"

"*Your* gown? I…it was…"

Georgiana looked at Jack for help, but he was too busy trying to think of a solution that would not end up with two enraged females fighting over him. Not that the idea didn't excite somewhat.

"You must have left it at the chateau last year." He took Danielle's arm and attempted to lead her into the more crowded ballroom. She was apt to do less damage there. "I shall have it returned to you promptly. This poor girl had nothing else to wear." He winced when a small fist met his kidney. He considered the possibility of sprouting wings and flying through an open window when one of his gambling associates appeared.

"You seem to be up to your neck in it, Waverley." The man's grin ate at Jack.

"Astute observation, Marcel. I would enjoy discussing how you beat me for a thousand francs tonight, but I am, as you pointed out, occupied. Perhaps you wouldn't mind taking one of these lovely ladies away from me."

Marcel eyed Georgiana with a smile anyone else would think was benign, but Jack was too aware of the man's reputation. He bowed to Danielle. "*Bon soir*, madame la comtesse." She returned his greeting with a flustered wave of her hand. He winked at Jack. "Who is this *très charmante* English rose? Your ward?"

"I normally appreciate your sense of humor, Marcel, but not this time."

Georgiana darted a look at Danielle, who glowered at both of them. "I am…his cousin."

Her response seemed to placate Danielle, who struggled to free herself from Jack's grip. She relaxed at Georgiana's introduction.

"You never told me you were bringing your cousin to France, Jack."

"It was a last minute decision. May I introduce Miss Waverley?" He nearly shook his head with the utter ridiculousness of the situation but decided to teach his little bride a lesson. Marcel seemed too pleased with the news and swept into a low bow.

"Enchanted, mademoiselle." He nodded at Jack. "Does your cousin dance this evening?"

"Oh, just try and stop her. She was complaining how she has been locked away in a dreadful tower with no entertainment." Before she could object, Jack took her hand and placed it in Marcel's. "Have fun, *cousin*." He didn't bother hiding his grin and pretended not to notice her narrowed eyes and tight lips. Danielle gave a little sigh and nestled her arms around his neck.

"You dance with me, Jack."

He extricated himself from her grip and took her hand. "I have a better idea." He led her into a darkened corridor off the ballroom, aware the entire time Georgiana was staring after him, her heart fully revealed on her face.

Guilt tore at him, but he shrugged off his discomfort. He would teach her a lesson she'd never forget. Even he knew marriage between friends was a bad idea.

Although he could suffer through the benefits if forced.

Chapter Twenty-Three

"Have some more wine, my dear." Marcel urged another glass on her. With her head and stomach reeling, Georgiana peered through the throng of dancers for a sign of Jack and Danielle, but they were gone. She smiled widely at Marcel and took the glass.

"I will at that." The liquid rolled down her throat. She'd lost count of how much she'd drunk in the past hour but didn't care anymore. Jack was clearly enjoying Danielle's attention somewhere else. Her eyes fogged with tears, but she forced them back with a throaty laugh that shocked Marcel almost as much as it startled her.

"Not so much. At least, not at once. We have all night." His words were spoken with more suggestion than she cared to notice. She set her glass down and opened her arms.

"Another dance, monsieur."

"I am happy to oblige you." Instead of taking her hand, he slipped his arm around her waist and led her through the throng of swirling couples. "This is a waltz. Do you know it?"

"I do now!" The ground spun beneath her slippers, and she soon forgot all about Danielle and Jack, but only for a moment.

Marcel's brown eyes remained locked with hers, and she lowered her gaze to stare at his lips, which were fuller and redder than Jack's. What would it be like to kiss those lips? She should do it for spite as well as in the pursuit of her education in the fine art of lovemaking. Jack could tease and mock her all he wanted. Marcel didn't know her as a little girl who'd pestered him. He wanted her as a woman, if the glances at her cleavage he didn't bother to hide were any indication.

She didn't object when Marcel took her for another turn around the floor and then smoothly exited the ballroom to the opened doors of a veranda, his arm securely around her waist.

****

Jack swatted away Danielle's hand as he took position behind a heavy curtain blocking his view from the ballroom.

"I can't see them." He pulled back a corner so he had full view of the dancers. He spied them immediately. Tall, handsome Marcel with his glossy black hair and Georgiana, petite and vulnerable in his arms as they waltzed away, Danielle's gauzy gown a blur as she swirled in his arms.

"I thought you wanted to be alone with me." She slipped her arms around his waist from behind and pressed her breasts against his back. "Do not worry about your cousin. She will be all right. Marcel never seduces on the first dance."

"This is their second." He turned around, trying to hide his annoyance. "Why do you not get us some wine? I will remain here."

She glared at him. "I am not your servant, Jack! Why are you so concerned about your cousin? You brought her to d'Oursy's, so you cannot be too concerned with her welfare."

"I didn't bring her. She followed me." The orchestra began another waltz, and he attempted to turn his attention back to the ballroom, but she tapped his shoulder, hard.

"I never knew you had a cousin, Jack."

Her steely eyes glared at him. He struggled to say something to placate her, but the time had come. He shrugged.

"All right. She is not my cousin. She is my wife."

Instead of spinning into a tirade of anger and emotion, Danielle merely laughed, as if he'd told her a simple joke.

"Your wife? Jack Waverley, a married man?" She shook her head patronizingly and patted his arm. "Oh, Jack, that is delightful. I would be jealous if you'd said she was your paramour. But I have little to fear from a *wife*."

He scowled. "I do not find it so amusing, Danielle. At this moment, another man is trying to seduce my wife, and he may very well succeed." He rubbed his jaw. "I have not been forthcoming with her, I'm afraid." He regarded her for a moment until she sobered. "Forgive me, Danielle. I intended to send you word, but…"

Her eyes flashed. "Please, do not tell me you are…Oh, merciful Father!" She laughed again, short and bitter. "Have you fallen in love?"

He scowled. "I would never sink so low as that, Danielle."

"Yet you avoid my advances. Ignore my letters."

"I've been…preoccupied." He mentally cursed his bad manners in not responding. One, simple message might have spared them all this trouble, and Georgiana would not, most likely, be contemplating an *affaire* with his longtime rival to spite him.

She snorted. "Yes, preoccupied! With your new bride who cannot take her eyes off you." She drew in a shaky breath. "I pity her, Jack."

"Pity her?" He laughed roughly. "I am so miserable a catch?"

"No. You will break her heart. You scorn the idea of love."

"Spoken by a married woman whose husband adores her, yet you are always chasing me."

They stared at each other in silence. Slowly, her frown disappeared until the barest, ironic smile remained on her lips. "I chase you because you cannot be caught. Goodbye, Jack. I'm sure you will send for me when you tire of this game."

He had no response. She spun away, the flounce of her hem swishing around her. He watched her, but only for a moment. When he turned back to the ballroom, Marcel and Georgiana were gone.

****

Marcel threaded her arm through his as they walked the spacious veranda. Large, sculpted planters overflowing with flowers bordered the edge, and she inhaled the scents of heliotrope and freesia.

"How long will you be in Bordeaux, mademoiselle?"

Recalling the way Jack had exited so blithely with his mistress, Georgiana squeezed Marcel's arm.

"Long enough."

"Ah." He abruptly stopped walking and faced her, his cheekbones casting shadows over his face in the moonlight. "I will have to make your remaining days here memorable. Your nights, as well."

His fingertip caressed with her cheek, and she nearly pulled away, but stiffened her resolve. "That would be nice."

The corners of his mouth lifted. "Nice? What a strange, beautiful thing you are. Fortunately, your cousin is not very good with a sword, or I would fear him in a duel."

"My…cousin?"

The black eyebrows lifted. "Jack. Forgive me, is he not your cousin?" The fingertip dropped from her face.

She shook her head, unable to bear the pretense any longer. "No, he is not."

Her vision blurred suddenly, and she stumbled away, looking for something to hold onto. Five glasses of wine—or was it six?—had affected her more than she'd thought. She reached behind for the wall and her hand was caught in a firm and familiar grip.

"Thank you for taking care of my wife," Jack said to Marcel. He peered down at her face. "You don't look too well, Pudding Face. Or should I say, Wine Breath?"

"Your wife?" Marcel grinned slowly, then bowed with a crisp gesture. "The pleasure was mine, Waverley."

Jack slipped his arm around her and led her toward the ballroom. He paused and looked back at Marcel, who seemed more amused than disappointed. "And you are mistaken, Marcel, as so many others have been. I'm more than competent with a sword."

Chapter Twenty-Four

"I can't believe how much wine I drank." Georgiana groaned and clutched her stomach as Jack helped her from the carriage.

"You possibly surpassed my limit, which is saying quite a lot." He paused when she stopped, leaned over and vomited the remains of her adventurous night all over the front lawn of his chateau.

"I'm so sorry." She wiped her mouth on the back of her glove. "If anyone saw my atrocious behavior, I will be ruined."

Jack stripped her gloves off her arms and balled them up, stuffing them into his coat. He shook his head.

"It's rather a scandalous society at the comte's parties. I doubt anyone will snub you. All that's transpired is a bottle and a half of wine you just deposited all over the lawn, and a waste of a perfectly good pair of boots." He clucked his tongue and hauled her upright. "You're very fortunate I found you before Marcel could have his way with you. When I came upon you on the veranda, you looked as if you were tempted to respond to his advances."

"Oh, dear," she moaned, but he shook his head in a friendly manner.

"Have no fear. I will not be meeting him at dawn in a deserted wood on the morrow. He would not have presumed to seduce you if he'd known you were my wife. He's more decent than I am in that regard."

His face shimmered in front of her. First, there were two Jacks and then there was one. He slipped his arm around her waist.

"Best to get you into bed, little drunkard, before you decorate the flower beds with the best Bordeaux has to offer. The next thing you know, dozens of drunken little bees and butterflies will be flying around."

She stumbled again, and this time, he swung her up into his arms and carried her into the house.

"I'm sorry, Jack." She squeezed her eyes shut but the world continued to spin. She wasn't aware they arrived at her chamber until he dropped her on the bed.

"Sorry for what?" He unfastened her dress and pulled it off. When he unlaced her stays, she took a refreshing deep breath. He lingered over her stockings, sliding his hands gently up and down her calves. "You've done no harm to me, little goose. Besides, now I'm in control of your thousands, I will order up ten new pairs of boots and send you the bill."

"I'm not talking about the boots. I said I was your cousin, because that woman…"

"What are you talking about?" He untied her garters and slipped off her stockings, kissing her toes in turn before drawing the coverlet over her. The quilt floated over her like a downy cloud. The room was still spinning, but Jack's presence relieved it somewhat.

"Danielle." The name hung in the air. "I saw the way she looked at you. She's in love with you." Her words came heavier now, slower. "You meant to be alone with her, and I ruined your evening."

He sank onto the bed beside her, and she closed her

eyes while he stroked the hair from her sticky forehead. "You did not ruin a thing, Georgie. I was not waiting for Danielle. I have not seen her since the last time I was in Bordeaux. Besides, it was utterly delightful to watch you flirt outrageously with Marcel. I believe you even made certain promises to d'Oursy's footman."

The dim edges of an encroaching dream filtered into her thoughts. "I wanted to make you jealous. I couldn't help myself." She lazily stroked the back of his hand and pulled it to her lips. "Forgive me, Jack."

"I do not forgive you," he said softly, curling his fingers around her hand. "I am jealous, little Pudding Face. Greener than you were out on the lawn. I can't stand the idea of any man looking at you or touching you…" He stretched out beside her on the bed. "And dancing is completely out of the question. From here on, I forbid you to dance with anyone but me, especially black-eyed Frenchmen. And dash it all if that offends anyone. If you ever dance with another man again, you will be duly chastised."

"How frightening! What will you do?"

"All I can say is it will involve much rolling about on the bed and seeking my own satisfaction while being completely oblivious to yours."

"You are a brute."

His caressing fingertips over her collarbone belied his words. "I will ensure you never recover from it."

"Then my wicked device worked."

"Yes, it did."

His heart beat reassuringly against her ear, and she drifted off to sleep, the low murmur of his voice singing to her or saying something; she couldn't tell which.

****

213

The wall pressed uncomfortably to the back of his head, but Jack ignored it. He didn't know how long he'd been sitting on the window ledge but guessed from the purple streaks in the sky that it was almost dawn. Across the room, Georgiana stirred in her sleep. He watched her hand search the bed, and when the object she desired was not found, she moved into the spot he'd vacated.

He should have written Danielle immediately upon realizing he no longer wanted to continue his passionate, though emotionally draining relationship with the volatile countess. Although he hadn't loved her and she'd made no similar protestation to him, it disturbed him he should have caused her any pain. The flash of jealousy in her eyes when she'd accused him of being in love with Georgiana could not bode well.

He swiped his hand across his face. His eyes burned as if he'd rubbed sand in them. Having a conscience was new and not entirely unwelcome. Danielle's mocking words still rang in his ears. He'd begun to wonder himself if it were possible he could ever give his heart away.

Georgiana was no courtesan or experienced paramour, but a remnant of his childhood and happier, easier times. It was obvious they were becoming closer than friends. Where once a kiss was forbidden, she now touched and kissed him with complete abandon. The physical intimacy was bound to have happened. He'd sensed something of his own insatiable passion within her that first night what now seemed ages ago, though only a week had passed since their spontaneous wedding. Even if she hadn't suggested losing her virginity to tighten their legal bond, he would have found a way to convince her to share his bed. This truth didn't bother him the way it should. The more time they spent together, the more voracious his need for her grew, affecting him the way no other woman ever had. She was intoxicating—an addiction.

But that was only part of his problem.

How would he explain himself to Lockewood, when they returned to England? Worse, what the devil would he do now, saddled with a wife?

"Jack?"

Georgiana's sleepy voice broke into his thoughts, and he nearly lost his hold on the ledge. Ghostlike, she hovered across the floor, her chemise floating about her like gossamer.

His lips parted to tell her to go back to bed, that he was only checking the security of the windows. No sound emerged. He waited for what seemed an eternity until she stood beside him, her fingers reaching out and touching the edges of his open collar.

Instead of making some excuse as to why they should spend some time apart, he held his arms open. She lay in front of him, curving her body into his. He drew his legs up around her, trapping her. The flowery scent of her hair and skin held a faint odor of musky sweat brought on from her earlier intoxication.

"What are you doing?" Her voice was soft and low, still heavy with sleep, though he felt the increase of her heartbeat with every passing second.

He stroked the damp tendrils of hair from her forehead, drawing it back over her shoulders so it hung in thick golden ropes over his hand. He pressed his cheek to the top of her head.

"Waiting for the sunrise."

"I'll wait with you, then." A moment later she murmured, "I am so glad you're not angry with me."

"Why should I be angry with you? What harm can a little goose like you do to me?"

She gulped. "I ought not to have followed you to the ball. It's none of my concern what your…activities are. I fear I embarrassed you."

Every man's eyes had been on her at the ball. He'd been struck at how powerfully the sense of protection and pride had grown in him. To think that Georgiana Lockewood, the celebrated beauty of the *ton* would even turn her sights on him was something he'd never imagined.

But it was not for his heart she'd chosen him. She needed to be tied to him for the very same reasons he needed her. Thirty thousand reasons, if truth be told.

"It takes much more than a flirtatious little poppet to embarrass me. In fact, your spitting and clawing only made me more desirable to certain females I wished to impress." It was a lie but would spare either of them from becoming too attached to the other, a thing he was dangerously close to becoming. Of course, holding her in his arms while both of them were barely dressed didn't help. And she had a disturbing habit of grinding her hip against his groin, already taut with anticipation and desire.

"Then you should be thanking me, instead of my apologizing to you."

"There is still the matter of my boots. And Marie and Philippe are going to raise hell when they find your mess in the morning."

She shuddered. "I have thoroughly humiliated myself, which shall be my punishment. Only, I do hope you won't tell Jonathan."

He tugged on her hair. "Yes, let me tell your esteemed brother how his little sister followed me to an orgiastic hell of a ball, where she proceeded to dance with a handsome seducer and imbibe massive quantities of the grape, while I, her supposed protector, was ensconced in a shady salon with a woman reported to be my lover." He stroked the back of her neck. "That should merit pistols at dawn, don't you think?"

She shook her head, very slightly, so he barely felt the motion. "Jonathan can have nothing more to say about my life. I'm a grown woman, a truth both of you need to accept."

"Your newly married status does not automatically grant you sensibilities, my dear."

She'd been stroking his arm during their exchange, and now pinched him. "And your superior age does not make you an authority on the subject, sir."

"Are you implying I'm not grown up, even at my superior age?"

"You can criticize my behavior tonight, yet you thought nothing of waltzing away into a private room with that…that…"

"As I recall, you granted your permission and approval for whatever activities I wish to pursue, without fear of retribution, retaliation, or, heaven forbid, tears." He'd wrapped a long strand of her hair around his fingers. He now began unwinding it. Her quickening breath fanned through his shirt.

"And you have not hesitated in taking advantage of your status."

He nearly laughed at her preposterous accusations. If she only knew how her antics with Marcel had tormented him.

"I am merely doing as my lady suggested many breakfasts ago, when you made me the most delightful offer of your thousands and the freedom to do as I liked. And I have not heard any protests from you. This arrangement of ours suits you as much as it does me."

"Yes, but…" She settled back into his chest again. "Never mind."

"You may tell me anything, Georgie."

"You will laugh at me. And say you told me so."

"I promise to remain as sober as a judge. I will laugh later, when you're asleep."

She pinched his arm again, harder. "Stop teasing, Jack! I am an adult, now. You forget I have had my share of experiences."

This time, he did not contain his laughter, though he did not intend his words to sound so sarcastic. "All borne out of my bed, so you cannot hold those over me."

"I was not talking about you."

Had she struck him across the face he would not have felt any less sting. Mitford's sly grin stamped itself in his mind. The thought of that dog pawing at her, kissing her, trying to seduce her… How far had he succeeded? He counted to three silently before he could respond. "Yes, you are a fully grown woman with her own mind." His heart began to pound in rhythm with hers, though his ardor dissipated. "But being all grown up does not mean you should throw yourself at every man who smiles at you."

She sat up with a jerk and faced him. A pink flush rose up her throat, and her eyes glinted. Her lips trembled as she caught her breath. "How dare you bring up Edward Mitford?"

He clenched his jaw hard. "For someone who swears she no longer loves the man, you do talk about him quite a bit. Besides, I was referring to your running off with Marcel tonight."

"I do not talk about him. Besides, it is not my fault he's here in France. As for Marcel, I only ran off with him because you wished to be alone with your...that woman. You couldn't wait for me to be out of your sight. You threw me at him."

"Then you should have stayed home, instead of chasing after me."

Shut up, shut up! His mind raced against his heart. He was treading in dark waters now and knew any more words would only hurt her and cause him further regret. He cursed himself for not leaving the chateau earlier when he'd had the chance. He could have been halfway to the *vignoble* by now and composing an apology to Danielle. Perhaps he should see more of her while in France. Was that not his original intent? To spend his nights in carefree passion, without reservation or restriction? Not to lock himself to one woman. Especially one whose eyes filled with tears and made him feel like the lowest snake in the world. With Danielle, there were no surprises. No expectations. No promises. Georgiana came with too many requirements. Too many working parts he hardly knew what to do with her.

"Chasing...after...you?" Her flush deepened. Her lips trembled. He ran his hands down her arms in an attempt to soothe her. She twitched away from him.

"Georgie...I didn't mean it."

She blinked rapidly in an attempt to quell the tears

already springing from her eyes. "I thought"—she hiccupped—"I thought you were different. Edward used me to get at my money. You were always so kind, so..." She stared into his eyes for a moment, then thumped his chest. "I should have known better! You tricked me into your bed on the guise of trying to help me. You're no different."

"I tricked you?" He wanted to shake her, but satisfied himself with holding her waist, as she squirmed to be free. "It was your decision we marry and also to consummate this spectacle of a marriage. If it were left to me, I would be living here alone, and you would be with Aunt Adele, where you belong."

"So this is my fault? None of this would have happened were it not for your lack of judgment before Lady Richmond!" Her jaw clenched. "You promised to help me, but all you've done is ruin my life!"

She broke his grip. With barely a conscious thought, he was off the ledge and behind her. He watched as if he stood apart from his body, reaching for and catching her chemise. She flailed in his arms, her swinging fist bruising his jaw. He trapped her hands and pulled her close, avoiding her raised knee and the soft battering of her bare feet against his shins. He swung her up into his arms after a brief struggle, avoiding her scratching nails but unable to shut out the strangled curses she cried out.

He dropped her unceremoniously on the bed, half expecting her to scoot away from him, but she reached for him, a new curse on her lips. He joined her a second later, pinning her with his weight while she thrashed, her teeth flashing white in the dim light from the rising dawn as she struggled to bite him.

Her lips were redder than he'd ever seen. Full and trembling, it was only natural to cover them with his mouth to stifle the choppy syllabic curses she spewed at him. Her teeth sank into his lip, but he fought the sharpness, ignored the tang of blood in his mouth. He released her hands to clutch her lithe figure, the cushioned softness of her breasts crushing his chest and sending him reeling with desire.

Blood from his torn mouth mixed with her tears, but he kissed her anyway, ignoring the salt and copper taste of her lips.

"I don't love Edward."

Each word was punctuated with a shuddering gasp. He was lost in time and space, his mind soaring through its own universe looking for a bearing. He found it in her, his child bride whom he'd loved from the start. It was why he'd avoided her at the Christmas party. It was why he'd offered to escort her to France. God knew it was why he'd dashed the remotest chance of her marrying Richmond or anyone else.

"I know that." The words squeezed out of him before he could stop them. "I know it. Oh, God, Georgiana..."

He bit back the words he'd never said to another human being in all his life. They remained stifled in his throat, buried deeply with the other feelings he could not dare drag to the surface. He could hold her for now and give whatever part of him she would take. It was the best he could do.

Hang it all. It was all he could do.

Chapter Twenty-Five

Finishing paperwork at the *vignoble* had kept Jack working far into the night, so it was well past midnight when he pushed away from the cluttered desk and rubbed his tired eyes. He'd been awake the night before, thoroughly making up with Georgiana until she'd finally fallen asleep in his arms. But he still had work to do at the *vignoble* and arrived late.

"I need a drink," he said.

Gaston took a wine bottle from a nearby shelf.

Jack shook his head. "Something stronger."

"I know a place. It's on your way home."

Jack grinned. "What are we waiting for?" He stood and stretched his back, grunting when it gave a satisfying crack. "I don't see any fault with the books, old friend. You've done a perfect job, as usual. Lord Waverley will be very pleased."

Gaston reached for their hats. "Why do you not call him your grandfather?"

They walked out the door. Jack took a deep breath of the warm, fresh air.

"Because this is business. Besides," he added, stepping into his waiting carriage, "I haven't called him anything but *sir* since I was a boy. Old habits, and all that."

"He always speaks highly of you." Gaston leaned back into the carriage.

Jack would have done the same but feared if he closed his eyes he would settle into a long deserved sleep. He had only himself to blame. Every night, he swore to himself he'd leave Georgiana alone, almost convincing himself she would be better off knowing him as little as possible. But every night, he was inevitably drawn to her, as the sea to the shore. She moved his pillows into her bed and he took it for granted they would share a bed. Amazing how the original intent of sealing their union for practical matters had evolved into something he could not live without.

He blinked. "What did you say? Oh, yes, I'm sure he speaks well of me. He doesn't have anyone else in the family he can trust to take care of his business. My cousin is a complete scoundrel on the fast road to ruin. We were running neck and neck for a moment there, but he has outlasted me."

"Thank the saints, your grandfather has you, then."

A moment later, they both laughed. "Where is this tavern you spoke of? I'm near sleep as we speak."

"Oh, it is not a tavern, Jack. It's a chateau. A very amenable marquise has the best parties. There is one tonight."

"Are we not a little late for a party?" The last he'd seen of his pocket watch, it was nearly two in the morning.

"The sun is not up for a few more hours. Besides, your work is almost done, and you will be a slave to your life in London soon enough. Your new bride will surely have you running around town, finding new ways to spend your money."

Jack snorted. "She has her own money and

certainly did not marry me for mine."

The chateau loomed in the distance, lit with hundreds of lamps illuminating the drive. Jack stifled a wisp of regret. A lively party was under way with no apparent end in sight. Laughter and music reached him inside the carriage, and he almost told Gaston to keep driving. He was loathe to spend more time from Georgiana than he cared to admit, even to himself. Perhaps this party was what he needed, to clear his head. Her enthusiasm in bed was probably a result of her newfound womanhood, and nothing especially to do with him. Once they returned to England, they would likely lead separate lives as planned, coming together for family occasions and the like.

The thought was positively dreary.

"I see a few friends." Gaston pointed toward a group in the courtyard. "Have a drink or two and make merry. Take the carriage home when you're ready, and I will find my own way from here."

Jack nodded. Georgiana was probably in bed by now. Lying on top of the coverlet because the night was so warm. Her chamber would be stifling, and she'd have thrown open the windows so the breeze wafted across her body as she lay in half sleep, waiting for him. He could picture her golden hair splayed across the ivory pillowcase. Feel her dewy skin, soft as rose petals, beneath his questing fingertips. Hear her murmured sighs and purrs as he stirred her desire to a feverish pitch.

He snapped out of his dream, almost annoyed with Gaston for not taking him home straightaway. A surge of impatience threatened to spill into his speech, but he remained civil.

"A few drinks then, but no gaming tables for me."

Gaston laughed heartily. "I never thought to see it, Jack. You are besotted."

It would be easier to deny it, but Gaston would not believe him. Hell, he thought ruefully. He hardly believed it himself.

He wandered through the salons and ballroom, recognizing a few faces. He nodded politely, avoiding conversation. One drink, he swore. One drink, and he would be on his way home, to finish the night with the one person he could not stand to be without.

Someone tapped his shoulder. Jack turned around, preparing for brief conversation. *God, let it not be Danielle.*

The stranger's eyes smoldered like coals against the backdrop of his red face. His rapid breathing ruffled his lace-trimmed cravat. Jack tried to place him, but was at a loss. He sized him up for a fight, subconsciously taking in the man's broad shoulders and clenched fists.

"May I help you?"

"*Monsieur*, you have insulted my wife. I demand satisfaction."

"I am sure you are mistaken."

Danielle emerged from behind a column, a smug smile on her rouged lips.

Jack sighed. The long night just grew longer.

****

"I'm not a baby, Georgie. You needn't coddle me." But he didn't push her hand away as she helped him into the copper tub filled with steaming water. "Send for a dusky servant girl to wait on me. I'll be myself in a while." He leaned back against a folded towel and closed his eyes. He opened them a second later when she poured a cup of cold water onto his head. "What was that for?"

"Forgive me," she said as sweetly as she could. "I'm not as able-bodied as a dusky servant girl."

He grinned, and she smiled hesitantly back, knowing he'd only spoken in jest, but her heart still writhed every time he mentioned other women.

"I suppose you'll do. I like my scalp massaged, if you please."

She settled behind the tub and poured a jug of warm bath water over his head. "No luxuries for you, Mr. Waverley. Fighting is a terrible habit. You need to give it up."

"Oh, the other fellow didn't come away so badly. Just a missing tooth, but it improved his appearance."

"And I suppose he deserved it?"

"I wish I could tell you how much." He closed his eyes with a heavy sigh and covered her hand, which rested on his shoulder.

She'd been shocked when he'd appeared in her chamber, his face bruised and puffy, his lip cut. He had not discussed his evening except to say he and Gaston had gone to visit friends before riding home, and he'd had an altercation with a drunken guest. She refrained from questioning him, even though she was dying to know what he'd been up to.

"Well," she said slowly, "it isn't proper for a gentleman to defend a questionable lady's honor."

"Why do you presume I was fighting over a woman? A questionable one, at that?"

"Were you?"

His jaw worked. "Yes."

She sniffed. "I'm not surprised. You possess a ferocious appetite when it comes to women." He irritated her further by laughing rather than apologizing. She lathered soap through his hair, tugging it more than cleaning warranted. "If you're getting into trouble here in France, I can only shudder to think what lies awaiting you in England." *And for me.*

"If it will ease your mind, we will be gone from here soon enough. My grandfather sent word to the *vignoble* my work here is done."

"Is everything all right?"

"I have no idea. I seldom see him upon my return from these visits. For some reason, he is asking to see me now." He splashed water on his face. "Damn Gaston and his loose tongue. He's probably written the old dragon about our marriage."

"Perhaps he's taken ill." She stroked the back of his hand, but he shook his head, dismissing the sentiment.

"Nothing would dare harm him. I don't think he's been sick a day in his life. Perhaps he's going to present me with another ultimatum, since he enjoys controlling my life so much." He entwined his fingers with hers. "So, my dear miss, I'm afraid your salacious rampage through my bedchamber must come to an end."

"How amusing you are." His teasing fell flat on her ears. She'd always known they'd return, but somehow, their peaceful days and exhausting nights had merged into one ecstatic blur she'd hoped would never end. Once back in England, she had no idea how their relationship would continue. Or if it would continue. There was so much unspoken between them, and every time she wanted to bring up the subject, a tiny voice in the back of her mind convinced her otherwise. The last thing he wanted was a clinging wife. Or, for that matter, any kind of wife at all.

"I've informed Philippe and Marie to start packing our things and closing the place. We can ride over to see Aunt Adele in the morning."

Her head was spinning. She pressed her fingers to her temples and gave herself a little shake. "I had word from her yesterday. She means to remain in France."

"That's probably for the best. Her sister is here, and now you are married, her chaperone duties are no longer required." He chewed his lip, appearing deep in thought, but she couldn't tell what he was thinking. He laughed suddenly. "Ferocious appetite! Good lord, Georgie! You say the most incredible things."

"You needn't act so surprised, Jack. Despite my secluded upbringing, I know what goes on between men and…and women like that Danielle." She chewed the inside of her cheek. Perhaps she ought not to have discussed the passionate woman who seemed more than willing to satisfy Jack.

"If you are right, and I do have such extravagant needs, what shall I do to quell them?"

"You need to stop fighting and seducing. The next time might cost you more than a bruised cheek." She couldn't help but stroke the purple bruise below his eye.

"And how am I to express my over-abundant ardor, Miss Pudding Face? Would you have a parson attend me daily, prattling on with dry, boring sermons until I'm bored into chastity?"

She was very happy to be perched on a stool behind his head so he would not witness the tormenting flames burning her face. "There are…advantages to our being married, you know."

"Advantages for whom? You would open your bedchamber to me every night, indulging every deviant whim and fantasy I might invent?"

She nearly drowned him with a fresh jug of water. Sputtering, he shook his head like a dog, splashing her with soapy water. As she muttered a suggestion to him while she dabbed at her wet nightrail with a towel, he turned in the tub to face her.

"If you recall last night and nearly every day since we married—" She drew herself up to her full height while trying to maintain her dignity. "—you would know I am not resistant to the idea of sharing your bed."

He was annoyingly masculine and exceedingly desirable, with the remnants of soapy water dripping down the firm column of his neck. A trail of tiny bubbles slid down the center of his chest and into the pool of water, just above his navel. Something hot and quivery seemed to strike her abdomen and moved lower down until she was tempted to grip the tub. His gray eyes mocked her, even though his tongue swept across his lower lip, as if preparing for a kiss.

"No, you are quite the opposite, Georgie. So much so, I fear your appetite is as—what was the word?— *ferocious* as mine." He grinned and held out his hand as if he were negotiating a contract. "I accept your suggested replacement for fighting and seduction. But we have only one point to settle."

"Which is?" She placed her hand in his, hesitating when he pulled her toward the edge of the tub.

"When does this new agreement begin? Tomorrow or…" He lifted her hand to his lips and brushed a light kiss across her fingertips. "Tonight?"

She longed to press her hand to her chest to quell her heart's rapid pounding but didn't want him to see how utterly disarmed she was. The low, burning ache had stirred so quickly at his touch she feared she would go mad if he didn't satisfy it.

Pretending nonchalance, she shrugged one shoulder. "Whenever you like. I wouldn't want you to suffer on my account."

"I do not intend to suffer another moment, then." Before she could stop him, he pulled her straight into his arms and over the edge of the tub. He quickly maneuvered her onto his lap, her back against his chest.

"What have you done? I'm soaked through!" She fought his hands to try to rise to her feet, but it was useless pushing against him. The linen quickly absorbed the bathwater until even her sleeves were wet. She squirmed on top of him until he wrapped his arms about her waist. His lips were against her ear, warm and ticklish.

"Keep moving like that all you wish. Or hold still. The first way is torturing me. The second will allow me to torture you."

"Torture? So violent, Jack…" She lost her train of thought then, because he'd released her to slide his hands beneath her nightrail and up across her ribcage to her breasts. Her head fell back against his shoulder, and she gripped his wrists. "Oh," was all she could manage.

"Who has the more voracious appetite, I wonder?" he mused, settling her firmly on his lap and wrapping his arms securely around her. "Perhaps we should be discussing how I may satisfy your decadent cravings, madam."

She brushed her mouth across his. "Perhaps we are the same, Jack."

"Then it is only fair you demand of me what I demand of you. We shall alternate nights."

"What do you mean?" She'd lost all thought of anything that made sense anymore.

"One night will be yours—you may do with me what you may. We can embroider little pillows, or I will accompany you on my violin while you eke sweet music from that ancient pianoforte." He raised his head to wink at her, a hard feat considering the acute concentrated look on his face. "Or you may summon me to your bed—or bath—and I will be yours to command. Conversely, on my nights"—his hands dropped below the water—"you will be at my mercy, my poor darling."

"Agreed. But I warn you, Jack. We shall not be sewing when it's my night."

Chapter Twenty-Six

Their last days in France were a blur of packing and saying goodbye to Aunt Adele. She'd given them a wonderful wedding surprise—the gift of her townhouse near Jonathan and Sophie's London home. Georgiana waited for Jack to comment about the house, but he'd kept silent, only thanking Adele for her thoughtfulness. She'd wanted to ask if he would live there with her, but the subject never arose during the coach ride to Calais.

He'd been uncharacteristically quiet during the ride, and she'd napped intermittently, putting his silence to the drama of arranging their rushed second wedding service at the British Embassy so they wouldn't miss the packet ship back to England.

"That's done it now, good and proper." The tension in his face eased as they reached the harbor. "No one can dispute the validity of two weddings. Not even your brother, should he decide to go the civilized route of forcing an annulment as opposed to the more obvious route."

She took his arm as they walked through the crowded dock to their ship. "What is the obvious route?"

His gaze focused on the sea beyond the outline of the ship. "To call me out." He left her side to speak to the dock master and returned a few minutes later. "We sail in a few hours. Are you ready to leave our dream behind and rejoin reality?"

She slipped her hand in his before he could present his arm. With their impending journey, it seemed their inevitable parting was upon them too soon. She wanted to make the rest of their time together as meaningful as possible.

"I shall miss Bordeaux." Unexpected tears filled her eyes, but she blinked to clear her vision. "I hope Marie and Philippe will be happy. She told me they hoped to marry one day."

Of all the things they needed to discuss, she had to bring up the servants. Perhaps she was so maudlin about her own marriage she wanted to find a cheerful outlook in the lives of others.

He glanced down as they walked up the gangplank. "I gave Philippe one of the cottages on the estate, and he is going to start working at the *vignoble*. I expect they'll marry by month's end."

"I never would have taken you for a romantic." She squeezed his hand, her spirits rising when he returned the gesture. A sailor showed them to their cabin, and she turned away to hide her blush when he glanced at her bare hand, not bothering to hide a smirk. Jack had neglected to give her a ring during either of their weddings. Strange how she'd never thought about it before.

"I'm sorry about the size of this cabin. The others were all taken, and we were lucky to secure this." Jack stooped to avoid knocking his head on one of the low-hanging beams. He pushed one of her small trunks with the toe of his boot, stowing it out of sight beneath the small bed. She would barely fit on the bunk, let alone both of them.

"It will be fine. We have a short voyage." She smiled uncertainly. He seemed distant, restless. Perhaps he couldn't wait to be rid of her. Jack Waverley was not accustomed to keeping company with the same woman for very long. She drew in a breath, and the dank cabin air assailed her nose instead.

Jack remained by the door. "We'll be under way soon. I'll leave you to freshen up. I'll be on deck." He closed the door behind him. The stairs leading to the deck above were outside the door and creaked as he ascended.

Did she need freshening? They'd only walked a short distance from the carriage to the dock. He wanted to be alone. Instead of saying so, he made an excuse to leave while appearing concerned for her wellbeing.

Releasing a shaky sigh, she knelt before one of her boxes and opened it. She would unpack a bit before joining him on deck as soon as enough time had passed so he wouldn't think her too attached to him.

She took her hairbrush and a few other items and laid them on a shelf over the bed. They would reach London early in the morning, so there was no need to unpack. Jack had also suggested they sleep in their clothes, so she didn't bother finding her nightrail.

She sat on the edge of the bed and sank into the sagging mattress. In a few more days, Jack would deposit her at Fairwood Hall before returning to his previous life. Perhaps he would visit on occasion, to keep up appearances. Many married couples kept similar arrangements, but never had she imagined it would happen to her. She'd always thought she would share her life to the fullest with a man she could love forever. Edward Mitford had seemed to be that man.

She gripped the shelf-like bunk, her knuckles whitening. She should be grateful to Edward. He'd taught her never to give her heart again so trustingly. Marrying Jack was the best thing she could have done. He was no Herbert Richmond, or any of the dandies she'd seen about town, selfish and degenerate. Jack was a trustworthy friend. A man who'd stood beside her family through all their trials. He never faltered, never gave in. His strength and courage were what she'd always depended on.

She could not have chosen a better husband if the Creator himself had molded him out of clay and left him on her doorstep.

What other man would gladly allow her to live as she pleased, without thrusting his own agenda upon her? Even Jonathan, as kind and considerate as he was, would eventually begin controlling Sophie and managing her life to the tiniest detail. It's what husbands did. She was fortunate to have a husband who didn't care about her domestication or her money. Who else could say the same?

The ship pitched forward. Fighting a wave of sudden seasickness, she resolved to go topside before nausea forced her to remain below. Memories of their crossing still lingered, and she fought a rise of bile in her throat before stumbling to her feet and out the door of the cramped cabin.

They'd left the warm, soft breezes of Calais far behind. Dark clouds rolled overhead and as far into the horizon as she could see. The waves, perhaps a foot or so high in the harbor, now slapped toward the bow. As the ship lurched forward again, she collided with a sailor.

"Steady, there, miss," he said, catching her arm.

She glanced up at his young, kind face, and smiled as best as she was able. "Thank you. Will the seas calm a bit, or are we fated to have a rocky crossing?"

"It won't be too bad, miss." His gaze dropped to her bosom. A blush warmed her face despite the cold sea spray on the wind. She sighed with relief when Jack made his way across the crowded deck to stand beside her.

"There you are, my dear." He took her hand and linked it through his arm. "Thank you for assisting my wife," he said pointedly, and the sailor tugged his forelock and moved on, his smile gone. Georgiana clung to his arm while they made their way to a low bench, somewhat protected by a bulkhead and some barrels on the other side. "Flirting with midshipmen, are we?"

His voice was teasing, but she noticed the firm set of his jaw. Could he be jealous?

"You know how we Lockewoods are," she teased, although her heart wasn't in it. "Always throwing ourselves at strangers."

"So now you're a Lockewood again? With two weddings, I thought you were as much a Waverley as I."

His words were teasing, but his eyes glittered the way they had when he found her with Marcel. It was almost comical to see Jack struggle with jealousy.

It couldn't be. He was merely protecting her from strangers, and, goodness knew she'd had enough problems with strange men lately. She tucked her hands around his arm, at first to soothe him, but then found she didn't want to lose their closeness. Too soon, he would be gone. She blinked against a sudden stinging in her eyes, unsure if it was tears or sea spray on the wind.

"I am as much a Waverley as you. Your grandfather should employ me, for all the wine I helped to make this summer."

"Stomping on a few grapes does not make you foreman at the *vignoble*." He tapped the tip of her nose. "Though you did look rather fetching in that peasant smock."

"Thank you." She hugged his arm impulsively, stopping a second later when she feared he might pull away. He moved closer.

"The weather should turn for the better. I was speaking with the pilot before you came up. I didn't want you to experience another dreadful crossing like the one we had from Portsmouth."

He'd gone ahead to gauge the crossing, not to leave her.

Relief flooded her. "I do hope so."

The sea breeze had disturbed his neckcloth, and she released his arm to straighten his knot, the back of her hand brushing across his jaw. "That's better."

"Gentleman Jack," he murmured, gazing down at her.

She didn't trust herself to look into his eyes. Her heart was full, and she feared all her fears and worries would pour out of her with his next kind word or look. She lingered over his lapels, smoothing the fabric, grateful for a pretense to touch him.

"You are a gentleman. Fighter or no."

"I rather enjoy what comes after the fighting. You've spoilt me with your ministrations, Georgie. I shall have to keep you close by when I resume my nebulous career."

Of course, he was teasing. She couldn't possibly accompany him to such a place. The very thought sent a shudder running down her spine. But something else inside her tingled, especially when she recalled bathing him in the tub and what followed after. His voice was low and soft, even with the noise on the ship and the snapping of the sails overhead. The masculine scent of his skin scent reached her nose, and her fingers tightened on his coat.

"I will always take care of your bruises, Jack." Her voice cracked, and she winced inwardly. She'd hoped to sound flirtatious and nonchalant, the way he always did, but she failed. "I will always..." *What are you doing?* It was too late. Surely, he could see every blind emotion, every hope and dream as clearly on her face as if it were stamped in ink upon her skin.

"You will always what?" He slipped his arm around her waist. Though they were a married couple, she didn't dare embrace him in public. A few sailors were watching, nudging each other and smirking, and she dropped her hands into her lap.

She forced the words from her lips. "I will always take care of you."

"I am very glad to hear it." The wicked grin returned. "I meant to ask when we boarded if your provisions for my fearsome appetite applies on ships, or just on land. Because, if you were to glance down, you would see your presence has stirred me, Mrs. Waverley."

A rush of heat flooded her face and burned through the rest of her. A small laugh bubbled out of her before she could stop it. "Even with the ship jostling us about and the prospect of that flea-infested bed, you can still ask?"

"If we were on the edge of Vesuvius and it was about to erupt, I would want you. If the world was about to end, and I had one chance to either save my soul or die a sinner in your arms, I would choose you." His teeth gleamed when he smiled. "You should know me by now."

He rubbed a circle around the small of her back. They hadn't shared a bed in the last few days due to his long hours at the *vignoble*, and she'd found him sleeping on a settee in his dressing room once or twice, having been too tired to climb into bed. She'd missed their closeness, the physical and emotional needs he met just by his nearness. Sleeping in his arms had quickly become a habit she was loathe to abandon.

He awaited an answer. His eyes, gray like the clouds overhead, glinted like metal. A delicious shiver crept into her belly, spreading downward until she wondered if she'd melt into the deck.

"My…provisions stand on land, sea, and the edges of volcanoes. But I do hope you choose your soul over me, should it ever come to that."

She held her breath, expecting a kiss and preparing to stop him before they created a spectacle for the interested sailors.

"Damn my soul. I'll take hell and Georgiana Waverley every time."

His Adam's apple bobbed as he gulped. She could almost feel the rush of heat emanating from him through his clothes. His hand behind her became restless. He slid it upward, finding a tiny patch of skin between the collar of her pelisse and her knotted hair.

She trembled at his touch and feared he would take her out there in the open, on that hard bench with the taste of salty sea air on their lips.

His mouth barely moved as he murmured, "Go down below. I'll follow you shortly."

Trying to hide her blush but flooded with relief at the knowledge he still wanted her, she rose casually from the bench and took her time as she made her way across the deck to the door that led to the stairs. The ship continued to rock, but the motions had lessened a bit, so she was able to walk quite easily to their cabin. Her heart pounding with excitement and an odd burst of shyness, she had barely removed her bonnet and hung it on a hook when the door opened and slammed shut.

She spun around, the greeting on her lips muffled by his mouth. He lifted her so quickly her toes scuffed the ground. Breaking away for just a moment to gasp a breath, she was nearly shocked at his expression. He looked almost fierce, his face flushed and his eyes bright. The ship rolled slightly to port, and Jack stumbled with her, falling onto the narrow bed.

"Are you hurt?" he asked anxiously, framing her face with his hands, while his heavy body pinned her to the bed. The mattress gave in spots and a knotty board pressed into her shoulder.

She only laughed in reply, and he gave her a quizzical look. "You are very exuberant, sir," she explained.

Chuckling, he hoisted himself to a sitting position and pulled her up with him. "I cannot restrain myself in your presence, madam." He tugged at her hairpins until her hair fell in waves over her shoulders and down her back. "Ah, Georgie," he murmured, lifting a lock and holding it to his face. "I pity poor sailors who must do without a woman's company for months. I think I would go mad if I were parted from you."

She wanted to explain he imposed their future distance, but somehow, all coherent words had abandoned her. He was with her now. She nearly choked on bated breath, waiting for him to start undressing one or both of them, but he remained as he was, her hair in his hand. As she was about to speak, he leaned forward, silencing anything she might say with a gentle, lingering kiss. She pressed her mouth to his, twining her arms around his neck and stroking her fingers through his hair, blown curly from the wind.

The ship rolled again and her belly rolled along with it. Gasping, she clutched her stomach and barely had time to scoot off his lap and vomit into a nearby bucket. He knelt beside her in an instant, one hand on her shoulder and the other holding her hair out of the mess.

"Sweetheart, are you ill? Is it seasickness?"

She groped for a small towel in her valise and mopped her mouth. Her legs trembled, but she rose with his assistance, leaning heavily on his arm until she sat on the bed.

"I haven't been ill, only it's just..." She didn't know what it was. The strangest feeling of sickness seemed to overcome her at the strangest moments. Once when she was in her bath. Another time when she was sitting at the pianoforte, daydreaming of him. She shrugged. "I'm fine now. It has passed." She forced a smile but he still frowned.

"We shall see a doctor as soon as we arrive at Fairwood Hall. I'll send word to your brother to have a doctor await us."

She squeezed his hand. He drew her close to his side, his arm protectively around her, almost too tight. "There's no need. It must be the fruit I ate this morning. The plums were a bit sour."

"Hmm." He took a bottle of water from the shelf next to the bed. "Drink a little of this. If you're feeling better, we can go up on deck again into the fresh air."

"I think I'll stay here." Despite the hard mattress and gray pillowcase, the bed offered some relief to the dizziness that often accompanied the feeling of a sore stomach.

He helped her lay down and she expected him to leave, but he sat beside her, stroking her hair from her damp forehead and alternately patting her hands.

"You're an old mother hen. You know that, don't you?"

His mouth twisted into a wry grin. "The only being I have ever nursed is you. Do you not remember the time you were down with fever, and your nursemaid couldn't keep you in bed?"

She closed her eyes, enjoying the sound of his voice. "She was a horrid old thing. She'd tell me ghost stories about the moors. Lost young women abandoned by their wicked lovers. I had nightmares for years."

"Is that why you stole into my chamber when you thought I was asleep?"

She cracked her eyelids open. "I thought you were asleep."

The bed creaked when he shifted his position. "I pretended otherwise so you wouldn't have to leave. I enjoyed the company, even if it was in the form of a little goose. I always wanted a brother or sister."

"And I was your little sister?" She couldn't help but make a face at him and he laughed, but the top curve of his ears reddened.

"No, thank heaven. I enjoyed running after you and playing with you, even when Lockewood urged me to accompany him. Perhaps I felt that you…"

His lips clamped shut. He shook his head and a lock of hair dropped before his eyes.

"What, Jack?"

"I felt that you needed me in some small way."

She held his hand to her cheek and pressed his fingers against her skin. "More than in a small way."

He leaned down slowly and she watched as if she were standing very far away as he came closer. She could make out the stubble on his jaw. The crease in his neckcloth. The silvery gray of his eyes, deep and filled with a meaning she could never fathom. She waited for a kiss, breathless with expectation.

His lips brushed across her forehead. "Rest now. I'll go back up and ask about the rest of the crossing. I don't want your sickness to return."

"Don't go. Not yet." She gripped his lapels and held him close, his chest hovering above hers. Her breath quickened with the realization he wanted her as much as she wanted him. "I do wish this were a proper bed."

"If it's a proper bed you want, I shall procure the biggest, softest bed in England." He kissed the end of her nose. "And we shall never come out of it."

She wrapped her arms around his neck and gave him a tight squeeze. "That sounds wonderful, Jack. But where will you put it? Your house or mine?"

His shoulders stiffened and he sat up. "We shall

have to procure two of them. One for each house."

"Will we..." She gulped, then pulled back a little so she could see his face. "Will we see each other once in a while?" She tried to keep her tone mildly interested, so he would not infer anything else from her question. "Or will your business keep you very much occupied?" She liked to pretend he was occupied with business rather than boxing and gambling and other shady things she hardly dared think about.

"I intend to see you quite often, Georgie. With the Season's balls and parties, you need someone to escort you and keep you out of trouble, do you not? And who else will be there to shield me from all variety of bewitching females luring me to my downfall?"

She'd forgotten about the other women. Incorrigible appetite, indeed. Still, she had him for now. He wasn't going anywhere for at least half a day. If she had her way, she'd ask the captain to circle England a hundred times before making port. It would take at least that many voyages to make her ill of his company.

Chapter Twenty-Seven

She'd never have thought she'd dread so much the sight of the English countryside, but by the time they were off the ship and away from the harbor, Georgiana was mired in depression. Jack seemed cheerful enough. He probably couldn't wait to resume his bachelor life and abandon her at Jonathan's home. She picked at her gloves so much he clasped his large hand over both of hers.

"Better now?"

She nodded, but wanted to scream. France was already a distant memory. Their long, sensuous nights were over. Here was reality. Two separate homes. Two separate lives.

Some of her pleasure returned as they reached the outskirts of Fairwood Hall's park. Familiar sights of trees and the moss-covered stone walls eased her anxiety a little. Jack nudged her knee.

"The old place hasn't changed at all."

"No." She didn't intend to be short, but a new worry loomed on the horizon. How would Jonathan react when he heard their shocking announcement? Would he threaten Jack? Berate her?

As if he could read her mind, Jack took her hand. "Lockewood always was a reasonable man," he said.

A slight tremor in his voice revealed his apprehension. She wondered if he spoke more to reassure himself than her. The inevitable could no longer be postponed. Within minutes, the carriage rolled to a stop in front of the house where a row of servants stood in neat lines. The footmen of Fairwood Hall unloaded the luggage as the front door opened wide. Jonathan and Sophie walked through it as one.

"Welcome home! How was the voyage? And Aunt Adele? Staying on with her sister, is she? Probably for the best. Wait until you see our little Sebastian."

Jonathan spoke so quickly Georgiana could not answer one question. She embraced him first and then Sophie, who had never looked more radiant.

"The voyage was to be expected," Jack replied. "Overcrowded and terrible food." He shook Jonathan's hand and kissed Sophie's cheek. "Congratulations on the birth of your son. We thought of nothing else while we were abroad."

Georgiana restrained herself from kicking his shin. She emulated his broad grin. "I cannot wait to see the baby." She linked her arm through Sophie's in order to move the group inside before the truth was revealed for all the servants to hear.

Jonathan seemed content to remain where he was. He clapped his hand on Jack's shoulder. "Thank you, again, Jack, for taking care of Georgiana and seeing to Aunt Adele. It is no less than what I expected and hoped."

"But you are grateful all the same I did not leave them stranded," Jack finished for him.

Jonathan laughed, but Georgiana noted his bashful grin. "As I said—you took as great care of her as I would. I am indebted to you."

"It was my pleasure." Jack scuffed the toe of his

boot on the ground.

"I hope the ladies did not distract you from your grandfather's business."

Jack's hands twisted behind his back. He suddenly appeared to be fifteen again, when he and Jonathan had been caught throwing apples at a passing carriage. Georgiana mentally urged him to remain silent, but he didn't look at her. His face flushed scarlet and he cleared his throat.

"They were no distraction. You may as well congratulate me, Lockewood. I found more than I bargained for in France."

"Let us go inside, shall we?" Georgiana said hastily, but her plea might have been spoken to the wind. Her brother remained planted in place, a carefully studied expression on his face as his gaze remained focused on Jack.

"Did you? Well, congratulations. I hesitate to ask for what I congratulate you. Knowing you, it could be any number of things."

"I assure you it is nothing sordid." He tugged at his neckcloth. "I am a married man now."

His words hung in the air. Georgiana pushed past her brother and tugged Sophie's arm. "Do show me the baby, dear sister! I can hardly wait…"

"Georgiana, please remain here a moment."

Jonathan gave her such a pleasant smile she was unsure what to do. She clung to Sophie for support. The moment she'd dreaded was upon her and she was helpless to prevent it from taking its inevitable course.

"That's wonderful news, Jack. Where is the new Mrs. Waverley? Did she accompany you back to England? We would all love to meet her."

His jaw steeled. Georgiana silently implored her sister-in-law with her eyes. Sophie's eyebrows rose slightly, and she patted Georgiana's hand.

"Jonathan, dearest, why not go inside and offer some refreshment to these two weary travelers?"

He and Jack remained passively staring at each other. To his credit, Jack stood with his shoulders thrown back and his chin high.

"As a matter of fact, she is right here." He held out his hand to Georgiana. Unsure of whom she feared more, she took it, avoiding her brother's gaze. "Lockewood, I do beg your blessing, and also wish to assure you of my…"

Jonathan turned on his heel and strode into the house without speaking. Georgiana let out a shuddering gasp as tears filled her eyes. Jack gripped her hand in his and gazed down at her.

"I forbid you to cry," he murmured.

"Perhaps we'd better go inside." Sophie linked her other hand through Jack's arm. "We will all have a nice lunch and discuss this in a civilized manner. Mr. Waverley, I also wish to thank you for taking such great care of Georgiana. Your presence in France was such a wonderful relief to Jonathan and myself."

Her cheerful banter continued as she led them into the house. As Georgiana crossed the threshold into her family home, a foreboding sense of doom enveloped her, and no amount of Sophie's chattering or the promise of seeing her new nephew could shake it.

****

"I never thought you to be as roguish as you'd have me believe, Waverley, but I admit I am stumped." Jonathan poured two glasses of brandy and handed one to Jack. "I do not know if I should call you out or slap you on the back."

"I'd prefer the slap, though I'm sure you'd prefer pistols at dawn." Jack drank his brandy in one gulp, and Jonathan followed suit, promptly refilling their glasses a moment later. "It is not what you think, old friend. I did not go to France with the intention of marrying anyone; least of all, your sister." He shook his head slightly. "That did not come out the way I intended. I only want to assure you my intentions are noble, such as they are." He swirled his brandy around the glass, scowling when he observed his trembling hand. "Believe me, marriage was the farthest thing from my mind."

"Yet you married her." Lockewood's voice lowered, and Jack recognized his friend's temper lurking just beyond the shadows of his amiable personality. "I might ask if there is a particular reason why you did, when you knew my plans for her." His bitter gaze met Jack's. "I received a letter from Lady Richmond, censuring me—most politely, of course— for not informing her Georgiana was betrothed to another man. She said she'd seen Georgiana abroad. I thought the old thing had lost her faculties, and we'd have a laugh when you returned. Apparently, the laugh is on me."

"This was in no way intended as a joke; either on you or the Richmonds."

"I suppose there is a good reason why you did it, although I can't imagine what it is."

Jack sipped his drink. The warm, buttery liquid burned a comforting trail down his throat. "Beyond the fact I love her, you mean?"

"Do you?"

"Of course." He placed his glass on a table with a louder than necessary clink. "Why else would I marry her?"

"This, from a man who, not three months ago, scorned the very concept of marriage? Sneered at love and swore he would never attach himself to one woman? But you need not worry about love, am I correct? Not when there are thirty thousand reasons why you'd risk the parson's noose."

Jack clenched the arms of his chair until the wood creaked beneath his fingers. "If you were not my dearest friend and a recent father, I would knock all the teeth out of your head."

Lockewood didn't blink. "You told me of your grandfather's directive. You had to be married by this time next year or your stipend would end. We even laughed about the wealthy little chit you'd have to convince to marry you."

"I said that then. I did not intend for that chit"—he bit off his words—"for my *wife* to be Georgiana."

"But she is wealthy."

"As am I." He ran his hand through his hair, fighting to keep his own temper. "You needn't worry about her security, Lockewood. She has her own money, and I have mine. I will draw up papers—hell, you may draw them up, and I will sign whatever you wish. You may control it all. I do not want her money. You need not give me her dowry. She is free to do as she pleases."

"As are you, I suppose." Jonathan chewed his lip. "Tell me, what kind of arrangement did you make with my sister that she would be sole retainer of her dowry?

It hardly seems likely a man forced to gamble and fight for money would merely snap his fingers at a fortune, because his heart has been so completely stolen away. Not that my sister isn't a beauty."

"Lockewood…."

Jonathan laughed bitterly. "Perhaps it is those fragrant summer nights in France I should blame. What did you do, Jack? Take her for long carriage rides out of Aunt Adele's sight? Show her around the *vignoble* and ply her with wine and God knows what else?"

His hand shook, and he set his glass on the table. They were both on their feet now. Jack's shoulders tensed as he waited to see if Lockewood would go for the heavy bust on the mantel first or if he should.

"I resent your accusations, Lockewood. I did not seduce her." He forced back his rising anger. "I love Georgiana, and she loves me. It has always been there between us."

"Really?" The dark eyebrows drew up in mock surprise. "It was there when she was ten, Jack? Twelve? Or fifteen, when you last took the time to visit with us? Was the attraction always there, even when you were fornicating and fighting your way through all sorts of bad company?"

He struggled to speak, to come up with any kind of reasonable reply. But he had none, as Lockewood well knew. Damn the man for knowing him better than anyone.

"I love her now, and that should be enough. In a few years, my grandfather will die, and all his fortune will fall to me. A grander fortune than even you possess. Despite my ways, there is no scandal or fudge on my name. Georgiana has married an honorable man, which is all you claim you wanted for her. Why should the name of Richmond be a better one for her than Waverley?"

Lockewood stared at him for an interminable moment before finally nodding. It was the briefest of nods, but Jack accepted it gladly.

"Very well. I will talk to her. If all is as you say, then you have my blessing."

"And if not, will you insist upon a divorce?"

"I wouldn't presume to scandalize both our families. An annulment would be…" His face blanched. "She is no longer…" He shook his head. "Of course, she would not be. Not if you had anything to do with it."

"Because I must have seduced her, you mean?" Jack's fists clenched automatically, but he quelled the urge to fight.

"You must admit your talent for persuasion is legendary, Jack. How often have your conquests been the subject of our conversation?"

"That was in my shameful past. Besides, if I had seduced her, why would I go through the trouble of marrying her? We had a proper wedding, and I will swear an oath there was no physical intimacy before the vows."

"Implying there was intimacy after the ceremony, I'll wager," Jonathan sputtered. "Speaking of the wedding, what kind of wedding was it, Jack?" His lips were drawn tight, and Jack watched with half an interest at a vein throbbing in his friend's right temple. "Did you happen across a vicar wandering the French countryside? Was Aunt Adele present? A lady who, by the by, has much to answer for. Now I know why she stayed on in France."

"We did not have a vicar." He snorted. "It is quite difficult to find the Church of England in France, as you well know. Rest assured, it was a marriage sanctified by God, and that alone matters. We had a civil wedding at the embassy in Calais. Aunt Adele had nothing to do with any of it. Indeed, she was as…" He almost said *shocked* but didn't want to use too strong a word. "She was as surprised as you but gave her blessing wholeheartedly."

"Because no woman has ever been able to resist doing exactly as you please."

"I wish I had these powers you claim for me." He was tempted to pour another drink, but a cool head was the better option.

"But…but Jack." Lockewood paced the room, shaking his head. "Why you? I mean, I know Georgiana is fond of you, but…why did she choose you, of all people?"

"I will ignore the obvious inference to my bad character. You go too far, my friend. I love her. I did not marry her for her money, so what objection can you possibly have? We have known each other all our lives, and I have cared for her since she was little. I'm the best husband she could have. Better, I dare say, than those fops and fools you'd have had her marry. We saw Herbert Richmond at a fête. If you had seen how he looked at her…" The hot flush spread upward to his temples. "I could not in all good conscience allow a match. You'd have thrashed him on the spot, had you seen him. You'll thank me one day."

"But you are Jack Waverley!" Lockewood thumped his hand on the table so hard the china ornaments on it wobbled. "I know how you treat women. I know of your expensive gambling debts, your nights in the gaming hells and those low boxing establishments." He sank into a chair, the very image of exhaustion. "Richmond is a fool, but he stays away from scandal."

"You should know me better than that, Lockewood," Jack said quietly. "I have never had any designs on your sister. Do you not remember how angry I was when you did not bring me along to Gretna Green so I could kill that whoreson, Mitford?"

Lockewood's face contorted. "Yes, I remember. He was another whom I'd trusted as a brother. Another I'd grown up with—and shared my home and family. Another who professed to love my sister more than the world."

"I am not Mitford." He gritted his teeth and nearly spat as he said the words. "Do not compare me in the same breath as that dog."

Lockewood's shoulders sagged. For a moment, Jack feared he would collapse, but then he raised his anguished face. "I love you as a brother, Jack. I needn't assure you my intentions for Georgiana have been in the sole realm of providing for her best interests."

"You love her so well." Jack walked to the window and flicked aside the curtain, though he couldn't focus on the serene view of the park. "You were ready to marry her off to the first ass with more than ten thousand a year, so you wouldn't risk a worthless lout marrying her for her money. My god, man!" He shook his head. "Is her fortune alone the reason anyone would want her? Have you never looked at her? She is beautiful and kind, talented and amusing. She's the kind of wife any man would count himself fortunate to have. The kind of wife I do not deserve, nor does any man."

He nearly choked on his words. He shook his head again, but this time it was to clear it of confusing thoughts. He almost convinced himself their marriage was based on mutual love and affection and had nothing to do with alternative motives.

Lockewood's sigh brought him back to the present. "If you swear you love her and will honor her, then…"

"You will see for yourself our affection for each other. That should set your mind at ease."

"I do hope so." He rubbed his jaw and stifled a yawn. "Forgive me, Jack. I am not myself of late. My ill temper is a result of being awakened throughout the night since the baby was born." He rose from his chair and held out his hand. "I have never lost faith in you, Jack. I know there's a heart beating behind that monstrously thick wall you've developed over the years. I'm glad Georgiana was able to knock it down."

He didn't know what to say. They shook hands, and Lockewood clapped him on the shoulder.

"Have you dined recently? We can find the ladies and order tea."

Accepting an uneasy truce, Jack followed Lockewood out of the study and into a sunny room filled with toys no infant could have any interest in whatsoever. Georgiana stood by a table, and he realized she'd been pacing as he had been. As it always happened when coming upon her, his heart skipped and his breeches grew uncomfortably tight.

"Welcome home, Georgiana. Or should I say, Mrs. Waverley?" Jonathan embraced Georgiana, and Jack noted the relief in her eyes.

"Will my husband live another day?" she inquired, and they all laughed, though Jack noted a slight hesitation on his friend's part.

"I have been vehemently assured of Jack's love and devotion to you. While I will not hide my disappointment at being left out of the arrangement, I am truly happy for you both. Whereas Jack will have proven us all wrong and show that love truly conquers all, he will also have you to control him, much as you always have done."

Georgiana glanced at Jack, a blush staining her cheeks. He tried to give her a reassuring smile, but something in her eyes made him pause. Was it a hopeful glance? A suspicious one? Why could he interpret the expression of every other woman in the world except for hers?

Sophie tilted her arms to display Lockewood's son. "Come and meet your nephew, Mr. Waverley," she said.

Relieved the baby's presence eased any remaining tension, he jiggled the baby's tiny foot. "I don't see what all the fuss is about, Lockewood. He looks a bit like a tadpole."

Chapter Twenty-Eight

At supper, Jack paid more attention to her than usual, taking a sip from her glass and forcing her to taste a spoonful of his soup. Georgiana poked his thigh and shot him a look, but he ignored it, laughing heartily at a mildly humorous thing she'd said. She glanced quickly at her brother and sister-in-law, but they hadn't noticed anything amiss.

"So, Georgiana," Jonathan said pointedly. "You haven't said anything about your wedding. Were there any guests?"

She set down her fork. "A few. Aunt Adele and Lady Priscilla attended, of course. Other than that, it was a very quiet affair."

"Hmm. Pity. Did Jack give you a present? I noticed you're not wearing a ring."

She almost gasped aloud. She'd meant to tell Jack about a ring after the sailor on the ship had given her that disgusting look.

"I have my mother's ruby I was going to have reset." Jack spoke so smoothly she almost applauded his quick thinking. "My grandfather has my mother's jewels. Have no fear," he added wryly, "Georgiana will be as adorned as your lovely Sophie." He raised his glass with a friendly nod at Sophie, who smiled in reply.

"Did you have a honeymoon?" Sophie asked.

"Paris can be so romantic. I should think you two had a lovely time. Riding through tranquil scenery, picnics on the Left Bank, strolling through the Tuilleries."

"We had a fine honeymoon." Georgiana sipped her wine, trying to forget the image of Jack's bloody knuckles after a night out, or the mess she'd left in the garden the night she'd followed him to the ball. "We didn't spend very much time outdoors, however." She hadn't meant to make it sound sordid, but Sophie coughed into her napkin and her brother's face flushed.

"What she means," Jack said hastily, "is we were occupied at home. The chateau had a marvelous pianoforte, did it not, Georgiana?" His question was followed by the slightest wink only she detected.

She ground her heel into his toe as her cheeks burned. "So it did. We spent many long hours playing." She steadied her nerves and smiled brightly. "Jonathan, did you know Jack is an accomplished violinist?"

"I am not surprised. I'm discovering something new about Jack every minute."

Sophie indicated Jack's full plate. "Is the food to your liking, Mr. Waverley?"

He dabbed his lips with his napkin. "It is superb, Mrs. Lockewood. I have lost some of my appetite since our return." He quirked his eyebrow at Jonathan. "But I am certain it will return to me in time for dessert." He tapped Georgiana's foot under the table.

She took a bite before anyone noticed her blush. "The baby is beautiful, Jonathan." She smiled at Sophie; too artificially, she feared. She was desperate to ease the tension between the two men she cared for most in the world. "Is he well-tempered?"

This was the distraction everyone needed. It was

endearing how enthusiastic the new parents were, and she wondered how she and Jack would fare as parents, should the day ever arrive. The thought of Jack dandling their child on his knee was so intriguing she nearly sighed aloud.

"Sebastian does love music," Jonathan said, his face brightening. "I'm going to bring in a master when he's older, just like you had, Georgiana." He grinned suddenly. "Perhaps Jack and you can entertain us later. If you're not too tired from your journey."

Wanting nothing more than to placate her brother, Georgiana smiled encouragingly at Jack, whose eyes had narrowed. "We would love to play. Would we not, Jack?"

He shrugged, finally giving in to a brief laugh. "If it pleases my wife, I will pick up the bow."

Georgiana nearly trembled with relief. Supper ended on a lighter note, and they retired into the drawing room, where Georgiana gasped with delight at the new pianoforte commanding the room. Before she could comment on it, Jonathan touched her elbow.

"It was meant to be a present upon your return." He laughed sheepishly. "I thought it would soften the blow when I urged you to consider marrying Herbert Richmond."

"Bribing her with shiny new instruments? How fortunate for your purse Georgiana can be placated so easily," Jack said wryly.

"It's beautiful, Jonathan. Thank you." She kissed her brother's cheek, and he squeezed her close for a moment.

Jack picked up the violin resting on top of the pianoforte. The maple veneer gleamed in the lamplight.

"This is a lovely instrument. I remember your father playing it."

Jonathan's expression softened with the memory, and Georgiana resolved later to kiss her husband out of gratitude.

"That was the Christmas after Mother died. He hadn't played in so long, but Georgiana wanted music."

"And Georgiana always gets what Georgiana wants." Jack's gaze fused with hers. His desire was too blatant. Surely, her brother would say something, but when she looked at Jonathan, he was helping Sophie arrange some pillows on a settee. The nurse brought in Sebastian, and Sophie and Jonathan fussed over him, murmuring and laughing with each other in a private little world so intimate Georgiana averted her gaze.

In the few times she'd ever dreamed about her future husband, she'd imagined a relationship like the one her brother and his wife enjoyed. How happy Sophie must be, knowing Jonathan's heart was hers. She didn't have to pretend to him or the rest of the world.

To disband her sudden melancholia, she sat at the magnificent pianoforte, taking a few moments to explore the scrollwork and designs. "This is truly splendid, brother. I hope my playing does it justice."

"I thought you were playing every day abroad. Was that not why you begged me to let you go?"

Before she could reply, Jack stood beside her, his presence solid comfort. "Do you honestly believe once we were married, we spent our days practicing duets?" This brought a raucous laugh from Jonathan before he collected himself. Sophie laughed behind her hand while Georgiana frowned at Jack, who merely wiggled his eyebrows at her.

He drew the bow across the strings and played a few practice chords. "Give me an A," he murmured to her, then nodded at Jonathan. "In truth, we didn't have much time together. I was on my grandfather's business, as you recall, and was occupied most of the time."

"Most of the time," Jonathan muttered. His mouth twisted in irony. "Speaking of that fine old gentleman, does he know of your nuptials, or do you intend on surprising him as well?"

Jack tuned the instrument before answering. "I am certain he will be as pleasantly surprised as you." He turned to Georgiana, and her heart jumped into her throat by the warmth in his eyes. "Play Boccherini. We will prove to your brother how compatible we are, even if it is only through music."

They began playing in harmony, each picking up the other's theme in flawless perfection. Jonathan wore a slight smile indicating he was contented and kissed his wife's hand.

Relieved, Georgiana glanced at Jack. Her heart thumped against her ribs. He played intently, but his gaze locked on her. They both knew the piece by heart, but it didn't matter anymore. She would have played anything so long as they could play together. Her skill matched his, and even when he added an extra flourish, she kept up, arching her eyebrow at his acknowledging grin. She stared into his eyes until the sweet, almost reverent conclusion.

Neither of them moved. Sophie clapped her hands. "That was beautiful. There is magic between you." She handed the baby to Jonathan and stood. "I believe I shall go to bed now he is quiet." She smiled serenely at her husband, who held the baby in one arm and slipped his other around her waist.

"A wise idea. Georgiana, I thought to put you in your old chamber, and Jack in his. But…" He shook his head, his grin widening. "Do as you please. I see now you truly are in love. I was a fool to doubt it. You are welcome, Jack. May our home also be yours, just as it ever was."

Jack carefully laid the violin back in its case. "I appreciate that, Lockewood."

Georgiana blinked back tears. If only it were truly so. She closed the pianoforte case and rose from the bench. "It has been a long day." She went to the little family and kissed her nephew's soft cheek. "Good night, Sophie. Dear brother." She kissed them both and turned to wait for Jack.

He offered his arm, and they left the drawing room. She was too nervous to glance behind, in case her brother was watching. They walked in silence upstairs and down the long gallery lined with austere family portraits. At the end of the hall was a new portrait of her baby nephew. His golden curls resembled Jack's. She imagined a portrait of her own child one day, hanging beside this one.

Jack opened her chamber door but remained outside. "Shall I stay in my old chamber, Georgie? I do not want you to be uncomfortable, with your brother just down the corridor."

She almost gripped his hand in her panic not to have him out of her sight. It had been torture to be near him all day, catching his musky scent in the air, staring at the hard slope of his jaw which had borne so many of her kisses. How she'd longed to kiss him and touch him the way her sister-in-law did so freely with Jonathan.

"I will not be uncomfortable." She bit her lip, fighting the blush that quickly rose to her face. He was standing too close, and at any moment, she wondered if he would take her in his arms right there in the corridor.

"Then I will stay with you. Although—" He pushed open her door and glanced meaningfully around. "I do not know if I can share that little girl's bed. We need to find someplace less filled with memories of you in ruffles and bows."

"There is my governess's old chamber next door. Will that do?"

He gave her a conspiratorial smile, then went to that chamber and opened the door. He nodded. "The bed is made, and we don't require a fire, anyway."

He held out his hand and she hurried to him, stifling a giggle as he pulled her into the room. Only when he'd closed the door did he sigh comically. He tugged at his neckcloth and wrapped the fabric around his hand to fold it.

"Make no mistake, Georgie. He saw right through us." He removed his coat and sat on the settee to take off his boots. "The jokes at supper, our playing together…" He pulled off his second boot and looked up at her. "If he asks to speak to you alone, it is probably to interrogate you. If he is not convinced, he may force me to abandon you altogether." He screwed up his face in a mocking attitude of despair.

She laughed, though her heart ached at the thought. She knelt at his feet and helped him with his boots. His stocking had a run in it. She pulled at a thread, which made the run worse.

"I think he was convinced. You seemed…" *Very much in love with me.* "You seemed sincere enough."

"As did you. Good job with your long, meaningful gazes. You almost had me convinced." He twined one of her long curls around his finger. She leaned forward, her hands sliding up his thighs, while his muscles flexed beneath her palms. His head lowered for a kiss, but she drew back, causing him to raise an eyebrow.

"Of what did I convince you, Mr. Waverley?"

"That you are madly and rapturously in love with me." He released her hair and ran his hands down her bare shoulders to caress her arms.

Her heart dropped into her stomach. Was there just the slightest expression in his eyes indicating he wished it so? She slid her hands up his chest and began unbuttoning his waistcoat. "Is that what my look meant when I passed you the butter?"

"Ah, Georgie," he breathed, skimming his fingertips across her décolletage, "never pass the butter to a man. It is a sign you want him to completely ravish you."

"Truly?" Her voice barely contained a sound. She pushed his waistcoat down his arms and began tugging at his shirt. His breath misted her face. Her eyelids flickered in expectation of the kiss he was purposely withholding to torment her. "And what if I passed you the pudding?"

"All that promise of creamy sweetness and sugared fruit? I'd have taken you right there on the table." He lifted her chin and leaned forward so they were only inches apart.

Her eyelids lowered in a thrill of expectation. She'd wanted to kiss him all day but didn't know how to request such a thing. In the bedchamber, she was free to do as she pleased. But when fully clothed in daylight, they were the friends who'd agreed to selflessly help each other.

"We shall have to convince Jonathan by other means." She freed him of his shirt and locked her hands around his neck.

He pulled her onto his lap and kissed her. His lips brushed over hers in a slow, delicious way, stirring the embers that never burned out completely.

Her blood rushed through her veins, throbbing in her head until she couldn't think or breathe. Each time she moved closer, trying to deepen the kiss, he moved slightly back, continuing the sweet torture. She wanted to laugh and scream at the same time, and pulled his hair with a sharp tug.

"Enough, sir."

His breath tickled her lips. "A kiss is much too quiet. They might think we're reading or doing some other such innocent activity as friends are wont to do."

She shifted on his lap, irritable and aroused at the same time. "You haven't quite kissed me yet." Again, she moved forward just as he pulled back, so that her lips met the air.

"Patience, my little bride. I intend to give you everything you want and need tonight. I just want you to feel a little of my frustration today. Did you know you have the most beguiling lips in the known world?" He traced his finger over her bottom lip and she sucked it into her mouth and bit it. "Every time you speak, or laugh, or berate me, I only think of the many things I want to do with your lips."

"I'm glad you suffered today, Jack." She raked her

fingers through his hair, ending at his ears, which she gripped, pulling him closer. "I've suffered, too." She pressed a kiss to his rough jaw, brushing her cheek across it. She felt his soft groan deep in his chest and bit his neck the tiniest bit. "All of this…this pretending to be in love with you has stirred my imagination."

"Oh, pray go on, Mrs. Waverley. Tell me everything." His hands slid restlessly over her chest and then down the length of her thigh. The silk rustled in protest at his questing hands.

She caressed his chest, exploring the hard, flat planes and lines of his body. She'd felt him a hundred times before, but each time was like the first. The hunger was always sated just enough to leave her wanting more. Every kiss was a prelude to the next. And the next….

"I do enjoy being married to you, Jack." She hadn't meant to whisper but had murmured his name as softly as if it were a lullaby.

"I intend to keep it that way." His heavy lids lowered, and he closed the short distance between them, silencing anything else she might say with a kiss. He suddenly rose from the settee, hoisted her in his arms, and deposited her onto the bed. She leaned back on her elbows to gaze at him as he stripped off his breeches, revealing his flat abdomen and the obvious sign of his desire.

"You could have been an artist's model."

He sat beside her, pulling her into his arms while he fumbled with the ties on her dress. "You may sculpt me if you like. But only after you allow me to do this…" His fingers brushed up her thigh. She hadn't even noticed he'd slid his hand beneath her skirt. She giggled, then clapped her hand over her mouth. He lifted his head to look at her.

"They might hear us."

"They bloody well better. Then, and only then, will your brother leave me in peace." He spoke a little loudly, and she pressed her hand over his mouth. He kissed it squarely, then hovered over her, his gray eyes gleaming. "Prepare yourself, Georgie."

"For what?" She didn't know if it was trepidation or excitement making her so breathless.

"Because I am going to make love to you until you cry out my name, so that every man in the vicinity of a thousand miles will know you are mine. Even the ghosts of Fairwood Hall will hear you."

She did not wish to inform him that Fairwood Hall had no resident ghosts. At this moment, he did not seem the least concerned with the presence of any spirit. Besides, the last coherent part of her brain thought, there might be a ghost or two lurking undetected behind the walls, and a little passion in the night shouldn't disturb them very much.

****

A butterfly landed on her cheek. Georgiana lifted her hand slowly, as if she were treading water. She brushed at it, and it flew away, settling further down on her body. Its multicolored wings fanned her silk gown, but as she watched, her gown vanished. She was lying in a flower-strewn meadow. Before she could wonder what she was doing in a meadow, the butterfly disappeared and she opened her eyes.

The top of Jack's head was inches from hers. His lips were the butterfly wings, only now they were lightly fluttering between her breasts. She drew in a surprised breath, and he lifted his head slightly.

"Good morning," he murmured, his lips tickling her skin as he spoke.

He rolled onto his side, taking her with him, as he always did. She nestled her face in the curve of his shoulder, breathing in his own natural scent and the musky perfume of their lovemaking the night before. She ran her hands down his back, enjoying the ripple effect of his muscles twitching at her light touch.

"What are you doing?"

"I wanted to express my appreciation, Mrs. Waverley."

"For what?"

He laughed softly. "I'm not certain, but I am sure you will do something nice for me today."

"So you are thanking me in advance?" She pulled away slightly to look at him.

He pushed a loose strand of hair from her forehead. "In actual fact, I wished to talk with you about our plans."

"We can stroll around the park this morning, and then play together this afternoon. Jonathan has some new music we can try."

"Beyond today, Georgie. We should go to my grandfather as soon as possible. It's about a two days' ride from Fairwood Hall to Stoughton Park." He gave an exaggerated sigh. "Of course, that will mean stopping the night in a cozy little inn."

He gave her a knowing look. A rush of heat flowed through her. "With a tiny room and a tiny bed?"

"Very tiny." He kissed her on the tip of her nose. "There's something else we need to discuss. Where we will make our nest." When she didn't reply, he cleared his throat. "Our living arrangements."

He twined a lock of her hair around his finger. He was no longer looking at her face but at her hair, as if it held some claim to his eyes. A chill prickled down the back of her neck. The warm feeling she'd had in her belly since she'd awakened faded as quickly as if she'd been doused with cold water.

She gulped to ensure her voice didn't rasp or vanish altogether. "Whatever you think is best, Jack. You have your rooms in town, do you not?"

"Yes, but that place is very small. Besides, they are for men only. So, if you wanted to visit me in the middle of the night, it would not be allowed. I thought you'd prefer to be near Fairwood Hall. I can find a larger place in town for when you seek entertainment."

Although she'd known the time to separate would come, it hadn't seemed real. Spending so much time together had changed things. Hadn't it? Or was it just her own foreboding sense of their eventual separation? She should be grateful their charade would soon end. It was a little tiring acting the part of the married woman when Jack so obviously could not abide being chained to her side longer than was necessary. He had given up so much of his life to help her, and it was time she gave it back.

She shrugged, trying to match his sensible attitude. "I don't have a preference. The country will suit me. And there's Aunt Adele's townhouse. We can take turns using it, so you needn't rent rooms somewhere else." She drew the coverlet between them, effectively shielding her body from his. Strange—she'd always dreamed of being mistress of her own home, with the furnishings and gardens just the way she wanted. Her dream would soon become reality, but rather than feel excited, she dreaded the moment.

The silence floated between them until she could bear it no longer. Before she could speak, he stroked her bare shoulder.

"You would be tired of my company, were I under foot too long."

She blinked, trying not to sniffle. The mattress shifted as he moved closer to her, pulling her against his chest and settling his arms around her.

"You are probably right. I can hardly abide your company now as it is." To prove her point, she pinched his arm.

He nibbled on her ear, and then his lips continued a teasing exploration of her throat, sending shivers of desire pulsating through her. "How tragic, as I find your company most distracting."

"Then you should find some other pleasure elsewhere. I would not wish to be the cause of any discomfort."

She bit her lip to stop the trembling, but it did no good. He reached beneath the sheet, skimming his hands over her body until she nearly shook with renewed passion. She marveled at how easily her body betrayed her.

"Fortunately, I do not mind a little discomfort."

She wanted to push him away. To shove against his shoulders and turn her head from his burning lips which trailed streaks of fire wherever they touched. He would leave her, just as she'd always known he would. Their marriage was truly one of convenience, borne of two friends pledging to help each other. The physical aspect of their arrangement was merely a pleasurable benefit, as well as a tool to bind them together so Jonathan could not tear them apart. She'd never expected to enjoy being with him so much, and he seemed happy to play the devoted husband, especially in the bedchamber. How wonderful life would be if they were in love.

Except he'd sworn never to love any woman, and she had vowed to never give her heart away again.

But even she knew her heart could make mistakes.

Chapter Twenty-Nine

"Your playing is lovely, Georgiana." Sophie glanced up from the baby who lay in her lap, his tiny legs kicking at the air. "Please, do not stop, unless you wish to. Sebastian likes it when you play."

Georgiana blew a strand of hair from her eyes and shifted her position on the padded bench. The new Broadwood had a marvelous sound, but her heart wasn't in her music.

"I don't mind playing some more," she said, and stumbled through a light sonata she could have played blindfolded.

Sophie rose from the settee, carrying Sebastian. "Perhaps some tea will revive us. My word, I do feel sleepy in this warm air." She rang the kitchens, and then carried the baby to the window. "Oh, look, my darling boy," she murmured, glancing quickly at Georgiana, "here comes Papa now. And he has your charming Uncle Jack with him, too."

Georgiana thumped the keys as she ungracefully scooted off the bench and hurried to the window, where she stood beside Sophie and peered into the park below. "They have their shirts off! Gracious, Sophie—they've been swimming in the pond!"

While she marveled at Jack's bronzed figure striding across the lawn, she was aware of a pronounced pounding of her heart. Sophie patted her hand, which she realized was twisting her skirts.

"Forgive me, dear sister," she said. "I believed you and Jack married for some different reason besides love. But I can see I am wrong."

"Of course I love him. That is why I married him." Jonathan might have asked Sophie to seek the real reason, but she wouldn't give him the satisfaction.

"No, you told your brother you loved Jack so he would not dissolve your marriage, and thereby have you marry someone else." Her slender eyebrow arched. "Your secret is safe with me. Jonathan believed both of you, but I saw through your protestations of love."

"There is no secret. Jack knows how I feel. He…" She stammered and blushed her way through a pitiful explanation, irritated at her sister-in-law's barely concealed grin.

"Jonathan assured me of your safety with Jack as escort to you and Aunt Adele. He said Jack would never marry, unless the circumstances were such that he was unable to resist." She frowned. "I feared at first he'd married you for your fortune, or that you had agreed to marry him to thwart your brother's plans. I worried you had taken a sacred sacrament and used it for your own ends."

Georgiana remained silent and turned her gaze toward the window again. Jack and Jonathan must have entered the house, because she couldn't see them anymore.

"That is ridiculous."

"Of course, it is!" Sophie linked her arm through Georgiana's. "I saw immediately you were both in love. I'm so happy I was wrong."

"Both of us?" She hadn't meant to sound so

surprised. Jack had been noticeably attentive in the Lockewoods' presence, but she'd put that to his worry her brother would still find a way to separate them.

"Why, yes. He cannot take his eyes off you for a moment. The other day, you left the room on some errand, and his gaze followed you out the door. He had obviously not heard a single word Jonathan said."

Georgiana pressed Sophie's hand. "Please, do not tell Jonathan! You are correct, Sophie. I had no wish to marry the suitors Jonathan chose for me, and Jack's grandfather forced him to take a bride. We…" Her words cut off as she remembered their passionate first night together. "We agreed upon a solution for our mutual problem."

"Well, it has worked out for the best, has it not? For now, you are both in love, truly in love. I could not be happier for you."

"He is only pretending to love me. For Jonathan's sake." A rush of heat flooded her face, and it was all she could do to keep her voice steady. "Ours is an unusual arrangement, but it suits us. We are the best of friends. I truly could not be happier."

"I did not mean to imply you were unhappy, dear Georgiana." Sophie seemed to study her, and Georgiana tried without some difficulty not to squirm before her frank gaze. "Your protestation leads me to believe you are unhappy, though you have certainly played the loving wife this week."

Georgiana clasped her hands together. "You should have seen Herbert Richmond, Sophie! You'd have done anything to stay as far from him as you could. And if there was a caring friend you trusted…" Her caring friend's passionate kisses filled her thoughts until her knees weakened. She gulped. "Do you think Jonathan has been fooled, then?"

"The question is not if your brother has been fooled, but if you are able to continue with this pretense. Are you both going to play being in love in public, but remain platonic friends in private?" Her eyebrow arched. "Or does the pretense continue into the bedchamber?"

It was on the tip of her tongue to protest they did not have a platonic friendship, but she couldn't speak of such things with Sophie. "I could not have found a better husband. Jack is kind and makes me laugh. He was so good to me in France." She stopped herself again from saying too much. It was better Sophie not know how she had come to stay at Jack's chateau in the first place.

"Then you are lucky, indeed. Many couples are never friends at all. Once the passion is gone…"

"He loves me in the best of ways," Georgiana continued, as if she had to convince both of them. "I am truly blessed to have such a warm friendship with Jack. You said so yourself." Then why did her eyes burn with unshed tears, and her throat ache with all the longing she wished to express?

"Say what you like, but I think you are wrong. He does love you, and not as a friend. A man could not feign the looks Jack bestows upon you. He is worse than your brother was, when we were courting." She laughed a little. "Jonathan found every opportunity to see me, even when there was no chaperone present. He once hid in the hedge beneath my window in hopes I would appear, but I never did. It snowed that night, and he was in a sorry state when my father found him in the morning."

Georgiana laughed. "I did not hear that story."'

"And he will never forgive me for telling you." Sophie stroked her arm. "You should tell him the truth, Georgiana."

"Tell Jonathan?"

"No." Sophie laughed gently. "Tell Jack. You both deserve a marriage based on the love between a man and a woman, not as brother and sister."

Footsteps and men's voices echoed in the corridor. Recognizing Jack's, Georgiana shook her head. "We cannot discuss this any further. Please, Sophie."

Sophie leaned in for an embrace. "Sooner or later, it will come out on its own." She straightened. "Did you enjoy your walk?" she asked as Jonathan and Jack entered the room, effectively ending their conversation.

"The water was splendid. I do hope you've occupied yourself in our absence." Jack's grin was infectious as they crossed the room to where the women remained by the window. He lifted Georgiana's trembling hand and kissed it loudly. "Look at her pink cheeks, Lockewood! Have you ever seen any woman so enamored of her husband?"

Jonathan brushed a soft kiss on Sophie's cheek. "If truth be told, yes."

"And what have you both been up to this afternoon?" Sophie asked.

"We walked the grounds and went for a swim. Jack was describing his grandfather's business. It seems very promising. I have ordered six cases of their fine burgundy."

"He wants me to succeed as a wine merchant and give up boxing," Jack whispered *sotto voce*, and they all laughed. He studied Georgiana for a moment. "Are you all right, my dear? You look flushed." He had never released her hand and now drew her to a settee, where he sat beside her.

She didn't want to look at him. Her heart seemed to flutter of late whenever they were in each other's close company. Surely, he sensed her struggle with their new life. But his mentioning of possible illness had brought her brother and Sophie near, and she hastened to assure them all.

"It is the warm weather, I suppose, and being so recently returned from our journey."

Forcing an easy smile, she was gratified when he seemed to believe her. "I am glad to hear it, then. One of the laborers we passed outside mentioned a fever in the village, and I hoped you would not catch it."

"Your concern is touching." Sophie sat opposite them on a comfortable chair while Jonathan sat on the arm, his hand on her shoulder. Georgiana wondered how Sophie had seen through her ruse but realized she should not have been surprised. One woman in love could always spot another.

"Perhaps this is as good a time as any to discuss the house," Jonathan said.

"What house?" Georgiana glanced down at her lap, where Jack's hand remained clasped around hers, without seeming intention of pulling away.

"I want you to have Rose Cottage, Georgiana. Mother always wished it for you, and I intended it to be your wedding present. It needs little upkeep, and the gardens are well-maintained. I took Jack over there today. He thinks it will suit you splendidly. You will have your own household while being right outside my door."

She avoided looking at Jack and fought hard to focus on her brother, whose visage shimmered before her blurry eyes. Jack did not want to live with her. Jonathan must have guessed some of it, much as his clever wife had, and wanted to spare her the indignity and pain of living in London in one residence while Jack took another. She blinked hard, grateful she had always been skilled at preventing tears when required.

"Aunt Adele has given us her townhome in London, so there's no need for me to move in next door." As much as she preferred the quiet countryside to town, living near Jonathan and Sophie would be that much farther from Jack. Even if he kept his rooms at the Albany, knowing they were at least in the same part of town was better than being away from him in the country. Perhaps she'd even see him at the theatre, or as a fellow guest at a party or ball. The thought of going anywhere alone and spotting him with someone else was sheer torture. She fought the urge to hug her stomach and bury her face in her knees.

"Well, it's there for you when you want it." Jonathan said amiably, but a frown creased his brow.

"Besides, Georgiana," Jack said, giving her hand a squeeze, "it might be nice to have a place to go when the blush of newly wedded bliss wears off and you are tired of me."

Their laughter turned his words into a jest, but she couldn't help but wonder if it was already the other way around.

Chapter Thirty

Georgiana stared in awe at the palatial residence that was Stoughton Park. Set back from the main road by several miles, it appeared suddenly when their carriage rounded a corner flanked by trees.

"This is where you grew up?"

Jack frowned. "Do not regard me with such surprise, Georgie. Did you think I lived in a stable?"

"Some sort of animal housing, yes." She leaned out the window to take in the view. "It is breathtaking, Jack. Has Jonathan ever been here?"

"No. Actually, I have not lived here since the old codger sent me off to school. As you recall, I spent most of my holidays with your family at Fairwood Hall." He squeezed her hand, which rested on her lap. She squeezed back and was mildly surprised but tremendously pleased when he continued to hold her hand all the way to the gate.

He tugged on his neckcloth, and she pulled his hand down to rearrange the knot. "Worry not. You look all the crack, Mr. Waverley," she teased.

His face was grim, and she smoothed her hands over the front of his coat. As always, his impeccable garments belied the pugilist within. The shoulder seams of his black worsted coat strained against his broad shoulders, and his buckskin breeches looked as if they'd split at any sudden movement. "Jonathan's valet

279

nicked you just there." She touched a spot on his jaw with the tip of her glove.

"I shall request he sack the old man." He stared past her at the house, which loomed over them like a fortress.

"You're clenching your jaw. Are you not pleased to be seeing your grandfather? When was the last time you spoke?"

"In person? When I left Cambridge. He shook my hand and gave me a note drawn on one hundred pounds and wished me luck." His gaze remained on the passing scenery, but Georgiana wondered if his mind wandered elsewhere.

"I cannot believe he would treat his grandson that way."

He shrugged. "There is nothing like being raised as a gentleman and then being forced to scrabble one's way up into the world. My luck changed when he was unable to make the yearly journey to the *vignoble* and asked me to take it over. Of course," he added bitterly, "I receive a set salary and am required to pay my own way across the Channel."

"How did you manage on your own? I can't imagine…" She shuddered.

He turned from the window. "Thank God for your brother. Lockewood came to see me in town and established me into rooms next to his at the Albany. I paid him back every penny, with interest." He chucked her on the chin.

"Jonathan has always cared for you."

His lips tightened for a moment. "More so in the past than recently, I'll wager."

"What do you mean?"

"He practically accused me of seducing you and turning your head." One eyebrow lifted comically. "He overestimates my charms and power over susceptible young ladies."

A hot blush flew up her throat and settled to just below her hairline. "Seduce?" She shook her head in dismay. "I never gave him reason to suspect something so base. When we spoke, I assured him of our mutual love and…and…" She gulped, flustered by the way he was looking at her. She gave herself a little shake. "Will your grandfather approve of me?" She tilted her head to the side and batted her eyelashes.

He tugged her earlobe from beneath her bonnet. "I approve of you, and that is good enough for me."

This caused another blush, though she did not know why. Unsettled, she gazed out the window until they stopped before the massive entrance of Stoughton Park. Two footmen assisted them from the coach. Georgiana wished she could stretch her back and stiff legs but restrained herself. Jack glanced about the grounds and the house, scanning the windows—for what or whom, she did not know. She took his arm before he offered it. He cast a distracted smile, leading her inside while the footmen struggled with their trunks.

"It will be like him to make us wait," he said in a low voice as they were shown into a parlor twice the size of Fairwood Hall's largest drawing room.

Georgiana was almost afraid to walk around and explore the busts and other objects in the room. The house had none of Fairwood Hall's homely charm and looked a bit like a museum—cold and empty. Jack seemed wedged in place by the fire, his hands clasped behind him. He'd thrown back his shoulders and held his chin high, but his left foot tapped a miniscule tattoo. No one had come to bring refreshment, and as Jack did not seem to expect anything forthcoming, she reconciled herself to a grumbling belly and dry mouth.

They stood in silence for several minutes. A few times, she'd wanted to say something, but the words died in her throat from the tension. She entertained herself by studying the portraits on the wall. One above the fireplace resembled Jack but the costume was from a different era.

"Is this your father?"

He nodded curtly.

"You look like him. He's quite handsome. Is there a portrait of your mother?" She glanced around the room, but he shook his head, a frown on his lips.

"No, there is none of my mother in this house."

Before she could question him, the door opened and a short, balding man of about sixty entered. His black coat was plain but well cut, and his waistcoat a muted dark gray silk. Ignoring Jack, he walked to Georgiana.

With a relieved smile, Georgiana removed her bonnet and handed it to him. "Thank you ever so much. May we have tea brought in? And perhaps some cake or sandwiches. Lord Waverley does seem to have kept us waiting."

Jack cleared his throat while the old gentleman cocked a thick, white eyebrow. "Grandfather," Jack said clearly, "I'd like you to meet my wife, the former Georgiana Lockewood. Georgiana, this is my grandfather."

****

She had been to the theatre once and saw a play where a trapdoor in the stage floor opened up, swallowing an actor on his descent into the pits of hell. The Persian carpet in the drawing room did not look as if it contained any such device, so she contented herself to blushing furiously and gingerly taking back her bonnet.

She curtsied, hesitant to raise her eyes. When she did recover, however, it was to find the old man's hand extended before her. She took it uncertainly, expecting him to kiss it, but instead, he turned her palm upward and ran his thumb across her hand.

"No callouses," he remarked.

She pulled back as if burned. "Certainly not!"

Jack chuckled, but his face belied no trace of humor. "She is of good stock, Grandfather. I have not seduced a scullery maid. You could not have chosen better for me, even had I allowed it."

Lord Waverley snorted, his gaze still appraising her until she knew how the horses in Tattersall's felt.

"Lockewood, you say? The Derbyshire Lockewoods?"

She nodded uncertainly, unsure if there was another family of the same name with whom he might be acquainted. "My brother's seat is at Fairwood Hall."

He nodded, his expression betraying neither interest nor disregard. Still studying her, he said to Jack, "I trust the wedding was legal, with witnesses?"

Jack strode to a settee and sat with a purposely sloppy gesture. "Yes, sir. And it was signed with genuine ink, not blood. I did have to rouse the drunken minister a few times, but we got through it just right, didn't we, darling?"

A dark flush shadowed his face. Georgiana gulped audibly. His temper was fearsome in any situation, but she had hoped the reunion with his grandfather would hold a little bit of cheer. She hastily sat beside him, moving his knee with a nudge of her leg.

"I have known Jack all my entire life, Grandfather Waverley. We fell in love…."

"What did you call me?"

She startled at the interruption but remained stalwart. Taking Jack's clenched hand, she unfolded his fingers until he held hers. "Why, I called you Grandfather Waverley. Isn't that what Jack calls you?"

A dry smile twisted his lips. "Yes, my dear. That is what Jack always calls me. Is it not, Jack?"

Jack was nearly immobile. She caught the scent of a fresh outbreak of sweat beneath his arms, and squeezed his fingers. Were it not for the vein bulging in his throat, she'd have thought him peaceful.

"Georgiana is as kind and genuine a lady either of us has ever met. If you continue to insult her…."

Lord Waverley raised his hands defensively. "I do no such thing. I was merely recalling the last name you called me."

"Do you mean the name I shouted as you drove away in your shining new coach and six?" He had spoken so pleasantly and quietly Georgiana was almost convinced he was not angry. But not quite.

"Yes. The very one. Always the artist with your words."

Before Jack could retort, the door opened and two servants arrived with a teacart. Georgiana poured the tea, as both men seemed more intent on staring each other down. She quickly thrust two plates of sandwiches and cake into their hands.

"He won't eat it. It's meant for us," Jack said.

His grandfather smiled tightly and carefully placed his dish on the table beside him. "I never eat luncheon," he admitted, then glanced at Jack. "Is she capable of entertaining herself while we speak?"

Jack bristled, but Georgiana smiled as prettily as she could. "Do you have a pianoforte in this fine house, Grandfather Waverley? I may entertain myself whilst you reacquaint yourself with your grandson."

Lord Waverley opened his mouth and closed it just as quickly. He scowled, then shrugged. "It has not been touched in quite a while, though it is routinely tuned. You may suit yourself."

Georgiana continued to smile at him, refusing to be brushed away. "Do you enjoy a particular piece, Grandfather? The sound will carry if I am close by."

"I do not care what you play." He puffed out his chest like a drawing of a penguin she'd once seen in a book. "Bach, then, if you have a firm hand. Otherwise, do not attempt him. You may play any of the silly tunes young misses are expected to know."

"Georgiana has been taught by the finest masters…" Jack began, but Georgiana waved his words away with a quick motion.

"Bach, it is." She rose gracefully from her seat and kissed Jack lightly on the lips. She then went to his grandfather. Before the old man could move, she kissed his pale cheek.

They watched her leave the room, and then his grandfather stared at him for a moment before taking an opposite chair.

"You always spoke out against marriage. I did not

expect you would obey me so quickly."

"I saw the folly of my ways. You only planted the seed of an idea."

A servant entered the room with hardly a sound, bearing a tray with the dry, almost tasteless cheese sandwiches his grandfather preferred. Jack ignored the food on his own plate while the old man watched him.

"You've done very well for yourself, Jack. I've heard only good news from Gaston."

"You sound surprised." He sipped his tea, noticing Georgiana had sweetened it with just the right amount of sugar.

"I am not surprised." He removed the top half of his bread and placed it on the plate, and then removed one slice of cheese. As long as Jack could remember, his grandfather had maintained the same routine. He didn't know why the cook could not prepare a single slice of bread with a single slice of cheese but was not about to question it now.

"I expected you to go into the law, Jack. Your cousin, Wilfred, has done well in the superior courts. He could have found you a position had you tried just a little."

"I did not want to turn into a dried up boor like Wilfred." The assorted cakes and tarts looked delectable, but he couldn't find any trace of an appetite. He placed his cup on the table and crossed his arms.

"You could have tried soldiering, Jack. Lord Nelson told me…"

"A bought commission. Yes, very noble."

"It's a far sight better than having your face rearranged! How many times have you broken your nose?"

"Twice, and I did not break it. It was broken for me."

"Still the same, aren't you boy? Quick-tongued and no respect for your elders."

Jack pushed out of his chair, deciding to leave before things were said that could never be taken back. He'd waited nearly fifteen years to tell the old man exactly what he thought of him, but did not want to do it with Georgiana in the other room.

"That's right, Jack. Run away. You always did, you know."

"I was not aware a six-year-old boy could run away and place himself in school."

"Sit down, sit down."

"I've done what you asked, sir. I found a bride. A wealthy one, as it turns out. I have no use for your money, as you can plainly see…"

"It wasn't about the money, damn you!" His grandfather's eyes seemed to burn in his head. His thin lips, drawn into a thin line, trembled. "It was never about the money. If it were, I'd have given you everything I had the moment you reached your majority."

"Then…"

"Sit." He waved at the settee.

After a pause, he sat. His grandfather poured him another cup of tea. "No, thank you."

Lord Waverley rose stiffly from his chair and opened a cabinet. He showed the decanter to Jack. "I suppose you're old enough to have a drink with your grandfather?"

Vibrating with anger, Jack gave a curt nod. His grandfather poured two cups, and Jack noted the shaking hands, peppered here and there with brown spots. He walked to the cabinet and took the cups from him. Together, they walked back to their seats.

"You're a damned fool, Jack."

"A trait, no doubt, inherited on my father's side."

His grandfather snorted, and for a moment, Jack thought he was going to laugh.

"Where are you keeping your wife?"

"Sir?" Jack tried to maintain a calm demeanor, but every nerve fought against it.

"It was a simple enough question, even for a man whose brains are knocked about his head every night. Do you share the same abode, or are you conveniently established in your rooms in town while she must suffer gossiping tongues?"

"We...I have..." Taken off guard, he blinked, as if that would clear the fuzziness.

"The reason I put restrictions on your inheritance was to force you into becoming responsible. I'd heard about your mistresses and how you spend your evenings in those so-called gaming hells."

"How do you come by this?"

"I have eyes and ears, my boy." He drank the brandy as if it were milk. "You're the grandson of Lord Waverley. Do not think I am deaf and blind to how you are squandering your life away."

Jack gritted his teeth. "I do not have to answer to you, or anyone. You may disinherit me if you wish. I make a tidy living with my sordid activities." He drained his brandy in one gulp and set his glass on the table with a louder than needed clink. "If you must know, I did not take a wife because of your command. I have loved Georgiana Lockewood all my life. Had it not been for her family's love and support, I should have perished my first year away at school. You need not question my marriage vows. I have sworn fidelity and love until I die, and I intend to honor those vows." He drew a shuddering breath, aware that his anger was gone. "Now, if you will excuse me, I am going to find my wife and order the coach. We will not disturb you any longer."

"Jack…"

"Goodbye, Grandfather."

"Stay where you are." His voice rang out as strong and stern as it had when Jack had trembled before it as a child. He motioned helplessly toward the settee. "Please."

The muted notes from the pianoforte a few rooms away carried through the walls and into the drawing room. Jack recognized the piano concerto in D minor, which was such an unlikely choice for Georgiana, whom he associated with light and airy pieces. For a moment, a look of peace overcame his grandfather's patrician features, and his eyelids almost lowered as the notes wafted around them, invisible flags of truce.

"I see you so seldom, and I admit the acrimony is mostly on my side."

"You must forgive my father and get on with your life. Stop punishing me for my parents' sins."

His grandfather turned sharply on him. "Is that what you think I've done? Blamed my own grandson for the faults of his parents?"

Jack dragged his hand through his hair. "You blamed my mother for Father's death."

The older man's face turned red and his hands shook. "He was a damned fool to take his own life. She was not the cause."

"She abandoned her husband and child for another man. A barrister, you told me once. Some would say that was cause enough."

"I have never blamed your mother for my son's death."

Jack swirled the tea in his cup until a few leaves floated to the top. "You could have fooled me."

"What say you?"

"You sent me away so you wouldn't have a reminder of your only son."

"I sent you away so you could learn what it is to be a man!" His voice rose, and Jack knew it killed him to lose his carefully governed self-control. "I spent thousands on your education, only to receive letters from the headmaster at every turn informing me how scandal-ridden my grandson had become. Seducing housemaids, drinking in your chambers, and all sorts of roguish behavior unbecoming to a Waverley."

"I was young and foolish."

"An excuse then, but not now." He gulped his brandy and remained quiet for a moment while Jack supposed he was trying to calm himself. "I am tempted to halt your allowance as I did when you were at Cambridge. Then shall you see what it is to take on responsibility."

"You may keep the allowance, Grandfather."

"What, and have you continue boxing and gambling? A worthy occupation for a gentleman."

"I have my salary from the *vignoble*, meager as it is. What do you pay Gaston?"

His grandfather sputtered. "More than you are worth! Gaston saved my life."

"Yes, I recall the story. You and he, on an island in the middle of the West Indies, both separated from your ships."

"Don't sound so flippant. He risked his life to save that of his enemy."

"He must have seen your pocketbook and made the decision."

"Gaston Gironde is the son of a gentleman and comes from a most respectable family in Paris." He pressed his hand to his chest. "You drive a man to distraction, Jack. I have forgotten what we were talking about."

"Salary. Mine."

"Very well. When you cross the sea to tend to my business, you will receive what I pay Gaston. Is that to your liking?"

Jack nodded shortly. "Honest pay for honest work."

Lord Waverley snorted. "I will have the papers drawn up; since I'm sure you will not accept my word for it."

"Your word is as good as any man's." He relented. "Perhaps more so."

"Then we are agreed." He poured another cup of strong tea and toasted Jack. "It shall all go to you when I'm gone, in any case."

"What will?"

"All of this." He nodded at the far wall. "The house, the estate, the *vignoble*." He pronounced the French word as Gaston did. "Oh, by the by, did you know that your cousin, Wilfred, is now betrothed to a very rich young lady?"

"No, but that doesn't surprise me. I always knew

his handsome face and lack of brains would even themselves out in the end. Good for him."

"Yes, good for him. Good for you, as well. Your mother's beauty and charm are evident in you. Always have been."

"But not my father's sensibilities."

Lord Waverley eyed him over the rim of his cup. "You have many of your father's qualities, Jack. Honor, being one of them." He rose stiffly, and Jack's heart panged at the physical reminder of the wounds his grandfather had sustained as a younger man at the hands of Napoleon's army. "Now, if you'd care to join me, I'd like to attend your lovely bride. She happens to be playing my favorite piece."

"She will be glad of an audience."

"Lend me your arm, Jack, will you?" His grandfather wrapped his thin arm around his as they exited the room. He shortened his stride to match his grandfather's, remembering another time when he'd barely outrun the old sod when he'd been caught for some mischief or other. The music grew louder as they walked to the drawing room where Georgiana sat, her back to them as she played. They paused to watch her for a moment before she sensed their presence and turned slightly to acknowledge them.

"She's as bewitching as your mother, when your father first brought her home."

"Yes." He didn't know how else to respond, because the old man's eyes had filled with tears as he swayed to the music, springing artfully from Georgiana's nimble fingers.

"I miss him," he said quietly, and Jack nodded, finally agreeing with him on some note. Although his grandfather could stand on his own, he remained with his arm on Jack's, softly humming along as Georgiana played.

Chapter Thirty-One

Georgiana danced around the ivory and blue-colored bedchamber. Heavy gilt-edged mirrors and picture frames adorned the silk-hung walls. An overstuffed settee was placed before the fireplace. She felt the beginning tremors of excitement at the sight of the large bed. Her sudden gaiety was the result of nervous excitement when Jack had quietly instructed a servant they would share a chamber. He'd also politely refused a lady's maid for her, and seldom used a valet anyway, so she was not surprised when the door was closed and bolted for the night.

Jack regarded her with a slightly amused look. It was the first glimpse of happiness she'd seen on him all day, and was grateful for it.

"Your playing was wonderful. He actually halted his tirade for a moment to listen to you."

"I am so glad. I haven't played Bach very often. One of my masters adored him, but the others favored Mozart. They said I was too young to play Bach."

"And infinitely too pretty and cheerful."

She gave him a little curtsy, and his gaze remained on her, as if he were trying to compose his thoughts. Gulping back a sudden wave of nervous energy, she motioned around the expansive room.

"Is this your old chamber?"

"This?" He laughed. "No. My quarters were a little

less extravagant. Grandfather believed in a rigid militaristic upbringing. I slept on a cot by the fire, which burned out promptly at nine and was not lit again until daybreak. '*Hot gruel and crusts, Jack! That will make you big and strong.*'" He'd imitated his grandfather almost perfectly.

Georgiana laughed, but her heart ached. They'd had such opposite childhoods. Memories of sweets and dolls and happy voices flooded her whenever she thought back to her childhood.

"He was probably being hard on you so you wouldn't be a soft little boy." How hard it must have been, to lose both parents so young. "That explains why you spent so much time at Fairwood Hall."

His face relaxed as a smile filtered through his gloom. "Those were the happiest times of my life. Lockewood promised to bring me home with him the moment we met. He said, 'Hullo, Waverley. I'm Lockewood. As you've no parents, you're welcome to my home at Christmas.'"

They both laughed. "That sounds just like him."

"Yes. Even at thirteen years, he was so like the man he's become. I've never quite thanked him for sharing his home and family with me."

They were quiet for a moment, and she wondered if he thought often of his parents. Perhaps not, she reasoned. Jonathan seldom discussed theirs with her, unless it was to cajole her into doing something she was loathe to do.

He removed his coat and gave her a pointed look, signaling it was time for bed. She hastened to the attached dressing room where their clothes hung in the wardrobe, even though Jack had insisted they would only stay the night. The door between the rooms had closed halfway behind her, and she was torn between closing it all the way and changing into her nightrail, or leaving it partly open so he would not think her a prude.

Her gown had a simple fastening at the back she could easily undo, and she quickly removed it and unlaced her stays with difficulty. She slipped off her chemise. The room was chilly, despite the warm evening, and she hastily pulled a nightrail over her head. She unpinned her hair, but then plaited it and stuffed it under a nightcap so it would be easier to arrange in the morning.

She emerged from the dressing room to find the lamps extinguished. Blinking rapidly to adjust her vision, she made out his shadowy form in the darkness. He'd removed his breeches, and stood with the long ends of his shirt covering him. She walked quickly to the bed and climbed under the coverlet, pulling it up to her chin.

"Are we leaving in the morning?" she asked, when the silence was too much.

He strode to the windows and pulled the drapes wide so more of a breeze would enter the room. He remained at the window for a few seconds, and she wondered if he was looking at something in particular or simply lost in thought.

"Hmm?" He turned and walked to the bed. "I suppose we can stay another day. He keeps mentioning a drain system he had installed. I think he wants to show it to me." He pulled back the coverlet and tossed it to the bottom of the bed. "It's too bloody hot." He lay on the pillows with a heavy sigh.

"He misses you. Does he have any other family

besides you?"

"I have a wastrel of a cousin and some distant relations we've never seen. He was an only child as was my father. My grandmother died years ago, before I was born."

"He's probably very lonely."

"A situation he helped to create."

She leaned up on her elbow to look at him. A faint light from the lamp on the table across the room illuminated him and she could see his eyelashes flutter.

"I've never known you to be so unforgiving, Jack."

"One of many aspects of my personality I hide from questioning little brides."

Again, the silence wrapped around them. She listened to his steady breathing, and realized he was still agitated. "Did you wish to talk, Jack? I don't mind. But if you'd rather sleep…"

He faced her, the movement causing the mattress to sink, rolling her into him. "No, no. Let's talk a while. Your voice is soothing."

She laughed softly. "I am so dull I put you to sleep?"

"Your voice has a pleasant tone. Lockewood's is the same. When one hears you speak, it is apparent you sing well. Which, by the by, you do."

"I never heard my mother sing. I don't have many memories of her, but I do remember she used to hum."

"That was because her singing voice was terrible. Thank God, you didn't inherit her lack of an ear. Your musicality is purely on your father's side."

"I'd forgotten you knew her better than I. Do you remember your mother?"

His silence revealed more than if he had spoken

volumes. "I was very young when she and my father died. It was all very sordid and caused a scandal back in the day. I told your brother about it years ago, but he obviously never spoke about it with you."

"How terrible," she murmured. "What happened?"

He was quiet for so long she wondered if he was going to respond. "She abandoned him. Me. For another. I do not remember much. My father killed himself shortly afterward. She later died, of an illness, I presume. It's not something I've told many people about."

"Oh, Jack."

He shrugged. "It doesn't affect me much. I remember little things about them. My father's laugh. My mother's voice, reading me stories when she put me to bed. Only then"—and he patted the quilt surrounding them—"I was in a chamber like this. Soft mattress, lots of toys. There was even a dog, as I recall. When they died, my grandfather got rid of it all. Even the dog. He moved me into a smaller chamber. He said I must become a man." His smile appeared as a shadow on his face. "I remember your mother. She was the kindest soul I've ever known."

Georgiana almost wriggled with impatience for him to tell her everything he remembered. "Jonathan said I look like her."

He traced his finger down the side of her face, tapping lightly on the nose. "Yes, you do. You both have her eyes—that silvery blue color. Yours are prettier than Lockewood's, however."

"Thank you."

"She was very beautiful. As are you."

"I am?"

He puffed a little breath of air, which stirred the hair that had come free of her cap. "Has no one ever told you that? I hardly believe it."

Her cheeks warmed with a blush. "My nurses always said I was, but I assumed they had to say it since I was their charge."

He pushed up one elbow, staring down at her with an almost incredulous look on his face. "My nurses made certain I knew how naughty and frightful I was. No, Georgiana, they told you that because it's true. You are the most beautiful thing I've ever seen."

"What is beautiful about me?"

He continued caressing her face, and then her ear, pushing back the hair that had emerged from her nightcap. Her eyelids lowered, and she waited, almost breathlessly, for a kiss. Instead, he chuckled, which stifled the burning embers in her heart.

"Fishing for compliments? Ah—let me see…"

She smiled against the fingertip skimming her lips.

"Your mouth is very kissable—puffy and fat. It feels like a little pillow when I kiss it."

She gasped in amused dismay. "That doesn't sound very nice."

"I am not a poet, Georgie. Would you have me compare it to a rosebud, instead?"

"That's a little more romantic."

"She wants romance now." He grinned, and the fingertips on her face slid down her jaw to her neck, where he tickled her lightly. "So much for the marriage of convenience."

"It is highly inconvenient either of us should have been forced to marry anyone." She rolled away from him. Confusion swept through her, mixing with an odd sense of despair.

His fingers twined in her hair, and she smiled with guilty satisfaction. She'd noted the heightened look of awareness in his eyes and could tell from the way his voice had grown huskier and his caresses bolder he probably intended to carry out his marital obligations. But if they were still keeping track of whose night it was, for the record, it was hers.

"Your eyes haunt my dreams, Georgiana," he said suddenly.

Her heart stopped beating.

"I go about my usual activities, and all I can think about is how you…" He seemed to stumble in his search for the right words, and swore softly. "I am a fighter, as you well know. I cannot spout pretty verses such as the ones your brother no doubt has in excessive supply with his bride. But I can tell you what I truly feel."

She faced him, and this time, moved right up against him. He grunted, then draped his heavy arm over her, pinning her in place, as if he didn't want her rolling away again.

"What do you feel?"

"I can perhaps show you more than I can tell you."

"A true Jackian response!" They both laughed, and she pressed her hand to his cheek, rubbing her palm over his scratchy whiskers. "Shall I tell you what I see when I look at you?"

"My broken nose? The scar on my eyebrow?"

She drew on his face with her fingertip the way he had done to her. "Your eyes are very handsome indeed. They aren't a true blue, but gray—like mist on the moors."

"You've never seen the moors."

"I read it in a book once." She explored the crooked spine of his nose. "Mamma told me she thought you'd grow into a handsome man, once you learned to give your heart away."

That seemed to halt something in him. He frowned slightly, and the hand in her hair stilled. "Your mother was very clever."

"She loved you as a son, Jack. I'm sure of it."

"I know. She used to call me Jackie. She was the only one who could get away with it. And"—his mouth quirked into a little smile—"she always kissed me first when Lockewood and I came home for holidays. He complained about it once, but she said…"

He abruptly turned onto his back. She could see the dim outline of his opened eyes from the moonlight streaming in through the windows.

"What did she say?"

A few seconds passed before he spoke. "She said, 'Jackie doesn't have a mother to embrace him. You do.'"

A light misting of tears blurred her vision, but she smiled at his shared memory. "That sounds like something she would say. I remember when she died. Jonathan came home at once, and you managed to come with him."

"I lied and told the head of our house my own mother was ill. He was new and didn't know she was already dead."

The urge to stroke his hair overcame her, and so she did, not caring if he moved away. She risked losing little pieces of her heart every time she was near him, but was powerless against the pull he extended on her soul. To her surprise, he didn't stop her, but faced her again, only this time, he lay a little closer.

"I found you in the library, curled up on your father's chair like a cat."

She was surprised at the sudden tears the onslaught of the memory brought. She blinked hastily. "You said, 'Hullo, little Pudding Face' and picked me up."

"Lockewood was with your father and other relatives. They'd seemed to have forgotten you in the confusion."

"I asked you to take me away. Do you remember, Jack?"

He laughed so softly she was barely aware of it, except that the bed moved a bit. "Yes. I asked you where, and you told me there was a castle in one of your storybooks, and you wanted me to find it. I think the boy in the book was named Jack, and you thought I was him."

"No, that wasn't it. I knew you weren't a prince from a book. I just wanted to go away with you."

"I wanted to care for you, Georgiana. I think a part of me was waiting for you to grow up, so I could marry you." He captured her hand that stroked his hair. His lips brushed across her palm, then held her open hand against his face. "I should have asked you to marry me, Georgie," he murmured. "And not in that silly way you proposed to me, but a proper proposal. You deserve it."

Her heart filled her throat. She inhaled slowly. "Then ask me."

He released her hand and plucked the nightcap off her head. "If you're to share a bed with me, no more nightcaps." He tossed it over his shoulder.

She stifled a laugh. "I thought you were going to

propose, Jack Waverley! Or should I say, *Ambrose.* Your grandfather told me you were named after him."

"Nobody calls me that and lives."

"I am still breathing." A bold recklessness overcame her, and she wriggled as close as she could to him. Her thin lawn nightrail and his fine linen shirt allowed her to absorb the heat emanating from him. He instantly reacted by lifting his leg over hers and sliding his arm beneath her.

"I have another condition, Georgie." He toyed with her neck ribbon, pulling it free. With a single nudge of his hand, her nightgown slid off her shoulder, which he then kissed. His feather light touch drew a long sigh from her.

"What is it, Ambrose?"

"No more nightclothes. Ever."

She pulled away to gaze into his eyes. They were glassy in the moonlight, and his mouth looked red and full. She skimmed his lips with her fingertips, and his eyelids lowered. "I shall have to remember your requirements."

"Please do."

His words cut off when she parted her lips to his insistent mouth. The rest of the night passed in a blur of murmured sighs and soft moans, gentle kisses and caressing hands, until she realized he had never mentioned the word love, but he wanted her. It was all he protested he was capable of.

Fortunately, she did not believe a whit of it.

****

"You are welcome to visit anytime," his grandfather said to them a week later as they prepared to leave. The days had flown by, and Jack was surprised he'd actually enjoyed his grandfather's company. Once they got blame and regret out of the way, they'd actually had a conversation about the state of the *vignoble*. He suspected the old man was pleased with his work in Bordeaux, but would never admit it.

"Thank you, Grandfather. We will." As they shook hands, the old man unexpectedly clasped his fingers in a tight squeeze. He turned to Georgiana.

"I enjoyed listening to you play. Perhaps next time, you and Jack will play a duet. I seem to recall Jack had a rather good ear."

"You never heard me play," Jack said almost petulantly. "I learned at school, with a private master."

"And who do you think paid for that private master?" he growled. He shook his head and sighed. "We must learn not to quarrel every time we see each other, Jack."

Georgiana was giving him a miniscule nod of encouragement, and he was forced to relent. "Agreed."

"Kiss an old man," his grandfather instructed her, and Jack couldn't help but smile as his wife leaned into the old man's embrace and kissed his cheek. "Take care of my boy," he said rather gruffly and handed Georgiana a small velvet pouch. "You may as well have these. They are part of the family collection. You shall have the rest upon my death, when Jack inherits all that I worked hard to achieve."

Jack bit his tongue to avoid responding in kind but noticed the corner of his grandfather's eye twitching in a wink. Stifling a grin, he turned to his wife, whose face revealed the pleasure felt by both of them at the gesture. He had wanted to ask for his mother's jewelry but feared his grandfather would accuse him of wanting to sell it. Georgiana emptied the pouch into her palm, displaying the blue diamond earrings and gold bracelets Jack knew so well. He had the ruby ring tucked inside his waistcoat and intended to give it to her once they were alone.

"They are beautiful," Georgiana said in a hushed voice. Her eyes sparkled with tears to match the glittering diamonds. "Thank you." She kissed his grandfather again and gave Jack a smile that went straight through his heart. "You must come to visit us in town, Grandfather Waverley," she began, but he shook his head.

"You don't want an old man underfoot, my dear. Especially when you are setting up housekeeping together, so recently wed."

"Yes, sir, please come. Perhaps you may attend me at one of my boxing dens and watch me rearrange some other man's nose."

Painful silence filled the air around them. Georgiana paled, but his grandfather's cheeks reddened. For a moment, Jack feared he would have a heart attack, but his grandfather embraced him tightly, laughing so hard he wheezed.

"I will! Jack, I will come and see you." He wiped the corners of his eyes and motioned them into the coach. "Godspeed and congratulations to both of you! Jack, you remember how to write, do you not? Goodbye, my dear girl! Take care of our boy!"

Jack sat back against the coach cushions with a loud heaving of breath. Georgiana was still laughing, and he handed her his handkerchief to wipe her streaming eyes.

"That went better than I thought it would," he

muttered, kissing her before she could say she'd told him so.

Chapter Thirty-Two

"Fancy you, Miss Pudding Face—the owner of her very own home."

Jack surveyed the newly furnished parlor of Aunt Adele's Kensington Gardens townhouse. Despite his affirmation the house was her sole possession, legally, it belonged to him. Georgiana had delighted in his solemn presentation of the keys to the property once they were out of the bank and in the new carriage she'd purchased. She'd wanted Jack to share in her newfound wealth, but he politely refused, reminding her again of their original agreement and insisting she need not give him a farthing.

Instead of being relieved everything was turning out the way they'd planned, she was melancholy. Somehow, it didn't seem right to be married yet so completely independent of her husband.

Since leaving Stoughton Park, they'd settled in Aunt Adele's townhome. At least, she had. Jack was staying at the Albany. Now, after a separation of a few days while he was purportedly involved with his grandfather's business ventures in town, they were together again. She'd missed him more than she wanted to admit. She wanted to run to him when he stomped up the stairs to her parlor but didn't wish to give her new servants fodder for gossip. She picked up an embroidered pillow from a chair and tossed it at him.

"If you are not nice to me, I shall have you thrown out. My new coachman, Roberts, looks as strong as you."

"Oh, really? As strong as me?" He cocked an eyebrow and peered toward the half-opened doorway into the corridor. "Send the blighter in to have a round. I'll wager a kiss from your tasty lips I can beat him."

She shook her head. "There will be no fighting here, my dear husband."

"In that case," he began. He stretched out on the settee. "If there is no fighting allowed, what shall be permitted? I am speaking of when you summon me once a week to service your insatiable appetite, madam."

"Summoned here once a week?" she sputtered.

He bowed his head. "Forgive me. I will come more frequently to indulge you."

She fidgeted with the teapot so he wouldn't see her agitation. He'd announced earlier he could only stay an hour due to pressing business, and the time was almost up.

"Indulge my appetites? Ha!" She swept across the room to the window and opened it. A bee flew from its leafy perch and buzzed about her nose. She quickly closed the window and turned around to face him. He looked as if he had no intention of going anywhere.

"You must admit, Georgie: our arrangement benefits you as delightfully as it does me."

"I would never be so base as to admit it."

He pulled the pillow from his face and regarded her with a smirk. "But you do admit it?" He rose to his feet and sauntered over to her, while she backed up against the wall. He was too close, towering over her with his spicy scent invading her nose and his fingers toying with the pendant around her throat. She tried to move, but he blocked her by planting both his hands on the wall, trapping her.

"You have no sense of boundaries, Mr. Waverley." She pressed her hands against his chest, but the feel of his heart pounding against her palms awakened a similar sensation in her body. She glanced up at him and realized the moment she did it was a terrible mistake.

His gray eyes gleamed like silver moonbeams. His lips were full and moist, and slightly parted in a grin. It was not his usual, teasing grin. It was the grin that always appeared right before he…

He didn't kiss her. She scowled. "Haven't you got your own home to see to, Jack? I'm sure there are all levels of female servants in your employ who miss their generous benefactor."

His amusement only deepened. "Why, yes, indeed I do. But my rooms are infinitely smaller and dingier than this place. Besides, I rather like the view in your house."

She sniffed with disdain, but her heart had begun hammering in her ears. "You mean the view *from* my house. You can stand all day by my window and look at the pretty girls strolling through the park."

"No, I meant *in* your house." His hand left her pendant, and he twisted his finger around one of her long curls that draped over her shoulder. "There is a living, breathing statue right in this very room. I must inform the British Museum immediately and advise them of its location. Some blackguard has stolen their most prized possession and supplanted it in

Kensington."

"Such a pretty speech. Tell me, Jack—have you always had to resort to lying in order to have your way with women?"

She hadn't meant to sound so brusque, but the entire arrangement seemed so sordid and troubling now. Her mentioning of his household filled with willing servant girls only added to her heartache. She wondered if he really did keep a bevy of maidens for that very purpose.

His brow furrowed though his smile remained intact. "You don't want me to go. Just say the word, and I'll stay." His voice was so low she wondered if she'd heard him correctly.

Her breath caught in her throat. "I don't care what you do. Go or stay, it matters not. As you said before, we are merely friends helping each other in a mutually satisfactory situation." Her hands remained on his chest. She glanced at his torso. She'd twisted her fingers in the fabric of his waistcoat.

"*Friends*. Well, when you explain our relationship like that, it does seem unpleasant. Hmm."

His breath warmed her cheek. His eyelids lowered, and she gasped her objection, but no words came. Against her will, her feet rose on tiptoe and she leaned into his solid frame, his desire evident in the pressure against her thighs. She'd released his waistcoat and now gripped him around the neck, desperate for his lips, which seared hers when they met.

The clock chimed loudly behind her, and she jumped. He licked his lips, sealing in her kiss.

"I do have to leave, my charming friend with whom I'm pleasurably linked in name and bed only.

But, if you like"—he stepped out of her embrace and straightened his coat—"we can meet at Lord Hetherington's masque this evening. Lockewood told me you were going with him and the missus."

She bristled, although she was secretly relieved her brother had invited him. She'd thought of making an excuse to Sophie about preferring to stay home, but now Jack was going, she wanted to go with him. It would be their first appearance as a married couple. She nodded.

"I'll see you at nine, then. Try not to miss me too much." He kissed her before she could object to his presumption.

She remained against the wall, her body aching with frustrated passion. "If I'm not otherwise preoccupied, I may come." She frowned. "But how will I find you if it's a masque?"

He paused at the door. "You will know me. I'll be the one with his heart on his sleeve."

She ran to the window to watch his carriage depart. What a strange costume he would have, with a heart decorating the sleeve! What manner of disguise was that? And what would she wear? Nothing in her wardrobe was suitable for a masque. Perhaps Sophie had a costume she could borrow.

As the carriage rounded the corner, he leaned out and waved. She waved back, frowning when she realized he'd known she would watch for him. Even so, she waited until he was out of sight before she turned from the window.

Chapter Thirty-Three

Georgiana entered Lord Hetherington's home on Jonathan's left arm, with Sophie on his right. The noisy chatter and laughter of the other guests distracted her from the restless feeling she'd had since Jack's departure. Her beaded mask tilted over her face, and she straightened it with a shove. Sophie had insisted on costumes reminiscent of the ousted French aristocracy, and Georgiana didn't know how she would maneuver the powdered wig reaching a good foot above her head. Not to mention, the wide panniers made entering a room the same time as the similarly costumed Sophie out of the question.

"Where is Jack?" Jonathan asked, too loudly.

Sophie patted Georgiana's hand. "Ignore him, dearest. He's irritable ever since he kissed Sebastian good night."

"I am not. I agree with you we need to separate ourselves from the bonny boy from time to time." His tone belied his words.

Georgiana would have returned Sophie's grin, but she was too anxious herself to be concerned with the new father's problems.

She searched the room, holding onto her brother's arm to rise on tiptoe, but there were too many people to find one man amongst the crowd. None of the men present matched him in breadth and height, nor were any costumed with hearts or any other organ on their sleeves. She wanted to abandon her party to search him out, but Jonathan detained her.

"I saw Jack at White's this afternoon. Is he not staying at Kensington with you?"

She'd always detested Jonathan's direct approach. With an airy shrug, she gave him her brightest smile. "He is keeping his set at the Albany to keep him close to his grandfather's affairs." Even to her ears, it sounded contrived.

Jonathan sniffed. "How convenient. I wanted to speak to him about it this afternoon, but…"

"Oh, please, Jonathan, do not!" She shook his arm. "Why can you not let us be?"

Sophie silenced them with a look that was neither critical nor censuring. Georgiana always marveled at her sister-in-law's ability to calm any situation, especially when it involved two of the hottest tempers in the family.

"Very well." Jonathan accepted defeat. He led them toward the main ballroom where a waltz already played. "Are you certain Jack is meeting you?"

"He must have been detained." Her face burned at Jonathan's direct stare. She shrugged, hoping to lighten his mood. "He will be here. He promised."

"Oh, well, then! Since he promised, he's sure to come."

"Why so surly, darling?" Sophie patted his cheek, giving a wink to Georgiana. "This is our first night away from the baby. Let us enjoy it."

"Speaking of babies, Georgiana, I wanted to ask you about your plans." His eyebrow arched.

Georgiana glanced around the ballroom. Everyone

else was dancing, eating, or drinking. Why could her family not have one pleasant evening? Ever since she came home from France a married woman, she'd had nothing but trouble.

"What are you implying, my dear brother?" she asked sweetly.

"I am still trying to reconcile the fact you are a married woman now. You declined having a season because of your supposedly fragile state after that despicable affair. You swore you would never fall in love, and I heard the same such affirmation from Jack. Yet, here you are, married, after a few months together in France. A pair of babies, both of you. Playing at a fantastic game." He shook his head and glanced at Sophie. "You remember, Sophie. Threatening to join a convent rather than consider marriage." He turned to Georgiana again. By now, she wished she could sink into the floor. "I don't know how you convinced Jack to throw off the mantle of bachelorhood, Georgiana."

"Why must I have convinced him of anything? Why could he not have come up with the idea himself?"

"They are in love, Jonathan," Sophie interjected.

Jonathan raised his hand. "My old friend has always done exactly what Georgiana wants him to do. She's dangled him from her little finger since the first time they met."

"In that case," Sophie said gently, taking his arm and linking her fingers around it, "let him continue to be swayed by the woman he loves."

Georgiana wanted to rage against their observations. Jonathan's ideas were too extreme. Sophie's were a fantasy she only wished were true. If she could control Jack, as Jonathan surmised, why was he not here, as promised? Lord knew whom he was with at this very moment, while she faced her brother's accusations.

Sophie's excited gasp broke the silence growing between them. "My dear, do you see the woman who just arrived? The one in the feathers and flounces?" Her voice rose in delight. "Is she not Mrs. Leister, the famous actress?"

Relieved the conversation had turned from her, Georgiana followed Sophie's gaze.

If she were not an actress or someone equally as flamboyant, the woman certainly had an intriguing sense of fashion. She was dressed from head to toe in violet silk, a headdress of black feathers gleaming against her raven-wing hair. A small crowd engulfed her. Jonathan's face flushed as scarlet as his waistcoat. He looked as if he'd walk away, but Sophie prodded him.

"I wonder if we may say hello. I did so admire her in *Agamemnon* last year."

"I daresay she has her own friends to keep her occupied." He cleared his throat and tugged on his neckcloth in the same manner Jack had when he was nervous.

"Yes, Jonathan, let us introduce ourselves." Georgiana rejoiced in his discomfort. Although she could not deduce why he would hesitate to meet such a personage, she wanted to punish him.

His eyes narrowed, but Sophie would not be swayed now she had a fellow conspirator. He sighed and shook his head.

"I can see we shall not have a pleasant evening until my two girls are satisfied." He pushed ahead and cleared a path for Sophie and Georgiana. They reached Mrs. Leister, who was entertaining the group around her with a story about an inebriated theatre patron who'd jumped from his box down to the stage.

Her laughter stopped abruptly when she noticed Jonathan. Georgiana could not mistake the flicker of surprise and recognition in the other woman's eyes. If Sophie noticed, she made no indication. Mrs. Leister sank into a graceful curtsy. Georgiana couldn't help but stare. Sophie, too, was mesmerized.

"Mr. Lockewood. How lovely to find you here."

Sophie gaped while Jonathan bowed. "Mrs. Leister, may I present my wife, the former Sophie Mallory?"

The women curtsied, and Mrs. Leister smiled at Georgiana. "This must be your sister, Mr. Lockewood. My, she is all grown up now."

"And a married woman," Jonathan added. He nodded at Georgiana. "She is now Mrs. Jack Waverley." He punctuated each syllable of Jack's name in an odd way.

Mrs. Leister's finely drawn black brows quivered against her ivory skin for a second. "Congratulations, Mrs. Waverley. I hope you will be very happy."

"I will…I am." She glanced at Sophie to see if she had noticed anything amiss with the other woman's reaction, but Sophie merely clapped her hands to her chest as if she had received the most marvelous present.

"We will not detain you further," Jonathan said after an uncomfortable silence.

Mrs. Leister gave Georgiana a little smile. "Perhaps we will meet another time."

"I would like that, Mrs. Leister." She returned the smile, but her face felt frozen. She clutched the edges of her skirt with stiff fingers. As she walked away with her brother and sister-in-law, Georgiana couldn't help but wonder if Jonathan had been hesitant to introduce her to the actress for a particular reason. A reason that had to do with Jack. Before she could question him, the group in front of her parted.

"There he is! Over by the punch." Her knees wobbled a bit at the sight of her husband's broad-shouldered form, bedecked in gaudy attire from a curly black-haired wig that reached his waist to the shiny tips of his leather boots.

Jonathan's lip curled. "A pirate. I should have expected as much. Go to your husband, then, my dear, grown up sister. We will finish our conversation another time."

Georgiana hurried across the ballroom. She concealed a frown behind her fan. Why would he surround himself with beautiful women rather than seek her? She took a quick breath and tapped his shoulder with her fan.

"I've been waiting for you, sir," she said breathlessly.

He turned around, his lips curled into a smile from the previous joke. The sapphire blue eyes gleamed at her. Too late, she realized the straight, Roman nose was not the crooked one she knew and loved so well on her husband's face. His costume was magnificent, but she doubted Jack was so skillful as to be able to change the curve of his cheekbones or the color of his eyes.

Edward Mitford swept the buccaneer hat from his head and bowed. "I've been looking for you, my lady."

She nearly fainted at the reach of her mistake. To confront a gentleman—to confront *him* in such a public manner—oh, God, if Jack were inside the ballroom and came across her speaking to Edward—

She hastily curtsied. "Forgive me, sir. I mistook you for someone else." She clutched the full skirts of her costume and swept it out of the way so she could make a quick exit. The layers of petticoats were unyielding and she stumbled.

Edward caught her hand. "I know that voice! Wait, my dear goddess. Do not go."

He led her to the middle of the floor, while she tried vainly to remain fixed in place. She looked around frantically for Jonathan and Sophie, but they were admiring the statuary along the walls. One statue depicted a mother and child, and she knew her brother would not turn his attention from the marble infant soon enough.

Edward's hand possessed her waist. She was grateful her mask prevented him from recognizing her.

"Are you not the delightful younger sister of Lord Aubrey? You caught my eye at Vauxhall last week."

She was nearly dizzy from the waltz. His hand clutched hers in an iron grip. Even through the layers of both their gloves, she fancied she could feel his heated skin.

"No, I am not." She fought for control while her mind tossed around ideas of how to break away without his being the wiser.

"Ah, you are going to play the coquette." His fingers caressed her shoulder just above the line of her protecting stays. She shivered and he mistook her trembling for something else. The blue eyes leered at her. "I know I have seen you before, sweeting. Pray, remind me, and let us renew our acquaintance."

They reached the edge of the dance floor. Before she could reply, a gloved hand tapped Edward's shoulder. His smile vanished, and they stepped to the side. Jonathan glowered at them from behind his face paint and mask.

"Unhand my sister, you scoundrel."

Edward stepped back, his face blanched. Georgiana nearly laughed at his cowardice. "Forgive me, Aubrey," Edward began.

"I am not Aubrey, you damned fool." Jonathan stepped closer.

Edward's head bobbed from side to side as he examined first Jonathan and then Georgiana, and back again. His lips split into a grin. "Lockewood! And his engaging sister. What a delight to see you both this evening." He bowed to Jonathan, who refused to return the courtesy.

Sophie tugged on Jonathan's sleeve. "Please, my dear. Not here."

His gaze remained fixed on Edward. "Sophie, please take my sister and go to the exit. I will join you shortly."

"Georgiana sought me. Did you not, Georgie?"

His hand dropped from her waist. Georgiana took refuge beside Sophie. "Jonathan, I wish to go home." She glanced around the crowded ballroom for a sign of Jack, her face on fire. How would she ever explain to Jack she had mistaken Edward for him?

"I will have words with you, sir," Jonathan said, his voice tight.

"You will ignore our agreement?" Edward clicked his tongue against his teeth. "How unlike the imperturbable Jonathan Lockewood."

"Our agreement be damned, Mitford," Jonathan hissed. The seams of his white evening gloves strained against his knuckles. "Stay away from Georgiana, or I swear to God, I'll…"

"What's all this? Come, come, gentlemen." Lord Hetherington's jovial voice interrupted Jonathan's threat. He offered his arm to Sophie. "I came to seek a dance with your lovely wife, Lockewood. Do you mind?"

Edward took the opportunity to walk away while Jonathan glowered after him. He turned his gaze to her. Something shriveled inside her. His lips pinched shut and he gave a slight shake of his head.

"I did not know it was him," she protested.

He closed his eyes for a few seconds and when he opened them, smiled gently at her. "It matters not. The man is a toadstool among roses, no matter where the garden may lie. You are pale, my dear. Let us find Sophie and return home. You may stay with us tonight."

She almost heard the unspoken words he wanted to say. *Because your husband is not here to protect you*. She followed him to the farthest salon away from Edward, who pointedly ignored them. Sophie caught her eye as she whirled around the ballroom with Lord Hetherington. Georgiana gave her a tremulous smile, and her sister-in-law appeared relieved.

"What did he mean by an agreement with you?" She hadn't meant to speak so suddenly. Jonathan's jaw clenched.

"I have not the slightest idea what you are talking about."

Georgiana picked at a tiny morsel of cake. Sophie's

doctor had assured her the daily nausea would pass. She'd sworn him to secrecy, assuring him she would inform her brother and his wife of her not-so-surprising news, but first wanted to tell her husband. In truth, she wanted to create a home with Jack before introducing a baby into their odd little family, but wasn't sure how to go about it.

She glanced at her brother. Jonathan's cheeks bore two red spots like apples. She recognized from childhood the telltale sign he was lying. "Edward said something about an agreement. Why would you have any dealings with him at all?"

"I have none. There are none. Change the subject, or keep quiet."

"I must have heard incorrectly." Her voice betrayed her hurt.

Before he could reply, Sophie joined them, breathless and bright-eyed, but concerned for them both. "I think we may leave now," she said.

Georgiana could not have agreed more.

****

The smoke-filled room made his eyes water and his throat scratchy, but Jack remained at his table, watching with pretended boredom as the dealer distributed the cards. Inwardly, he cursed the late hour. Georgiana was probably dancing the evening away, enjoying her time with Lockewood and Sophie. He should be with her. But a man could not keep a roof over his head nor settle his debts with his tailor when he relied on a pittance from a grumbling old miser. Nor would he rely on the charity of the bewitching little wife he'd somehow acquired.

He paused a second before looking at his cards.

The queen of hearts stared mutely up at him. Her golden hair tumbled down her bosom, so like Georgiana's. Scowling, he sorted the cards in his hand, tucking the queen to the back.

"Tough luck there, old man," Lord Winston murmured, drawing on his pipe before washing down the smoke with a gulp of brandy.

"Pardon?"

"You looked dismayed for a moment. I wondered if it was your cards, but you never lose. Must be that delectable bride you took a few months ago. Lockewood's sister, am I right?"

"What about her?" Jack leaned back into his chair and slowly twirled the stem of his glass between his fingers.

Winston placed his hand on his chest. "Nothing, Waverley. I wonder why a man so newly wed into a fortune would choose to gamble every night as if his life depended upon it."

"Lockewood has his sister's fortune on a tight leash," another man muttered.

Heat rose rapidly up Jack's throat, settling somewhere between his eyebrows and his hairline. "Wonder all you like. I see no need in changing my old habits."

"Forgive me, Waverley. I meant no disrespect." Winston mirrored Jack's pose. He was nearly as big as Jack, which didn't worry Jack in the least. But it was Winston's penchant for revealing a cleverly hidden knife at the last minute of fisticuffs that did unsettle him.

"Fortunately, Winston, I am not of a mind to fight this evening. I came here to lose the remainder of my fortune."

"Then, I am your man." Winston settled in his chair and loosened his cravat. An hour passed, and then another. Lord Winston finally pushed back from the table and stretched, yawning elaborately. "Well, I'm off to my own lovely bride, though it's been a good twenty years since I called her so. Waverley, should you not also attend your wife? She's probably been weeping lo these many hours in your absence."

"Probably weeps when he's at home," Viscount Atherton, another player at the table, said with a smirk.

The others laughed, and Jack allowed the corner of his mouth to curl into the semblance of a grin.

"She doesn't weep at all, if you must know." He tucked his winnings into his purse, stuffing it inside his coat. "I have a marvelous understanding with her."

"She allows you to do as you please?" Atherton drained the last of his brandy. "My own wife promised just the same, and that was…oh, five years ago. I could gamble as I wished, and she would turn a blind eye to any…" He twirled the stem of his glass and winked at Jack. "…indiscretions."

"They are always accommodating in the beginning, Waverley," Winston interrupted. His eyes widened in sudden hilarity. "Aha! I see it is so! Have you advised your paramours to stay away? Paid off any Cyprians who may cause trouble at your hearth?"

The other men in the room had taken an active interest in the conversation. Some looked amused, while others shook their heads in sympathy. Flushing, Jack pulled at his neckcloth for air.

"Fortunately, I do not entertain half the poxied mistresses as you, Winston, so it was fairly easy to accomplish."

"Well, he hasn't had to give up gambling," Atherton remarked.

Winston nodded. "That will be next week. And wait until she's carrying one of his brats! I'll eat my hat if he doesn't vanish from all the gaming hells in the city before next Friday."

"I'll provide the broth to boil your hat, Winston." Jack rose from his chair, preparing to leave. Atherton guffawed.

"I will take that bet! Good luck, Waverley! Kiss your bride for us." He leered at Jack. "On second thought, do not bother. I'm sure she'll be most appreciative of companionship outside the marital bedchamber after a few more weeks of marriage to you."

Jack had never liked Viscount Atherton. Couldn't stand him, if truth be known. So he hardly minded at all when the viscount pretended to stumble against him when he rose to leave. He nearly sighed with satisfaction when the man raised his fist to strike, as it gave him an excuse to bury his fist into Atherton's stomach, dropping the man to the ground.

Chapter Thirty-Four

Jack appeared ghostlike in the misty garden. Georgiana blinked a few times until her vision cleared. The gravel crunched beneath his feet as he approached her, and she hastily swiped at the tears on her cheek.

"Did you receive my note? I sent word I'd miss the ball. I'm sorry I wasn't there." Jack unwound his neckcloth and stuffed it in his pocket. "It's beastly hot out here, Georgie. Why are you sitting outside with all the buzzing creatures of the night?" To prove his point, he swatted at a moth.

He sat beside her on the stone bench, but she rose a second later, taking a few steps away and keeping her back to him.

"I wasn't expecting you before midnight, and thought I would take a walk." She was glad her voice sounded steady. Involuntarily, she placed her hand lightly on her abdomen. Whether it was to reassure the tiny being within her or her own tattered nerves, she didn't know.

"I will join you, then."

She quickly faced him, wiping all traces of misery from her face. "No, please. You've been busy all day and probably wish to rest. I will be inside shortly."

He gazed down at her, the moonlight reflecting off his eyes until they resembled pools of mist. She fiddled with the edges of her skirt, her breath catching in her throat. Why would he not walk away but continue to stare at her like that? His hair was mussed, and she wondered if it were from his own restless fingers or one of his many paramours.

Miserable, she lowered her gaze and stared at the front of his chest. She pointed at his waistcoat.

"You've blood on your clothes, Jack."

"It isn't mine."

She lifted her eyes, questioning him with her silence. He brushed a strand of hair from her face, a smile touching the edge of his lips.

"Were you boxing again?"

"I never look this pretty when I've been boxing, my dear." His laugh faded when she turned and started for the bench again. "Are you in such a hurry to be rid of me, Georgie?"

She hissed through her teeth, her nerves shattered. "I do wish you'd stop calling me that. I have a proper name, you know." She clenched and unclenched her hands. No doubt, he'd been fighting over a woman. *Again*.

"I do know. In fact, I have made good on my promise to you in France to come up with a name more befitting the proper married woman you've become."

He wrapped the end of one long curl hanging down her shoulder around his finger and gave it a little tug. She tried to pull away, but he reached for her waist with his other hand, drawing her close even though she stumbled to remain where she was. She pressed her fists against his chest, but she might have been pushing against an oak.

"Do you not want to know what it is?" His voice was husky and low. She fought the quivering sensation rolling through her limbs.

"Most probably a variation on some embarrassing exploit you remember from my childhood. Perhaps you're going to remind me of the time I cut the whiskers off the stable kittens, and the spanking I received afterwards." She was horrified to hear the tremor in her voice. Even though she wanted to push away, she was drawn to him. It was inevitable as the moon controlling the tide.

He brushed his thumb across her cheek without commenting on her tears. "No, I think you will like this one. Although that story about the kittens is rather amusing. I'd forgotten until you reminded me."

She sighed with exasperation, though it was more to do with her own feelings than with him. "Please, do hurry and tell me. I wish to go back inside."

"I thought you were taking a walk."

"I'm...I'm done with my walk." In another moment, she would make a dreadful scene. She gulped quickly. "Tell me the ridiculous name so we may both have a laugh, and then we'll go into the house." *Until sunrise, when you'll leave me again and go to God knows whom. Perhaps the actress with the violet eyes.*

"I must whisper it in your ear."

He wore a decidedly smug grin on his face, which only deepened her agony. Another joke. Another endless string of teasing. This was her reward for marrying a man who was her older brother's friend. A man who remembered her in ruffled petticoats and her hair tied up in bows.

A man who could enjoy her company in bed but would never take her seriously as his wife.

She closed her eyes, heaving an irritated sigh as his

head lowered. His breath fanned her cheek, and she felt the lightest touch of his lips against the outer shell of her ear. Her heart thudded dully as she waited for him to speak.

"You are still my little Pudding Face, and always will be," he murmured, depositing a light kiss on her ear. She tried to back out of his arms, but he was infinitely stronger. She gave up trying to fight him. "And you will always be my Georgie." His lips brushed her cheek and swept across her face to her mouth, which trembled. "But you are also my Mrs. Waverley, and that makes you my heart…"

He kissed the left corner of her lips. "My soul."

Another kiss dropped on the right side. "And my love."

She forgot about pushing him away, because his lips were moving over hers. She stretched her arms to encircle his back, clinging to him so hard the buttons on his coat pressed into her skin through her silk gown. His hands skimmed her back and up to her face, holding and caressing, tugging at the hairpins until her hair tumbled in long waves about her shoulders. He parted her lips with a soft groan, kissing her deeply until she almost lost her balance from the force of her rising passion.

She wanted the moment to last forever but could not keep her secret from him any longer, regardless of the consequences.

"Jack…oh, Jack, I must tell you something." She was grateful for his tightening arms around her.

"Anything. What is it?" He framed her face with his hands, his lips a tantalizing inch or two away.

"I hardly know how to say it."

"Is it a dreadful secret, or something wonderful?"

Her heart felt like it had moved from her chest into her stomach. "Both."

"Ah. The very best kind. You may tell me anything."

She drew a deep breath, inhaling the fragrant roses in the garden and his musky scent at the same time.

"You must not gamble anymore. Or stay out all hours of the night with other women. And you must relinquish boxing, no matter how much you love it. I do not want you to injure yourself, because…because I need you." One sandy eyebrow rose on his forehead, but he remained silent, waiting for her to continue. "And your child needs you." She whispered this last, and dropped her head to his chest again.

He seemed frozen in place, and she feared he hadn't heard her. She stepped back, hesitating before looking at his face, dreading his reaction.

"Tell me again, my love, for I fear you just told me we are going to be parents."

She nodded uncertainly. "That is what I said."

"But—I do not understand. Why is it so terrible?"

"Because…" She broke away this time, and crossed her arms over her chest, shivering in the cool night air. "I cannot pretend anymore, Jack. Not to Jonathan, or…or to you." She drew a shuddering breath. "Especially to you."

He frowned. "What are you pretending?"

"This…this marriage between us. I know I proposed the idea to you and you were friend enough to assist me, but…" Her lip trembled as she forced back her tears. "It doesn't work. You were right, Jack." She laughed shortly. "I never thought I would say you were right about anything! But the kisses, and sharing a bed…and seeing you as a man, not a friend…" She blushed through her stammering. "I don't know how to explain it, but it changed our friendship, as you warned me it would. I laughed at you, but you were right, because…"

She stopped pacing. He walked to her and gripped her shoulders in his large hands.

"Just say it, Georgiana. I told you once, you can order me to do anything, and I will obey you." He was smiling but wasn't teasing her anymore. She sensed all humor from their youth had vanished between them, replaced with a new awareness and understanding.

"I do not wish to give you orders. I want you to feel it in your heart as I do."

"I am listening."

"It was always you." The words rushed from her before she could stop them. "Even with…with Edward, my heart has always been yours." She blinked rapidly, and he matter-of-factly brushed her tears with his fingertips. "I wanted to be your wife because I couldn't bear the thought of being anyone else's. At first, I thought it was because you had always rescued me in the past and could rescue me again. And…I know…" She couldn't look into his eyes anymore. His expression had grown far too serious for Jack Waverley. "I know you married me to save your inheritance, and I admit I have enjoyed sharing a bed as part of our arrangement…"

The sob tore from her before she could stop it. Horrified, she stifled the next with her hand, but he pulled it away and replaced it with his lips.

She expected the kiss to end in a few moments, but

he continued holding her, his lips drinking from hers as if she were his very sustenance. Her emotional outburst had exhausted her, and it was so comforting to be held in his strong embrace.

Gasping his name, she twined her fingers in his hair and tugged at his shirt with an overwhelming urge to feel his bare skin. He must have had the same urge, because he tugged at her bodice, pulling her gown past her shoulder until his lips burned the rising swell of her breasts.

"I love you, Jack."

His head lifted, and he regarded her in the moonlight. The buzzing insects and noisy frogs were silent. His eyes glittered like falling stars.

"That's all you've ever had to say, my little goose," he finally said, stooping to slide one arm behind her knees and pick her up. "I share your feelings."

"Then say it."

"I've been saying it all along. You've just not heard me."

She gazed into his eyes, her fears and doubts melting in the force of his love. "I hear you now."

"It's about bloody time." He lifted her easily and carried her into the darkness.

Chapter Thirty-Five

Jack restrained himself from singing aloud as his carriage took him from Kensington to his set at the Albany. He never thought he'd be so ready to abandon his bachelor quarters for gentle domesticity, but the moment had finally arrived. He planned to take his most important papers and personal effects back to Georgiana's home. His houseman would send the rest of his possessions to the new home he was happy to share with his bride.

The days since her revelation had passed in a blur. Jonathan and Sophie were ecstatic at the news; Jonathan, more so. Every time someone approached Jonathan at White's, he was the first to blurt out Jack would soon be a father. Jack even tempted fate and sent word to his grandfather, announcing the blessed event. He was mildly surprised but pleased when the old man sent a heartfelt letter in return.

For the first time in his life, Jack was blissfully aware he had proven the world wrong. He was in love. He wanted to shower Georgiana with every bauble and trinket he could, but it was obvious she only wanted his company. He was happy to oblige her, and if a pulled groin muscle and bruised lips were the price he paid for marital bliss, he would happily pay it.

His houseman was surprisingly absent, but Jack didn't mind. He whistled as he jogged upstairs to his drawing room. The door was ajar, and he heard the clinking of a glass against a crystal decanter.

"What the devil?" He stopped in his tracks and stared at his visitor.

Edward Mitford swallowed the finger of whiskey in his glass and gave Jack a half salute. "Hope you don't mind, but I let myself in."

The devious smile and narrow eyes had not changed much since they were schoolboys. Jack's right thigh muscle twitched. He'd forgotten the small knife he always carried in his boot. The life he'd led had carried with it a certain element of danger he was glad to give up but now regretted giving it up so soon.

"Help yourself to a drink."

"I did." Mitford settled into Jack's favorite chair.

"Let's not bother with pleasantries, Eddie," Jack said, purposely using the nickname the man detested. "What the hell are you doing here?"

"Straight to the point, as always." Mitford leaned his elbows on the arms of the chair. "First things first, Waverley. I must congratulate you on making a very fine match. A very fine match, indeed."

Jack envisioned walking across the parlor and seizing the man about the throat and shaking him until his mocking eyes bulged out of his head. "I thank the Lord every day for the blessing that is my wife."

Mitford's mouth twisted in a gloating smile that made Jack queasy. "I know some of the pleasures you're experiencing, Waverley. She was always a spirited girl. Especially where it counts."

Though his jaw hurt from grinding his teeth, Jack walked to the window as casually as he could and fiddled with a loosened latch while he scanned the street below. Except for the broad-shouldered behemoth standing watch by what he presumed was Mitford's carriage, there were few passersby. If he acted quickly, he could grab Mitford and dangle him out the window by his ankles until the wretch begged for mercy. Hell, he could even smash him to the pavement before the behemoth made it halfway up the stairs.

"Though I will not sink to your level, which would require me to dwell below the sewers of Cheapside, I will point out an obvious fact of which you are well aware. We both know Mrs. Waverley's reputation was *intact* when I married her." He couldn't bring himself to speak her name in the cad's presence.

"Oh, come now, Jack! We are both men of the world. Ladies may have *intact reputations* but may still enjoy other pursuits that would leave no physical evidence of their occurring."

Jack pictured Mitford's eyes popping out of his skull the tighter he choked him. He wondered if the man would soil himself when the final moment came and had to shake his head to dispel his murderous thoughts.

"If you have a wish to die by my fists or pistol, say so now. I'm available at any hour or location of your choice. This conversation and your presence are exceedingly tiring and revolting." He picked up a small bust of Plato and put it down again, realizing he was unconsciously considering hurling it through the front of Mitford's head. Splattered brains all over his carpet would require an explanation to the servants.

"I did not come here to provoke you, Jack, though I've always enjoyed bandying words with you. The last we spoke was…when was it?"

Fire rose to his jaw, but he held his tongue. Mitford's eyes widened, and Jack was reminded of the intensely charming, but always troubled younger man he'd known long ago.

"Ah, yes, you remember. I was up for the prize in Latin, which meant a well-placed position in the law. Someone—how the mind does fog a little with the onset of age—informed the master of my…proclivities. The prize went to someone else. Oh, yes, I do now recall who it was." His voice rose. The dark eyes went darker still, and Jack stifled a shiver at the transformation.

"It was you, Jack."

"You raped a coalman's daughter. You didn't deserve any sort of prize."

Mitford's lip curled. "She made up that lie because I would not marry her."

"Your word against hers. And she sported a bruised cheek and bloodied nose. Not very usual for a woman in love."

"Since when do you care about a servant?"

"Since when would any decent man allow a scum like you to debase another human being?"

He picked up the statue again. This time, he turned off the muttered warnings of his subconscious.

"I must say, Jack, your sense of honor has not wavered since you were a lad. You even married a woman of questionable reputation. Good for you."

"There has never been a speck of inquiry against her. You've known her and her family as long as I have. Say it again, and you will come to know Signore Plato very well." He hefted the bust.

"I apologize, then. Believe me; I did not come here

with a mind to provoke you. Your reputation far exceeds my own when it comes to brawling and murderous rampage."

"I can always hide your body. What's one more bloated carcass dragged out of the Thames?"

"I thought you might say that." Mitford looked too smug for Jack's taste. "You probably noticed a very large brute standing outside. If I do not walk out of this structure in half an hour, he is to summon the authorities to look to you." He clasped his arms in front of him. "Tell me, Jack—what would happen to *Mrs. Waverley* should you meet your demise at a hangman's noose?"

Forcing slow, even breaths, Jack glared directly into Mitford's eyes. "You have one second to explain your presence before I throw you out the nearest window, hangman be damned."

"There is a child, Jack. A bonny little boy kept in a very safe place with a young woman who will do anything I request. She has signed a statement attesting the child was left to her care by a wealthy young lady who wished to remain anonymous."

Jack snorted. "And you expect anyone to believe the child is Georgiana's?"

"They won't have to believe it, Jack. But the rumors and scandal it will cause her, Lockewood, his wife, and your old grandfather will be enough to censure them forever. Oh, the problems it will wreak with Jonathan's place in society. He will never forgive his sister. And poor Georgiana!" He clucked his tongue. "She will be devastated by the knowledge her husband could have helped quiet a tiny scandal but chose not to."

"What do you want?"

Mitford leaned back into the chair, settling his hands across his stomach. "I always took you for an intelligent man, despite being a snobbish brute. Five thousand pounds will ensure my lifestyle continues in the manner into which I've become accustomed."

Jack erupted in laughter. "I wondered how you acquired your extravagant lifestyle. Attached yourself to a rich widow, have you? Some dowager duchess paying you beneath the bed skirt while you enrapture her with loving attention?" He shook his head with disgust. Mitford's eyes hardened.

"My income is provided by someone close to you, Jack." His smirk revealed his white, sharp teeth. "If you wish, you may take away his shame and worry. Being that you are such a loyal friend."

"Even if I wanted to pay you, my inheritance is locked away until my grandfather dies. Can you wait another fifteen or so years? Waverleys are known to pass ninety."

"Clever, Jack. Georgiana is sitting on a fortune. She won't even miss it. You are her husband, and all her worth is tied to you. Besides, your generosity will take Lockewood off the hook with me."

A rushing noise in his ears nearly knocked him over. "You have been blackmailing Lockewood? Over what matter?"

"Your brother-in-law ensures I do not remember his sister's near-elopement with me. That, and other secrets he would rather his wife not know."

"If I pay what you ask, what is to prevent you from making a similar request a month or two hence?"

"I will give you the statement, and you may do

with it as you please. The bonny boy and his mother will continue their quiet, simple life out of the shadows of Kensington." His eyebrows rose with a false expression of earnestness. "What is your wife's comfort worth? Surely, you would not want her disturbed in her delicate condition. And Mrs. Lockewood must also be considered, Jack." He shook his head. "I pity the effect such terrible news will have on two women newly introduced to the purity of motherhood."

Before he could think, Jack seized Mitford by the lapels. To his credit, the man didn't flinch. His face only an inch or two from Mitford's, Jack had to restrain himself from strangling the bastard on the spot.

"What is it to be, Waverley?" Edward's voice choked out.

Struggling with his emotions, Jack finally released him. He dragged his hand across his jaw as if he'd received a physical blow, when Mitford had not touched him.

"I will have the funds deposited in your account tomorrow. I trust you have the information somewhere on your person?"

"As fate would allow, yes." Mitford removed a folded paper from inside his coat. "As soon as I am notified the funds are there I will deliver the statement to your club. I would not want it to fall into the wrong hands."

"If you don't have it, you'll beg for death when I'm done with you."

"Funny. Those are the same words Lockewood said when he found us at Gretna Green. Pity he didn't arrive an hour later. Georgiana was nearly panting in her state to remove her clothes."

Jack opened the door, almost ready to shove Mitford onto the landing below. "Unlike where my brother-in-law is concerned, mine is not a threat. Jonathan should have beaten you. I'd have killed you."

"Unfortunately for Georgiana her brother was too much of a gentleman."

Jack's hand clenched before he almost realized it. His bicep tensed as he drew back his arm and slammed his fist into Mitford's nose. He gave a satisfied grunt at the squishing sensation as his knuckles crushed the cartilage. Mitford doubled over, clutching his face while blood rapidly stained his ivory waistcoat. Jack flexed his fingers.

"Unfortunately for you, I am not."

Chapter Thirty-Six

Jack had not returned home. At first, Georgiana thought friends or business had detained him, but it was unlike him not to send word, especially if he knew she was expecting him. She walked restlessly around her bedchamber, straightening the drapes for the tenth time. When he hadn't appeared the first night, she put it down to his being busy. The next night she feared he was lying in a dark alley somewhere. Three nights later and still no sign of him could only mean one thing.

She sipped a cold cup of tea she'd forgotten earlier. Her body felt as if elephants had trampled her into the ground, leaving only her skeleton to walk the earth. Every sound or knock on the doors downstairs made her jump, but it was only a delivery or a servant coming and going.

She left her chamber and walked listlessly to the parlor. Her worst nightmare had come true. Their recent admission of love had been all on her side, as she'd feared. She had to know the truth, even if it killed her. The not knowing was the worst part. To hear him tell her he didn't love her was better than not knowing his mind at all. If he didn't come soon, she would go to the Albany herself in the morning and confront him.

Her butler appeared in the doorway and announced Jonathan's arrival. Almost giddy with relief for a familiar face, she met him in the doorway before he removed his hat. One look at his scowl made her heart stop.

"Are Sophie and the baby well? You do not bring bad news, I hope?"

Jonathan paced the floor while a servant brought in the teacart. "All is well at my house. I wish I could say the same here."

Georgiana felt a sudden urge to rub her throat. "What do you mean?"

"How did five thousand pounds vanish from your account?"

Had he shouted, the words could not have echoed more loudly in her ears. She had to force herself to remain upright rather than cower in the presence of his barely controlled rage.

"I haven't the slightest idea." She fought the icy flow of panic rising within her. "There must be a mistake. Banks make mistakes all the time." Jack had sworn off gambling, but even if he had returned to his old ways, it was not like him to take her money when he never had before.

"The Bank of England does not make mistakes." He leveled his gaze. "Where is Jack?"

"Jack?" She gripped the back of a chair to stop the room from spinning.

He snorted. "Yes, Jack. My best friend who is now your husband. The man who beguiled you and stole your innocence."

Her anger rose to his level. "He has stolen nothing. He wouldn't take the money, Jonathan. He and I…" Now would come the explanation that sounded so preposterous when she spoke it aloud.

"He and you what?"

"We…I…there's an agreement between us." If a blush could burn her skin and leave a mark, she feared a blotch on her face would appear any moment.

"An agreement."

She took his hand and kissed it. His fingers were stiff. "Please, dear brother, do not worry. He assured me he would never touch my money. He receives money from his grandfather. He promised to give up gambling and…" She chewed her lip. Perhaps it would be best if she didn't mention his former paramours. Her chest rose with a shaky breath. "If Jack did take the money, I'm sure it was for a good reason."

"He was seen last night in a rather unsavory gambling hell, as well as associating with the sort of people you'd rather know nothing about." She must have paled, because his face softened. He brushed a kiss across her forehead. "When do you expect him home?"

Unable to admit she hadn't heard from him, she turned her attention to the pot of tea, pouring two cups with a trembling hand. "He should be home shortly."

"I inquired of your butler, and he told me Jack hasn't been here in nearly three days."

She turned on him, though it was more from her own self-loathing than anger toward him. "That was not your place to do so! I am not a child, Jonathan, and you are no longer my guardian."

"Fine." He strode to the door and paused in the entry. "However, you are still my sister, and apparently, I am your only protector. I will make some inquiries. If Jack is up to no good, he will answer for it."

She clasped her hands, but they continued to tremble. A shiver began in her shoulders and coursed through her, rattling her bones. A look she had never seen before in her brother's eyes filled her with dread. She swallowed to moisten her tight throat.

"What are you going to do, Jonathan? Call him out?"

"For my sister's honor and that of her unborn child, yes." He stormed out of the room before she could beg him to change his mind.

****

Someone had stuffed cotton in his mouth. Try as he might to spit it out, it remained there. Sitting up in bed, Jack glanced around his room, trying to remember how he'd gotten home the night before.

A cool hand stroked his brow, and he blinked to clear the lingering traces of fog in his head.

"Look who's alive! My, but you gave me a scare, Jack."

"Sarah?" In a flash, he remembered seeing her at the Haymarket. Had they gone to supper afterwards? He fumbled beneath the coverlet and discovered to his relief he was still fully clothed. "What are you doing here?"

"I came by this morning to reassure myself you were still alive. I've never known you to drink until you couldn't stand."

She sat on the edge of the bed, almost prim in her posture. If he hadn't known she was the scandalous lady of the stage with not two, but three lovers in the House of Lords and a rumored husband no one had ever seen, he would have thought her a charitable society dame come to look in on a degenerate.

Slowly and painfully, the events from the past few days came back to him. Requesting Mitford's fee from the bank. Sitting at the first open table he found at the Cocoa Tree in order to win it back. Losing all he had with new debts to boot. Unable to return to Georgiana, he stumbled into the theatre as if a past memory had urged him. He must have gone to Sarah's dressing room afterwards and vaguely remembered sharing a coach with her, but there his memory ended.

He kicked his legs over the side of the bed. "I must get up. What time is it?"

"Almost noon. Are you certain you're not ill? Shall I summon a doctor?"

He brushed her hand away, following with a smile so as not to hurt her feelings. "I do not need a doctor. Thank you for coming. I shall be all right."

"I can make you something to eat. I have not forgotten my domestic skills."

He regarded her silk gown with matching pelisse and fur-trimmed collar. Diamond ear-bobs gleamed beneath her shining black hair. "You've done well for yourself, Sarah. You're a rich, successful woman. I hardly recognize the skinny chit on the stage, pouring out her heart for a few guineas a night."

She toyed with the satin trim on the coverlet. "It's been a long time in coming, Jack. Tell me…" Her dark blue eyes gazed into his. "Do you need any assistance? I heard you lost at Lord Wrothingham's table last night. I can make a loan to you."

He winced at the sudden pounding in his head. "I do not need any money, least of all, yours."

"I didn't mean to insult you. As an old friend…"

He leaned on his dressing table and stared at his haggard face. His eyes were bloodshot and heavy-lidded, and a mysterious bruise stained his jaw. "As my friend, Sarah, I beg you to stop worrying. All is well."

"I have a right to worry about you. If you are in any trouble…" She pressed her hand to her heart. "You are in trouble, aren't you?"

"Sarah, it's good of you to stop by, but I do not need your help. I don't need anybody's help. I'll figure this out for myself."

She rose from the bed and walked to the door. "Do you know what your problem is?"

"I'm sure you're about to tell me."

"You refuse to let anyone in, Jack. So many people care about you, yet you can turn your back on them in an instant." She snapped her fingers. "I know you are a caring, wonderful man, and yet…"

"You shared my bed years ago, Sarah. Forgive me, but that does not make you an authority on my life." His words hung heavily in the air. He regretted them the moment he spoke, but could not take them back.

She stared at him, giving him the same look he recognized from her performance as Lady Macbeth. "I know you better than you do. Tell me, Jack: is it blackmail or an error in enterprise to blame for your downfall?"

"Why must it be either?"

"Because you and I move in the same low circles, my dear. I was dining out before the play last night and overheard a man boast how he'd taken down his most hated enemy. Can you guess who this was?"

He heaved a sigh. "I have many enemies. One cannot seduce married women or clean out a gaming table without garnering a few enemies."

But she wouldn't be swayed. Were it not for the way she worried the doorknob between her fingers he'd have thought her as calm as a parson.

"It was Edward."

He did not respond. After a few moments of silence, she nodded briefly. "I'm going to send for tea, and then I'll let myself out."

She left him gazing at his reflection, though he no longer saw his face. Georgiana's trusting eyes were all he could see. He dropped his head, too wracked with shame to think on her. How would he ever face her again? How could he ask her forgiveness? He'd betrayed her as Lockewood predicted he would. Worse, he'd done the very thing he'd sworn never to do. The same thing Mitford had done.

Taken her trust and cast it aside.

"Jack?"

He knuckled his eyes fiercely in the hopes when he was finished he would recognize the man in the mirror. "I'll be right there, Sarah. Give me a minute."

There was a pause. "I'm not Sarah."

He turned slowly to face his wife.

Chapter Thirty-Seven

Georgiana struggled to see through the cold mist that threatened to suffocate her. The man before her could not be Jack, his face bruised, his linen rumpled. She'd been shocked when Mrs. Leister wordlessly showed her into the parlor. At first, she thought she had the wrong address, but the woman's nod of recognition assured her she was in the right place.

Despite his promise to give up his vices, it was obviously another lie in an apparent string of them. If Jonathan had not discovered the truth, how long would she have remained in the dark? Until all her money had vanished, presumably gone toward gambling and other women?

"Good day, Mrs. Waverley," Mrs. Leister said, as politely as if they had met at a garden party. "I'll be leaving, then." She stepped past Georgiana and went downstairs without looking back.

Jack stared at Georgiana. She hardly recognized him with his bruised jaw and dark patches beneath his eyes, whether from fighting or lack of sleep, she couldn't tell. His hair hung about his face in lank strands. But it was his eyes that made her wonder if she were really looking at the man to whom she'd so recently committed her heart. Dark and red-rimmed, they looked nothing like Jack's eyes.

"Would you care for a drink?" His voice cracked.

She gripped the edges of her skirt so tightly her hands were numb. "No."

"That was…"

"I know who she is. Jonathan introduced us at the masque."

He stared at her in silence for a few seconds. "You didn't tell me that before."

"I didn't think it important. At the time." She was inanely proud of herself for her steady voice and dry eyes. "I am here about an entirely different matter."

He poured himself a glass of brandy and drained it in one gulp. He didn't even bother to offer further explanation of his sorry state or his absence from her home. A small part of her felt she no longer cared.

"What is it then?"

"Five thousand pounds."

He set the glass on the table and gripped the edges, his shoulders hunched over. "Let me guess—your brother poked his nose into your business."

She refused to let her temper control her. "Someone needs to look after my affairs." Her voice sounded foreign, as if she weren't used to speaking. "Apparently, you are too occupied with your own. You promised you'd given up fighting and gambling, and…" She stopped before her voice threatened to shake from the force of her feelings. "And women like that tart who just skipped out of here. I suppose you'll say the dark shadow on your face is smudged dirt, and not a bruise."

"It isn't what you think." He turned around and fumbled with his shirt in an attempt to make himself look presentable. She crossed her arms to stop them from shaking.

"You have no idea what I think, Jack Waverley."

"Trust me, my dear, you have the wrong idea."

His betrayal nearly rocked her off balance, but she maintained her composure. Her gaze flickered to the open bedchamber door. "Had I come a half hour ago, I'm sure I'd have proven those words lies. Fortunately, I was detained by my brother's arrival."

He muttered a curse and set his hands on his hips. "I've no wish to quarrel, Georgiana. Sarah is not a tart…well," he flushed, "she is, but we do not have that sort of relationship. She's been a friend of mine for years. Were actresses part of your acquaintance, I'd have introduced you long ago."

"You seem to have a penchant for acquiring female friends, Jack. Was I not also your friend?"

In the past, he'd have laughed at her accusation and kissed her fears away. A shadow crossed his face, making him look older, sadder. "I have loved you all my life, Georgiana. And not only as a friend."

She gulped hard. "Why not have her around for tea, then? Perhaps she plays the violoncello. We could make up a trio."

He exhaled slowly. Funny, she almost wanted to see his familiar, almost mocking smile when she was wrong about something.

"You have nothing to fear from Sarah. She only arrived a few minutes before you did, to look in on me. I was going to leave this place and come home, but…" His flush deepened. "I was ashamed to see you, if you must know."

She took a step toward him and stopped. "We are family now, Jack. At least, I thought we were."

He nodded. "Exactly. I do hope we continue to be

349

so." His gaze flitted to her middle, and she instinctively folded her hands across her abdomen.

"Why did you take it?"

"I thought you didn't care about the money."

"I don't. In fact, you may have the lot of it."

"I do not want it." He sighed and shook his head. "I cannot tell you," he said quietly. "I wish I could, but…as horrible as it sounds, it is not something I want you to know. I've been trying to win it back these last few days, but it seems my luck has run out."

Her legs wobbled, and she gripped the back of a chair. He was at her side in the space of a heartbeat and wrapped his arm around her waist for support, but she pushed him away. A strong reek of his unwashed body reached her, and she turned her head away.

"I forgot I am not allowed to ask you about your private affairs."

"I have no private affairs. I told you the other night…when was it? Wednesday?"

She sniffed, trying to sound aloof, but instead sounded as if she had a cold. "How sweet of you to remember the night you first told me you loved me. Forgive me. You never actually said the words. My memory is as unreliable as yours."

Without responding, he returned to the sideboard and poured another glass of brandy. "Drink a little of this."

"I do not want anything." Tears filled her throat, straining her voice. He handed her the glass, and she took it despite her protestation. The liquid seared her throat. "It's not about the money. You lied to me. The fighting, the…" She took another drink and sputtered. He tapped her on the back, but she ignored the gesture.

"All I ever wanted, Jack, was…."

He took the glass from her and clasped her hands. "I have done nothing to break my vow to you, Georgiana. Believe me, there have been no other women since I escorted you to France."

"But…but Danielle…"

The corners of his eyes crinkled. "I wanted you to be jealous."

"Why?"

"Because you swore never to love me, and I couldn't accept it."

"If you accept it now, then tell me why you took the money."

His shoulders sagged. "I cannot, but believe me, it wasn't anything to do with us, or to harm you in any way. Quite the opposite, in fact. I swear it on my father's grave."

"Do not swear, Jack." She shook her head. "Jonathan is very angry. He thinks you are no better than Edward was. Worse, perhaps. I'm inclined to believe him."

He swore beneath his breath. "I am not the man your brother and you fear. I will explain everything soon, but not now. Please, do not ask me."

"I won't." She turned on her heel and walked unsteadily toward the door. "Goodbye, Jack. You needn't return the money. In fact, you may have it all, to throw away on whatever or whomever you like. I will not stop you."

"Where are you going?" He followed her.

She opened the door and stepped into the corridor. "To Jonathan's. I will be out of your way."

He caught her elbow; too roughly. She raised her

hand to strike him. He released her, but the look in his eyes told her he almost welcomed the blow.

"You can't leave, Georgie."

"I can, Jack. I can do anything I please. Remember? That was the sole foundation of our arrangement."

He gripped the door, and she noticed the bruises on his knuckles.

"You have everything you ever wanted, Jack. All of my fortune, gambling as you like, boxing, and your women." It took the last bit of her strength to stare directly into his eyes. "Congratulations. All it cost you was a few months playing the husband to a silly, infatuated girl."

No trace remained of the humorous friend he'd always been. If pressed, she could not explain how he looked but wished she'd never have to see his expression again.

"You don't know how very wrong you are."

"But I do, Jack. I was wrong to try to make you into something you are not. Something by your own admission, you never can be."

"What is that?"

"My husband."

It was torture to stare into his eyes. She waited for him to look away, but he didn't. A muscle quivered in his jaw, and she longed to bury her head in his shoulder while he assured her everything would be all right.

But he did not speak words of love or beg her forgiveness. She would have taken any confession or explanation, regardless of how preposterous, but he was silent. She turned before he could see her tears.

"Goodbye, Jack. Thank you for helping me in

France. I will always treasure those memories. I like to believe not all of them were lies."

With a little shrug, she slipped through the doorway. In her mind, he was already behind her. Running down the stairs, taking them two at a time, to catch her. Clasping her in his arms before she climbed into the waiting coach. Covering her face, her eyes, her mouth with burning kisses. And she melted into him, her lips answering his.

The stairs echoed only one pair of footsteps. The door closed behind her soft as a whisper. He had not followed.

Chapter Thirty-Eight

"This is all rather untoward of the bank to discuss these matters with you, Miss Lockewood." Mr. Chadwick leaned forward on his steepled fingers to shove his wire-rimmed spectacles up his nose. Georgiana arched an eyebrow and sat up straighter.

"It's Mrs. Waverley now, Mr. Chadwick."

He flushed. "Yes, of course." He opened his hands, palms out. "I regret I am still unable to tell you…"

"The money belongs to me, regardless of what the bank says, Mr. Chadwick. My husband has specified to the bank I have joint control." She clenched her hands in her lap. It wouldn't do to anger the banker. She tried a different tack. Fluttering her eyelashes, she touched her cheek with her gloved fingertip, as if she were swiping a tear. "My poor husband has been struck with apoplexy, and the doctors have no idea when he'll recover. He wanted me to take an accounting of the funds recently removed from the account. I do not know what will happen if I return without it." She buried her face in her hands and gave a loud sob.

The screech of the chair on the parquet floor assured her of her convincing act. A spotless white handkerchief was poked into her hands.

"Please, Mrs. Waverley—do stop crying. I will see what I can do to assist. Your family's business has always been a priority with our bank."

She patted his hand. "Dear sir, I am indebted." She allowed the tears to slip unchecked down her face, unsure of how many of them were in pretense or because she really did want to cry.

He cleared his throat and bowed. "It will take me some time, ma'am. I will send in some tea." He scurried from the room and she couldn't blame him. Not many men were comfortable around a weeping woman.

The second the door closed, she wiped her face and took a deep breath. She must remain calm and not allow emotion to get the better of her, especially now it seemed she would be on her own. Wincing at the unbearable thought, she rose from her chair and peered out the window at Threadneedle Street below. A sea of black hats floated amongst the carriages and horses. Jonathan might even be among them. Jack would surely be out of place among these men of industry. Her chest constricted, and she wished she could loosen her corset, but that was impossible, here in the venerable building. The modiste had altered her wardrobe to accommodate her budding figure, but it never seemed enough. Thoughts of the baby melded with the dull, throbbing ache of her loneliness for Jack.

No longer having to fake her depression, she returned to her chair as Mr. Chadwick entered the office, a sheath of papers in his hands. His forehead gleamed with perspiration, and a whiff of body odor settled around her as he walked past her. He placed the papers on the desk.

"I have the answer for you…for your husband, I mean." He fidgeted with the edges of a page. "I hope this is not a delicate matter, but it appears the sum of five thousand pounds was written into an account held by one Maisie Smith."

She blinked. "Who?"

"I do not have any more information, Mrs. Waverley. Perhaps—" He appeared to study her trembling hands, and she realized she'd probably blanched at the news. "Is there something amiss?"

"Uh, no. No, everything is fine." She stood hastily, nearly knocking over her chair. "I had forgotten about my husband's cousin, Maisie Smith." She nearly choked on the lump of tears rising in her throat but regained control of her emotions, at least as far as displaying them. "Indeed, my husband has asked me to place a visit to her at once. Can you tell me where I might find her?"

"I will have to search for that information. I do not know if I have an address. These papers only reveal a name."

She smiled so broadly her teeth hurt. "I am sure a clever man like you can find it if he wanted to." Her eyelashes fluttered delicately against her cheek, and she watched the slow flush burn his face until he tugged at his collar. He cleared his throat.

"I am sure something may be done. I will have this information in a day or two, Mrs. Waverley."

"That will be too late." She clutched her hands together. "I must pay this visit today. It is imperative."

The sigh emitting from his lips was barely noticeable. He nodded. "Very well. If you will excuse me a moment, I will see what the clerk can find out." He bowed before exiting the office.

Georgiana collapsed into her chair, covering her face with her hands. Every hope of a happy life with

Jack had crumbled like burned toast. She didn't know what was more upsetting—that he'd gone ahead with the freedom she'd promised or that she was surprised he had. Hadn't he warned her of this very thing? He had lived a sordid bachelor life for so long she was a fool to think he could give it up for a childhood friend he enjoyed teasing occasionally. Not to mention, a baby on the way to further tie him down.

Mr. Chadwick's return interrupted her thoughts. She fought to remain silent while Mr. Chadwick took his time walking around his desk before handing her a slip of paper.

"Not a very nice neighborhood, I'm afraid. Still, it is generous of your husband to care for a relative."

Georgiana scanned the paper quickly. "This is exactly what I need. Thank you very much."

"I'm glad to be of service to you and your family."

She folded the paper and stuck it in her reticule, then paused at the door. "Please, Mr. Chadwick, keep our meeting confidential. I would not want my poor brother to have the wrong impression."

"Is Mr. Lockewood unwell, too?" The bulbous nose crinkled.

She feigned another attack of nerves. "Ah, yes. Yes, he is. It is so very sad."

"Very sad, indeed." He opened the door for her. "Please give my warmest regards to your husband and your brother." She held up her finger to her lips and arched her eyebrow. He nodded hastily as sweat broke out on his balding pate. "Naturally, you will not, since this meeting never occurred." He gave her a conspiratorial wink, and she held out her hand.

"Thank you, dear Mr. Chadwick."

He bowed over her hand.

A few minutes later, Georgiana sank back into the cushioned seat of her waiting carriage.

"Home, ma'am?" Roberts asked.

She pressed her fingertips to her eyes. "No. I have another stop. In Cheapside." Roberts took the address from her as easily as if she'd asked him to drive her to Grosvenor Square. She stared out the window with blurred vision as the gray buildings and crowded streets flew by. If only she could order Roberts to keep driving and never stop until he reached the sea.

Where she would throw herself into it.

Chapter Thirty-Nine

Men loitered in the alleys and huddled in the narrow doorways of Harkham Street. A few women walked slowly down the street in pairs or singly, and Georgiana met the gaze of one as her carriage drove by. The smeared cosmetics, the blowsy hair—underlined by her absent corset and stained gown—answered any questions she might have had.

She leaned back into the confines of her carriage, shivering beneath the rug. What business could Jack have had in this neighborhood? Maisie Smith, that's what.

Almost nauseated with nerves and her growing condition, Georgiana jumped when the carriage halted before a weathered building, its windows streaked with soot and grime. Roberts opened the door for her, not even bothering to hide his suspicious glance.

"Shall I accompany you inside, ma'am?"

She squared her shoulders with more bravado than she felt. "That will not be necessary." A few men looked at her with leering interest, and she touched Roberts' arm. "Stay close."

He tugged his forelock and remained beside the carriage, his arms folded across his barrel chest. Were her nerves not so on edge, she might have laughed at his fierce demeanor.

She walked up to the door and straightened her

bonnet, then rapped smartly on the wood. The plaintive wails of a baby inside made her pause, and just as she changed her mind and prepared to turn back, the door opened a crack. A girl about her age peeked through the opening, her wide brown eyes offset by a smattering of freckles on her nose and a mop of red curls poking from beneath her dingy cap.

Her face brightened as she took in the sight of Georgiana on her doorstep. "Come in, my lady." The girl bobbed a nervous curtsy, patting the loose strands of hair hanging over her forehead. "Please excuse the clutter. It's not very tidy, I'm afraid. We don't have many visitors."

Georgiana wanted to be cruel, but the feeling died at the girl's earnest smile. She stepped into the tiny foyer, and they stared at each other. "You must be Maisie Smith." She didn't know why she'd said such a preposterous thing, but the girl bobbed another curtsy. "Surely, you must know who I am."

"Oh, yes, my lady. Of course." Her lips quivered into a smile. "He said you'd come by. That I was to accept any help you could give."

"Help?" Her fingers tightened around her reticule string. "Oh, with the baby, you mean." The gall of him! That she would assist in any way with his bas...

The crying baby she'd heard before began wailing again, the sound almost vibrating the thin walls. Maisie turned on her heel with a backward glance. "He's in here, milady. Do you want to see him?"

"I'd rather not," she said sharply, but the girl looked so crestfallen, she relented. Georgiana followed her into a cramped parlor that also doubled as a bedroom. She wrinkled her nose at the squalid conditions. "When are you moving?"

"Eh?" Maisie picked up a wrapped bundle from a woven basket. "This is my home, milady. I know it ain't much, but it's a roof over my head." She indicated the baby with a nod. "This is him, milady. This is my Tibby."

"Tibby?" Good lord, could Jack not suggest a more proper name? Even if the child would never follow its father into society, at least he could bestow a proper name on it. A wave of nausea swept through her like a whirlwind. She gripped a table edge. Maisie frowned.

"Are you all right, milady? Would you like to sit?"

Georgiana sank into a chair that creaked in protest. "Thank you," she murmured, unable to keep up her stern visage any longer.

The girl leaned forward, the baby in her arms. "Would you like to hold him, milady?"

"Not really. No, thank you." But she was too late. The bundle was thrust into her arms. Blinking back sudden tears and fighting the urge to give the child back, she stared at the round, pink face. "He's rather beautiful, isn't he?" she asked, startled at the realization. She wondered if her baby would resemble its little half-brother with the wide, blinking eyes and rosebud mouth.

"He is, milady." Maisie knelt by Georgiana's feet. "He's the image of his father. The same eyes and hair," she added proudly.

Biting her tongue, Georgiana could only nod. "I wonder why you are still in this household, miss. I thought…he…" It was impossible to use Jack's name to this girl. "I thought he was moving you to better quarters."

Frowning, Maisie lowered her gaze. "No, milady. He said I must stay here until he has the funds to set us up proper."

Muttering under her breath, Georgiana stopped when Maisie's gaze was upon her again. "Apparently, five thousand pounds doesn't go very far these days." It wasn't Maisie's fault. She seemed an ignorant country girl who could easily be seduced by a man half as charming and handsome as Jack. Could she really blame her? But her words were disturbing. Could Jack really be thinking of keeping house with such a creature? It would mean the ruin of him.

And of her.

"Have you no family?" *Besides my cheating dog of a husband, of course.*

The curls bounced on Maisie's shoulders as she shook her head. "None, miss. They're long dead. Tibby and his papa are all I have in this world."

Georgiana's throat constricted and she cleared it before speaking. "Something must be done for you and Tibby. I will ensure that it happens."

The pale cheeks flushed pink. "Oh, thank you, milady, thank you! I never dreamed the Charitable Angels would help with more than some food and nappies."

Georgiana stared at her. "The what? Angels, you say?" The girl nodded. "Do you not know who I am?"

"You are from the…the Charitable Angels. Edward said he'd sent…"

"Edward?" Georgiana almost cried out the name. "You mean Jack."

"Jack?" Her rosy blush faded. "Who's Jack?"

"The father of your child."

Their raised voices awoke the sleeping infant. The lower lip, so plump and full, quivered. His paper-thin eyelids crinkled, and Tibby let loose with a lusty cry. Georgiana jiggled him slightly. Maisie reached for him and held him to her shoulder.

"You are mistaken, begging your pardon, milady. His father's name is Edward."

"Perhaps that's what he calls himself to you," she retorted. "I should know, for I am his wife."

"His wife?" The girl's face screwed up like her baby's, and Georgiana hastily patted her arm. "He told me he would send one of the Charitable Angels 'round. Not any wife."

"I am not an angel." Georgiana stood briskly and fumbled with her reticule. "I can leave you some money. See that you buy some food and things for…for Tibby."

"Oh, thank you, milady." Maisie clutched her baby with one arm and wiped her tears with the sleeve of her other. "He's a good baby, is Tibby."

"I'm sure he is." Blinking back tears, Georgiana headed for the door. "I wish you well. You and…and little Tibby."

"Thank you, milady." The girl's voice was a whisper. She lifted the baby onto her shoulder, and pulled off his cap to stroke his hair. His curly black hair.

Georgiana frowned. "I thought he has his father's hair."

"He does." Maisie giggled, her earlier tears forgotten. "All that thick, dark hair. Black as a cat's." She smoothed her hand over the little head. "Just like his father."

Georgiana released the latch on the door. "No, miss." She stepped back into the room, a sense of hope merging with relief that almost weakened her legs. "Jack's hair is golden."

The girl's eyebrows lifted. "No, no. It's black as this, milady."

Inhaling slowly, Georgiana stood in front of her and tentatively patted Tibby's firm little back. "My husband's name is Jack Waverley."

The girl frowned. "That wasn't his name at all, milady. Tibby's father, I mean."

"What is his name?" She knew the answer before the girl uttered it.

"Edward. Edward Mitford's 'is name."

****

Roberts stopped at the Albany, but Jack wasn't home. Impatient to find him and admit she'd misjudged him, Georgiana decided to wait. She paced the parlor, avoiding the crates and trunks of his belongings, which had not yet made their way to Kensington Gardens. The sight of his worldly possessions packed in a few boxes tore at her heart. Had it only been a few days ago when they'd spoken of their future together?

Taking a seat at the desk by the window, she stared down at the busy street, barely aware of the action below. All she could hear was Maisie's voice, proclaiming Edward the father to her son. None of it made any sense. Why would Jack give money toward the wellbeing of a woman he so obviously did not know? More to the point, why was he funding Edward's child?

She rubbed her temples and focused on the street, hoping without any real conviction to see Jack, carefree and smiling as usual. There was no sign of him. Sighing, Georgiana lay back against the chair and tapped her fingers atop a stack of letters. His grandfather's signature on one caught her eye. She pulled it free and shot a glance at the door to ensure no one would catch her reading his mail.

In brief, harsh terms, his grandfather begged Jack to reconsider his stipend. *"Accept what is rightfully yours. A gentleman cannot survive on boxing and gaming."*

She replaced the letter, confusion outweighing her surprise. Why would Jack decline his allowance? If he refused her money when she'd offered, why would he then take it behind her back? Most vexing of all was the connection of Edward and Maisie, who were somehow involved.

"Mrs. Leister, ma'am."

The butler's voice made her jump. Before Georgiana could question the woman's audacity to come to her husband's home, the butler staggered against the doorframe as the actress pushed past him, expertly sweeping the train of her dark blue gown out of his way.

Georgiana's hands clenched at her sides. She pushed up from the chair and leaned into the table edge for support.

"Mrs. Leister…."

The actress nodded curtly. "I've no time for pleasantries, missus." She dismissed the butler with a sharp nod. "I would have sent a message, but there's no time."

"No time for what?"

Mrs. Leister reached into her beaded reticule and

withdrew a folded paper. She handed it to Georgiana. "I found this."

Georgiana scanned the note, trying to interpret the strange instructions and times contained upon it. "I don't understand." Her irritation at the woman's presence dissolved. Jack's former—whatever she used to be—was certainly not at the Albany for a tryst. It was almost as if she'd come to see Georgiana, not Jack.

"It's Jack's instructions to his second, Talbot Reynolds. He must have made another copy. This one was crumpled up." When Georgiana still hadn't registered the information, Mrs. Leister pursed her lips. "Jack is going to have swords with him."

She didn't have to ask with whom. She sank back into the chair. "Edward." Shock and disbelief mingled as she struggled with the reality of what was about to happen.

"Yes." Mrs. Leister paced the room, the heels of her shoes marking the worn carpet in front of the hearth. "Before you came the other day, Jack told me what he'd done."

Georgiana shook her head, as if the motion could also clear her worries. "I don't understand."

"Edward blackmailed Jack. You suspected something about your missing money. Jack told me Edward came to him and made certain accusations he could not ignore." Her carmine lips curled into a sneer. "I'm not surprised at how low he'd sunk. He was always the most unmitigated scoundrel."

"I had no idea you knew him."

Mrs. Leister laughed softly. "I knew them all, dearie, when they were students. Jack and Edward and...your brother...used to come to the theatre to see me. I was friends with them all." She spoke this last in a dignified manner, as if she dared Georgiana to judge her.

Georgiana bit her lip. Whatever happened in the past was long over. Besides, there wasn't time to be jealous or suspicious. Jack needed her.

"What do we do to stop him?"

Mrs. Leister's sigh revealed she was helpless in the matter.

Georgiana stuffed the note into her reticule. "May we not go to the authorities? Surely, there must be something we can do."

"I do not know where they will meet. Short of killing Edward ourselves, there's not much we can do."

Georgiana hesitated. She had never hurt a living thing in her life. Couldn't bear the sight of little Tibby, Edward's bastard child, living in dismal surroundings. So why did the idea of killing Edward not disturb her in the least?

"Where is Jack now?"

"I don't know. Preparing for their duel, I expect."

"Then I shall find Edward."

Mrs. Leister's brows drew together. "He cannot be reasoned with, Mrs. Waverley."

Georgiana laughed sharply. "I do not intend to reason with him."

"It won't matter if you find him. His enmity with Jack began years ago. He's already made his decision, and once Edward Mitford makes up his mind, there's no stopping him." She shook her head. "You don't know him like I do, dearie."

Georgiana rang for her carriage. "And you do not know me."

Chapter Forty

The carriage circled St. James's park twice, but Georgiana was unable to locate Edward. Roberts inquired at Edward's usual haunts, generously provided by Mrs. Leister, but they had turned up nothing. The opinion at Edward's club was that he took a daily constitutional in the park with his newest conquest: a rather plain widow in possession of a large fortune, but it seemed as if the park would also yield nothing.

The day was unusually sunny, the clouds scattered enough to allow children to run through the grounds, their shrieks filling the air, but Georgiana hardly noticed. Within the course of a week, her life had gone from filled with the promise of a future with Jack and their unborn child to a nightmare threatening their happiness. She hoped to end the nightmare by addressing its personification.

One good thing had come of Edward's deception. She'd sent her housekeeper to fetch Maisie and Tibby and bring them safely to Kensington Gardens. Heaven only knew what she'd do with them, but her conscience would not allow her to leave Maisie to the squalid life to which Edward confined her.

She was about to give up her search and tell Roberts to take her home when a small crowd parted across the green. Edward's tall, unmistakable form was visible among them.

Roberts stopped the coach and a footman handed her out. Straightening the short edges of her spencer, Georgiana ambled across the path toward him, pretending she was just another lady of quality enjoying the park. Edward didn't notice her. He leaned down to speak to his companion, a richly dressed older woman who clutched his arm and giggled at every word he spoke.

She wished she could take the woman aside and tell her exactly with whom she was involved, but it wouldn't make a difference. Edward could be quite charming when he wished. She of all people knew that.

He dressed more elegantly now than when she'd known him, what felt like a lifetime ago. If Jonathan hadn't come after her—if there hadn't been a delay at the crossroads when another carriage had broken a wheel and they'd stopped to help—it could be her, instead of poor Maisie Smith, caring for his child. She stifled a shudder and forced herself to place one foot before the other. Each step brought her closer and closer to the thing she dreaded, and her courage began to fail.

His companion noticed her and said something to Edward, who glanced at her twice before stopping in his tracks. Dark violet bruises beneath his eyes and a crooked set of his nose marred his usual beauty. He bowed extravagantly when she stood before him.

"My dear Mrs. Waverley."

She curtsied, every bone in her body rebelling at showing him any civility.

"I'd like a word with you, Mr. Mitford, if you please." She gazed directly into his eyes. His mocking smile threatened to disarm her.

"I am your humble servant." He glanced at his companion. "Will you excuse me, Blanche? I must see to this charming lady's demands."

The woman curtsied uncertainly at Georgiana, who nodded back. When she'd gone on a few paces, Georgiana turned to Edward, whose icy gaze hadn't wavered.

"To what do I owe the honor, Georgiana? Or have you already tired of that rogue Waverley? I'd be happy to service you in any way you desire."

She drew in a slow breath so he wouldn't notice her agitation. "You will stop blackmailing my family immediately."

He chuckled as if she had told him a joke. "Your esteemed brother and husband have been making false accusations."

"My brother?"

His brows furrowed. "Did Jack not tell you everything?"

"He didn't have to. I've met Maisie Smith."

"Who?"

"The mother of your child."

"Ah, yes. You are referring to the mother of Jonathan's child. Or the caretaker of yours." His smirk returned. "I can never remember who the little bastard belongs to."

"My child? What are you talking about?"

He seemed taken aback. "I thought you said Jack told you."

Her lips parted to speak, but she couldn't fathom any sort of response. He sighed in a show of boredom.

"I informed your husband of the sorry truth that he is married to a woman who, in the impetuosity of youth, bore a child out of wedlock. The unfortunate Maisie Smith will sign a statement affirming she is raising the child as a favor to the Lockewood family." He smiled slightly, his eyes narrowing. "He didn't tell you."

"A preposterous lie does not merit a reply."

"Your husband didn't seem to think so."

She almost felt a physical blow in the pit of her stomach at the realization of what Jack had done. His nights of gambling and boxing had not been a result of his refusal to accept responsibility but as a means of replacing the money before she noticed it was gone. Just as he had said.

"He was not paying you to save his face, but mine." Her voice quavered. She lifted her chin, every nerve sparking with action. "It matters not whose child he is. You will cease your threats, or pay the consequences."

"If I am arrested, you can be assured your husband's and brother's pasts will come to light. The respectable Jonathan Lockewood may not want you to open a trove of his indiscretions. Nor will Jack's esteemed grandfather be pleased with revelations his heir has married an immoral girl. Tell me…" He rubbed his jaw, staring directly into her eyes, trapping her. "Does Jack know the extent of your wantonness? You were quite the eager one in our carriage ride to Gretna Green."

She gritted her teeth. "We both know nothing happened. You were drunk." Memories flooded her, all sour and bitter. "And cowardly," she couldn't help but add.

His eyes flashed. "You didn't seem to mind, then. And from the way you are looking at me, probably wouldn't mind now. Jack's extramarital activities must be taking their toll. Did you know he once shared the beds of five different women in a single week?" He clucked his tongue. "I don't know how you can stand being married to such a rogue."

"I did not come here to discuss the past with you, Mr. Mitford. Only the future. You may say what you will about Jack or me. Do what you like with spreading scandal. But I believe Maisie will take my side. Especially since she is now under my protection."

He didn't have to speak. His eyes widened almost comically, but he didn't reveal any more of his feelings. "Bravo, Georgiana. You've solved the issue of Maisie's brat. However, your brother always had an eye on rising through the government. It's a pity how a scandal can destroy a man's aspirations. One false word carries more weight than the truth."

"My brother is secure in his marriage and his friends. You, unfortunately, do not have such security and must rely on deceit to move forward. I wonder what lies you've told that poor woman." She indicated his lover with a nod.

"Since when did you become a supporter of the downtrodden? Spoiled Georgiana Lockewood, who stomped her feet and cried her way through life until she got exactly what she wanted?"

She rocked forward in her desire to scratch his eyes out. "I grew up, Edward, which is more than I can say for you. You are still the conceited, self-serving boy you always were."

"And you loved me in spite of it."

It was the only weapon he had, and he knew it. A lump rose in her throat, but she realized with surprised relief it was not of tears. It was determination and conviction.

"Yes, Edward, I loved you." She chose each word carefully. "Or what I thought was love. I only discovered what true love is when I married Jack. You will never know how precious that can be. You will remain alone, regardless of how many rich widows you entice, or how many innocent heiresses you connive upon. You will die alone and unloved."

He stared at her with a mixture of amusement and confusion plain on his chiseled features. "That's a pretty speech. But how will you accomplish saving your brother's and husband's futures?"

"You will not receive another penny from either Jonathan or me. Write the newspapers. You may advertise around the country my brother's and husband's supposed misdeeds all you like. I do not care what you do. But you will stay out of our lives from here on."

Turning on her heel, she walked deliberately away from him, keeping her back as straight as a pole even though her insides quivered.

"What if I do not obey? Perhaps we can come to our own special arrangement."

Before she considered her actions, she spun around and walked back, her heels squishing into the damp grass. She looked directly into his eyes.

"If you ever speak to me or my family again, I will see it is the last thing you do. Further, you will abandon this duel you've arranged with Jack."

"Fighting his battles for him, are you? A cheap little thing like you?"

An image of Jack appeared starkly in her mind as

373

he demonstrated the punch that had knocked out *"the biggest Irishman I'd ever seen, Pudding Face. I drew back my arm like so…"* Her bicep tensed as she lifted her arm. *"And then I crunched my fingers into a hammer."* Her knuckles cracked as she gripped an invisible ball in the center of her hand. Her nails dug into her palm through her thin gloves. *"The poor bastard didn't know what was coming."*

Edward's high-pitched scream broke the still afternoon. Blood streamed between his fingers and spattered his waistcoat as he clasped his re-broken nose.

Georgiana shook her hand and gingerly flexed her fingers. "I now understand why my husband is so enamored with boxing. It was rather enjoyable crushing your nose. Thank you, Mr. Mitford, for being such an amenable object of demonstration."

Some boys playing on the grass laughed and pointed. One elderly gentleman out for a stroll tipped his hat. Edward's companion pointedly turned and headed the opposite way. Georgiana hastened to her waiting coach.

Roberts handed her in, his face carefully blank as if he'd just fetched her from a social appointment. "Home now, ma'am?"

"No, to my brother's house. And not a word of this to anyone."

Roberts cleared his throat and shook out his handkerchief, which he handed to her. "You've a spot of blood on you, ma'am."

She brushed at the red drop on the front of her pelisse. "So I do."

Chapter Forty-One

Jonathan got into the coach without a word, as if he sensed Georgiana's arrival was of an urgent matter. She told him all she knew in two minutes. When she was done, he shook his head, his eyes sorrowful.

"I should have told you both what Mitford had done to me. But I was…" He clasped Georgiana's hand. "I was ashamed. My past is something I wish to keep from Sophie."

"It isn't worth it, dear brother," she whispered, squeezing his hand. "Sophie will forgive you anything. You should have told Jack when Edward first came to you."

"How could I?" His eyes were shadowed and creased. "After I'd accused him of marrying you for your fortune, how could I tell him I was living my own lie?"

"He cares for you as a brother."

"I know." He kissed her forehead. "We should get you home, dear. I will seek out Jack myself. This night air is not good for you or the baby." Georgiana silenced him with a look. He grinned. "I keep forgetting you are an old married woman and need not listen to a bossy big brother any longer."

"I keep reminding Jack the very same thing." At the mention of his name, her heart threatened to burst through her chest. She was nearly bouncing in her seat, stricken with anxiety and the urge to find him soon, soon, soon...

An hour passed, and then another. Bleary-eyed, she'd nearly fallen asleep on Jonathan's shoulder when he gently shook her. Sitting up straight, she peered through the carriage window at the darkness by the edge of a wooded park. The eerie silence assured her they were far from London.

"Edward told me about this place long ago. He'd had one duel already. God knows how many others he's had since. But I thought we would try here first, as I assumed the leopard would not change his spots." Jonathan pointed to a spot beyond the clearing. "There," he murmured.

A small group of figures stood by three carriages, their shadows flickering in the light from the carriage lamps.

"Is Jack among them?"

"I'm going to find out. Wait here." He rapped on the roof, and Roberts brought the horses to a halt. Closing the door quietly behind him, Jonathan disappeared into the blackness.

Her chest squeezed so tight she could barely breathe. She gripped the edge of the window, straining to see. A figure suddenly appeared before her, and she stifled a scream behind her gloved hand.

"Didn't mean to startle you, dearie." Mrs. Leister's face appeared ghostly white in the darkness.

"What are you doing here?" Georgiana hissed.

"I've come to stop them, the same as you."

Georgiana opened the door and stepped down, taking the woman's offered arm. She spoke before she could stop herself. "You love him." Then, as if she should clarify her statement, "You love Jack."

Mrs. Leister nodded briefly, her lips pinched tightly together. Georgiana found she no longer had the urge to hate the woman.

"Then, help me."

Together, they moved through the trees and bushes, hiding in the shadows although no one noticed them. A flash of steel caught the lantern light and Georgiana gasped.

She would have been relieved they were not using pistols, as both men were dead shots, until she recalled Edward's boastful words years ago, when he was a schoolboy.

"I won the prize for fencing. Jack and your brother were green with envy. Neither of them can touch me. Our fencing master said I should make a great pirate."

Jack and Jonathan had teased him to no end, provoking him into giving a demonstration of his exceptional skills with a blade. Decidedly proud of his friend, Jack had clapped him on the shoulder, his face beaming. *"I pity the unfortunate soul who ever comes upon you in a fight, Mitford,"* he'd said.

Mrs. Leister's voice brought her back to the present. "I do not see anyone else coming, Mrs. Waverley. Perhaps it is a legitimate fight."

She had no sooner spoken when a clattering of horse hooves in the distance reached them. The two women sprang back into the bushes, Georgiana clutching her companion's arm for balance. "It's a patrol," Mrs. Leister hissed in her ear, holding her low to the ground. "I suspected he lured Jack out here to have him arrested for dueling."

Georgiana twisted away and scrambled to her feet.

"We must get Jack away! Quickly!"

Without considering the prudence of her actions, she broke through the bushes and ran toward the men. Jonathan was already there, and his voice rose above the noisy group of men, pleading and threatening for the fight to cease.

She pushed past two men jostling for position and halted in her steps as if she'd struck a wall. Gasping back her fear, she took in the terrible sight.

Bereft of coats, Jack and Edward were in a grim fight for their lives. Their sabres clanged together, swishing in dangerous arcs within inches of their marks, but even still, Jack's shirt was torn and bloodied in long slashes, whereas Edward bore only a cut on his left arm. Out of breath and panting, Jack doggedly stumbled around the makeshift circle of men, swinging too wildly one moment, coming up short the next. Edward whooped with triumph before slicing close to Jack's ear.

Mrs. Leister wrapped her arms snugly around her waist. "Stay back," she whispered, her voice cracking. "Do not distract him."

Panic threatened to overcome her. Georgiana clutched her hands into fists, helpless to do anything but watch the gruesome scene. Any second, Jack would falter, and Edward would deliver the deathblow. She could not save him. She could not stop the fight. She met Jonathan's pained expression, and he shook his head slightly. *Let it be*, he silently told her. *I will not*, she replied.

"Edward!"

Her voice crackled in the moonless night. Edward's foot struck a rock as his head swiveled toward her voice. Without turning to look at her, Jack nimbly slashed at his opponent's arm, and Edward cried out as he dropped his sword. Jack held the tip of his bloodied sabre at Edward's throat.

"Leave…my…family…alone."

Edward nodded rapidly, his Adam's apple bobbing as he gulped for air, sputtering and sobbing his penance. Jack carelessly tossed his sword to Jonathan and picked up Edward's, throwing it as far as he could into the nearby thicket. He then faced Edward again and drew back his arm and…

Looked at Georgiana.

The breath strangled in her throat as a thousand or more emotions ran through her. She took in everything—the triumph in his eyes, the shirt hanging in tatters over his broad shoulders. His face looked bruised, but nothing worse than what she'd seen before. The glimmer of a smile tugged at the corners of his mouth.

"You owe my wife an apology."

As Edward sputtered the words she didn't care to receive, she broke from Mrs. Leister's grasp and reached her husband. Before she could kiss him or do anything but cling to him, the patrol appeared. Jonathan shoved Georgiana and Jack toward the woods, where Roberts waited in the darkness with the carriage.

Jack almost threw her inside and slammed the door behind them. Roberts urged the horses in the opposite direction. The last thing Georgiana saw before Jack swiped the curtain closed was Jonathan and Mrs. Leister disappearing into the night, while Edward remained on the ground, surrounded by the authorities.

****

"What the devil are you doing here?" Jack's lips were cracked and bloody. Chest heaving, he leaned back against the padded wall, sweat dripping from his face and mingling with a hairline scratch across his cheek. She dabbed at the cut with her handkerchief, ignoring the tears sliding down her face. He gently grasped her wrist and pulled her hand down.

"I came to rescue you."

They were both silent until they broke into matched spontaneous laughter. He kissed her hand and held it firmly on his thigh.

"How did you know where to find me?"

"Mrs. Leister—" She gulped and closed her eyes for a second. "She told me what you'd planned. Jonathan and I have been searching for you all night."

He was quiet a moment. "There is nothing between Sarah and me."

"She loves you." Her eyes filled with fresh tears, although if they were from relief or regret, she didn't know.

"I am aware of that. She also loves your brother, so I only possess half her love." He winked to soften the intimation. "So…." He let out a long sigh. "The two bumbling babies I've always rescued have become my own heroes." His hand trembled slightly as he stroked her cheek.

"You had better get used to it, Jack."

"I agree, especially since I've officially given up fighting from this moment forward. This little bout with Mitford has winded me. By the way, did you see how badly the scoundrel's nose was smashed? I daresay he received another blow after I did the honors."

Her knuckles burned at the memory. "I would not

be surprised. He has a bad habit of crossing the wrong people."

He quirked an eyebrow. "I don't suppose you would know anything about it?"

A giggle escaped her although she didn't know how she could possibly find amusement given the recent situation. "Perhaps I made my point a little too clearly."

"One of my boxing supporters happened to be strolling through St. James's and mentioned it. Of course, he assured me the girl in question only resembled my innocent bride and could not possibly be Jonathan Lockewood's esteemed sister." He kissed the back of her knuckles, and she winced. He grinned, but his smile faded a second later. "Georgie, I have to ask. Why did you call his name and not mine?"

The old jealousy was back. He would never forget she'd once loved the despicable man who'd nearly been the ruin of them all. At least she could assure him now.

"I knew he would turn at the sound of a woman's voice and you would not. You've always said how focused you are in a fight."

"And I thought you were only pretending to listen to me until you could drag me back into your bed."

"There is that." She leaned against his chest, his heart thudding beneath her ear. "I should have trusted you, Jack. The fault is all mine."

His arm squeezed around her, pressing her face into his damp shirt. "Forgive me. I should have told you the truth from the start. I'd hoped to return the money before you found out."

"I'd have given it to you freely."

A heavy sigh shook him. "I never wanted to touch

your money, my love. I only took it to stop Mitford from blackmailing us. His lies would have ruined you."

"I do not care about anything he could say. Do you not see, Jack? You're all that matters to me."

He kissed her forehead, then broke their embrace. "I'm covered in blood, dearest. There will be plenty of time later." A familiar glint in his eyes made her laugh despite her emotional turmoil. "Besides, I must be careful with you in your delicate state." A faint dimple appeared in his cheek when he tried not to smile.

She thumped him lightly on the chest. "Do not be too careful with me, Jack. I warn you I will not be careful with you, once you are patched and cleaned up." She slipped her fingers between his shirt buttons and caressed his chest.

"Hmm. I'd forgotten how spirited you Lockewoods are. Must not forget again."

"I'm a Lockewood no longer, if you'd be so kind as to remember. I'm your wife and always shall be."

She twined her hand around his neck, forcing him to lower his head. He brushed a light kiss across her lips.

"That you are." He pulled her onto his lap, wincing only for a second before clasping her firmly. "I never knew how stubborn you can be," he whispered.

"Almost as stubborn as you."

"My sweet Pudding Face. What a commanding mother you shall be to our offspring." His hand skimmed down her side, fingers spreading to encompass her growing belly.

"Harrumph." She slapped his hand, but lightly, since even his knuckles bore scratches from Edward's sabre. "At least one parent shall maintain control and order in our house."

His chest vibrated with silent laughter beneath her ear, and she closed her eyes, content in the knowledge they'd weathered the worst of the storms together. Now, they only had to look forward to a peaceful existence with their new family. She could hardly wait.

"I've finally decided what name you may call me."

"What? No more Pudding Face?"

She shook her head. "Never again."

"I suppose Georgie is out of the question."

"Only when I'm in a particularly good humor."

"I shall ensure it shall always be the case." He shifted her into a better position on his lap. "Tell me then, what you've decided."

She framed his face with her hands and caressed his cheekbones with the tips of her fingers. She touched his lips, which kissed her back.

"Yours."

Epilogue

"He looks very much like a tadpole but, fortunately, possesses the handsome Lockewood eyes," Jonathan said, not bothering to hide his grin while he examined the baby cradled in Jack's arms. Aunt Adele, who had left Bolbec once Georgiana entered her confinement, clucked her tongue.

Jack frowned. "Come now, man! Ambrose has the sturdiest legs I've ever seen. Do you not agree, Aunt Adele? And his hands…have you ever seen such a strong grip? Look how he grips his papa's finger. As if he would pull himself up."

Jonathan clapped Jack's shoulder. "Welcome to fatherhood, old friend." He stooped to hoist Sebastian into his arms and walked over to Georgiana, who reclined on a chaise, holding back her laughter while she watched the interplay between the two men she loved best. "How is the new mamma?"

"Tired, but happy. Poor Sophie—you are going through with this again."

Her sister-in-law laughed as she touched her belly with a caressing hand. Her expanding waistline was the result of another little Lockewood on the way. "I only hope your brother will be content with two children for a few years, at least."

"At the very least. I intend to have an entire battalion of the little devils. Just as long as they have your temperament and beauty."

They kissed, and Georgiana averted her eyes from the tender scene, her heart full with the amount of love in the room. If asked a year ago if she thought her life would turn out this way, she'd have laughed. Who could ever have predicted the girl who'd protested she would never fall in love would now be the happiest woman in the world?

Jack sat on the edge of Georgiana's chaise and relinquished the bundle in his arms. "One week old and already he has commanded my heart. Much as his mother did, so many years ago." He twined a long curl of her hair around his finger and gave a gentle tug.

"It took you enough years to acknowledge it," Jonathan muttered.

Georgiana laughed at the attractive flush spreading up her husband's throat to reach his solid jaw. The scratches and cuts inflicted by Edward months ago had healed, and hardly a trace remained of their origin. Edward had not fared as well. Jonathan heard that Edward's latest mistress had banned him from her house, and he was now living abroad in Paris, having been declared *persona non grata* in London by those irascible patronesses at Almack's. Georgiana could only hope he would not return to England any time soon.

When she stroked her husband's cheek, the ruby ring on her finger sparkled. Jack had presented it to her with much fanfare when his grandfather brought over the remaining family heirlooms upon Ambrose's birth. As if her thoughts summoned him, Grandpapa—as Tibby and Sebastian dubbed him—strode into the room, carrying Tibby on his shoulder as if he had been born to the task. Maisie was close behind, alternately scolding the little boy and apologizing to Lord Waverley, who merely laughed.

"How are you today, milady?" Maisie gave up on separating the old gentleman and her son and fussed over Georgiana with the tenderness of a sister. Her shyness was gone, and she flourished in her new position as nursemaid to the littlest Waverley.

"I am wonderful. In fact, I think I will relinquish the sick bed today and have a walk around the garden."

Aunt Adele pushed another pillow beneath Georgiana's feet. "You must not move an inch, my dear! You are still in a very delicate condition."

Lord Waverley set Tibby on the carpet and began pouring the tea. He handed Aunt Adele a porcelain cup. Georgiana noticed a certain giddiness about her aunt whenever Grandfather Waverley was around.

"I think she is robust enough to enjoy the sunshine, so rare this time of year. Perhaps we may accompany her."

Georgiana stifled a laugh with a discreet cough. Aunt Adele simpered and batted her eyelashes like a young girl.

"Perhaps. But I cannot stay for long. I must return to my packing."

"You aren't going back to France so soon, Aunt Adele?" Jack asked.

She sighed. "My poor sister wants me. Nevertheless, I admit I dread the crossing, my dears. I think this will be the last time I make the voyage."

A journey of a few days had become an epic adventure. Before Georgiana could suggest her husband escort the dear soul, Lord Waverley cleared his throat.

"If I do not intrude, I would like to offer the use of my sloop, dear lady. As it happens, I am long overdue in paying a visit to my old friend, Gaston. He has had the running of our *vignoble* all to himself for much too long. Would you not agree, Jack?"

Jack nodded in an effusive show of concern. "Undoubtedly. He requires your acumen in certain matters of business."

Lord Waverley grunted. "Just as I thought." He bowed slightly to Aunt Adele. "If you would prefer to travel in comfort, madam, I would be most honored if you'd allow me to take you across the Channel."

Georgiana avoided Jack's amused gaze, knowing she would burst into laughter if she caught his eye. Aunt Adele appeared to think about it for a few moments, but Georgiana already knew her response.

"If it would not be too much trouble, Lord Waverley." She sipped her tea, the tip of her pinky quivering.

"Please, call me Ambrose. Why, we are practically family."

Tibby wandered over to Jack, who promptly scooped the little boy onto his lap.

"You must take care of little Ambrose, Master Tibbs," Jack admonished with mock seriousness. "He will be prone to finding trouble, much as his dear mamma did in her youth."

"I never found as much trouble as when you were around, Jack."

"How very true." Jonathan winked at her and motioned to Sophie. "Come, let us all repair to the garden, so the new parents may relish this time together."

Lord Waverley offered his arm to Aunt Adele, who made such a blushing display over the gesture Georgiana sensed the old dear would not remain in France for long. Maisie collected Tibby and closed the door behind them.

Georgiana tried to convey the deepest reaches of her heart to her husband with one glance. "I hope you know how much I love you."

"I will strive to deserve you for the rest of my life."

She settled the baby in her arms, amazed at how quickly three individual souls had merged into a family. She kissed Ambrose's petal-soft cheek. "He looks like you, Jack."

"No, my dear—I beg to differ. He looks just like you." His voice trembled with pride.

"But he will be strong like his father."

"And have the musical ear of his mother."

"Oh, Jack! You play brilliantly." She'd have said more, but his meaningful look told her no more words were required. She shifted her position so Jack could recline beside her, the baby between them. Jack stroked his downy cheek with a fingertip while Georgiana caressed her husband's hand.

"Your grandfather is so proud."

"He wants me to take over his enterprises here and abroad. This trip to Bordeaux is a ruse so he may accompany dear Aunt Adele."

"They will be good for each other. He seems so happy."

"I know," he mused. "I keep expecting a lecture on how to be a good father to his great-grandson, but he hasn't spoken one ill word."

"He only wants what is best for you."

"I know what is best for me."

He tilted up her chin and brushed his lips across hers. She was about to tease him into asking what he meant, but was distracted by the taste of her husband's mouth and the surge of desire his nearness always inspired. The baby's soft cry interrupted them. Jack gave him the tip of his finger to suck. He pressed his cheek to her forehead.

"Well done," he murmured.

She gazed up at him, her eyes brimming over with tears she no longer had to hide. "It's not done yet, Jack. We've only just started."

A word about the author...

Anna Small wrote her first romance novel when she was sixteen. Her mother's only criticism was not to have any love scenes. Anna was sorry to disappoint her.

Several books and years later, she happily writes heartwarming, sensual, historical and contemporary romances which capture the imagination of her readers. Sharing the journey are her husband (who serves as a willing research participant for the love scenes) and their two children, who support her dreams and put up with a messy house.

She is a member of Romance Writers of America and the Sunshine State Romance Authors chapter.

You can visit her at:

http://www.annasmallbooks.com

Thank you for purchasing
this publication of The Wild Rose Press, Inc.
For other wonderful stories of romance,
please visit our on-line bookstore at
www.thewildrosepress.com.

For questions or more information
contact us at
info@thewildrosepress.com.

The Wild Rose Press, Inc.
www.thewildrosepress.com

To visit with authors of
The Wild Rose Press, Inc.
join our yahoo loop at
http://groups.yahoo.com/group/thewildrosepress/